FOR SUCH A
TIME AS THIS

"Travel to the town of Bountiful with Christian author Ginny Aiken, where romance, intrigue, and even a few childish pranks converge. *For Such a Time as This* offers readers all of the elements they love in one beautifully written, Esther-themed tale. Highly recommended!"

> —Janice Hanna Thompson, author of
> *Love Finds You in Daisy, Oklahoma*

"Popular author Ginny Aiken has created a wonderful new heroine in Olivia Moore, protagonist of *For Such a Time as This*. Courageous and level-headed, Olivia is a heroine readers will love, and Aiken does a masterful job of evoking life in a small Oregon town in the 1870s. Readers won't want to miss this first book in Aiken's Women of Hope series."

> —Marta Perry, author of the
> *Pleasant Valley* Amish books

"The Biblical story of Queen Esther meets the West in an engaging historical romance. A hurting hero you'll root for. A steadfast heroine with a big heart who will steal yours. A poignant story of overcoming past betrayals through faith, forgiveness, and finding true love."

> —Vickie McDonough, award-winning author of
> the Pioneer Promises series and coauthor of
> the Texas Trails series

FOR SUCH A
TIME AS THIS

FOR SUCH A TIME AS THIS

A WOMEN *of* HOPE NOVEL

GINNY AIKEN

New York • Boston • Nashville

FaithWords
Hachette Book Group
237 Park Avenue
New York, NY 10017

www.faithwords.com

Printed in the United States of America
First Edition: August 2012
10 9 8 7 6 5 4 3 2 1
RRD-C

FaithWords is a division of Hachette Book Group, Inc.
The FaithWords name and logo are trademarks of Hachette Book Group, Inc.

Library of Congress Cataloging-in-Publication Data

Aiken, Ginny.
  For such a time as this: a women of Hope novel / Ginny Aiken. — 1st ed.
    p. cm.
  ISBN 978-0-89296-848-0
  1. Frontier and pioneer life—Oregon—Fiction.   I. Title.
PS3551.I339F67 2012
813'.54—dc23
                                                    2011048560

*To the Lord of Lords and King of Kings,
who makes everything in my life possible, and to
my family: my husband, my sons, the lovely young women
in their lives, my parents and sister, and my grandsons,
who, in spite of my deadlines, still love me.*

...Who knoweth whether thou art come to the kingdom for such a time as this?

—Esther 4:14

Chapter 1

Bountiful, Hope County, Oregon—1879

Olivia Moore swiped the back of her hand across her cheek. She slapped away a trickle of tear, the only moisture visible as far as she could see in all directions.

Drought.

Such a simple word, but, oh, how complicated its reality was to her family. And not just to her family. All the other farmers and ranchers scattered across Hope County were suffering as much as Mama and Papa, with no hint in the cloudless sky of any relief to come.

"Oh, I hate this," Leah Rose, Olivia's youngest sister, complained. "I hate it, I hate it, I hate it!"

Olivia hitched the willow basket more securely onto her hip, crammed down another one of their father's shirts with the rest of the laundry, and prayed for patience. "Nobody likes to fight the wind when they're trying to work. But we must get the clothes inside before they get dirtier than before we washed them. You don't want to scrub them again, now, do you?"

Leah rolled her eyes then yelped and rubbed her nose, her eyelids, and her mouth.

Another blast of hot air buffeted Olivia right then, its texture rough and sandpapery with the tiny grains of dry dirt it picked up as it gusted across her family's ravaged land. She wrapped her arm tighter around the tree limb where Papa had tied one end of the wash line. The bark rasped her skin.

Not ready to go back inside the house quite yet, she propped the basket between her hip and the bare trunk then shielded her eyes with her free hand. The wind whipped her calico skirt into a froth against her legs, the flapping another unwelcome irritant.

Leah Rose muttered something, but the rising wind carried away the words. Olivia suspected it was just as well. More grumbling that echoed her own misery didn't appeal just then.

She didn't want to gather still-damp laundry any more than Leah Rose did. Still, Olivia couldn't be too hard on the girl. She, too, wished things were as they'd always been, that the old rhythm of their pleasant lives still determined their daily schedules. In previous years, that late in the summer, nearly September, had meant days filled with the mad busyness of preparing for winter. Olivia had always worked with her mother as Elizabeth Moore canned, dried, salted, and helped her husband smoke the results of their efforts, the fruits of their land. The hardworking couple had made certain their family would have enough provisions to see them through the dark, cold months ahead. Olivia admired her parents' diligence.

That year, however, diligence would not be enough.

"Oh, Livvy, I can't stand it another minute!" Leah Rose threw a petticoat at Olivia, but before she could catch it, a gust of wind snatched it and turned it into a tumbleweed, rolling and bouncing just out of her reach.

She sighed and hurried after the voluminous white garment. "Go on in, then. I'll be right behind you. When I'm done with the wash, you understand. Let Mama know for me."

Leah Rose bent against the wind, dramatizing a bit more than necessary, and ran to the house. Once on the porch steps, she glanced back over her shoulder. "I will. And do hurry, Livvy. I want to show you my latest project."

Leah Rose had the ability to turn needle, fabric, and thread into exquisite things of beauty. Olivia, while a competent enough seamstress, couldn't come close to producing the fine needlework at which her youngest sister excelled. "I'll be happy to see what you've accomplished so far as soon as I've finished out here."

She chased after the elusive petticoat, the willow basket on her hip hampering her steps. But if she set it down, the contents would likely capture the swirling dirt. With every step she took, her irritation rose. Just as she came within a finger's length of the renegade piece, the wind caught it, tossed it up and over, and then flung it against a large rock that in previous years Elizabeth and her girls had ringed with cheery blossoms. This August the flower bed around the boulder lay bare, the soil as dry and dusty as everything else.

Olivia rushed the garment, but the next blast of wind snatched it away again, whirling it across the rear of the house. Finally, when she was about to give up on ever capturing the infuriating piece of clothing, it slammed up against the privy wall and sagged in a pile onto the dirt at the base. Olivia grabbed the petticoat, shook it out, grimaced at the dirt stains

Ginny Aiken

it had gathered, and finally stuffed it in her basket, resigned to
another session with hot water, lye soap, and the washboard.

Her temper didn't tamp down as easily as the fabric did.
Frustrated by her family's situation, and aggravated by the
rebel slip, she squared her shoulders and marched back over to
the clothesline, her every step propelled by her resolve.

With renewed vigor, she yanked a pillowcase off its moor-
ing, reached for a pair of socks, and then an old towel. In
moments, she had stripped the rest of the wash from where
she'd hung it not so long ago. When she reached the post at
the end of the line, she leaned on it and paused to catch her
breath, a difficult endeavor as the gritty air continued to bat-
ter her face. Through narrowed eyes she looked out over the
Moore property—Papa's pride and joy.

Olivia's heart constricted, and she fought again for breath. As
awful as the scorching, dusty wind was, she knew it wasn't wholly
to blame for her misery. Her distress stemmed from watching
her dear parents work, work, work, and then, by virtue of a twist
of nature's fickleness, see all their efforts come to nothing.

In the years since they'd come to Oregon Territory, her
father had plowed and planted his fields as soon as spring
deemed the land ready. For the last two years, however, the
plants had battled to drink what little moisture the land provided, and when the sturdy shoots had broken through to the
sunshine, they'd been ravaged by the sudden arrival of swarm-
ing airborne beasts that descended on the young crops. The
ravenous grasshoppers had left nothing behind.

Despite the weather, Olivia lingered outside. She couldn't
bear to see the worry that drew deep lines down either side
of Mama's mouth again, nor hear the strain in her mother's

voice. She didn't know what she would do in an hour or so when Papa dragged himself inside for whatever Mama put together and passed off as that night's supper. The ruts etched across his forehead and those that fanned out from the corners of his eyes made her heart ache with futility.

Mama and Papa hadn't meant for Olivia to overhear their late-night conversations. But she had. At the age of nineteen, she was no child. By all rights she should have been married already, and maybe even a mother, as well, like her friends Adelaide Tucker and Rosie Thurman. But so far she hadn't been tempted to take that step with any of the very few marriageable men in town, and her parents hadn't pushed, to her great relief. She'd yet to meet the man who appealed to her enough to make her consider the momentous change.

She'd been happy to stay home. She helped Mama with the younger children, and with the never-ending work around the house. She also helped her father and the boys with whatever she wheedled Papa into letting her do out in the barn.

But even those welcome chores had vanished with the last of the grasshoppers. Papa had been forced to sell Olivia's sheep when he no longer could provide properly for them. There was little feed anywhere, and whatever could be found came at a dear cost indeed. Faced with the choice of feeding animals or feeding his children, Stephen Moore hadn't even blinked. He'd sold a fair number of the Moores' prized cattle as well.

The small sum Papa had realized from that sale hadn't stretched far enough. Olivia wasn't supposed to know what her parents had resorted to, but she'd struggled with sleeplessness during the last couple of months as their circumstances had worsened, seemingly by the day. Papa's anxious words during the late-night conversations had confirmed her unsettled feeling.

He'd been forced to mortgage the property.

"Livvy!" Leah Rose called.

"Coming—" Olivia tried to respond, but her dry mouth turned the word into a croaked rasp. She ran her tongue over her parched lips, grimacing when she tasted the dust there. She started toward the house and gave her answer another go. "I'll be right there."

At the top of the porch steps, she cast a final glance down the long brown drive. It was as dry and dreary as it had been the last time she'd looked that way, scant minutes earlier.

"Well, Lord," she said. "I trust you will show me what I'm to do at a time like this. I'm not a child anymore. Surely you have something for me to do. I refuse to be nothing more than another mouth for them to feed here at home. Show me, Father, but please don't take too long. Our situation is dreadful. Winter isn't far off now. And when it comes…"

She couldn't let herself think of that right then. She had to focus on solutions rather than the frightening what-ifs. There had to be a way for her to help her father and mother. Even if she had to leave the home and family she loved.

"Livvy!" Leah Rose cried again, impatience in her voice. "You said you were coming."

As Olivia closed the front door behind her, a sharp pang crossed her chest. She was going to miss her little sisters…her brothers…her parents…their home…Once she discerned the Lord's leading, of course.

Until then, she'd relish every minute she was blessed to spend with them.

"Here I am, silly!" she answered, drenching her words with more enthusiasm than she felt. "Let's see that needlework of yours."

Sunday morning, Reverend Alton delivered a thought-provoking sermon on 2 Corinthians, third chapter, third verse, where he exhorted his congregation to be living scriptures for the lost world, flesh and blood illustrated lessons on God's abundant blessings. After the final hymn, Olivia followed her family outside the church, her Bible hugged close against her chest, her soft drawstring leather purse slung from her right elbow. The fierce winds of the past week had finally calmed, and the fine dirt that had roughened the air had settled down once again.

While the sky remained as relentless in its clear blue brightness and the ground as persistent in its dusty brown dryness, the temperature had dropped enough to make midday almost bearable. Olivia had dressed in her best slate-gray serge skirt, white blouse, and fine blue fitted jacket. She appreciated any chance to dress up, since at home, with work always needing to be done, simple cotton calicos made the most sense.

Before the Moore family left home for the service that morning, Olivia had told her mother and father that Adelaide Tucker, her dearest friend, had invited her for lunch—and, of course, for Addie to show off three-month-old Joshua Charles Tucker, Jr., her pride and joy. Olivia missed Addie since her friend had become a married lady. As much as there was at home to keep Olivia busy, Addie had far more on her plate, what with all her responsibilities as wife and new mother.

"You'll meet us back here by three, right?" Papa asked after Olivia's two brothers had left to find their friends. Mrs. Alton approached Mama and the younger girls, since the pastor and his wife had invited the remaining four members of the Moore clan for the noon meal.

"Oh, yes," Olivia said. "I'm sure Addie will be tired by then. She's told me Baby Josh keeps her up for hours most nights, and she must steal naps whenever he sleeps. She and Joshua have been trying to teach their sweet little one that nights are for sleeping, but that lesson seems to hold no interest for him."

Mama traded glances—and knowing smiles—with the pastor's wife. "It does happen with some little ones. I suppose you might have been too young to remember, Livvy, but your sister was like that, too. Marty took almost a year to figure out what sunset meant."

"Poor Addie!" Olivia shuddered. While no one could accuse her of laziness, she did enjoy crawling under her blankets, and most nights she dozed off right away. "I won't tell her about Marty—"

"Hey!" the Moore family's tomboy yelped. "I learned, didn't I?"

Olivia fought a laugh. "Of course you did, Martha Jean. And, I'm sure, not a moment too soon for Mama and Papa."

Chuckling at Marty's glare, and aware of the time passed as they'd visited with Mrs. Alton, Olivia set off toward Addie and Joshua's neat clapboard house. While the church sat on the eastern edge of Bountiful, Joshua's parents had built their home in the center of the small town, next to their thriving livery stable. Now that the elder Tuckers were in heaven with the Father, Josh ran the business, while Addie ran their household with easy efficiency and good humor.

Olivia enjoyed any opportunity to catch up with her friend as much as Addie did playing hostess.

Her stroll from the church to Addie's place had her crossing the road a few houses down from Reverend and Mrs. Alton's home. A final glance back showed Leah Rose and Marty standing to a side while Papa helped Mama up the front steps and into the generous-sized white house. Her younger brothers were...well, Olivia hadn't heard where the boys planned to spend the afternoon, but she suspected they might be with the Carters, since that family abounded in high-spirited boys.

As she hurried down the wooden sidewalk toward Addie's home, a burst of children's laughter at Olivia's left caught her attention. A chorus of shrill girlish cries followed, as they evidently headed toward her.

The loud guffaws grew more raucous.

The frantic screams grew more frenzied.

The commotion resounded from the alley up ahead. She quickened her pace, curiosity piqued. Before she reached the mouth of the alley, a trio of little girls, around the age of eight or nine, burst into the street, white-faced, their wails near to hysteria, their shoes kicking their Sunday dresses into a froth of skirt and petticoat.

Seconds later four boys, in their Sunday best as well, darted out from the alley and surrounded the girls, fencing them into a huddle in the middle of the street. Fortunately, Sundays saw little traffic once churchgoers left for home.

"We got 'em now, Luke!" a freckle-faced, red-haired imp

yelled as he ran circles around his anxious victims. "Hurry up afore they get away."

The towheaded boy with chocolate eyes joined in with his own taunt. "Fraidy-cats."

All four closed ranks around the girls, their laughter destroying the afternoon's peace. The high-spirited quartet made for a lively, if frightening, cage for the captives.

As Olivia marched toward the children, a new sound joined the cacophony. Grunts and snuffles grew louder, ushered in by a dusty dervish that stampeded past her. A dervish otherwise known as . . .

"A pig!" Olivia backed up flat against the front window of Mrs. Selkirk's charming new millinery store. She was not about to step into the swine's path.

A fifth boy, this one with jet-black hair tumbled down over a pair of brilliant blue eyes, followed on the heels of the monstrous hog.

"Go on, go on, *go on*!" He yelled, stomped his feet, and smacked two sticks against each other, urging the filthy creature along.

His cronies laughed so hard that the red-haired one fell in a heap onto the dusty road. The little girls tried to flee through the opening his fall created, but the hog went for that exit route at the same time. As the girls ran past, three pretty Sunday dresses picked up dirt from the pig's coat.

The girls' wails multiplied.

The boys' laughter did as well.

The hog tore off between two buildings, his hooves kicking up a dust storm all their own. "I'll get him!" hollered the black-haired boy as he chased after it around the corner.

She'd seen enough. Olivia tucked her Bible between her elbow and her ribs as she hurried toward the children before the other boys ran off as well.

When Eli locked the door of the bank, the usual thrill at the sight of the gold-foil letters on the pane of glass sped through him:

BANK OF BOUNTIFUL
ELIJAH WHITMAN, JR., PRESIDENT

He breathed a prayer every single day, thanking his heavenly Father for helping him save the enterprise he and his late father had worked so hard to build. He'd come too close to losing everything two years earlier.

As he pushed away the memory of that painful time, he heard children's squeals and laughter from not too far away. Then, a clear feminine voice called out, "Gentlemen."

Silence descended.

He wished he had that kind of effect with his two youngsters every time he spoke to them. He slipped the key into his pocket, sighing. Things were fast approaching a desperate stage at home.

He stepped down to the sidewalk and glanced down the street. A young woman marched toward a group of children gathered in the middle of the road. The picture they painted piqued his curiosity. What parent would allow youngsters to run wild in the middle of town in their Sunday best?

Eli headed toward the group.

"Gentlemen," the lady repeated in a firm, stern voice as he approached. "Which one of you would care to explain what this"—she gestured to encompass the entire scenario—"is all about?"

The boys grew mute.

The girls rushed to the lady's side.

"Oh, Miss Livvy!" cried a petite blonde with bouncy curls. "They're horrid, these boys. Look. Just *look* at what they did to my lovely new dress."

The young lady—Miss Livvy as the girl had called her—dropped down to the child's level, clearly more concerned about the besieged girls than about the possible soiling of her gray skirt.

"I saw what happened, Melly," she said. "Go home now, girls. But as you do, would you please stop by Mrs. Tucker's home and let her know I'll be late? I might not even make it today after all."

All three nodded and stepped away. Before they left, however, Miss Livvy seemed to have another thought. "If any of your mamas is upset with the state of your clothes, please have her speak to me. I'll vouch for you."

With a chorus of agreement, the girls scampered away. The young lady then turned to the tight knot of boys. "Now, gentlemen, what do you have to say for yourselves?"

"Ah..."

"Um..."

"Er..."

"Hm..."

When none of them responded, Miss Livvy prodded, "Well?" Silence reigned on Main Street.

She went on. "Aside from the apologies you owe the three young ladies—"

"Aw..."

"Nah..."

"Really?"

"But..."

"Aside from the apologies you owe the three young ladies," she repeated, "there is still the matter of that runaway pig."

Eli stifled a laugh. A pig? He crossed his arms, enjoying the moment.

"Oh, no!" the red-haired boy cried. "Pa's gonna kill me if he sees Rufus's not back in his pen."

Rufus. Eli smiled, he couldn't help himself. Albert Brown, a friend of his son Luke, would soon be facing a dressing down, if not a switching, from his father. Mr. Brown put a lot of stock in his pigs.

Miss Livvy seemed to agree with his assessment, as her lovely features brightened with her own smile. "Perhaps you should have thought of that before you decided to torment the girls," she told Albert.

"Uh-huh." He took a step away from the gathering. "Reckon so. Yes, ma'am, I do."

Miss Livvy crossed her arms, Bible and purse hugged close. "Not so fast. You have some friends here, don't you?"

With a lingering look in the direction of the offices of the *Bountiful Scribe*, the town's weekly paper, and the school-house, Albert stopped. He wiped the dusty toe of one shoe on his other trouser leg. "Yes, ma'am."

The other boys donned differing levels of worry.

"And did your pa say for you and your friends to chase his swine around town?"

He blushed under his freckles. "No, ma'am. He don't rightly know Rufus's gone."

"Then it would seem that you gentlemen could well be called thieves. You took a hog that didn't belong to any one of you. After all, Rufus wasn't *given* to you."

"Oh, but—"

"That ain't how it happened—"

"Not so—"

"Nah—"

"And," she said as though they hadn't argued, "thieves are fair game for Marshal Blair, don't you think?"

Four pairs of eyes opened wider than ever. The boys began to argue, their statements indecipherable since they spoke one over the other.

She went on in her calm, even voice. "So. What'll it be, gents? Shall I send for the marshal or will you set things to rights again?"

"SOOO-oo-eeyyy!" shrieked the aforementioned porker as it reappeared, galloping back down Main Street toward Miss Livvy and the boys.

"There!" the lady cried. "A chance to do your duty, gentlemen. Catch him—Rufus—and return him before I'm compelled to fetch Marshal Blair."

The boys pelted off after the squealing swine, each determined to beat the others to their quarry.

Eli caught sight of the three girls peering out from around the corner of Metcalf's Mercantile. Apparently they'd stayed to watch the boys get their just deserts.

The hog darted toward them.

The girls squealed.

The pig did as well.

The boys pursued the animal, one of them managing to get a hand on its ear, but the creature changed direction, and the would-be captor fell to the dirt.

The girls laughed.

Jonathan Davidson, another of Luke's friends, bounded upright and dusted off his clothes. "That's not funny."

"Neither was chasing us, Jonny!" said the small blonde. Her headful of ringlets bobbed with her indignation.

Miss Livvy donned a slight smile and seemed to settle in to observe.

Eli followed suit.

Young male glares flew toward the girls as they tried to capture the pig who, after his taste of freedom, did not intend to be caught. He darted and weaved from street-side to street-side, the boys in hot pursuit. The girls found the situation hilarious.

No matter how hard the boys tried, each time any of them came close to laying hold of the animal, the pig wriggled out of their clutches. The would-be trappers grew grimier with every pass, as the girls giggled and cheered on the elusive prey.

"Miss 'Livia!" Albert bellowed after he, too, landed face-first in the dust. "It ain't funny. Make 'em stop laughing!"

Miss Olivia arched a brow. "The young ladies didn't find being chased by runaway livestock particularly humorous, gentlemen."

The pig turned back toward the way he had come, but a fifth boy, dirty and breathless, blocked his escape.

Eli recognized the fifth trouble-maker. In a flash, he stomped down the street, anger and frustration burning in his belly.

"Lucas Andrew Whitman!" he roared from just behind Miss Olivia. "What is the meaning of this?"

Chapter 2

Olivia spun to see Mr. Elijah Whitman, owner of the Bank of Bountiful, glaring at the madness in the middle of the street.

The silent boy, the one with the black hair and blue eyes wide and full of alarm, stood frozen before the man. "He-hello, Papa..."

Olivia could almost touch the change in the air. "Mr. Whitman?"

"Yes?"

Those eyes...goodness! They seemed to see right through her. A shiver ran through her. Olivia tried to bring her reaction under control. A woman couldn't help but admire Mr. Whitman's rugged features, his broad cheekbones, square jawline, high forehead, and shiny black hair. He was a most imposing figure of a man, blessed with wide, strong shoulders, a superior height, and an undeniable air of competence, power, and skill. He looked as if he would be as comfortable on horseback as he surely was behind a desk in the elegant bank.

A lesser woman would be forgiven for a swoon in his presence.

Oh, Olivia, how silly. You're no simpering ninny, so stop behaving like one.

"If...uhm...you would allow me, sir? I—ah...I believe I have this matter under control."

"Control?" The banker gestured toward the children, the hog, even the appalled milliner, who'd stuck her head out the front door of her store. "This hardly seems under control."

Nerves struck then, but Olivia went on. "Oh, but it is, sir." She tipped up her chin. "And if you'll allow me a moment, I'll be happy to explain."

Mr. Whitman's brows drew close. "That should be good. Proceed, Miss Livvy...Olivia"—confusion altered his expression—"just who *are* you?"

"Miss Moore." She blushed at his pointed scrutiny. "Olivia Moore."

He nodded. "Go ahead, then, Miss Moore. I look forward to that explanation."

A gnawing took up residence in the pit of her gut. *Oh, Lord Jesus. I do need your help. Please don't turn a deaf ear on me now.*

Only too aware of the male scrutiny, Olivia urged the scamps in the street once again to recapture the creature. "Work together, gentlemen. I'm sure you can come up with as good a plan as your earlier one, especially since this time, it will be the right thing to do."

As the boys doubled their efforts, she turned to the girls. It was their turn to appear sheepish. Olivia fought yet another smile. "I think you'd all best go home. This time, for certain.

Your mamas will be wondering where you are. I will see to everything on this end."

The former victims skipped off, smiles wreathing their sweet faces.

Within seconds, the boys' renewed efforts bore fruit, and the swine was surrounded. They urged Rufus back toward the alley from where they'd all originally come with the same cacophonous results. But before the boys and their prize vanished, Olivia extracted a promise from the other four to return and report to her once each had apologized to the hog's rightful owner.

As the scoundrels went on their way, Olivia released a heartfelt sigh.

"That challenging?" The man at her side didn't mask his amusement.

"Indeed!"

As soon as the word escaped her lips, heat flooded her cheeks. What must this important man think of her? First, he'd found her on Main Street with a group of squabbling children and one filthy pig. Then, she'd almost confessed she'd met her match in the handful of youngsters and the ornery swine.

He laughed, a cheery, robust sound that made Olivia feel better, to her surprise.

"I do understand," he said. "I have a daughter as well as Luke, and they trounce me more often than I care to admit."

She responded with a rueful smile. "They do have nimble minds, don't they?"

"And overabundant energy." He sighed. "I don't know if others have the same experience, but ever since I was widowed—"

"Oh, I'm so sorry."

A faint grimace, as though he'd swallowed something distasteful, twisted Mr. Whitman's attractive features. He shrugged and averted his gaze. "I appreciate your condolences, but they're not necessary. Life is full of unexpected trials and difficulties. A man must just...cope."

His words surprised Olivia. Especially their flat, emotionless timbre, not what she would have expected from a bereaved man. "I...see."

Mr. Whitman looked on the verge of saying more, but he shook his head and stared toward the alley where the kids had disappeared. "I only wish," he said in a strained voice, "that everyone was as willing to accept children's unique peculiarities as you have been."

What an unusual thing for him to say. Taken aback, she repeated her bland, "I...see."

He turned, and his bright blue eyes, so much like his son's, met Olivia's. His smile, although void of humor, revealed his intent to keep their conversation pleasant. She appreciated his effort.

"No," he said. "I don't think you do, but it's very nice of you to try. My children are only twelve and ten, but they're certain they've grown beyond the need for supervision and adult care. They have chased away the three highly qualified nannies I've hired so far."

The memory of Luke beating sticks to drive the hog along burst into Olivia's mind. She couldn't stop the chuckle that bubbled up. Yes, the boy was a rascal, but an older and wiser adult should try to think like a youngster every once in a while. That would help figure out how best to deal with them. Goodness knew her two brothers and two sisters had enough mischief in them to fill even Mr. Whitman's Bank of Bountiful vault.

"I wouldn't cast all the blame for your predicament with the nannies on your children," she said. "I suspect the nannies must have been lacking in one way or another."

He arched a jet-black brow. "Were *you* that generous when the boys and the pig—"

"We're back!"

Although Olivia had been ready to explain how her large family had taught her a number of lessons on handling children and the scrapes they got into, she was relieved when the four boys ran up and halted in a line before her, their grubby faces beaming with self-satisfaction.

"And...?" she said.

"And we returned Rufus and we apologized and we watched Mr. Brown yell at Albert for taking his hog." The blond-haired one the girl had called Jonny had clearly enjoyed his friend's discomfort a mite too much.

"Consequences," Olivia said. "They do follow our actions. While you fellows have returned the stolen pig, apologized for the theft—"

"It weren't no theft—"

"We just *borrowed* Rufus—"

"And he's back now. No harm done—"

"Excuse me!" It took some doing to make herself heard over their statements. "It strikes me that you're in no position to argue. At least, not right now. It's likely time for you gentlemen to return home, don't you think?"

Three of them nodded and nudged each other along, more than ready to escape the scene of their crimes. The fourth,

Luke Whitman, darted nervous glances toward his father. He must have reached a decision, since with a grand display of bravado, he hooked his thumbs into his trousers front pockets, and sidled off after the others. That is, he tried to sidle, but didn't get far.

"Lucas," Mr. Whitman said, "you really do not want to wander off again today, young man. You and I have some talking to do. About pigs and girls and the proper activities for Sunday afternoons."

The three others picked up their pace.

"But, Papa…" Luke's voice held a lot of pleading and a dose of dismay. "We already apologized."

"Like Miss Moore said, there are consequences to a man's actions. I'm not so sure an apology is quite enough, son."

His comrades in crime broke into a run.

Luke hadn't taken his gaze from his father's serious face. "Aw…"

"I appreciate everything you've done, Miss Moore," the banker said. "But please, should Luke misbehave again, just bring him to me. I won't have him trouble you further."

Out of the corner of her eye, Olivia caught the mutinous glare Luke sent his father while the man was looking at her. The boy's crossed arms suggested more trouble to come. But it would be Mr. Whitman's problem.

"I understand, sir." She gave Luke a pointed look. "I'm sure whenever we meet again Luke and I will do just fine. We understand each other, don't we, Luke?"

The boy responded with a series of vigorous nods. To emphasize his answer, he added, "Yes, ma'am."

"It's been…interesting," she said to the two Whitmans, "but now, I must be on my way, too."

As she stepped up onto the sidewalk to resume her walk to Addie's house, she heard Mr. Whitman sigh. "It's no wonder you've chased off every nanny I've hired," he told his son. "Just what do you have to say for yourself?"

"They've been just *awful*, Papa. 'Sides, Randy and I *don't* need a nanny. Nannies are for babies. Randy's practically grown up, and I'm no baby. And they smelled nasty, too, like vinegar and sour milk."

Stifling a laugh, Olivia slowed her steps.

"All three of those ladies came with the best recommendations, Luke. I must assume the trouble lies with you and Miranda."

"Nah. It was them."

"I can see we're getting nowhere. We'll discuss the matter again when we get home. After we have dinner. Let's just make certain you offer the next one your full cooperation and you treat her with the proper respect."

"The next one? Who're you gonna bring home now?"

Olivia forced herself to walk, head forward, gaze on the sidewalk below. She couldn't let her curiosity take over.

"I don't know, Luke," Mr. Whitman said, sounding tired. "I really don't know. I suppose I'll have to put another advertisement in the Seattle paper. Perhaps in Portland and San Francisco as well."

"Oh, no, Papa! Don't do that. I got an idea. A *better* idea."

Olivia paused in front of Selkirk's Millinery to stare at a confection bristling with feathers and bows.

"Really, Luke?" Mr. Whitman said. "An idea? About a nanny."

"Uh-huh."

"That would be . . . ?"

"It's simple, Papa. You just have to hire the *right* nanny this time."

"And just who would that be?"

"Um . . . how about her? Yeah, I want *her*."

In the reflection of the store window she saw the boy, arm extended, index finger pointed straight at her.

Goodness! What an awkward moment. In the middle of the most awkward of days. What could Mr. Whitman possibly think of that? She really shouldn't have lingered to listen. Pretending not to have heard or seen, she resumed her walk, her heels clicking a brisk pace against the wooden sidewalk.

After Cooky cleared away the dinner dishes, Eli headed for the parlor, well aware that his son had fled upstairs as soon as he'd swallowed his last bite. Just outside the oak pocket door, he paused. "Luke! Please come back down here. I did tell you we would discuss this afternoon's disaster after we ate."

He headed for his favorite armchair to wait for the boy. Long minutes later, he heard slow, heavy footsteps on the stairs, accompanied by unintelligible grumbling. Luke appeared in the doorway, brows drawn down, eyes narrowed, lips bunched up into a knot. Eli braced himself. It looked as though they were headed for another unpleasant argument. Not something he had the stomach for, but something he knew he had to do.

Weariness struck. While his marriage to Victoria had been

a phenomenal disaster, and the children showed evidence of years of her...indifference, the situation with the children had only worsened since her death. He'd come near to the end of his rope. And yet, he still didn't know how to reach Luke and Randy. Both were driving him to distraction with their unruly behavior, their unwillingness to listen and mind their elders, and their unreasonable antipathy toward the well-qualified, experienced nannies he'd hired.

Luke crossed his arms, his expression more closed, if possible.

Eli studied his son for a handful of minutes, hoping Luke's appalling stubbornness would fade. But as the tall case clock in the entry hall ticked off the minutes, he recognized that the boy was digging in his heels again, just as he'd been doing whenever Eli attempted to discipline him for quite a while now.

Regardless, he couldn't let his son grow up as a rowdy ruffian. He loved Luke too much. "I asked you a question back there on the street," he said. "What in the world were you thinking?"

Luke's only response was a slight shrug.

"How could you ever torment those three little girls? Would you like someone to torment you?"

"Doesn't scare me," Luke answered, his voice full of bravado, his jaw jutted out. "Wouldn't make me squeal like no pi—" He stopped himself when he realized what he'd been about to bring up.

Eli crossed his arms and arched a brow. "Do continue, son. Finish what you were about to say. Please."

A scarlet flush crept up Luke's cheeks. But just when Eli thought the boy's conscience and discomfort would make him admit his wrongdoing, he pulled himself up to his full height, shoulders back, chin up, eyes flashing defiance, lips clamped tight.

Standing, Eli slammed a fist into the open palm of his other hand. He began to pace. "I know things haven't been their best since...since your mother died."

He shook his head. To be honest, things had been going from bad to horrific back when Victoria had betrayed him, and had actually settled down some since her passing, to his relief. But he'd always kept his feelings about that dreadful episode from his children. He wasn't about to change now.

"I know you miss your mama, but nothing can bring her back."

Luke shrugged again. "Don't mean I hafta have a nanny."

"And I don't either." Eli's eldest, Miranda, flounced into the parlor, her expression haughty, her blue eyes flinty. "Hello, Father. You must realize I'm practically a full-grown woman now. Why, I'm turning thirteen soon, and I *don't* need a nanny. Nannies are for babies."

A mischievous spark flashed over Randy's features as she glanced at Luke. "Perhaps Luke does."

Eli stopped inches away from his daughter. "And you, young lady. Where were *you*? I left Luke with you for...oh, no more than ten minutes. Next thing I know he's taunting little girls in the middle of town and he's even found himself a pig."

At first, Randy flinched, but then, when she heard the last of his words, her lips twitched and a very unladylike but wholly childlike snort escaped her. "Luke was playing with a pig?" She tossed her black braids off her shoulders, her façade of maturity back in place. "How...how dirty-little-boy of him."

" 'How' is an excellent word. How did your brother wind up in the middle of the street with his gang of hooligans?" He let out a frustrated gust of breath. "Where were you, Randy?"

She tapped the toe of her shoe in a show of impatience. The image of Victoria flashed into his mind. A chill ran through him.

"Answer me, please," he said in a low, iron-tough voice.

His tone wasn't lost on his daughter. The façade vanished. She laced her fingers together and twisted her hands. "I... ah... I went to Metcalf's Mercantile with Audrina Metcalf. You know she's my dearest friend and her papa had told her he'd just gotten in a shipment of lovely boots and belts for ladies and Audrina invited me to go see the new things and they're ever so much more interesting than watching a dirty little boy who always finds trouble with his dirty little friends and—"

"Enough!"

As frustrated as he'd been with his children these past few months, he'd never raised his voice to them. Right then, he roared.

A fleeting memory of the calm, competent, and winsome Olivia Moore dealing with the five boys and three girls shot through his thoughts. He wished he could be that effective with his mere two.

He shook his head. No time to waste on foolish wishes. "It's more than obvious that you both *do* need a nanny. I cannot leave you alone—even in each other's company—for a solitary second without you scaring up some kind of trouble." He let out a heartfelt sigh. "I will be looking for another nanny, and this time I will brook absolutely no shenanigans like before. Understood?"

Luke made a face. "But—"

Randy stamped a foot. "Papa—"

"No. I will have no frogs in bureau drawers, no grasshoppers in bed linens"—*please, Lord! No more grasshoppers. All of us in Bountiful have suffered enough*—"no sour apple cider vinegar in anyone's scent bottle, no pebbles in boots, no hidden spectacles, no vanishing hatpins, button hooks, or"—he glared at Randy, his cheeks blazing with mortification—"missing corset laces. There will be no more running away and hiding, and under no circumstances will I tolerate any more sassing your elders. I want not a single complaint brought to me about either one of you. That is as clear as a man can make his position. Do you understand?"

"I toldja how we can fix the nanny thing," Luke said, defiance flashing from his eyes. "Miss Olivia is the *right* nanny for us. She's pretty. She smiles. She don't holler. And she doesn't smell funny. All *you* hafta do is bring her home."

Randy shrugged and tossed her braids over her shoulders. "I don't care who you bring. *I'm* taking care of myself. *I* don't need the nanny. You can bring Luke's Miss Olivia home any time you want."

Faced with their obstinacy, Eli's anger and frustration crashed down into that barren weariness he'd struggled against so often of late. It was only too clear that he might as well have been talking to the parlor wall for all the good his scolding had done.

He stood still as a tree, wishing things were different, wishing he knew how to solve his children's obvious unhappiness, wishing he had a solution to his dismal situation. As he stared, Luke slunk out of the parlor. His son's misery stung him to his very core. He understood. Of course he did. But what

Luke really wanted and needed was the one and only thing he wouldn't—couldn't—give his children. After what he'd barely survived at the hands of his late wife, he'd never marry again.

Never.

As Randy scurried away, he collapsed into his armchair again. He brought his hands to his face, covered his eyes with his open palms. Things were bleak, indeed.

Oh, Father. Victoria failed us—all of us. I can't do the same. They're my children. I love them and I must raise them right. But...you see what I have here. Please show me...what am I going to do with them?

Late Sunday night, Olivia lay in bed next to Leah Rose, unable to scour the images of the day's events from her mind. Had she really been that bold before the owner of Bountiful's bank? One of the most important members of their small community?

Every time she thought about her actions—and words— her cheeks heated. Goodness! She could scarcely recognize herself.

Then, to make matters worse, when she'd thought she was done for the moment, that rapscallion Luke Whitman had managed to make things even more awkward. By a lot.

I want her...

She rolled over again, clutched a pillow close to her heart, then propped her chin on the downy softness.

While Mr. Whitman's face had shown his surprise at his son's words, it hadn't revealed his opinion of the outrageous pronouncement. It was clear the boy only wanted to distract his father and avoid further scolding. Still, Olivia didn't think the banker had thought too highly of the suggestion.

How could he have? She wasn't quite sure what she thought of it herself. While she did love children, and she had spent her whole life helping Mama with her younger siblings, she was no nanny. She could never pretend to be one.

What must the man think of her?

Her cheeks burned again, and she rubbed her face against the pillow one more time.

She would have to face Mr. Whitman in the coming days anytime she had to run errands in town. She'd often seen him walking in or out of the bank, and from time to time at church. Now, even something that meaningless would make her blush.

While Luke hadn't been happy about heading home with a displeased father, she didn't think the boy was frightened of Mr. Whitman. Instead, she suspected he had a tendency toward mischief, as his father had said, and that tendency had landed him in trouble a time or two or maybe more, as it seemed to have done with the nannies. It was too bad the Whitman children no longer had their mother with them. Olivia couldn't imagine growing up without her own dear mama to guide her, comfort her, teach her, and encourage her along the way. After all, could a nanny, even the best of nannies, really do the job of a mother? Could any hired help offer Luke and his sister the love they needed? Was that what had been lacking in the women who'd failed the Whitmans?

Enough.

Olivia fluffed up the pillow, then flopped onto her back. She could drive herself mad turning the whole thing over in her head, and still not get anywhere. Besides, why should she?

It wasn't any of her business. The most she could do, and the best thing for her to do, was to turn the matter over to her heavenly Father. Surely he knew what the Whitman children, and their busy father, needed most.

She slipped down to the side of the bed, knelt, and poured her heart out to her Lord.

Before too long, however, in the deep silence of the peaceful farmhouse, the sound of her parents' hushed voices reached her. Anxiety threaded their words as they again discussed the state of the family's finances.

"I don't know," Papa said. "I just don't know where to turn. We have very little money left from the sale of the livestock, and you know I've mortgaged every last acre of the property already. There won't be any help there."

Mama's response was unintelligible, but her voice sounded as strained with worry as his.

Papa sighed. "Oh, Elizabeth, I'm so very sorry. I never meant for you to think I was scolding you. I don't know another woman who could manage as well as you have done with so little in hand. All these years, ever since we left Baltimore, you've been an incomparable companion. I don't know what I would have done without you and your wise ways. Now this. After all you lacked during wartime, after all the misery I witnessed in the Deep South, I was determined to make sure you—our family—never went without."

Another murmured reply from Olivia's mother.

"Oh, but I'm sure you will do wonders with what supplies you have left. You always do, my dear." Papa's pause went on and on. Finally, he continued, his voice shaky, his tone uncertain. "Although, we both know eventually you will run out of even the last scoop of flour and the last scrap of dried beef. Then…"

"Well, then," Mama said, her voice louder with crisp determination, "I'm sure the Lord will provide as He always has. I have faith."

"So do I, Elizabeth. Still, a man can't help but worry about his family. And I see a bleak winter coming toward us only too soon."

"You don't know that it will be bleak," Mama argued. "I'm certain the Father didn't lead us out here to Oregon, to this particular piece of land, only to wrest it from us. Or to let us starve. Something will come up. Something will occur to you. I trust you."

"If it were only the two of us, I wouldn't worry quite so much," Papa continued. "It's the children that concern me. What if Olivia meets a man who'll court her and win her heart? How will we pay for a wedding? What kind of man can't provide that for his daughter?"

Olivia's heart squeezed. Tears rolled down her cheeks.

Her father's voice, roughened with emotion, rose through the black depths of the night. "Then there's the boys— young men, now, seventeen and almost sixteen. Have you seen how short their trouser legs have grown these last few weeks? And beyond that. I must be thinking of their futures. Right now, I can provide them with land, but it won't provide for them as they need. It won't offer them the means to support themselves and the families I'm sure they want to build. After all the things I saw while fighting… I pray the Lord doesn't leave them only the option of a military career. As honorable and distinguished as our men in uniform are, my love, I wouldn't wish the horrors of battle on our sons."

"Please don't fret, dear." Mama's voice now drifted up softer, more soothing but still louder and clearer than at first. Olivia knew her mother well. Elizabeth Moore was determined to keep her husband from sinking into another of his dark spells. At those times, he would go about his chores and then come inside and sit in a cloud of sadness. Mama insisted the spells were due to his time fighting the Confederacy.

She went on. "Worry won't help the children, and it could fog your thinking, which is never good. Come, now. Let's get some sleep. Tomorrow is another day, with another set of troubles. We need to be rested so that we can tackle them wisely. At the very least, I need rest so that I can let out those pesky, rising hems."

"You're right, dear heart. How did I ever get so fortunate? How did our God know to bless me with a woman so wise as well as beautiful?"

"Oh, pshaw! There you go again, Stephen, flattering a girl..."

As their voices faded, another tear rolled down Olivia's cheek. Her anxiety grew to where nausea threatened. Up until tonight, her parents' discussions had centered on their efforts to raise the funds they needed to buy feed for the animals and seed to sow in the fields and the garden. Olivia hadn't realized they could run out of food.

She crawled back into bed. She couldn't go any longer without standing on her own two feet, without doing something to relieve her parents' situation. She could never live with herself if she stood by and did nothing.

But what could she do? She wasn't a trained nurse and she didn't have the money to get the schooling. And while Mama, who'd grown up in Baltimore, had taught her children, making sure all of them benefited from her excellent education and proper manners, Olivia lacked the preparation needed to work as a schoolteacher. Besides, Bountiful already had a teacher.

Should she leave Bountiful—Oregon, even—to seek employment?

Restless, Olivia rolled over on her other side, careful not to disturb Leah Rose, who shared the bed. She was a competent seamstress, so she supposed she could hire out as a garment factory worker back East, but if she did, she'd still have to afford herself a place to live and food to eat. What would she have left after tending to her immediate needs to send back home? What help would she be to her family?

Then, too, she'd learned from Addie Tucker that their friend, Suzannah Arnold, with her new husband's blessing, was opening up a dressmaking shop in their front parlor. Suzannah's skill with her needle was legend and left Olivia's efforts quite a bit back in the distance.

While a number of new shops were opening up in the growing Bountiful, Olivia didn't have any particular talent to market, like Suzannah. She could do a number of housewifely things well enough, but she was nowhere near as accomplished as even the recently widowed Mrs. O'Dell. Everyone in town eagerly awaited the day she opened the bakery she'd begun to set up since Mr. O'Dell died a few months ago.

She'd heard some women took in laundry to add to their husband's earnings, but there were few unmarried men in Bountiful—all of Hope County, as a matter of fact. Those few bachelor fellows bartered services or a few coins for their friends' wives to help them care for their clothing. No one who set herself up to do the dirty, steamy, backbreaking work would earn enough to do any good.

She flopped over onto her back. The last possibility left to her was domestic work. As Elizabeth Moore's daughter, Olivia did take pride in her ability to run a household. She and Mama worked shoulder to shoulder to keep the Moores fed, clean, and in good health, and the house in as near to perfect condition as possible. She could handle any kind of housework, and she got on well with everyone she knew.

That meant she could, of course, try to hire herself out to a busy boardinghouse owner back in...oh, say Denver or Kansas City, but that still left her with the matter of her own food and housing needs. She'd have to make sure the position included a room and meals.

Still, if she did that she'd wind up ever so far from Mama and Papa...her brothers...the girls. A twitch of anxiety and a wagonload of sadness overwhelmed her.

"Oh, Lord Jesus..." Her heart clenched yet again. "You know just how serious things are. Please help us. If nothing else, please show me what I should do to help. I feel so useless, as though I'm failing Mama and Papa..."

But no matter how fervently she stormed the throne of heaven with her pleas, Olivia felt no easing of her fear. After more long minutes than she cared to count had passed, she was able to thank the Father for his provision up until that point. "And while I'm still worried, I'm more than ready to let you change my worry into joy. I know you're the only one who can do so."

With a sigh, she tucked her fist under her pillow and closed her eyes, determined to find that elusive sleep.

But within seconds, two matching pairs of bright blue eyes popped back into her thoughts. Those Whitman men...

And then, Luke's words came at her with a strength they'd lacked before. *"I want her."*

Olivia bolted to an upright position. "Father...Lord God? Is that it? Did you provide the answer to my situation earlier today without me noticing?"

A question remained, however. Could she do it? Was she in any way qualified? And, of course, did she dare even ask?

Olivia sighed. It was quite obvious, she would never know unless she asked. She would never know until she tried.

Her stomach turned a walloping cartwheel that stole her breath away. As crazy as the notion was, Olivia saw no other alternative.

Turning onto her other side, she enumerated her other options. She could, of course, marry—should have married already, but none of the men who'd approached her after church or while she went about her business in town had raised in her the slightest bit of interest. The thought of binding herself to and sharing her life with someone she didn't...cherish turned her stomach. She'd much rather live out her days as a spinster working in...in a...even a slaughterhouse. If they'd have her.

She suspected Mama knew how she felt, and she thanked the Lord her parents hadn't pushed her into that kind of marriage, in spite of the difficulties they'd been experiencing.

Yes, she could go east in search of work, but that would mean she'd have to live far, far away from her family and all she held dear. Growing up in a new town like Bountiful, where everyone was intent on building the region, making it flourish, she knew no one who'd gone into service. The prospect, while it might be her final decision, made her middle tighten into a hard knot.

It had to be her last resort.

She only saw two immediate possibilities. On the one hand, she could continue to live at home, consume the family's meager resources, and drain their provisions, since she couldn't contribute a thing in return. On the other hand, she could gather up her gumption, seek out Mr. Whitman, and offer her services as a nanny.

"Those three ladies came highly recommended."

She could let the banker's words intimidate her. That would mean her faith was too weak for words. She could instead choose to see God's hand in everything that had happened after church, no matter how absurd, and take courage from the Father's presence in her life.

The worst that could happen? Mr. Whitman could laugh her right out of his office.

The best that might happen? He might offer her the position, even if on a trial basis.

What a relief that would be for Mama and Papa.

Olivia sighed. Her choice was made.

But...had she ever really had a choice in the matter? It seemed as though the Lord's hand had been there guiding her the whole day long. Only the Almighty could have worked in such an unconventional fashion. Only the King of Kings could have turned a mad encounter with a runaway pig into a bright, shining opportunity.

All Olivia had to do was trust.

And obey.

Chapter 3

"But, Olivia, dear—"

"No, Mama. Please don't ask me more questions right now. Do believe me, though. I must go to town today. That's why I need the wagon, and I'm sorry I won't be here to help you this morning. I expect to be back by early afternoon. I'll tell you everything then."

She didn't reckon Mr. Whitman's clear and resounding "no" would take too long to convey. But even though she had no lofty expectations for the meeting, she knew she had to do it, she had to ask. She had to follow through with what every corner of her heart said her heavenly Father was leading her to try.

She trusted the Lord for the outcome, whatever that would be.

Mama sighed, then wiped her hands on her apron, a sign of nerves on her part, something she did to steal the time to gather her thoughts.

For a second, Olivia wished she could wear an apron to her

meeting with the banker. She had no doubt many spells of nervous anxiety would strike as she pressed Mr. Whitman for the opportunity to care for his daughter and son.

Her mother shrugged. "I suppose I must trust you. You're no longer a child, Olivia, and you've always had a good head on you. Go ahead, dear. Go tell your papa what you're planning—or as much of it as you're willing to share."

After a quick kiss to her mother's cheek, Olivia hurried outside, tugging down on the waist of her blue jacket. Papa and the boys were likely in the barn. She didn't much like going in there wearing her jacket and other good skirt, this one a lightweight flannel in a lovely deep plum. The barn offered too many chances to soil nice clothes. But it couldn't be helped. She needed to be on her way if she was to catch Mr. Whitman early in the day, and then return home before too much of the afternoon was gone.

Papa's response to her request was similar to Mama's. While he wanted details, and to that end asked myriad questions, in time he decided to trust her. Before long, Olivia was on her way into town.

After she left Maizie and the wagon with Josh Tucker at the livery stable, Olivia hurried down Main Street, her every thought on what lay ahead. Her gaze, too, was focused on the next step before her, and then the next, as well. She feared if she let herself stray one whit in thought or action she might chicken out, run back to the stable, gather horse and wagon, and beat a hasty retreat home.

That would honor no one. Certainly not her Lord.

Every time her thoughts turned to the many arguments why she should not do this, she shoved them away, determined to obey what she felt to be the Father's call.

At the solid and attractive oak and glass door to the Bank of Bountiful, Olivia paused one moment to breathe a final prayer for courage and favor and dry hands. She missed that apron a whole lot already.

"May I help you?" a red-haired gentleman in a black suit and rimless spectacles asked as Olivia stepped into the bank.

Lord Jesus, help me, please. "Yes." Her voice wobbled only a touch. "I...ah...I'm here to see Mr. Whitman. The president. Of the bank, that is. Not of the nation, of course."

Hush, Olivia. You're blathering.

She straightened her spine and held her chin high, waiting for the gentleman's response.

Skepticism colored his expression. "Do you have an appointment to see Mr. Whitman?"

The doubt in the man's face told Olivia he knew quite well the answer to his question. Nonetheless, she responded. "No, sir. But Mr. Whitman knows I'm due to meet with him, just not when. He knows we have something to discuss. About his son. Please let him know I'm here."

He drew his brows together, shuffled his feet, and wrung his hands. "Just who might you be?"

"Miss Olivia Moore, sir. The lady who handled yesterday's swine situation."

She could have bitten her tongue when blinking and blatant disbelief—a mite of horror, too—blossomed on the man's face. She didn't blame him. Embarrassment seared her cheeks.

"I see." The man's spectacles dropped down to the end of his thin nose and he shoved them up with an ink-smeared finger, which left a streak all the way to the bridge.

"Please, Mister...?"

"Colby, madam. Mr. Lawrence Colby, at your service."

She gave a tight nod. "Mr. Colby, then. Please let Mr. Whitman know I'm here. Let him decide if he'll see me."

In the meantime, she would pray and pray and pray that he did.

With abundant distaste on his features, Mr. Colby nodded, then stepped to a door at the back of the large lobby of the bank. He knocked, entered, and closed the door, leaving Olivia to study her surroundings. Papa always attended to business matters and she'd never been inside the bank before.

The main chamber spoke of serious responsibility and abundance. A spot for each one of the two tellers was located on either side of the room, the openings protected with thick brass rods. The gentlemen behind the bars wore neat white shirts with black sleeve garters, proper black ties, and smart-looking green-billed visors over their foreheads. Olivia wondered why they'd wear hats indoors, but she didn't think her curiosity was important enough to satisfy that day. Maybe she'd ask Papa once she went back home.

A muted conversation caught her attention. One customer stood before the teller to Olivia's left, patiently watching the teller count bills into separate, tidy stacks. She took note of the man's crisp gray trousers and well-tailored coat, gleaming black boots, and fine-looking slate-hued hat held loosely in his left hand. From where she stood, she thought it might be the recently arrived German shoemaker, Herr Schmitz.

Moments later, she verified her guess as Herr Schmitz strode past her and nodded respectfully in greeting, a spear of light from the nearest window catching the gleam of his blond hair. At the door, he donned his elegant hat before stepping outside.

As she looked around again, Olivia found plenty to admire. The two windows, tall and ample, graced each side of the generous-sized chamber, and the brilliant August sun poured in, brightening the mood of the otherwise solemn business establishment. The scent of wax polish rose from the gleaming floor, and the tang of lemon oil told Olivia that someone cared enough to make sure the abundant wood wainscoting on the walls and all the desks' surfaces were as well tended.

Olivia grew more nervous by the minute, as she continued to wait for Mr. Colby to return with the verdict. After what seemed a minor eternity, Mr. Colby emerged from behind the door, followed by Mr. Whitman.

"Miss Moore," Luke's father said, a question in his voice, curiosity in his gaze. "To what do I owe this pleasure?"

Olivia tugged down on her navy jacket, wiping her nerve-dampened palms against the fabric at the same time. "If you don't mind, sir, I would prefer we speak in your office."

Mr. Whitman's eyebrows shot toward his hairline, and he and Mr. Colby traded glances. "Very well," he said. "If you'll follow me, please?"

Olivia did so cautiously, unwilling to trip over her own feet because of her anxiety. The most important thing to remember was the worst that might happen, and making a fool of herself as Mr. Whitman refused her offer wouldn't be too horrid an outcome. Embarrassing? Yes. Devastating? No.

Well, embarrassment was the immediate worst that might happen, but in reality, the worst that would happen was her inability to help Mama and Papa in their hour of need. She couldn't bear that thought. So she pressed on.

When she and the banker stood on either side of the solid

desk in the center of the room, Mr. Whitman turned his brilliant blue eyes on Olivia. "I must admit, Miss Moore, my curiosity is quite piqued. Is this about Luke's discipline?"

She took a deep breath. "In a way, but not exactly. If you'll allow me, sir, I have an offer for you."

Again, surprise overtook the man. "This should prove interesting."

"I hope so." She set down her purse on an upholstered brown chair, then faced the banker, her gaze direct, her back straight, her chin tipped up. "It would seem you're in a pickle of sorts. When it comes to your children, that is."

"Ah...the nanny situation."

"Precisely." *Go on, Olivia. Get it over with.* "I don't know of many candidates for that position in Bountiful or the surrounding area."

He nodded, his head tilted a tad to one side.

That was when it struck Olivia. Goodness. She was outgunned when it came to negotiating with this man. Not only was Mr. Elijah Whitman a respected pillar of the community, a prominent businessman, and well-to-do, but he was also a very handsome specimen of a man. On the other hand, she knew nothing of business and she didn't know much about men. At least the subject she wanted to discuss was one she understood. By virtue of who she was, she knew more than a bit about youngsters, an ordered household, and family matters.

Still, she had to face those eyes. They glowed with the intensity of the clear August sky outside, and even the black lashes that fringed them didn't do a thing to dim their radiance. "Miss Moore?"

She blushed—yet again. This just wouldn't do. She couldn't

let herself be distracted by his stature in town or his good looks. If she did, she would surely make a mess of her attempt to seek employment, something she very much needed to manage well. She needed the job he had to offer. She had to make him see she was the woman he needed just then, not a weak girl who would fold at the first sign of trouble from his two rambunctious youngsters.

She gave another tug to her jacket's hem. "Very well, Mr. Whitman. I came to speak to you about an idea that occurred to me last night. As your son said yesterday, he and his sister haven't been charmed by your choice in nannies thus far. Am I right?"

He gave a wry laugh. "I doubt any choice in nannies would please those two. How they've come to believe they're ready to manage themselves, I don't know."

Thinking of her brothers and sisters, Olivia smiled. "Adolescents see themselves as more capable and wiser than they really are."

He crossed his arms, a touch of skepticism in his expression. "You have the kind of experience with adolescents that would lead you to say that?"

His piercing gaze made her warm and twitchy all over. As unexpected and unfamiliar as her response was, Olivia had to believe it came from nerves. She squared her shoulders. "Why, yessir, I do. I'm the oldest of five children, and I've always helped Mama with the younger ones. My two brothers and two sisters have put me through my paces when it comes to coping with youngsters."

A spark of interest caught fire in his gaze. "Do tell."

"Indeed." She smiled. "That leads me to my suggestion.

Since I have the experience already, and your son Luke was so daring as to suggest that I might be an adequate nanny—"

"I was afraid you might have overheard that. If I remember correctly, Miss Moore," he said, amusement in his voice, "my son is certain you're *the* right nanny for him and his sister."

While he'd barely leashed his laughter, Olivia sensed no malice in his humor. She went on. "As I was saying, since Luke is already well disposed toward me, and since we agree"—she hoped—"I have the experience needed to cope with children his age, I would like to offer my services as your next nanny."

As soon as the words left her lips, she felt her middle do a colossal flip, her knees grow weak, her palms dampen again. A sensation that felt suspiciously like a swoon was taking over. Well, she'd never fainted in her life and was not about to try it now. Who would have thought she'd prove such a coward in a situation of such importance? Or so bold as to create a situation that revealed her weakness to begin with? Mercy. What could she have been thinking?

Dear Lord, please...

Although she tried, Olivia couldn't quite come up with a petition that would express to God what she needed right then.

Silly! What you need is for Mr. Whitman to hire you. And your Almighty Father knows that well enough.

The silence in the room seemed to take on a life of its own. Like a blanket, it surrounded her, covered her, threatened to smother her as she stood before the scrutiny of those blue, blue eyes.

A scrutiny that continued to make her more aware of herself than she'd ever been. What must Mr. Whitman think of her?

And why was he taking so long? Why didn't he answer?

The longer he took to think, to stare, the closer Olivia came to that threatening swoon, just like one of those weaker women she'd looked down on moments earlier. But she wouldn't. She couldn't. No one would hire a swooner to chase after two unruly children. If Luke was anything to go by, she doubted his sister would be the shrinking sort. Olivia had to present a strong, competent front to her potential employer, a man of substance.

"Well, I suppose I would be the nanny, but what I'd like to do is call myself your children's companion, since it seems they've developed quite an aversion to the title itself. I'd like them to see me more as an older acquaintance who has their best interests at heart rather than another of their much-despised nannies. That is if you wouldn't object. And if you decide to hire me."

Still, he continued to stare but didn't respond.

"I suppose..." he said when she was about to explode with anticipation, his words slow and deliberate, drawn out, "you couldn't do much worse than the ones who came before you." Olivia breathed yet another prayer, this time aware of the spark of hope in her heart. She thought it best to let the banker think things through without further comment on her part. She doubted he would like to bring a chatterer into his household.

If he hired her.

Before too much longer, he seemed to come to a decision. "Very well, Miss Moore. We can give your suggestion a try. How about if we agree to a trial period? Say...three months?"

Her heart soared. "Oh my, yes! That would be"—

she stopped herself before she scared him off with her enthusiasm—"that would be quite appropriate, sir. We should know by sometime in November whether this arrangement will work for all of us."

"That's what I think." He gestured for her to take a seat in the chair across the desk from him, and then pulled up his own large leather chair. "Now, about the details. Let's begin with your starting date. How soon can you join us?"

"Join you?" Olivia hadn't dared to dream he would ask her to live with his family. The arrangement would offer greater relief for her parents.

"Yes, Miss Moore. If you're to care for the children, you'll be needed at all hours of the day. I never know when a business meeting will delay me well into the evening hours or when I might need to leave town for a few days...or weeks. You do need to live with our family." He held out a hand to stop any possible comment. "Please don't worry about proprieties. I have a housekeeper and cook who also lives with us. You will not be alone in an unmarried man's home."

Although she hadn't thought that far ahead, Olivia felt a great deal of relief at the notion of female companionship in the Whitman home. "That sounds acceptable, sir. I'll only need a few days to gather my belongings and move into town. How soon would you want me to start?"

"Tomorrow?" The word seemed to burst out unbidden, since as soon as he said it, Mr. Whitman's eyes widened and he shook his head. "I'm sorry. I'm afraid matters at home have reached the point where I cannot even think clearly. Of course, tomorrow is impossible. How about if you join us in a week or two?"

"A week from today, next Monday, will be fine."

"Excellent. That would be excellent, indeed."

Now he seemed as enthusiastic as she had been moments earlier. Olivia took it as a good sign, but until he repeated his agreement, she refused to let her heart soar on just the possibility. "Then we're agreed, right?"

"Yes, Miss Moore." Their agreement seemed to bring him a measure of relief. His shoulders relaxed and the fine line across his forehead was no longer visible.

"You have no idea what a blessing your words are, sir. Now that we've agreed, I must be on my way. I have a great deal to do before I can come next Monday and take over Luke's and—" She drew up short. "I'm afraid I don't know your daughter's name."

"Miranda, but we have called her Randy since the start." His lips took on a wry twist. "Although, since she's about to turn the ripe old age of thirteen in a few months...well, she's decided Miranda's far more appropriate."

Olivia smiled. "Why, of course, it is. She's practically a grown woman, sir."

"But—"

"Never fear, Mr. Whitman. I was only speaking from Randy's point of view. That's what she believes, isn't it?"

"Well, yes..." Reluctance dragged out his response.

Olivia stood and began to pull on her gloves. "But *we* know the truth, don't we?"

His appealing smile put in a return. "Aha! I understand. We do, indeed, know the truth. I suspect I may have made a better bargain than I could have hoped for."

She slipped her leather bag to the crook of her elbow, and

reached out to shake her new employer's hand. "I hope you continue to think so, sir. And now, I'll be on my way. Do have a pleasant day, Mr. Whitman."

"Miss Moore," he said, not taking her hand. "We have yet to speak of wages, duties and responsibilities, or specific arrangements. I'm sure you'd like to know all of that."

Olivia blushed and let her hand dangle at her side. Oh, dear. The simple fact of being hired had so flustered her she hadn't bothered with any of those truly important matters. "Of course, of course. But, I'm sure I'll be quite satisfied with your customary arrangements. With your previous nannies, I mean. Not that I'll be the nanny, right? I'll be the children's companion."

A crooked smile tilted his lips upward at one corner. "Yes, I do believe we'll call you the children's companion. And since you're so agreeable, then perhaps it would be just as well if we discuss the details when you come to the house next Monday."

She gave a deep sigh of relief. She hoped that by then she'd be better prepared to handle this business of being a woman in the banker's employ. "Certainly, Mr. Whitman. That will be quite fine. And—well, I really must be on my way now."

When his long, sturdy fingers surrounded hers, Olivia shivered. The warmth, the strength of his clasp, surprised her… mostly with the pleasure she felt. Not to mention her reluctance to let go. Which would not do, certainly not now that she worked for the man.

His rapid blinking as he stared at their clasped hands suggested he also felt a similar awareness, which flustered Olivia even more.

Oh, my!

Then he shook his head an almost imperceptible bit. He stood taller, firmed up his shoulders, and gently and slowly released her hand. "Yes, Miss Moore. I'm sure I—ah...will. Have a good afternoon. And thank you. My greatest problem has been resolved. Thank you very much, indeed."

That pulled her out from the pleasurable moment of—was it connection?—between them.

He'd resolved his greatest problem by hiring her. Really?

If only Olivia's greatest problem could be as easily solved. All she hoped for as a result of the step she had just taken was to ease her parents' burden a bit.

She sighed. Then she noticed he was waiting for a response. She shrugged. "I'm glad to be of service, sir."

Once on the sidewalk again, Olivia's knees began to melt. She leaned against the sturdy brick wall of the bank, certain she couldn't support herself for another minute on her own strength.

"Thank you, Jesus. Your mercies *are* new every morning. You've just made it so real to me once again."

A sense of peace settled over her, even though it did nothing to remove the overwhelming impression the banker had made on her. Mr. Whitman was such an attractive man. Even if she never should have taken notice of his appeal, his masculine strength, his handsome face, and his resonant voice. Her exquisite awareness of him might make working for him uncomfortable.

Perhaps. But it couldn't be helped.

Olivia took a deep breath and started down Main Street toward Tucker's Livery Stables. Mr. Whitman himself was yet another matter to take to the Lord in prayer. She certainly couldn't take back her offer then run away now that she'd achieved her goal. She had to move forward down the path she'd chosen.

A path that presented yet another hurdle for her to overcome. She had to face Mama and Papa. Something told her it wouldn't be quite as easy as approaching and persuading Mr. Whitman had been. As if that had been easy in any way.

She prayed all the way home.

Chapter 4

Olivia managed to keep Mama and Papa's questions at bay until after supper. When the younger children had gone to bed, she approached her father. "I'd like to tell you and Mama about my visit to town today. It's important."

Papa nodded. The slight smile he gave her didn't fully erase the concern in his eyes. He turned to Mama, extended his hand, and they both followed Olivia into the kitchen. The scent of cinnamon-dusted fritters still lingered in the air.

"Would either one of you care for a cup of coffee? Tea?"

When both shook their heads, she took the teakettle Mama always kept on the back of the stove and poured boiling water into the china teapot where she'd already measured the aromatic leaves, letting it steep longer than usual to make up for the sparing quantity she'd used. Moments later, she sat across from her parents, the teapot on a folded kitchen towel in the middle of the large round table, a cup and saucer in front of her spot.

"Well, Livvy, dear," Mama said. "You've kept us in suspense long enough, don't you think? It's time you told us what you've been up to."

Olivia nodded as she poured a cup of tea. With her gaze on the curl of steam that rose from the fragrant liquid, she began.

"I know how difficult things have been for you both these last two years—"

"Olivia," Papa said, "that's not for you to fret over. Your mother and I do have matters under control."

Control? It didn't seem that way to her.

"I do understand, Papa. I also know how hard both of you work. I just feel as though I haven't carried my weight. I'm not a child anymore, as Mama said earlier today."

Her mother's golden brown eyes narrowed and she shook her graying head. "I never thought you'd use my own words against me, Livvy."

"I'm not using your words against you. I'm stating the obvious. As an adult, older than you were when I was born, I need to make something of myself. Today, I took the first step in that direction."

Mama's eyes opened wide, while Papa's narrowed. Neither spoke as they waited on her.

Olivia tipped up her chin. "I have found myself suitable employment. I begin work next Monday, and there's a great deal I must do to be ready in time."

"Employment!"

"You've become a hired hand? Where?"

Olivia laughed. "No, I haven't become a hired hand, Papa. That's not the only kind of work there is, you know."

"It's the only kind I know of around Bountiful."

"Not exactly." She stirred a golden lozenge of honey into the hot tea. "There is another kind of work, quite appropriate for a woman like me. I'm happy to tell you it was offered, and I accepted the position."

"Very well, Olivia," Papa said. "Please tell us what you've done."

"I've agreed to become the new nanny for the bank owner's children."

The depth of silence in the kitchen was greater than anything Olivia had ever known. While she'd suspected her parents would be surprised by what she'd done, she hadn't imagined she would shock them as much as she evidently had. But it couldn't be helped. She and Mr. Whitman had reached an agreement. She couldn't back out now.

"I . . . I don't know what to say," Mama murmured, a frown on her otherwise still smooth forehead. "I knew he'd had trouble keeping a nanny, but I can't imagine what would possess you to offer your services."

Papa wouldn't even look at Olivia, so she focused on Mama's statement. "Simple. I've been helping you with the boys, Marty, and Leah Rose all these years. I know how to work with them. And . . . well, there was an incident yesterday on my way to Addie's house. I met Mr. Whitman's son and a group of his friends while they were making mischief, and I handled the situation quite well."

At least, she thought she had. Evidently, so had Mr. Whitman, enough to have given her the opportunity to prove herself.

"Then last night I prayed, and after a while, I couldn't discount the strong leading I felt. God seemed to call me to help out the Whitmans. It didn't hurt that I'd be able to help you at the same time."

"Oh, but, you really don't have to—"

"Why would you think things are so—"

"Please!" She held up a hand. "Let me tell you the whole story."

Olivia went on, and when she finished describing her meeting with the banker, her parents seemed dumbstruck. Neither uttered a word. She pressed her advantage.

"It would seem an excellent solution for everyone. I will feel productive, and I'll be able to help you with the finances. I won't be a drain on the family's resources, since I'll be living with the Whitman's cook in their enormous house, and the Whitman children won't have to put up with another nasty nanny."

After a moment, her father crossed his arms. "What, pray tell, does Mr. Whitman gain from this arrangement?"

Olivia shrugged. "I wouldn't know, Papa, since Mr. Whitman wasn't my main concern. Perhaps he'll benefit from happy, well-behaved children. Especially, a son who won't have the opportunity to terrorize the town when boredom strikes and his papa's not able to chase after him. There's a lot to be said for peace of mind, I'm sure."

Her parents traded glances. Olivia couldn't read what had passed between them, but she knew neither was happy with her decision. She wondered how strenuously they would oppose the plan.

"I can't say what you've done sits well with me, Livvy," her father said after a bit. "But I don't suppose I can change your mind, can I?"

She shook her head and took a sip of tea to hide her nerves.

Mama's frown deepened. "Would you at least arrange to make this a trial? So that you can leave gracefully if after a while you want to quit."

Olivia allowed herself a smug smile. "Already done, Mama. That's what Mr. Whitman and I agreed to. We'll give this arrangement three months. If it doesn't work out, there's no harm done. I'll come home and Mr. Whitman will advertise for a new nanny."

Papa slapped his large, work-roughened hands on the table. "Well. It looks as though you've thought of everything. Now all you have left to do is pack. I'll drive you to town next Monday morning."

Mama gave her a wistful smile. "I'm proud of you, Livvy, but I will admit, I'll miss you."

"Oh, please, don't say that. You'll make us both sad, and instead, I want us to be happy. I've done something good. I'll be helping you and Papa. The Whitmans, too. It's a blessing. For all of us."

She hoped.

The memory of Elijah Whitman's blue eyes seared her thoughts again, followed by the exceptional sense of awareness she'd experienced when he'd taken her hand in his.

Olivia hoped she hadn't mistaken her enthusiasm, reading more into it than was there, seeing it as leading from above. She hoped she'd been listening to the will of the Father. If not . . .

Oh, Lord Jesus. Keep me honest, on the right path, and in your will.

*   *   *

"Miss Moore," Mr. Whitman said when Olivia arrived at his home the next Monday morning. "Please, do come in."

He gestured and she followed, Mama's old and battered satchel clutched in both hands. When she entered the large entry foyer, she had the immediate sensation that she'd stepped into another world. While the Moore home was reasonably roomy, comfortable, and pleasant, it looked nothing like this.

Warm golden oak floors gleamed underfoot, and a cream, blue, and gray wool rug graced the center of the area. On the wall to the right, a small table sat beneath a carved mirror with brass candle sconces on either side.

Awed by the elegance of the Whitman home, Olivia glanced to her left. There she spotted another pair of sconces, these framing a tall case clock made of a dark wood, most likely walnut, since she'd heard that wood was quite deep toned.

She blinked, unaccustomed to so much finery. How did folks live here? Weren't they leery of even touching the elegant items? Of stepping on the thick, soft-looking rug?

How would *she* manage to live here?

Had she made a mistake by asking for the position?

"Are you all right, Miss Moore?"

Startled, a squeaky "Oh!" escaped her lips before she could prevent it. "Ah...yes, yes. I'm quite fine. I was...I was just admiring your beautiful home."

There she went again, sounding foolish and inexperienced. Was this when Mr. Whitman took back the offer? Then what would she do?

Olivia shook herself, pulled up to her full height, and set

her shoulders in a firm line. She couldn't afford to let this opportunity escape just because she'd never done anything like this before. One had to start somewhere in life, and she was going to start right then and there.

But what should she say? Especially since Mr. Whitman's brilliant blue eyes remained fixed on her.

Oh, yes. They had left certain matters unsettled.

"I believe, Mr. Whitman, we agreed to discuss matters of duties and expectations and living arrangements once I arrived. Well, sir, I'm here now."

The banker tipped up the corner of his mouth in another of those crooked smiles that betrayed little of his thoughts. He extended a hand to grasp her satchel, and Olivia relinquished the heavy bag.

"I'll see this gets to your room. Now, please follow me into the parlor, Miss Moore. I'll have Cooky bring us some fresh coffee, and we can discuss everything we need to in comfort there instead of standing here."

They started down the hall. Past the end of the stairs, lovely with their gleaming treads and banisters, her new employer stepped into an open doorway on the left side. When she followed, Olivia found herself in another room of exceptional beauty. Deep plum velvet upholstery covered a graceful sofa nestled against the far wall between two generous-sized windows whose draperies, a shade darker than the sofa, had been pulled open to welcome the sunshine, giving the parlor a rosy glow. To her right, a fireplace with a tall oak mantel looked ready for the chilly days to come. At her left, a couple of broad armchairs in slate gray upholstery sat on either side of a small round table topped by a brass oil lamp, its glass globe decorated with a smattering of colorful blossoms. A handful of small tables dotted the room, a bookcase full of tomes graced the wall across from the fireplace, and beneath everything lay another wool rug, this one in shades of black and cream and deep rose.

Olivia couldn't wait until she could tell Mama about the Whitman home. Surely this compared quite well with the places Elizabeth had told her children she'd visited with Grandmother Hodges back in Baltimore.

And yet, as splendid as the house looked, Olivia had to wonder. How did all this luxury wind up in tiny Bountiful? Kansas City or even Denver, she could understand. But here in Hope County most folks struggled to scratch a living from the soil or raise cattle for the beef, chop forests for the lumber, or mill wool from the various flocks of sheep. True, the town had a handful of merchants, but no one she knew had this kind of wealth.

Then it dawned on her. She'd heard Mr. Whitman, Sr., had struck gold years ago, when he'd first come out west. It appeared the man had indeed done well enough to enable his son to keep a home like this.

A home like the one she still stared at like some uncouth creature. She waved a hand. "Please excuse me, sir. As I mentioned before, you've a lovely home."

This time, his smile thinned and tightened, and his eyes narrowed. "My late wife... *preferred* the finest things."

Oh, dear. She'd done it again. She'd made this poor widower think of his loss. She would have to take time to consider what she might say in the future. It wouldn't do to just blurt out any old thing that came to mind.

"I'm sorr—"

"It's fine, it's fine," he said, but his voice sounded as tight as his lips appeared. "Please, take a seat. I'll ring for Cooky to bring in that coffee I promised."

As Olivia perched on the sofa, Mr. Whitman sat in one of the plush armchairs. He rang a small brass bell Olivia hadn't noticed on the side table.

Moments later, a plump lady with white hair and a plain black dress walked in, a large silver tray loaded with cups, saucers, spoons, coffeepot, and various other items in her hands.

"There you are, Mr. Whitman, sir. A nice coffee for you and your guest—" The woman clamped her mouth shut the moment she laid eyes on Olivia. Those eyes narrowed, and her nose twitched.

Cooky, as the banker had called her, was not pleased to find Olivia in the room. She wondered why.

"Thank you," Mr. Whitman said. "You can leave the tray here at my side."

Once she'd done as asked, Cooky turned, gave Olivia a once-over, then left, her sniff impossible to miss.

What could she possibly have done to displease the woman to such an extent? She hadn't even begun to work as yet.

Before she could think too much on the possibilities, Mr. Whitman spoke. "How do you take your coffee?"

"Cream and sugar, please."

Moments later, he stood before her, extending a steaming cup. Glad for something to occupy her hands, Olivia took it and smiled. "Thank you."

He returned to his seat, poured himself some coffee, took a drink, and then turned to her again. "Shall we get started?"

At her nod, he continued. "Your duties are quite simple.

I expect you to prepare the children for the day—daily for school, of course, and Sunday for church. You'll also be responsible for their rooms and their belongings, although Cooky's daughter, Kate, does most of our actual cleaning and laundering. Once Luke and Randy return from school in the afternoon, you'll need to supervise their assignments and join them for their meals, making sure, of course, they behave and display appropriate manners."

Olivia drew her brows together. "Do they not eat with you?"

"Those times when I'm home, yes, they do. But business keeps me late at the bank oftentimes, and I do travel a good amount. They need someone with them on a regular basis, to keep the wagon-wheels well oiled, so to speak."

Unusual, but not unreasonable. Then it occurred to her. "You—do you expect me to take my meals with *you*?"

He laughed. "I promise I know how to use my napkin and I don't chew with an open mouth. I won't make it too great a hardship on you."

Olivia's cheeks burned. "Oh, dear. I'm sorry. I didn't mean anything of the sort. Of course, I'm sure you have lovely manners and know how to act at all times, but it's just…well, I didn't think folks who hired help would then eat with them."

Mr. Whitman shrugged. "I suppose in fancy social circles, especially back East, that would be the case, but I'm more interested in getting my children to mind. You saw Luke the other day with those boys. I'm sure you would agree he needs reining in."

Olivia forced herself to relax; not easy, true, but at least she didn't have to stay bolt upright. "That's the whole point, sir. I don't think Luke is all that different from most other little boys. Remember, Luke wasn't alone on that street with that hog. You and I saw a group of them making mischief. He needs chores and activities that will keep him too busy to find trouble, wouldn't you agree?"

"Precisely. But I'm sure you understand that my work prevents me from doing that. There lies my need for a nanny—"

"Companion, remember? We don't use that dreaded word anymore. We want to start off on a happier note this time."

"Indeed." After he set down his cup, he leaned forward, elbows propped on his knees, hands laced between them. "I know they're a handful, but I also know they can do much better. That's why I need you to supervise their evenings, as well. Bedtime has become a battle of enormous proportions. Luke insists he doesn't need to sleep as much as I know he does, and Randy…well, she's certain she's too adult to even have a bedtime."

"Completely normal."

He arched a brow. "We'll see how you feel after a few days with them." Sitting back, he picked up his cup, his gaze fully on Olivia again. "Finally, I intend to set your wages at the same level as our former nannies." He named a sum far greater than she'd hoped for. Before she had the chance to react, he went on. "As far as your personal quarters, you'll have the room at the end of the upstairs hall, right next to Cooky's. While it is small, I'm sure you'll find it adequate. None of the other nannies found fault with it, but if there's anything else you need, please make sure you ask Cooky."

Sure, she would. After the woman had made her disapproval more than evident, Olivia would go without just about everything she could envision before she asked the Whitmans' cook for even a pin.

"I'm sure it will all be fine, sir." She made a point of glancing around. "Where are the children? I haven't seen them, and I've yet to meet Randy."

"I wanted us to have this time alone," he said, "to discuss these details, but I'll fetch them now. They need to be at school by nine. You'll have little time to prepare them today, but they were supposed to be getting ready on their own."

"Do they expect me?"

To her surprise, he blushed. "Er...no. I thought it best not to give them time to prepare a frontal attack before you arrived."

Or to avoid unknown consequences if I didn't show up.

Olivia chuckled. "They really do seem to have things in an uproar here, don't they?"

"And how!" He shook his head, a sheepish grin on his lips. "Now that I've painted the most unattractive picture of my children for you, let me go for them. I hope you can do more with those two than the others before you have. Otherwise... well, I don't know."

As he crossed to the doorway and stepped into the hall, Olivia felt another pang of apprehension. *Oh, Father. What have I done? Are these youngsters the wild beings their papa has described? Am I up to this challenge?*

Before she had time to ponder the possibilities her imagination had begun to conjure, footsteps announced the children's descent on the stairs.

"Please join me in the parlor, Luke, Randy," Mr. Whitman said. "I have someone for you to meet."

Luke whooped. "We're not going to school today!"

"Not so fast there," his father cautioned. "You are headed for school, today and every other day, but right now you need to meet someone—"

"Miss Olivia!" the boy shouted when he saw her standing by the sofa, a wide smile on his face as he rushed to her side. "You *did* come!" He paused, sniffed. "You don't stink of sour milk and smelly lini—nilli—oh, that rubbing stuff for rheumy spots."

She might as well start her job. "That's liniment, Luke. And I'm happy to see you again, too."

"Uh-huh. That stuff." Alarm widened his eyes. "You don't use it, do you? 'Cuz if you do..." He went back to sniffing.

"I don't use liniment."

"Lucas!" Eli called from the doorway. "What are you doing? You don't go up and smell folks. Please apologize to Miss Moore right this minute."

"But I wasn't doing nothing wrong!"

Olivia placed a hand on the boy's shoulder. "That's anything, Luke. But you're right. Mr. Whitman, we were having a discussion on the faults in the usual smell of liniment."

"Still, Miss Moore, sniffing you like...like a dog? That must stop, Luke."

"I'll make sure he understands what's appropriate," Olivia said. "This time, as I mentioned, we were having a specific discussion."

Wearing a doubtful expression, Eli raised his hands in defeat. "If you insist—"

"Papa!"

The girl in the doorway was lovely, and she would one day

blossom into an absolute beauty, as long as she didn't wear the frown she now displayed. Her black hair gleamed like her father's and her blue eyes matched those of both men in her family.

This could only be the heretofore absent Randy.

"So you did hire another nanny," she said, her nose high in the air, her chin tipped skyward, disdain in every line of her being. "I suppose Luke does need someone to keep him from wallowing with pigs on a Sunday afternoon."

Olivia stifled a chuckle. Randy's description went much too far, and her posture and attitude broadcast her troublesome attitude. She clearly considered herself the lady of the house. Still, as Mr. Whitman had said, the girl was not yet thirteen. Olivia would have her work cut out to deal with her, never mind win her friendship and cooperation.

But she would do both.

She had to.

Stepping forward, she held out her hand. "I've been looking forward to meeting you, Miranda. I must correct one detail, however. I'm not your new nanny. Your father merely hired me to be a companion for you and your brother since he works so much and travels some, as well. I'm counting on your expertise to help me learn the ropes around your home."

Randy blinked. Then she narrowed her eyes, crossed her arms, tapped a toe. Finally, she tossed the lengths of her thick, dark braids over her shoulders and turned to her father. "I suppose, if you must have someone to watch Luke at all times, she'll do. But I'm no child, Papa. *I* certainly do *not* need a companion."

As Mr. Whitman's lips tightened, Olivia caught his gaze,

wishing she could warn him not to push his daughter too far right from the start. Olivia had to win the girl, not force her.

He must have understood Olivia's silent plea, because he eased his shoulders and lightened his expression. "Miss Moore is here because I need to make sure there's an experienced adult in the house when I'm not here. She'll make sure to make your days run smoothly, and she'll also make certain you both have everything you need."

His vague answer pleased Olivia. It gave her a great amount of leeway with the children, and she planned to take advantage of it. "I'm sure there's a good deal that must be done before we start out for school," she told the children. "Now, if your father will excuse us, let's see what you both need for the day."

As she walked out of the parlor, she came within inches of her employer. He looked a touch perplexed, but she much preferred that to the frustration he'd revealed out on the street that other Sunday.

"I'll be sure to check with you when I come home from the bank this evening," he said. "You'll find your things in your room. Cooky or the children can show you to the right one."

With that, Olivia stepped out into her brand-new life, a measure of trepidation in her heart and a quiet prayer for strength and wisdom on her lips.

Chapter 5

By the time Olivia closed the door to Luke's bedroom at eight that night, she felt as though she'd spent the day fighting an angry mama bear and still had lost the bout. As she drew a deep, heartfelt breath, every ounce of oomph drained from her exhausted body and she sagged against the wall to keep from folding into a lump on the floor.

For her to litter the hallway at the end of her first day of work did not strike Olivia as the best way to give her employer a good impression. If he'd finally come home.

While Mr. Whitman had said that morning he'd speak with her once he returned from work, she'd yet to see the man.

Perhaps it was for the best, what with Luke breaking his bread into small bits and rolling them into lumps all through the evening meal. He'd then lobbed the tiny missiles at his sister, who'd not been one bit pleased. In the end, Randy had excused herself with her lofty attitude firmly in place, and

Olivia had been reduced to removing Luke's ignored supper from the table, then sending the boy to his room.

That did not seem to fill the bill when it came to her employer's expectations. She'd followed the young Whitmans upstairs, which hadn't ended any better.

Randy, sitting at a pretty dressing table brushing the bread out of her glorious black mane, had reminded Olivia that she hadn't started the altercation, and that she could indeed take care of herself. As she'd informed her papa, and Olivia herself, that morning.

"So please close the door behind you," the child had said.

Olivia had called upon her last drop of patience to not take the brush from the girl's hand, send her to change into her nightclothes, and supervise until Randy crawled under the covers. But she'd known that wouldn't serve her in her ultimate goal. She wanted to win the girl's cooperation. A confrontation over a trifling matter wouldn't further her end.

So instead she'd marched into Luke's room. There she found the boy sprawled on the floor, spinning a red-painted wooden top across an uncarpeted corner. If she hadn't known better, she would have said he was a deaf-mute, the way he'd failed to react to her requests. Finally, she'd done what she hadn't in Randy's case. She'd snatched the top before it stopped whirring, before Luke could wrap the string around it and snap it back into action, and pocketed the toy.

At her charge's wail, she'd clapped her hands as if they'd been covered in dust, then crossed her arms. "You shall have it back in the morning, once you've apologized to Randy for tossing sticky bits into her hair."

"Won't."

Two could play, of course. "Then I suppose I've just acquired an excellent top for myself."

His eyes narrowed. "That's stealing. I'll tell Papa."

Aha!

Olivia smiled. "Are you sure you want to do that? You understand, don't you, that your father will, of course, want to know why I felt the need to take the top."

He blinked.

She smiled wider.

"Um...well, I'll tell him she was being super—super-silly again. Good night, Miss Moore."

Olivia fought a chuckle. He'd obviously listened to his father try to correct Randy's haughty airs before. "That's supercilious, and I don't think he's going to accept that answer any more than I did."

" 'S what I said, super-silly. And I know he will. He's always after Randy to stop being...super-silly. And you said it was bedtime. Good night."

So. After he'd told his father he wanted her for a nanny, now that she had the position, he could hardly wait to be rid of her. Too bad. She had a job to do.

"But," she said, "I know he has never tossed sticky things into her hair to get her to stop."

The eyebrows drew close, the brow furrowed, the lips pursed. "Fine. He hasn't. But he'll make you give me my top. *After* we wake up in the morning. G'night."

She again ignored the dismissal. "If you insist...why then, there's nothing to do but wait until the morning and tell him the whole story. We'll let your father make the decision. Right now, I need to see your school lessons."

"I only had a spelling list." He walked to the small table before the window and picked up a sheet of paper. "Here." A sly look crossed his face. "Now will you give me my top? And go to sleep?"

"You'll have the top as soon as you get back from asking Randy's forgiveness."

He grunted and flung himself onto the bed. "Not gonna do it."

Olivia chose to ignore his negative response and instead studied his spelling words. Luke had written them out in a squiggly, childish hand, five times each.

"Let's see, now. How about if I quiz you on them? That way we'll make sure you get all of them right in class."

Luke raised his head a fraction. "You'd do that?"

She nodded.

"But, why?"

"Because I want to help you do well in your studies. It's important to learn everything you can. A young gentleman must be well-educated, you understand."

Although he still seemed suspicious, when she called him a young gentleman his expression brightened a touch. By the time they'd worked their way up and down the list twice, his face glowed with the sparkle of achievement.

And he hadn't tried to run her off again.

Olivia also felt good about their accomplishment, but at the same time she felt exhausted. Now it was time to make sure Luke went to sleep, and early, as his father had told her he wished.

"Please wash up," she told the boy. "And change into your nightclothes. It's time for bed."

Although he grumbled about being perfectly clean, he stepped to the washstand near the small armoire and splashed water in the bowl. Hands then dove into the water, dabbed around his chin and forehead, and then reached for the towel.

"I do believe there's a bar of soap right next to the pitcher. You need to use it."

"But I already toldja. I'm clean."

"One can always be cleaner. You know that's what that small cloth is there for, right? To soap up and use it to scrub, even behind your ears. Please do the right thing, Luke."

With an angry glare, he started over, this time lathering the cloth, rubbing his cheeks, and splashing even the wall behind the washstand.

After a lick with the dry towel, he spun around. "There. I'm going to bed. *Good night*, Miss Moore."

"The nightclothes, please."

"But I'm only gonna have to change again in the morning."

"Of course. That's what everyone does. Please change."

"But—"

"Young gentlemen don't argue what's right. They simply do it at the right time. Especially when they're asking for something in return."

He slanted a narrowed look her way. "The top?"

"The top depends on your apology to your sister. Your cooperation decides whether I report your behavior to your father or not. I have no idea what price he'll expect you to pay if you fail to cooperate, as he asked you to do. It's best if we work together."

With much grumbling, he yanked open the door to the armoire, rummaged inside, then brought out a wad of blue and green plaid flannel. To allow the child his privacy, Olivia turned her back while he changed.

"Done," he said moments later.

Olivia turned to see him crawl under the covers, his garments spread over the rug. "Not so fast, my dear Luke."

He frowned. "Now what? Thought you wanted me to sleep."

She pointed at the clothes.

"Huh?"

"Please pick them up, fold them, and place them neatly on the chair."

With even more grumbling, he did as asked, then he turned to Olivia. "*Now* will you leave—er...let me sleep?"

He sounded more like Randy by the minute. "As soon as I've heard your prayers."

He let out a frustrated sigh but slid onto his knees at the side of his bed. After a number of 'Please blesses' and a couple of 'Thank yous,' he murmured a hasty amen. "Now?"

"Good night, Luke. May our Lord bless your sleep."

She'd left him then, and now she scarcely could find the strength to walk to the room the children had identified as hers. She had yet to see it, but as long as it contained a bed, she'd be more than satisfied.

The strain of dealing with two children who didn't particularly want her in their lives, despite Luke's proclamation on the street the day of the pig, and the difficulty of facing Cooky's unexplained dislike had completely worn her out. With a sigh, Olivia drew herself up to her full height. She was no quitter. Certainly not after only the first day on her job.

She dragged herself away from the supporting wall and

took a step toward her new room, then another step, followed by more steps that felt as though her feet had grown heavier than the massive anvil in Mr. Woollery's smithy. Only when she reached out for the doorknob did she feel a measure of anxiety. What was the room like? Would she find any comfort inside? Or would it be stark, cold, unwelcoming?

The longer she stood outside the door, the greater her apprehension grew. Silly, really. All she had to do was open the door and step into her private little space.

She would, however, miss her little sisters. The three Moore girls had always slept in the same room, ready to chat, to comfort one another, to offer a prayer, and to never let any of them feel all alone.

As Olivia was in the Whitman home.

I will never leave thee, nor forsake thee...

The familiar Scripture verse bubbled up, and Olivia felt a warm sensation in the vicinity of her heart. She really had nothing to fear. She had the Comforter, the One her Lord had sent after He'd been crucified. He'd promised to never abandon her. She was not alone.

With her last drop of determination, Olivia opened the door. She slipped inside, then leaned against the closed door. Someone, Cooky more than likely, had lit the oil lamp on a small table next to the head of the bed. The golden glow illuminated a room of small dimensions, where a bed took up most of the space, Mama's satchel waited for Olivia at its side.

The oak bed, while plain with its flat headboard and footboard, looked inviting. A couple of plump feather pillows beckoned, and a pieced quilt in muted shades of blue and gray and white added a note of cheer and the promise of warmth.

Against the right hand wall stood a tall bureau with six drawers, plenty of space for her belongings. On the left, a small washstand, very much like the one in Luke's room, stood at the ready, the pitcher giving off a tiny bit of steam.

Hm...although Cooky had been anything but pleasant, at least she'd provided nicely for Olivia. Perhaps the woman wasn't quite as opposed to her as she seemed.

If that were the case, then she had hope of befriending the older woman. Maybe Olivia could offer to help while the children were at school. Surely another pair of hands couldn't do any harm...and they might do a world of good.

It was time to turn to the Father. Otherwise, she'd succumb to the errant if persistent thought that had hovered in the back of her mind the entire day.

Had she made a mistake? Would she fail? Would she have to return to Mama and Papa, a burden once again?

Determined to avoid giving in to her foolish fears, Olivia marched up to the satchel and plunked it on the bed. In a handful of minutes, she'd emptied it of its contents and slid the case under the bed. She separated her undergarments from her blouses, her skirts from her stockings, and then, with her unmentionables in hand, strode to the bureau.

She opened the top drawer and something leaped out at her.

It grazed her cheek and she dropped her armful of items.

Her shriek stopped in her throat at a loathsome sound.

A grasshopper.

That invoked anger rather than fear. As if those nasty creatures hadn't already harmed her and her loved ones enough. How on earth had that...that *thing* found its way into her new room? Into her bureau drawer? Surely, Mr. Whitman's house wasn't infested with the greedy, chirruping beasts.

Then she knew.

The intrusion had nothing to do with a plague. It had everything to do with a boy. One who'd already tangled with a pig. Now, he'd captured a grasshopper.

No wonder Luke had done everything short of pushing her from his room. He'd been counting the minutes until she ran into the hall, squealing in fear of a hapless insect.

Little did he know how many grasshoppers she'd dealt with these last two years. True, the insect had startled her when it bounded from the drawer, but she wasn't afraid of it. And just as grasshoppers didn't frighten her, a ten-year-old boy didn't frighten her either.

She smiled. Luke had a lot to learn about her. Tomorrow was the perfect time to start the lessons.

Chapter 6

Although the heavy velvet silence and the lonely emptiness of her room left Olivia with tear-crusted cheeks the next morning, something she'd never admit to anyone, she rose early, washed up, dressed, and checked her small silver pocket watch once ready. After she gathered all her gumption—as well as the small parcel on top of the bureau—she headed down the hallway.

She knocked on her youngest adversary's door. "Time to rise, Luke. Please get dressed. I'm sure Cooky has breakfast ready so we can leave for school on time."

She took the muffled sounds behind the door as agreement.

Then Olivia stepped to Randy's door. But before she could knock, it opened and the girl sauntered into the hall, fully ready for the day. "I told you I *don't* need a nanny—excuse me, a *companion*. You do understand, don't you?"

If she hadn't known of the girl's loss of her mother, the rudeness would have infuriated Olivia. Randy needed time to see Olivia as something other than a threat. Then, and only then, would anything pleasant grow between them. She had to trust the Father's wisdom and wait on His timing. She could botch everything if she barged ahead, acting on her feelings.

"I'm glad," is all she said to Randy.

In the dining room, she set down her small package in front of the plate at her place at the table. She made sure her clean hanky covered everything.

As Randy sat down, Luke shuffled in, eyes sleep-heavy, hair in a bird's nest of a mess. Then Mr. Whitman walked in. He greeted first Randy, then Luke, placing a kiss on each dark head.

Once done, he turned to Olivia. "Good morning. I hope everything was acceptable in your room."

"It's clean and neat, and the braided rug and quilt on the bed are lovely. It suits me very well."

Luke looked at Olivia, a puzzled expression on his face. "Huh?"

"I just said my room is fine."

"I know," the boy said. "But—"

"In fact," she continued, "it even provided me with the most interesting topic for conversation this morning."

Three pairs of blue eyes focused on her.

"You don't say," Mr. Whitman murmured. "Please do tell us what you mean."

She smiled. "You see, Mr. Whitman, I had company last night in the room. I didn't have to miss my family." Not *too* terribly much.

He looked as puzzled as his son. "I'm glad, but...company? That wasn't part of our agreement, Miss Moore."

She shook out her napkin, spread it across her lap, then waved away comment. "I should probably have said I had a visitor. A very small and interesting one. One who reminded me of life on our land these last two years."

Alarm widened Luke's eyes.

Olivia's smile broadened.

The boy wriggled in his chair, his cheeks reddened, and he gestured wildly to catch her attention.

She ignored his attempts.

With greater dramatic flair than she usually displayed, she flipped her napkin off the upturned water glass from her room to reveal the grasshopper. It had taken some doing, but she'd scooped it with one hand and with the other, clapped the glass on top. She'd set the hanky over the mouth of the glass, and then tied it in place with a boot lace.

"Isn't he fascinating?" she asked. "I'm happy to bring you from my bureau an insect to examine this morning—"

"Ooooh!" Randy cried. "Take that disgusting thing off the table! Make her, Papa. Please."

"Uh...yes, Papa," Luke added. "I can help. I'll take it outside. Wouldn't want...er...for it to—well, I don't want it to bother Randy. Yes. That's right. I'll take it out."

Olivia focused on not laughing.

Never a fool, Mr. Whitman sized up the situation in seconds. He arched a brow her way.

She smiled again and shrugged.

"I do think Miss Moore has an excellent point," he said. "It would be interesting to discuss the grasshopper this morning. Tell me, Luke, how do such insects travel? They must be mighty wise, since this fellow made his way indoors and into a piece of furniture."

"Indeed," Olivia added. "All the way up into the top drawer of my bureau, as a matter of fact."

Luke slouched lower in his chair, cheeks a blazing-hot red.

His father's eyes betrayed his humor. "You don't say?"

"Oh, yes," she answered. "I'm thankful I'm not prone to apoplexy, you know. It startled me so when it sprang out as I stored my clothes."

"I can very well understand," the banker said. "Just look at its legs. What do you think, Luke? It must have jumped high and far, what with those legs. They're awfully big for his body. It must have shocked Miss Moore."

"All right, all right, *all right*!" the boy cried. "I'm sorry. I put it there. I just...well, I thought it'd be funny to hear her squeal like Randy does all the time. Only..."

"Only Miss Moore didn't respond like your other nannies did. I do remember an incident with a frog—"

"I said I was sorry, Papa. Really, I am." He scooted his chair back with a loud screech. "Look, I'm gonna take it outside right away." As he raced to Olivia's side, the boy went on. "I'm sorry, Miss Moore. Honest. I didn't mean nothing bad by it."

"I understand pranks," Olivia said, her hand on the glass. "but if the grasshopper had startled me enough to make me fall, I might have hurt myself."

He gulped.

Mr. Whitman stood. "That's a valid point, Lucas. I do remember asking you to cooperate with Miss Moore. Do you?"

Dismay, a touch of fear, and even a hint of desperation chased over Luke's face. Olivia suspected he was remembering the incident with the lumps of bread the night before. She figured he'd suffered enough for the error of his ways.

"I accept his apology, Mr. Whitman. I do think it would be best if he rid us of the insect's presence."

In a flash, Luke scooped up the glass and the grasshopper, and raced out in the direction of the kitchen. Moments later, a door slammed. As they waited for the boy's return, she caught the stunned expression on Randy's face.

"Are you well?" she asked the girl.

Randy snapped shut her gaping mouth. "Ah...yes, of course. It's just...he apologized! Luke apologized, Papa. You didn't even switch his behind to make him do it."

Out of the corner of her eye, Olivia saw Mr. Whitman smile. "He did, Randy. He did, at that. Not that I've resorted to the switch as often as you might think, dear."

He turned to Olivia. "I'm impressed, Miss Moore, and far more comfortable telling you I must leave town for the next two weeks. I'm sure you'll manage quite well in my absence."

"Thank you, sir."

While Olivia's voice rang clear and firm, a tremor of unease ran through her. She might have convinced him she could handle this companion thing, but if Randy and Luke decided to challenge her in his absence, she couldn't be sure of anything at all.

Just then, Cooky banged the tray in her hands against the door on her way into the dining room. "Here I have your nice, warm breakfast all ready, I do, and that boy goes and runs off like a coyote after a hare." She tsk-tsked. "I'm a-hoping he doesn't plan to go off to school all hungry-like and all."

She plunked the tray with its bowls of cooked oats, biscuits, a jar of honey, and a pitcher of milk on the table. Then, with a glare at Olivia, she let out a disapproving sniff. "Wonder what chased him out like that, I do, Mr. Whitman, sir. A body does have to wonder."

She might have handled the grasshopper incident well enough, but Olivia still felt no confidence at all. How would she handle the children with their father gone, much less the cook?

Trepidation shot through her. Had she made a colossal mistake by assuring Mr. Whitman she could do the job?

On Wednesday, the day after the banker left, Olivia's mettle faced another challenge from the Whitman children. And perhaps Cooky, as well, since she suspected the older woman had turned a blind eye to the mischief.

She got the children to school on time and with a minimum of complaint on Luke's part. Then, when she returned to the house, she sat in the rocker in the corner of her room to work on the shawl she was knitting for Mama's Christmas gift. She planned to skip her noon meal, since she doubted the cook would be pleased with her presence in the kitchen. But when the sun reached the crest of the sky, Cooky called up the stairs.

"I've set a plate for you, I have, Miss Moore. Please, and be coming down now."

Although it sounded more like a command than an invitation, Olivia was relieved. She'd grown hungry in the time since breakfast.

Downstairs, the dining room table sat empty, so she headed to the kitchen, braced for whatever the cook had in store for her, a prayer on her lips. That room, too, was deserted. On the table in the middle of the utilitarian space, however, a plate with a generous portion of fried potatoes with bacon, a dish of applesauce, a thick slice of fresh bread, and a glass of milk awaited her. Olivia sat, prayed, and enjoyed the plain but hearty fare.

When done, she took dishes and utensils to the washbasin on a table under the back window. The water was warm, and a cloth sat on the edge of the basin, a bar of yellow soap in a chipped teacup just inches beyond. Only too aware of the cook's disdain, she didn't want to give the woman any more reason to dislike her, much less become the source of additional work. She washed and dried everything she'd used, and then wiped the table clear of all crumbs.

That afternoon, she went to wait for her charges at the schoolhouse gate. When they saw her, their smiles faded. Randy tipped her nose up in the air and Luke drew his eyebrows close and pushed his lips out. Not the greeting Olivia wanted, but she reminded herself she needed to exercise patience if she hoped to win the battle of wills.

Before going for the children, she'd asked Cooky to prepare a small snack. Back at the house, Luke and Randy ate as though they'd missed their last five meals.

"How was your day?" Olivia asked.

Randy shrugged and Luke mumbled through a mouthful of cheese and bread.

She wondered if a more pointed approach wouldn't work better, so she spoke directly to Luke. "How did you do with the spelling words we studied the other night?"

A spark lit up his expression. "Good. I did them all right. Every last one."

"I'm glad. Please let me know the next time you have spelling words. We can work on them together so you do as well again."

He didn't respond, but also didn't refuse. Olivia counted it a victory. A tiny one but, as Mama said, a wise woman took encouragement wherever she found it.

With the snack finished, she sent the children to play. That turned out to be the wrong word for Randy.

"I'm too old to play," she said as she started up the stairs. "A young lady entertains herself with more...grown-up... um, things. Surely even you know this."

"Yes, Randy," Olivia said, voice tight, words clipped. "I do know that, but I also know that a young lady, a mature one, does not go out of her way to be unpleasant or rude. Perhaps you can try showing me—and your father—how grown up you are with your sweet nature."

The girl's cheeks turned apple red. Fury blazed from her eyes, and she ran up the stairs, feet pounding the steps in a most unladylike way.

"I—I'm gonna tell my papa!" Randy cried. "He's going to send you packing. Right as soon as he gets home."

Olivia clutched the newel post and stared after Randy. Things had gone from bad to worse with the girl. Was this attempt at earning a living doomed to fail?

Oh, Lord. Please help me. Help me win over these children

*before Mr. Whitman comes home. It's not a long time, I know,
but you know how I need this position. Still…your will, Father.
Show me your will.*

She went back to her room, eyes burning with tears, heart
heavy with worry. Fortunately for her, the knitting pattern
she'd chosen for Mama's wrap wasn't especially complicated,
since concentration eluded her. All she could think was how
she didn't want to fail, didn't want to be a burden on her family again, how much she did want to help.

And how she didn't want to confess to Mr. Whitman how
she hadn't been as capable as she'd claimed. The thought of
those blue eyes judging and finding her lacking was more than
she could bear.

When Olivia heard Cooky call them back down for supper,
she realized she'd failed once again. She'd spent so much time
nursing her bruised feelings that she'd never once checked on
the children. Who knew what kind of mischief they'd found
on their own.

On her way downstairs, she asked the Lord's forgiveness,
asked Him for strength and for the courage to do what was
right, what she'd committed to do. She also asked Him for the
grace to confess to the two Whitman hooligans. She hoped
they wouldn't see it as a weakness, for then they'd be sure to
take advantage of it and drive her truly mad.

On the other hand, she doubted any of her predecessors
had apologized, much less asked forgiveness, of the children
for failing them. Maybe that would throw them off kilter
enough for her to reset the balance of their relationship.

To her surprise, she found both at their places when she

walked into the dining room. "Something smells good," she said to break the ice.

Randy shrugged.

Luke rolled his eyes. "I s'pose."

Standing by her chair, Olivia cleared her throat. When she had their attention, she forged ahead. "I owe both of you an apology."

Randy gaped and Luke leaned forward.

She continued. "I became distracted this afternoon and failed to keep you company. We could have spent the time doing something interesting, but instead you both had to entertain yourselves on your own. I gave your father my word, and I'm afraid I didn't follow through. Please forgive me."

As she'd suspected, she'd caught them by surprise. For a moment, neither spoke. Then they murmured responses that she took for agreement. She nodded, took her seat, shook out her napkin, and smiled.

Cooky marched in. As soon as the older woman had filled their plates, both children made faces at the food. While the cook remained in the dining room, Olivia didn't pursue the matter. But she wondered about the complaints. Were they so accustomed to a life of plenty that they couldn't appreciate decent food and that in generous quantities?

She hoped not. She hadn't forgotten the conversation she'd overheard between her parents where both worried if they'd have enough to feed their family until they harvested another crop.

Cooky served Olivia hearty, simple fare. Boiled potatoes and dried beef, creamed hominy, more of the same good bread she'd enjoyed earlier that day, and red-cheeked apples would nourish them well, if not elaborately. It did surprise her some that the family didn't eat fancier foods, but it was more than adequate.

"Shall we pray?" Olivia said.

The children bowed their heads while she asked the Lord's blessing over their meal, but then, once they'd said their amens, neither one of the youngsters bothered to take a bite. Olivia didn't follow their example, whatever the reason for their odd behavior. She ate.

Simple, true, but quite edible.

After slow minutes went by, Olivia broke down. "Is something wrong? Is there a reason neither one of you is eating tonight?"

Randy scraped her chair away from the table. "I can't bear it! Not one more bite of this tedious, wearisome food. I'd rather...um...*expire* than be bored with this kind of meal again."

While Olivia was pleased to see Bountiful's teacher was earning her salary when it came to the children's vocabulary lessons, she had a time controlling her amusement. Randy Whitman was nothing if not dramatic.

When she turned to Luke, his sly expression caught her by surprise. "Do you agree with your sister?" In her experience with boys his age, they weren't picky about their food. They simply wanted plenty of it, and often.

He blinked, then nodded. "Sure. Cooky always makes potatoes and hard meat in soupy stuff and other mushy white things." He scooped up a spoonful of hominy and let it plop back down. "Like this."

She couldn't argue with Luke or Randy's assessment. The

meals she'd shared with them had all been...well, bland and boring. Cooky seemed to lack inspiration in the kitchen, something Olivia had never experienced before, since Mama excelled at cookery. She'd have to give the matter some thought.

"It's not bad enough to chase you away," she said, stabbing a fork into a still-tough piece of beef. Or was it pork? She couldn't tell.

Luke rolled his eyes again. "I s'pose."

While this response echoed his earlier comment, he did start in on his meal. Before long, he swiped at his mouth with his napkin, pushed his chair back, and headed for the door.

"It's polite to ask to be excused," Olivia said in a gentle tone.

He shoved his hands in his pockets, that sly expression on his face again. "So, c'n I be?"

"Of course. I'll stop by your room to see how you're doing with your schoolwork." But before she finished her words, he darted out.

Olivia took a final sip of water, dabbed her lips with her napkin, and pushed away from the table. Then she stood.

At least, she tried.

To her dismay, she found herself stuck to the chair. She twisted, turned, then braced herself against the table and pushed up. The chair came with her. A heartbeat later, it dropped to the floor with a loud *thunk*, throwing her off balance. She banged her knee, an elbow, and worst of all, her ribs and head against the table.

"Oooh..."

Refusing to let a chair get the better of her, Olivia blinked the tears from her eyes, grasped the chair with both hands, and pushed it away. It let go of her skirt with sticky reluctance.

Once freed and fighting the stinging pain, she righted the chair to see what had caused her problems.

Sure enough, a thick gloss of what looked—and smelled—like honey covered the wooden seat. Fury threatened, but her bumped head hurt more than her bruised dignity, so she rubbed the spot, wincing when strands of hair stuck to the minuscule amount of sweetener her fingers had picked up.

A snicker sounded from beyond the door.

Another prank, of course.

No wonder the other nannies had fled this madhouse. After the unpleasant attitudes, the welcoming grasshopper, and now this, Olivia was hard-pressed to keep from heading for the door and running until she made it home in time to kiss her sisters before they crawled into bed. But she was responsible for these children. No matter what they did.

She followed the chuckles, her sore knee making her limp. There, she found Luke, arms around his middle, trying to muffle his laughter.

Before she could speak, Cooky stomped out of the kitchen, a tin pail in her plump hand. "And, pray tell, what have you done with this whole new pail of honey, Lucas, my boy? It's a sweet tooth you're after having, but not nearly half this bad ever before."

Olivia's knee gave way as she turned to face the cook. She groaned.

"Uh-oh," Luke said.

"What's wrong, miss?" the older woman asked, alarm in her voice, disapproval on her face. "I'll be having you know, we don't cotton with tipsy folks around here, we don't."

Drawing herself up to her full height in spite of the pain,

Olivia donned a thin smile. "I'm so very glad to hear that, Cooky. I fully agree with you. I...had an accident with the... furniture."

"Oh, dear!" She dropped the pail and stepped up to Olivia, wrapping an arm around her waist. "Here, child, and let me be helping you to a chair in the parlor, now. I'm thinking, and we should be a-fetching Doc, don't you know?"

"Oh, no. That won't be necessary. I'm sore, but I'm sure I'll be fine soon." She turned to Luke, whose eyes had widened in dismay. "I can't take a seat anywhere until I change. I do seem to have found the missing honey."

"Really, miss? And just how would that be?"

"It found its way from the pail onto the seat of my chair. When I tried to stand, my skirt was stuck in it."

Cooky let go and plunked her fists on her rounded hips. "Lucas Whitman! Have you not learned yet, my boy? Your papa will be after switching you, I'm sure."

"Before we let Mr. Whitman know about the traveling honey," Olivia told the cook, "Luke has a mess to clean off that chair. Could you please see he has a soapy cloth, Cooky? A bowl of clean water and a dry towel, as well. In the meantime, I'll go upstairs and change."

"Aw...really?" Luke headed for the stairs. "Do I hafta? I didn't mean nothing by it, Miss Olivia. Weren't my fault your clothes stuck. Honey's kinda sticky, you know."

"As do you, Luke. I believe you need a reminder about actions and consequences. Please go with Cooky to fetch the things you need to clean the chair. I'll be right down to check on your progress."

"You won't tell Papa if I clean the chair, right?"

"It depends on how well you cooperate from now until he comes home."

"Aw…" He shuffled away behind Cooky. "Ain't no fun at all."

Perhaps cooperation wouldn't be fun, but if she persuaded him to work with her, Olivia might find a bit of peace. And the boy might learn a valuable lesson.

She started her hobble up the stairs.

Please, Lord, just a bit of peace.

Chapter 7

On Friday afternoon, as Olivia walked the children home from school, she noticed a group of boys, among them Luke's partners in pig rustling, following them down Main Street. Every few steps, one or another hissed at her charge.

When they were only steps away from the Whitman house, one of the ruffians called out in a sing-song voice. "Luke is a sissy."

Another added, "Walks home with *gurrrls!*"

A quick glance revealed a mortified Luke, his face flushed, even to his ears. At the taunt, he ran into the house, slamming the door in his wake. Olivia and Randy followed at a more respectable pace.

Although she'd established the successful snack routine in the days since she'd come to the Whitman house, Luke didn't show up when it came time to eat. Olivia felt bad for him, but she had agreed with his father to walk the children home from school to prevent any mischief.

Still, there had to be something she could do to ease the apparent disgrace he felt her presence brought down upon him. What should she do?

Thinking of her brothers, an idea took form. Every boy she knew loved the outdoors. Most of them also loved fishing. While she didn't know if the season was right, she decided to take Luke and his band of would-be bandits to the nearby creek the next day. As a further bribe, she would bring along a fine picnic. How she would persuade Cooky to go along with her plans, she didn't know quite yet. She prayed for inspiration.

At Luke's closed bedroom door, she knocked, expecting no response. "I'd like to invite you to an adventure tomorrow," she said. "How would you like to go fishing? You can bring your friends, too."

"Fishing?" His voice came through muffled by the door.

"Yes. Have you gone before?"

"Nah. Not really."

"Would you like to?"

"You go fishing?"

She hadn't in a few years, but she knew her way around tackle and hooks. "Um-hm."

He opened the door a crack. "And Jonny and Albert and Tommy and Daniel can come?"

Five boys. Was she up to the challenge?

It didn't matter. She had to be. "I told you they could. Would you like to go invite them?"

Suspicion narrowed his eyes. "You coming with me?"

"I have some errands to run, so we can start out together, but as long as you stay close enough and don't go looking for mischief, you can ask your friends on your own."

He agreed, and while Olivia stopped at the Mercantile for string and hooks, Luke went from friend's house to friend's house. All the boys, clearly intrigued by the thought of a lady who would go fishing, accepted Luke's invitation.

In the morning, she shocked the boy even more when she took him outside just after dawn to dig in the earth for worms. It wasn't spring, so they only found two sad specimens, but they would do. In a pinch, so would small bits of bread.

Which led her to Cooky. Olivia still had to persuade the woman.

However, the episode with the honey must have had an impact on her, and when Olivia offered to prepare the lunch for the boys, Cooky offered no objection. She helped Olivia pack cold slices of last night's fricasseed chicken, a hunk of cheese, thick slabs of bread, sweet butter, and six juicy pears. They also prepared a large bottle of tea, chilled and sweetened with the remaining honey. Pickled cucumbers found their way into another small jar, and together with the utensils, the women tucked it all into a large woven willow basket. All in all, a feast.

The outing proved a roaring success. Olivia stunned the boys with her lack of squeamishness around the worms, especially when she set them on the hooks. Then, when she opened the picnic basket and handed out the treasure, she had them all smiling and munching.

While they didn't catch a single fish, everyone had a splendid time, and each boy thanked her for the afternoon when she herded them toward town. Buoyed by her success, Olivia led her new friends home to wash up and sit in time for dinner. As a fitting end to a successful day, Luke flabbergasted Cooky when he thanked her for the picnic lunch.

Then Sunday morning arrived. Olivia awoke, happy to head for church and thankful for the opportunity to greet her family after the service. She gathered clean bloomers, petticoat, her navy blue jacket and gray flannel skirt, and humming a hymn, she slipped her right leg, still sporting a nasty bruise from the chair, into her bloomers.

Her leg stopped when it reached the end of the fabric. It had become solidly shut at the bottom.

Dismayed, she checked the other leg and found it similarly altered. She turned to her petticoat, shook it out, and found the side seams neatly taken out. The pieces of fabric hung in flapping independence, quite useless to her.

With no alternative, she donned the garments she'd used the day before, even though they were less than fresh after the fishing expedition. While it seemed she'd thawed the air a bit with the cook, and appeared to have conquered one child, she still had a ways to go.

This was Randy's doing. How would she win the girl?

Two weeks. Two long weeks away from home, and Eli had no idea how things were going. Although he felt the need to travel, to bring further investment to Bountiful, he feared what kind of trouble his two wild offspring might find in his absence. After all, they never failed to cause mischief while he was around, trying to control them. But when he walked into his house, trepidation in his heart, wondering what he'd find this time, the house echoed with the peaceful hum of normal domesticity. From the kitchen at the back of the home he heard the clanging of pots and kettles, the welcome sound of food preparation. Then, as he hung his hat on the hall tree, a merry laugh rang out upstairs. His son appeared to be in a pleasant mood.

As he often did after work, Eli stepped into the kitchen, drawn by the scent of food close to ready to eat. His stomach rumbled, even though he suspected he'd be served the same kind of plain, bland food Cooky prepared on a regular basis.

"Hello there, Cooky. I must say, the smells are a pleasant welcome home."

The widow, who'd been a fixture in his household since Miranda was a babe in arms, blushed. "Ah, Mr. Eli! It's but a joy to work for you. A widow-woman doesn't have many choices, and you're a decent man." Cooky flapped a small white towel at him. "Get going and clean up now, Mr. Eli, sir. I have plenty to do yet, if you're wanting me to serve your supper soon, that is."

Eli chuckled on his way out of the kitchen. But as he ascended the stairs, a dervish barreled past him, a dervish with a strong resemblance to his son. He narrowly avoided the collision.

"Whoa, there! And where might you be off to in such a hurry, Lucas?"

The boy came to a complete stop. "Oh! Hello, Papa. I'm hungry, and I hafta see how long Cooky's going to keep us waiting."

"Did Miss Moore send you?"

Luke's forehead crinkled. "Miss Moore? Why would she send me to the kitchen? Nah. I'm jist hungry." He stepped down toward the end of the hall. "Um ... it's nice you're home. And ... well, I s'pose I'll see you at the table."

Before Luke disappeared into Cooky's domain, Eli offered a word of friendly advice. "If you think you're going to wheedle a morsel to tide you over until Cooky serves, then you're mighty mistaken, son."

Luke stopped then and rolled his eyes. "You jist don't know how to do it right, Papa. I always get snacks from her. She says I'm hungry 'cuz I'm a growing boy, and need every bite she can get into me."

Again, Eli laughed as he resumed his way to his room. "You're one step ahead of me, son," he said as Luke opened the kitchen door. "*You* are a growing boy. I'm not. Enjoy whatever you manage to cadge from her."

There was a lot to be said for coming home to a happy child. Eli couldn't remember the last time he'd returned after work and not found yet another complaint about Luke.

As he walked into his room, Eli whistled a lilting tune and allowed himself a smile. He hung up his jacket, loosened his tie, and then approached the washstand between the tall wardrobe and the window. As usual, Cooky had filled the pitcher with fresh water. Years ago, Eli had developed the habit of washing away the troubles of the day, and it never failed to help him relax upon coming home.

A short while later, when Cooky rang the bell to announce that the supper table had been set, Eli hurried down. To his surprise, he was the last one to arrive at the dining room. Miss Moore, lovely in a crisp, long-sleeved white blouse with a plum-colored ribbon at the throat, stood by a chair. Randy, still girlish in her yellow dress, and Luke, the image of mischief with his hair in its usual tousled mess, were already seated and waiting for him. The silence sat thick and tense over everyone, and the expression on Randy's face was enough to curdle the glass of milk the cook had already set before her. Eli sighed.

He pulled out the chair at the head of the table, opened his napkin, and covered his lap. Turning to Miss Moore, who still stood by her chair, he gestured for her to sit. "It's good to see you," he said. "Please, join us."

"Are you certain, sir?" she asked. "I...I can eat just as well in the kitchen."

"I thought we'd covered this on your first day. I prefer for you to join us."

She hesitated, then nodded and took her seat.

Moments later, Cooky bustled into the dining room and set a large white tureen on the table; Eli asked the Lord's blessing; Miss Moore and the children said their amens; and then he ladled up bowls of what appeared to be potato and dried beef stew, one of Cooky's most frequent offerings. As he glanced around the table the tension assaulted him. He picked up a slice of Cooky's excellent bread, and breathed a prayer. He asked the Lord to show him how to turn the situation around, since he didn't have any idea how to do so.

The only thing he knew was that deep sense of certainty when he looked at Miss Moore. The way she'd taken charge of Luke before gave him hope. He sincerely hoped his faith in her wasn't misplaced.

Hours after he'd gone to sleep, Eli was yanked awake by an earsplitting clang and clatter outside in the hall. He bounded out of bed, smoothed down his nightshirt on his way out, and struck a match to light the oil lamp on the table next to the door.

His lamp illuminated an unexpected scene. The door to Miss Moore's bedroom stood partially open, a couple of tin pails littered the hall, and his new nanny lay on the floor propped on her elbows and wearing a frustrated expression. Utter silence filled the darkened house.

Which in itself said a lot.

No one could have slept through the din. His children were awake, he was sure. And yet...neither one had come to investigate.

While he knew he'd have to discipline Luke and Randy, he had to see to Miss Moore first. He knelt at her side, setting the oil lamp on the floor close by. Its golden glow illuminated her face, the even features pale at the moment, and her rich, golden brown eyes, wide with shock. Her lips, most often in a cheerful smile, were clamped tight, the edges white from the pressure.

In spite of all that, the most inappropriate thought crossed Eli's mind. Miss Olivia Moore was indeed a beautiful woman.

Long seconds passed, and then, she began to move. Eli called himself all kinds of fool. The lady had fallen, and here he'd been admiring her instead of offering a helpful hand.

"Are you hurt?" he hurried to say.

She shook her head, her lips clenched tight. "As is often said, only my dignity."

"Allow me to apologize for my children. And please let me help you up."

"I'm sorry, Mr. Whitman." A blush brought a rush of color to her cheeks. "I realize you're trying to make amends for what's happened, but it's not necessary. And..." She turned even redder. "Well, sir, it's not proper at all, you being a gentleman and me...well, it's just not. I'll take care of myself."

Only then did he realize how inappropriate the moment was. He excused himself and stood, determined to get to the bottom of this latest prank. As he made his way to Luke's room, Cooky's door flew open.

"And just what, pray tell, is a-happening in this madhouse *now*, Mr. Whitman, sir? Can't a body be getting a lick of rest around this place anymore?"

The plump older woman made quite the picture of indignation. She'd flung a scarlet wrap around her white nightshirt, and her long white braid flopped over one shoulder, bristling all its length with strands escaping their bounds. Her frown made Eli stand straighter, glad he'd left his lovely nanny's side before the cook found them in a possibly more compromising position than it already was.

"I was on my way to learn precisely that." Heat flooded his cheeks, as well. "It appears Luke has quite a bit to learn yet."

The boy's door opened with a bang against the wall. "Nuh-uh! It weren't just me, Papa. Randy's the one with the idea. She jist wanted to make Miss Olivia look clumsy now that you're home. She said clumsy ladies can't be good nannies. I told her a lady who can stick a worm on a hook's the best kind of nanny ever!"

Eli rubbed his forehead. Clumsy ladies...worms on hooks... nothing made sense at this hour of the morning.

Best to send everyone back to bed, and try to get to the bottom of this in the morning. "I think, son—"

"She's too clumsy to care for anyone," Randy said in her

most disdainful voice. "Why, she can't even make her way around a couple of itty-bitty empty pails."

As tired as he was, he couldn't just let Randy's unpleasant assessment pass. "I imagine in the dark anyone could trip on a booby trap. I don't suppose Miss Moore set it for herself, now did she?"

"No, sir," Luke said, his voice earnest. "Randy made me find her empty pails. Then when Miss Olivia went—" His eyes popped open wide and his mouth formed a large O. "Well, when she...um...needed to...er...use the—oh, *you* know, Papa. That's when Randy set the pails in place. And it's dark. And Miss Olivia didn't expect them." He pointed at Randy. "*She's* the one. She made me help her."

Eli turned to his daughter. "Is he right, Miranda Marie?"

Randy gave a sniff, turned, and marched back into her room, closing the door with great precision.

"If you think this conversation's over," he said in a louder voice, "then you're much mistaken. We will handle this in the morning. Now, everyone, back to bed."

As he tried to fall asleep, however, the only thing in his mind was the vulnerability he'd seen in Olivia's eyes. It touched him in a deep, private place he thought he'd shut tight two years ago.

In the morning, Miss Moore surprised Eli. She was waiting for him outside the dining room when he went downstairs for breakfast.

"Could I have a moment with you, sir?" she asked.

The sinking feeling went all the way to his toes. She was

leaving. What would he do now? He'd tried all along to avoid sending his children to boarding schools back East, but if he couldn't find anyone who would stay in spite of their antics, he'd have no alternative.

"Of course, Miss Moore. What is the problem—aside from last night's deplorable disaster? Please rest assured I'll take care of those two wild—"

"That's exactly what I wanted to address this morning."

Here it comes. Eli braced himself. "I'll understand if you wish to leave."

What looked like fear flashed in her eyes. "Oh, no, sir. I don't want to leave. I wanted to plead with you to let me handle Randy. I'd like to work with her to reach a reasonable discipline, but without turning her against me any further. I'm afraid if you appear to punish her harshly that she'll be more determined than ever to fight me."

He frowned. "Are you sure? After all, I'm her father."

"Of course, Mr. Whitman. But you've hired me to work with your children. It appears to me I won't ever succeed if I can't find a way to smooth things between Randy and me. I've made progress with Luke, even if last night was a step backward. Please, sir, I would greatly appreciate another opportunity to reach out to your daughter."

Her earnestness touched him. None of the other nannies, those with the long lists of recommendations and years of experience caring for children, had ever voiced interest in, as Miss Moore said, reaching out to his children. Besides, her plea meant she was still willing to stay. A relief, since he couldn't afford to let her go.

"Very well," he said. "Let's see what you can do with her.

Goodness knows, I've been unable to do much in a sadly long time."

She caught her bottom lip between her teeth and nodded. "I'll keep you updated, Mr. Whitman. I wouldn't want to do anything that might go against your wishes."

Her zeal impressed him. So did her interest in operating within his preferences. "Very well, I'll go along with your plan, and I appreciate your interest in keeping me informed. But if matters go like this much longer, I'll have to intervene. I cannot allow my children to risk injuring you."

"Thank you, sir. I'll let you know if I need your assistance."

Breakfast, to Eli's surprise, went by in relative peace. Randy appeared unusually subdued, and Luke chattered to Miss Moore about, of all things, fishing and worms. It struck him that perhaps he'd found a woman cut from very different cloth. As young as his new nanny was, and as delicate as she looked, she seemed nonetheless made of far sturdier stuff than the others.

Perhaps he'd found the one that would last. He hoped so. For his children's sake, as well as his own.

That afternoon, on the way home from school, Olivia told the children she needed to stop by Metcalf's Mercantile. Neither responded as she'd hoped.

"Do we hafta?" Luke asked.

Randy stuck her nose up in the air and glared.

"I won't be long." Olivia hoped once Randy saw the reason for the stop she would change her attitude.

Luke donned what Olivia had come to think of as his

I'm-coming-up-with-trouble expression. He grinned, mischief dancing in his eyes. "C'n I go see Papa at the bank? He does let me, Miss Olivia. You can ask him tonight."

By tonight it would be too late, but since Randy didn't say a word, Olivia had to assume it was something Luke had done before. If Mr. Whitman was busy, she was sure he'd send the boy home. And she'd hear about her mistake later that evening.

"All right. But please meet us here in ten minutes so we can all go home together. Understand?"

"Yessss!" His footsteps pounded against the wooden sidewalk as he ran off.

Randy sniffed. "Such a child."

Olivia decided the better part of valor would be to ignore the comment. "Let's hurry," she said instead. "That way we'll be ready to leave once he joins us again."

Although Randy hadn't commented on the stop, she did seem curious about the reason for it. And since punishment hadn't been meted out after the pail incident the night before, Olivia figured the girl felt she'd gotten away with the prank.

Not at all.

"Let's look at the linen Mr. Metcalf has," she said.

Randy strolled ahead, clearly familiar with the dry goods side of the store. "Here it is," she said. "Together with the muslin and a stack of bolts of dimity. In all kinds of lovely colors, too."

Aha! Olivia had guessed right. "Hm...you're right. But I don't need the dimity right now. I'm after some good, plain linen to do some needlework. Embroidery, you know."

Randy wrinkled her nose in distaste. "That's boring."

Exactly what Olivia thought the girl would think. "Oh, I don't know. Every lady must know certain things, and fine needlework is one of them. My mama taught my two sisters and me how to embroider when we were little. How about you?"

A tiny wrinkle appeared between her brows. "No. My mama didn't do anything like that. She wore pretty things and she took trips to visit family and...well, she scolded us a lot, too."

It sounded like a less-than-lovely situation for children. It was way past time someone taught Miss Miranda Whitman a few ladylike arts. "I see. Well, it strikes me as just the perfect time to learn. You seem to have far too many empty hours, and they give you the opportunity to concoct schemes that are less than exemplary. Mama always said idle hands were the devil's playground."

Randy's relatively open expression shut down like a curtain. "I don't have too many empty hours. I'm fine just as I am."

Olivia slanted the girl a measuring look. "It seems to me it took you a good amount of free time to think up and carry out your tin pail trap."

She had the decency to blush. "Not that long. Luke found the pails."

"But you asked him for them, right?"

Randy turned to the dimities. "He found the pails."

"And, Randy, how about my undergarments? Did Luke sew my bloomers shut and cut open my petticoat?"

The girl blushed a furious red. "Shh! A lady doesn't mention her"—she dropped her voice to a whisper—"*unmentionables* in public. Don't you know that?"

"In fact, I do. And that's the reason I didn't speak of that episode with your father. I'm sure he'd rather not have to hear such an embarrassing tale, don't you think?"

Randy crossed her arms and frowned even more.

"So, then, how about if we agree to cooperate? I can teach you a few ladylike accomplishments, and keep you busy that way. I can assure you, there won't be much time to think up scrapes that do nothing but bring your papa a great number of headaches. We will keep that matter between the two of us, agreed?"

With a shrug, Randy flounced to a display of vanity sets.

It appeared this would be all Olivia would extract from her charge at the moment. Still, she'd learned enough to know she was on the right track, even with the stubborn Randy.

She asked Mr. Metcalf for a yard of the nice, sturdy, cream-colored linen, and then chose an assortment of J & P Coats embroidery thread. Mr. Metcalf put the items on her brand-new account, which she would cover once Mr. Whitman paid her.

With the package tucked under her arm and the moody Randy at her side, Olivia went out to wait for Luke.

A few minutes later, they made their way home without incident.

That was how Olivia intended to keep things.

With the Father's help.

The next evening, when everyone sat for supper, another issue came to the fore. Cooky brought in the inevitable white tureen, and when Mr. Whitman took off the lid, it became more than obvious that she'd made her trademark potatoes and dried meat—pork, this time. At one side, the older woman had a large bowl of cooked cabbage, and when one set it next to the putty-toned potatoes and meat and bread, it made for a somewhat off-putting meal.

Olivia, who'd never had reason to turn down food, came close to rising and going upstairs with an empty middle. But since she wasn't fond of a growling stomach, and as she didn't want to present a bad example to the children, she served herself modest quantities of the day's Cooky Special, as she'd come to think of supper.

Randy had no such qualms. "No!" she cried when Cooky had left the room. "I'm not eating this…this sticky stuff. Can't she *ever* make something good?" She marched out, leaving the room under a pall.

Mr. Whitman rubbed his forehead, sighed, and then glanced at Olivia. "I'm sorry, Miss Moore. This has been an ongoing issue with Randy—"

"I don't want it either," Luke said, pushing away from the table. "I'll go hungry and starve and that'll show Cooky."

Olivia bit the inside of her cheek to keep from laughing out loud. Then she caught her employer's frustrated expression. Her stomach sank.

She hadn't really made that much progress managing the dreadful situation with his children. She still had to prove herself. In no way did she want Mr. Whitman to send her back home to Mama and Papa, as much as she missed them.

"I'll make sure to save the children something for when they're hungry later on." She offered a silent prayer for heavenly help in meeting her goal.

"But that's making more work for you," he countered. "And it's letting them misbehave."

"Not really. I remember it was a powerful way to learn about consequences in my family. Luke and Randy get the same food later, only colder and even pastier, since it has sat around for so long. Believe me, they'll eat. Children rarely go so far to make a point as to make themselves any more uncomfortable than necessary."

Her comment elicited an interested look. "I suppose you speak from experience with your brothers and sisters."

"And my own." She made herself smile even though inside she felt the strain of worry. "I once refused to eat, and Mama held my food aside. It was dreadful to eat that cold mess once the grumbling in my middle came to bother me later on. I didn't pass up supper again."

Although he seemed skeptical, Mr. Whitman agreed, and they finished the meal in silence—an awkward silence. As soon as she was done, Olivia excused herself, hurried to let Cooky know her plans, and then went to supervise the children's schoolwork and the rest of their evening routine.

Before too long, however, both Luke and Randy returned to the kitchen and consumed portions of the congealed concoction they'd refused in the first place. When they tried to voice complaints again, Olivia reminded them they'd been the ones who'd chosen to wait.

"This is what happens when food sits around," she told Randy, who'd asked again for something different to eat. "Perhaps you'll remember next time you decide the meal is too boring for you."

With a glare, the girl tucked in, while Luke continued to mutter about Cooky's uninspired offerings. Olivia felt sorry for the children. She agreed in that regard, and deep inside knew she could remedy the situation. Unfortunately, she didn't know how to do so without erasing the slight progress she'd made with the cook.

It would take prayer and a kindhearted approach to come up with a solution. But she had to do it soon. She had to find a way to become indispensable to the Whitman household if she was to keep her position. She couldn't fail. She couldn't go back home.

This was her opportunity, the time to succeed. With God's mercy and the Holy Spirit's wise guidance she could do it.

She had no other alternative.

Chapter 8

Saturday morning, Olivia sent Luke to scrub the back steps. While she did everything she could to avoid the appearance of a punishment, she knew that was how he viewed the chore. She, on the other hand, knew she had to keep him busy, otherwise he'd find trouble sooner than not.

As soon as she set him up with a pail of hot water and melted yellow soap, and a stiff-bristled brush, she hurried inside to snag Randy before the girl found her own kind of mischief.

"Do I really have to do this?" she asked when Olivia set out scissors, the length of linen, and the embroidery floss on the dining room table.

Olivia breathed a prayer for that ever elusive but always desired wisdom only God could provide. "No, of course you don't. But young ladies do need to master certain arts, and needlework is one of them. Surely you're interested in fashionable clothing, but I wonder if you know enough to discern the difference between quality goods and lesser pieces. Learning to use needle and thread will help you do that."

While Randy didn't argue, her expression didn't show any great enthusiasm, either. Olivia persisted.

She blocked out letters on the linen cloth for a basic sampler. "What would you like to put in this space?" She indicated an empty spot above the alphabet.

"What do you mean?"

"Mama always had us draw something we liked on our samplers so that we could learn fancier stitches. I drew one of the trees near our house. One of my sisters drew the house. The other one, a horse. What would you like?"

"I would like one of the lovely hats at Mrs. Selkirk's Millinery, with flowers and ribbons and feathers, too."

Now, there was a challenge, but Olivia couldn't back off. She'd offered and would find a way to come up with a reasonable copy of the confections the newly established lady constructed.

To her surprise, the endeavor captured Randy's interest, and the girl put her heart into her project. A couple of hours sped by. Before Cooky had to set the table for the midday meal, Olivia gathered up the supplies with a satisfied smile. She'd just taken another step in the right direction.

As they ate the dishes of applesauce they'd been served as dessert, pounding on the front door broke the calm. Olivia saw Cooky run to answer, her cheeks flushed, a kitchen towel in her hands, a prayer wafting behind her.

Anxious voices came through, even though Olivia couldn't understand what they were saying. She didn't, however, need anyone to elaborate on the cry Cooky let out.

Mr. Whitman stood. "Please wait," he told the children and Olivia. "This does sound serious."

A glance at the children revealed pale faces and fists clutching the table. It struck her then that the alarming situation out front could be a vivid reminder of their mother's death. She had no idea how the late Mrs. Whitman had met her end, but as young as she must have been, it could have come about as a result of an accident or an unexpected ailment.

She had to help. "Cooky sounded quite upset. Would you both like to do something for her?"

Despite their disdain for the woman's cooking, both children nodded, still intent on listening to what might happen next out front.

Olivia stood and held out her napkin. "Good. Here, Luke. Take all of these, and gather up the silverware, too. We're going to clear the table for her." She turned to his sister. "Since you're older, Randy, why don't you gather the dishes and carry them to the kitchen table. I'll take the tureen and the other empty bowls."

Once the table was clear, she set up operations in the kitchen. "Luke, you can hand me plates and cups to wash, one by one, or a handful of silver at a time. Randy, please take a clean towel from the shelf by the pantry door, and dry as I hand things to you. We'll stack it all on the table, and if you'll help me find the right places, we can put everything away for Cooky."

Although the children still looked concerned, in a short while, Olivia had the three of them working like the wheels of a locomotive. To lighten the mood, she led them in a series of cheery songs, beginning with "Camptown Races," going through "Oh, Susannah," and on to "Listen to the Mockingbird."

Scant minutes later, Mr. Whitman entered the kitchen, lines pleating his brow. "Cooky's daughter, Kate, had an accident at her home. She's been taken to Doc Chambers's, and they sent her husband to fetch her mother. I assured Cooky we'd all be fine, and I see, Miss Moore, you've beaten me to making good on my word. Thank you."

He laid a hand on Randy's shoulder and ruffled Luke's hair on his way back out. "It's a comfort to see this kind of cooperation. I'm looking forward to it continuing."

Olivia released her held breath. Relief made her weak in the knees. Who would think that something so common as washing up after a meal would prove to be such a great measure of progress?

As evening approached, Eli began to worry. Cooky hadn't returned, and he had two children who needed food. He supposed he could root around in the kitchen for whatever he might find, but he'd never had to put together a meal, and he knew he wouldn't be able to do so now.

Still, it looked as though he would have to—and soon. As the house still had a vague aroma of their dinner, he figured hungry bellies wouldn't fail to catch the scent. The children would come down soon, looking for supper.

As he headed toward the kitchen, he heard the familiar sizzling sound of food cooking. Had Cooky come home and not let him know? He opened the door, and instead of his cook, found his nanny at the large black stove, wooden spoon in one hand, a folded kitchen towel in the other. While he watched, she took hold of the iron skillet and stirred a mix that released a savory scent.

"I'm sorry, Miss Moore," he said, "I never expected you to shoulder even this responsibility."

She turned, spoon still in hand. "It's no bother at all." She waved all around the kitchen with the spoon. "Cooky keeps a well-stocked larder, and it's nothing elaborate, just sausage, apples, and biscuits, but it will do until Cooky returns."

He smiled. "Whatever it is, it smells wonderful, and I appreciate your willingness to step in. Let me know when I should call the children to the table."

Her cheeks tinted an attractive rose. "You can go ahead and ask them to wash up whenever you wish. The biscuits are about done. I'll have everything on the table in minutes."

"We'll be there, and again, thank you."

She looked away, clearly embarrassed by his praise. "You're welcome, Mr. Whitman."

As he hurried to find Luke and Randy, Eli marveled at his good fortune. None of the previous nannies had been the kind who would have helped in an emergency like today's.

Then, when they sat to eat, he received another pleasant surprise. The savory scent in the kitchen should have alerted him, but the first bite of sausage and potatoes burst in his mouth with more flavor than Cooky had produced in the last month. To make sure he wasn't imagining things, he took a bite of the apples, golden brown at the edges, tender, and with a hint of molasses, cinnamon, and cloves.

He slanted a sideways glance at the woman who'd put the meal together and saw her studying Luke. It struck him she might be worried his children wouldn't enjoy her food, since they'd been so critical of Cooky's fare. But as he was about to pay her a compliment, Luke spoke up.

"This is *good*! What'd Cooky do to make it so good tonight?"

Eli smiled. "It is very tasty, isn't it? But Cooky's not back yet. Miss Moore surprised us with this fine supper. Why don't you thank her for her help?"

Luke shoveled in another mouthful, chewed, swallowed, and then nodded. "Miss Moore, this is...it's better than good. C'n you show Cooky how to cook? Her stuff's like—well, it's like the whitewash Papa had Mr. Webber put on the outhouse in the summer."

Miss Moore looked horrified. "Oh, no, Luke. That wouldn't be nice at all."

Luke shrugged and, before he went back to his food, added, "Would help."

Eli turned to Randy. "What do you think, dear?"

She gave her lips a dainty dab with her napkin. "I can eat it." She swallowed—hard, and refused to meet the nanny's gaze. "Thank you, Miss Moore."

Olivia's cheeks reddened as she glanced up and met his gaze. A heartbeat later, she turned away, smoothed her hair, picked up her napkin, and brought it to her lips.

She was modest, too.

It occurred to Eli that Miss Olivia Moore might be the best bargain he'd ever struck.

*   *   *

The next morning, as Olivia smoothed her hair into the usual knot, someone knocked on her bedroom door. Hurrying across, she found Cooky on the other side.

"Good morning," she said. "How is your daughter?"

Cooky twisted her hands together. "It was a bad burn my Katy-girl got on her right arm. But Doc says it should be a-healing just fine, miss, if she takes care, you see. But it sure did hurt the poor thing, it did." She looked down at the floor. "But that isn't why I'm here. I . . . I just wanted to say I'm sorry for the way I've been, and all. Here I was thinking you'd be just like the other highfalutin' nannies, but you've been nothing but sweet as just-pulled taffy and even helped when I was gone, at that."

Olivia took the woman's hand. "Please don't worry about it, Cooky. Mr. Whitman explained what happened, and I was more than happy to help. I'm glad you could be with your daughter. I know I would have wanted Mama with me if I were hurt bad."

"But I didn't ever welcome you or even say a kind word, I didn't. It dawned on me, it did, when I was with my Katy, that I'd have been steamed with anyone who'd been so stiff-necked-like to her. Wasn't right, Miss Moore, it wasn't. Good Lord knows I've been an old fool—"

"How about if you do *me* a favor, Cooky? How about if you call me Olivia, and we'll call it a day. Please don't think about it anymore."

The teary-eyed cook wrapped Olivia in a warm hug, and for the first time since coming to the Whitman home, she felt as though things might work out. Who would have thought a skillet of sausage, potatoes, and apples would pave the way?

On Monday morning, Eli had an unexpected visitor at his office. "Nathan! How are you? It's been a while since I've seen you. How's the logging camp?"

The son of Eli Whitman, Sr.'s business partner, Nathan Bartlett, had inherited his father's share of the Bank of Bountiful. He ran a hand through his dusty-brown hair in a clear effort to remove the deep mark his hat had left. "It's a world of hard work, but Father left me that land, and now that we have the means to get the lumber down to market over the Columbia River, I'm going to make the most of what I have."

A pang of apprehension struck. "Are you telling me you need to withdraw funds? I realize it's a costly enterprise."

Nathan hesitated. Then, "May I sit?"

"Please. You're part owner this bank, after all."

"It's never felt that way. I'm not cut out to sit at a desk and count folks' money. I need to be outside, to be in the best part of God's Creation."

Relief made Eli chuckle. "We're different men. I'd be lost out there."

"You're where you belong, and Bountiful needs a bank. Which is the reason I came."

And here Eli thought he'd made it past peril. "You don't say?"

Nathan leaned forward, his expression earnest. "I don't know how else to do this, so I'm just going to say it. I'm sure you know as well as I do how farmers and ranchers are hurting this year. All their properties...I've heard tell they've come to you for mortgages, that you've helped them all. Is that right?"

"I couldn't let them fail—the bank holds too many notes. Of course, I helped them."

"How are the bank's funds after you've made these loans?"

"I won't lie to you. We're on a tight margin of liquidity. We can't make hasty decisions or mistakes. But we should be fine—"

"Should the Lord bring us rain, right?"

Eli shrugged. "It can't be dry forever."

"What about the grasshoppers?"

"Two plagues are more than enough, don't you think?"

"Sure, that's what I think, but it might not be what happens. What if they come back? If they eat all the plantings as they have the last two years? What then?"

"Then I'll have to trust in the Lord's provision, just like everyone else."

Nathan stood, his tall, strong frame dwarfing the room. He paced from the chair to the door and back. "I trust in the Lord's provision, but I also use the caution He's given me. I can't afford to let my money stay here if the bank's going to be wiped clean by another drought. If the loans aren't paid back, I won't be able to count on my deposits, will I?"

"No need to worry. I know these men. As do you. They're honorable, hardworking, and determined to pull through."

"Grasshoppers are just as determined, and they're always hungry. No one's managed to fight them off with any success." He gripped the back of the leather chair where he'd sat. "If these men begin to default, I won't be able to sit back and wait. I—I'll have to withdraw my funds."

Lead landed in the pit of Eli's stomach. "Please don't say that. Give us time to see things turn around. Don't make a hasty decision."

"I can't risk everything my father worked for."

"He believed in this bank. Our fathers were partners. He worked for this—"

"Hello, Papa!" Luke cried, opening the door and pelting in. "I came to see you. Miss Olivia and Randy are at the Mercantile. Cooky wanted a sack of beans and salt and other boring stuff, so I came to see you."

"So sorry, Mr. Whitman." Samuel Holtwood, Eli's right-hand man and the bank's head cashier, stood behind Luke. "I know you've asked us to keep interruptions to a minimum, but I couldn't stop him before he ran in."

"Uncle Nate!" Luke cried when he spotted the lumberman. "You coming home with us tonight? Please?"

Eli didn't know whether to be exasperated with Luke or grateful for the timely interruption. He needed to gather his thoughts, to come up with an argument to persuade Nathan to not leave the bank high and dry.

"Not today," Nathan said. "I came to town for supplies for the camp and to talk to your papa."

"So, then," Holtwood said, a hand on Luke's shoulder to lead him back toward the door, "since they were talking, you and I are going to let them continue with their business. You can visit your father another day."

"Bu—but—"

"No, son," Eli said, "Mr. Holtwood's right. Go on with him." He turned to the cashier. "Please give Luke a penny for candy. I'm sure Mr. Metcalf has something on the counter he'll enjoy."

"G'bye, Uncle Nate. Please come back soon."

"I will. I promise." When the door closed, Nathan faced Eli again. "Very well. I'll wait, but not for so long that the bank is drained as dry as the land around these parts."

"Thank you. I appreciate it." Eli crossed to Nathan's side, hand outstretched. "I know we're on the way to better days. I have faith."

Nathan clasped Eli's fingers in his strong, warm grip. "So do I. That's why I'm willing to give you—and the others—more time."

"I won't let you down. And . . . if it looks as though things are going sour, well, then, I'll send word. You can come withdraw your part."

"I'm sorry it is this way, but I must steward what Father left behind. Thank you for understanding."

As his friend left, Eli's temples began to pound. Between the bank, the matters at home, and now with Cooky's daughter injured, he felt as though he were being torn in two.

A knock came at the door. "May I come in?" Holtwood asked.

"Of course."

"I sent young Lucas with a handful of pennies. He promised he wouldn't eat all the candy at one time."

"Thank you. I appreciate your help—more than I can say."

Silence thickened. Seconds ticked by. Eli wondered what his serious, highly efficient right-hand man wanted. Holtwood was rarely at a loss, so this perplexed him.

"Can I do something for you?" he asked when he could no longer bear the wait.

"No, sir." The cashier met his gaze head-on. "I'm hoping I can help you. It's about Luke. I understand how difficult it has been to care for him and your daughter since—well, the last two years. But I must say, you've been distracted of late, and I suspect it's because of the children."

"I can't deny it. They weigh heavily on me. I don't know how to be both mother and father to them."

"Then let me make a suggestion. I have a friend back East. He's the headmaster at the boarding school where I studied. I can contact him for you, make sure he has a spot for Luke. There is also a young ladies academy nearby. I'm sure they'll be glad to have Miranda."

Eli dropped his pencil onto the blotter on his desk. "I know, I know. I've thought about it many times. I suppose it's the most practical solution, and may be what's best for them. Perhaps I'm being selfish, but I can't imagine an empty home every evening."

"You must understand, considering the importance of your negotiations with the railroad, you must not let anything distract you. Not right now."

"You're right, but . . . I'm not ready just yet. Besides, I've hired a new nanny—companion, we're calling her, since the children feel they're too old for a nanny. She seems quite promising."

"I hope the promise bears fruit, and soon. We can't let this opportunity slip by us."

Eli sighed. "You're right. Negotiations are at a critical point. I'll keep your offer in mind. I won't wait too long before deciding."

Holtwood gave a quick nod. "Do remember, Mr. Whitman, I'm here to help you. In any way you might need."

"You have been for years. You can't imagine how I appreciate your help. Especially at a time like this, when things are so difficult." He clapped a hand on Holtwood's back. As he walked him to the door, a piece of paper on the corner of his desk caught his eye. "Did you see to the letter for the railroad?"

"Yesterday. I have it with the rest of the correspondence for you to sign. I will admit, though, my penmanship's not nearly as excellent as Harry's was, but right now, we must make do with my attempts."

Harry O'Dell, secretary at the bank since Eli's father had opened the doors, had died six months earlier. They'd been doing their best to manage since then, but Eli realized he'd put off finding a replacement for too long.

He chuckled. "Then perhaps you'd enjoy penning one of your last missives today. Please prepare an advertisement I can send to a number of newspapers. It's past time I replaced O'Dell."

"I'll be happy to."

"I'm sure of that. I'm sorry I let it go on for so long. You've been doing too much for one man. I hope we find a secretary soon."

"I'll see that we do, Mr. Whitman. Let me get right to it."

Eli closed the door behind his head cashier—truthfully, Holtwood was far more than just a cashier, a run-of-the-mill employee. The man had been there for Eli's father, and in the years since the older Whitman had died, he'd also been there for Eli through even the worst moments.

He realized he'd been consumed by his troubles since

things began to go wrong in his marriage to Victoria. Unfortunately, he wasn't the only one who'd paid for his late wife's sins. Not only had his children suffered, but Holtwood—the bank—had also borne the consequences.

Regardless, he had to make sure the bank didn't go under.

Nathan had said he didn't want to lose what his father had worked for. Well, neither did Eli. He just hadn't had the heart to let the farmers and ranchers go under when weather and insects had ravaged the land. He hoped doing what he believed had been the right thing didn't cost him everything his father had left him.

Chapter 9

Working for Mr. Whitman provided Olivia with more benefits than she'd hoped. She was no longer a burden to Mama and Papa, and she earned a reasonable wage. While the banker's children were...well, challenging, they were also intelligent and, occasionally, a joy to work with.

Olivia counted her new relationship with Cooky as a promise for the future. The older woman had a down-to-earth approach to life and, since their truce, she'd noticed the cook had a way of finding the humor in many circumstances, something to be treasured when working with children.

Finally, working for Mr. Whitman offered her the opportunity to live in town, which meant she could visit Addie on a regular basis.

That Wednesday afternoon, after Olivia and Cooky finished their lunch of cold lamb slices from Sunday's roast, a wedge of good cheese, Cooky's fresh-baked bread, and the crisp apples from Mr. Newton's nearby orchard, she donned her navy jacket, pulled on her gloves, and then gathered her leather drawstring purse to make her way down Main Street to the Tucker home. The crisp fall air bore the spicy tang of the season, and the bright sun lifted her spirits.

At the Tuckers' home, when she clanged the doorknocker against its brass plate, an unhappy Baby Joshua wailed his response. Moments later, a harried-looking Addie opened the door.

"Oh, dear," Addie cried. "I'd so looked forward to a lovely afternoon with you, Livvy, but my little man won't stop his crying, no matter what I do. Honestly, you don't have to stay and put up with all this howling. I understand if you choose to leave."

Olivia stepped past her friend and into the attractive entry to the Tuckers' comfortable home, tugging off her fresh gloves. "I should leave you to cope with it alone? What kind of friend would that make me?"

Addie gave a weak laugh. "A wise one."

Joshua gave a particularly sharp cry.

His mother went on. "Who in her right mind would subject herself to this when she doesn't have to?"

Olivia removed her hat and placed it, together with the gloves and purse, on a chair in the parlor. "A real friend, Adelaide Tucker. Here. Give me that sweet boy of yours. Let's see if a change of arms will do him any good."

While Addie looked doubtful, she handed Olivia her unhappy son. "I think you've gone completely mad. This nanny position you've taken seems to have affected your sanity."

"Did *you* ever think *me* particularly sane?"

The chubby little boy halted his screams when Olivia

cuddled him against her shoulder. A waft of sweet baby scents drew her to the crook of his neck where she nuzzled him. He let out a surprised giggle.

She did it again, and he responded with delighted laughter. "You like that, do you? Then maybe you and I should go giggle in the kitchen so that your poor, tired mama can take a short nap. I suspect she needs one, since you don't strike me as though you've been of a mood to sleep much lately."

Addie snorted. "Sleep? I doubt this rascal has any recollection of that pleasant, wonderful activity."

"Go ahead, then," Olivia urged Addie. "Do lie down for a bit. I'd love to entertain Joshua. Besides, I'm sure you'll feel like a new woman after a nap. If I can get him to fall asleep, well then, that will be all the better."

"Oh, but Livvy, that's not fair to you. You spend your days chasing after those wild Whitman children. The last thing you want to do on a free afternoon is to cope with my little one."

"Let me decide that." She glanced at Joshua, who was making interesting gestures with his rosy mouth. "I suspect he's teething. If you trust me, I have a trick or two Mama used with Leah Rose when she went through the same thing. Go ahead and lie down. I'm sure Josh, Sr., will be happy to come home and find his beautiful bride all rested and happy to see him."

Addie blushed a pretty pink that made her fair skin glow and set off her green eyes. "I suppose you do have a point. Josh has come home to a screaming baby and grumpy wife too many days now." With amusing eagerness, she crossed to the stairs. "Who would have thought things would turn out this way for you?"

Holding onto the newel post at the bottom of the stairs, she paused to study Olivia. "I do believe you've come into your own these last few weeks. Working for the bank president seems to suit you. Better still, those two youngsters don't appear to be having too dreadful an effect on you."

Olivia shrugged, a hint of heat filling her own cheeks. If Addie only knew what she'd been going through since she arrived at the Whitman home. "They're not that bad, Addie. They're at loose ends, what with their mother dead, and all. Then Mr. Whitman hired three elderly matrons, each one without a smile to her, and much too full of strict rules, from what I've heard. How much sense does that make to you?"

Addie started up the stairs. "Not much, if what you say is indeed the case. But I say it's still a surprise how well this position suits you. You're blooming like your mother's garden—"

"You do mean Mama's garden *before* the drought and the bugs, right?"

"Oh, Livvy, I'm sorry. I didn't mean to remind you of all that. Let's not talk about dreary things. My thoughtless comment is enough to convince me to take you up on your offer to watch Joshua. Oh, and that nap, as well. Maybe sleep will put a leash on my words."

Before Olivia could comment, Addie bolted halfway up the stairs. "Don't let me sleep too long," she pleaded. "I wouldn't want to take advantage of you. No matter what you say, you do spend enough of your time watching other folks' misbehaving little ones as it is."

Olivia shooed her friend all the way up the stairs, and then sat in the lovely maple rocker near the window in the parlor, little Joshua babbling away against her shoulder. Addie did have a point. It was remarkable how well the job suited her. Remarkable, but true. As troublesome as Luke and Randy could be, she was coming to love those two scamps. Every day they found a way to nudge deeper into a corner of her heart.

Every day she thanked the Father for putting in her mind the idea to approach Mr. Whitman. She also would forever be thankful that Mr. Whitman had, in turn, agreed to this trial period.

She hoped he felt the same way. She hoped he didn't regret bringing her into his home.

After a two-hour nap, Addie seemed to fly down the stairs, a smile on her lips, the normal glow back in her face. "Thank you so very much, Olivia. I can't tell you how much good the nap has done me—"

"Shh! You might wake him up."

"He's asleep?"

"It looks as though your little one simply wore himself out. It had to happen sooner or later."

Addie hurried to the cradle on the far side of the sofa to see for herself. "I can't thank you enough."

She came to sit on the sofa, Olivia in one corner, Addie in the other. As moments went by in silence, Olivia watched her friend's expression change. From cheerful and animated, she turned somber and concerned.

Olivia grew alarmed. "Addie? What's wrong? Do you feel ill?"

"Not in the way you mean. But there is a situation that's making me ill, if you understand my meaning."

Olivia couldn't imagine what might be troubling her friend. It was hard to imagine, but one thing came to mind. "Are you and Josh no longer getting along?"

"No, no. Of course, we are. It's something else." Addie stared at her hands, knotted together in her lap. "I...I went to Mama's the other day. She was hosting the Ladies' Bible Society, and I was there to help her. Oh, Livvy, those old biddies and their gossip made me so mad!"

"Addie! How could you call them such a thing? That isn't like you one bit."

She met Olivia's gaze, her green eyes sparking with anger. "I wanted to pull their ears, like spoiled children, they made me so angry. They had the nerve to talk about you."

She gasped. "Me? Why?"

Addie's cheeks blazed. "That's what bothered me so. They were talking about you and—" She drew up short, clamped her lips, shook her head. "Oh, Livvy, I'm so sorry. They were saying horrid things about you and Mr. Whitman. They made it sound frightfully inappropriate for you to work for him, to live in the house with him."

Olivia clapped her hands on her own scorching cheeks. "But I'm not living with him. Not *that* way. Besides, there are children in the house. Cooky's room is next to mine. She's always there with me. He and I are never alone."

"Mama said so, but they wouldn't listen. They had made up their minds. Nothing we said swayed them." She took Olivia's hand. "You may have to consider leaving your position. You can't let your need for wages sully your reputation. You have to watch what these sour cats say."

"But I can't, Addie. You know how things stand with Mama and Papa. I can't burden them again. I need this job."

"You need to keep yourself above reproach."

The ache in her heart grew so deep that Olivia struggled

to draw another breath. How could it all have turned out like this? Now, when things seemed on the right path for the first time?

She had a clear conscience, and the Lord knew her heart. She simply had to persevere. Those women needed chores to keep them busy, as she'd busied Luke and Randy these last few days.

"I suppose I'll have to think about it," she said, "but I can't let frivolous gossip keep me from helping my family. I'll have to trust the Lord to see me through."

Addie nodded, a rueful smile on her lips. "I can't say I like your point, but I understand. I'll always stand behind you, you know. I'll always defend you."

"I'm so glad you haven't even asked—"

"What? If there's anything to the rumors?"

Olivia nodded.

"Pffft!" Addie waved. "I know you better than that. You're a decent, moral, godly woman. You'd never do anything like that. Besides, as you said, there are children in the house. Those women need their hands slapped."

Olivia gave her friend a weak smile as she stood. "And I need to get to the school. The children will come out any minute now, and Mr. Whitman wants me to walk them home every day."

"I must say, since you started there I haven't heard a single word about them getting into more scrapes. You're doing an excellent job."

She hoped.

Addie grabbed her hand, squeezed her fingers. "But promise you'll think about what I said."

"I gave you my word, Addie. I'll think about it. Only don't expect me to change my mind."

Addie nodded, but said nothing more. There was nothing left to say. They walked to the door in silence, each one somber, Olivia fighting tears.

Eli left the bank early that afternoon with a troubled heart. At some level, he knew Nathan was right, but he didn't have it in him to let down the men who'd asked for his help.

Holtwood also had a good point. If matters didn't settle down, he risked losing a splendid opportunity for the town. He'd never live with himself if his distraction cost Bountiful the chance to really flourish.

As he closed the front door, Cooky bustled to meet him. "You've a visitor, Mr. Whitman, sir. I did show him to the parlor, and served him a good cup of coffee, I did. He's a-waiting on you there."

How odd. He wasn't expecting anyone. He'd come home early, seeking time to think and pray.

"Well, well! Reverend Alton," he said, surprised to find the man in his home. "To what do I owe this pleasure?"

The reverend stood, hat in hand, his expression one that spoke of anything but pleasure. "I'm afraid, son, that I come on a difficult errand."

"Please, do sit. You've intrigued me. How can I help you?"

"Actually, Eli, I'm hoping I can help you. There's been talk around town, nasty talk, and you're at the center of it."

"I never let gossip bother me, Reverend. I don't have the time to waste on that sort of thing."

"This time is different. It involves more than you."

"I'm not following. I'm a plain-spoken man, and I'd rather you come right out and spell it out for me."

"It's about you, and Olivia Moore."

Eli couldn't believe his ears. "There's talk about my children's nanny and me?"

"Afraid so."

"What could they possibly say? My wife died, I've hired a number of women to work with my children, who ran them all off. I was at wits' end, and reckoned a local woman might be for the best. Besides, I'm away a great deal of time. Please tell anyone who's come running with tales that they're wrong."

"You don't have to defend yourself to me, and you shouldn't have to defend yourself to them, either. But folks are that way. They see something curious, and they're bound to make much of it. You're a young, well-to-do man, and Olivia is a beautiful young woman. Both of you are unmarried, and she lives in your home."

"It's not as though we're alone. The children are here, and they keep her busy all the time. Cooky is here, too. We're properly chaperoned."

"I understand, Eli. Believe me, I do. But you cannot continue like this. You cannot let your situation tarnish Olivia's reputation. Even the hint of scandal will ruin her for life."

Eli ran a hand through his hair. "But I can't let her go. She's done more with my two than anyone before her. I need her here."

"You need her, you say?"

"Without her, I'd have to send Luke and Randy to boarding school back East. I can't care for them while I'm at the bank or away on business. Cooky can't watch them, either. Her hands are full with the house and the kitchen."

"The way I see it, son, you have two choices. You either send Olivia back home to her parents or..." He stood and looked away. "Or you marry her."

Eli bolted upright. "Absolutely not! That's madness. I couldn't up and marry that woman. She's practically a stranger. Besides, you know what I went through before. I'm not about to do that again."

"Olivia's not Victoria. Many, many good marriages begin for the sake of the children. Tender feelings grow from common goals and after longer acquaintance. The Lord blesses those who do the right thing, you know."

Eli could scarcely believe his ears. This was madness. "You think the right thing is for me to marry my children's nanny?"

"You could also send her home."

"I need a nanny for my children, and perhaps someone who'll help with the occasional social event—but those are rare. I haven't hosted one since...well, since Victoria died. I don't need a wife."

"I'm sure Olivia will excel at both."

"Madness," Eli murmured, although he did agree with the pastor on at least one detail. Olivia Moore was indeed a beautiful woman.

"Much of life starts out as madness, but then, Scripture says that all things work together for good to them that love God, and are called according to His purposes."

That brought Eli up short. Could there be wisdom in Reverend Alton's suggestion? While his parents had married for love, he also knew others who'd married for various practical reasons. Most of those marriages were far more productive and peaceful than his to Victoria had been.

He knew in his heart that God could work miracles in the oddest of circumstances. He'd been a believer since he was very young. "I suppose that is something to consider."

"Please do that, son. A young woman's future is at stake."

"As is my children's."

"You're correct. They need a mother more than they need even the finest nanny."

As they walked to the front door, Eli heard Luke laugh. Again. The boy hadn't laughed much in longer than he cared to count. Since well before his mother died, as a matter of fact.

"Is that your boy?" the reverend asked.

Eli nodded.

"Is he alone?"

"I doubt it. Before you ask, I believe he is with Miss Moore."

Reverend Alton patted Eli's shoulder. "That speaks volumes. Think about what I've said."

Eli nodded. He would think about it; he doubted he'd think about much else in the near future.

Another laugh floated down the stairs, this one bell-like and feminine. Olivia Moore did indeed look better and better every day.

Chapter 10

"Oh, no! No-no-no-no-no-no-*no!*"

In the dark interior of the privy, Olivia couldn't believe the door was stuck. How?

She'd come outside, as she always did before changing into her nightgown and going to bed. The door had been open, nothing had been in the way. She'd taken care of her needs, and now...well, now she couldn't get out.

She didn't want to face the suspicion looming large in the back of her mind, but she supposed she had to. Could either Randy or Luke—or both—have done this? Had they thought this funny or were they still rebelling against her presence? Were they this serious about ridding themselves of the hated "nanny"?

Of all days. After that disturbing conversation with Addie.

Olivia didn't know how much more she could take before she broke.

It was fall, and a cold spell had come through. While the

outhouse walls kept the wind from striking her, she could feel the advancing cold. Since she hadn't planned to spend much time outside, Olivia only had on her regular clothes, and hadn't brought a wrap with her. She never brought a candle, unless it was a moonless night—unlike tonight. The utilitarian structure was pitch dark. A shiver ran through her. She didn't want to spend the night out here. In fact, all she could think about was curling under her blankets and shutting her eyes. Blessed sleep wouldn't come too soon for her after this horrid, horrid day.

She wanted...she wanted...

She wanted to go home, to Mama and Papa, to where she knew she was wanted, treasured, respected. She didn't want to continue to fight the children's stubborn rejection. What had she done to make them lock her in? Did they resent an outsider so much that they felt the need to show her she would always stay outside the circle of their family?

Did they think she was trying to worm her way in?

On top of that, she didn't want to defend herself before a gaggle of gossiping fools. Even if some of them were Mama's friends. If they could think such awful things about Olivia, then they were fools.

Tears burned her eyes. She hadn't sinned. She hadn't even overstepped her place within the Whitman family. At least, she didn't think she had.

"Lord Jesus, what did I do wrong? What did I fail to do? It's clear I'm failing, no matter how hard I've tried. You know how much I need to help Mama and Papa. I need to stand on my own two feet. I need to make this work."

How could she fail at something so simple? This was what

she'd done her whole life, she'd helped out at home, cared for her sisters and brothers. Surely she could handle two children.

Couldn't she?

A mocking voice set up a refrain in the back of her thoughts. *Failure, failure, failure.*

Her spirits sank to the lowest depths she'd experienced. When he heard the rumor, and saw how incapable she really was, Mr. Whitman was sure to send her home. Once she was no longer employed in Bountiful, she would have to seek work elsewhere. The thought of leaving her family to move to Kansas City, Denver, or Minneapolis made everything inside her freeze, and not from the piercing chill. To be unable to see her family at church on Sundays, to know she couldn't go home and visit—it was more than Olivia could stand.

A sob rose and broke past her lips. She brought a fist to her mouth to stifle the next one, and then the next.

"Oh, Father God. How could you have let me fail?"

Ever since Reverend Alton had left, Eli had done nothing but think about their conversation. By the time Cooky served supper, myriad images of Olivia Moore had alternated with those of Victoria in his thoughts. Could Reverend Alton have been right? As much as Eli wanted nothing to do with marriage, he couldn't deny his children's need for a mother.

He also knew no better candidate than their nanny.

Each time he reached that conclusion, his stomach roiled. Since his late wife's betrayal, he couldn't bear the thought of making himself, and by extension, his children, vulnerable again.

Supper had been a silent affair. The children had had little to say, which had suited Eli just fine. Each glance past Olivia toward them had left his cheeks warm and had made a dozen what-ifs shoot through his mind.

By the time he'd finished the surprisingly good dried apple fritters Cooky served after another bland chicken fricassee, he'd nearly run from the table and ensconced himself in the parlor after closing the pocket door. The children knew better than to disturb him when he did that, so he'd known he could count on peace and quiet for a few hours before he went to bed.

He'd pulled out his pipe and tamped down a bowl of his favorite cocoa-flavored tobacco, opened his Bible, and immersed himself in the heavenly Father's Word.

A while later, when he went upstairs to bid his children good night, the peaceful hush in the house soothed his nerves as little else had that whole day. While praying, he'd come to a decision. Problems didn't solve themselves by ignoring them. He had to talk to Olivia. He kissed his children, and then walked to the end of the hallway. To his surprise, when he knocked on her door, Olivia didn't answer. He tried again, this time louder, with the same lack of response.

She hadn't been in either of the children's rooms, so he thought she might have gone to the kitchen for something to tide her over until breakfast the next day. He hurried down, hoping he'd find the right words to express what lay heavy on his heart.

He found the kitchen dark and empty; neither woman was there. He checked the dining room, and while he'd left the parlor only minutes earlier, he even looked there

No sign of Olivia Moore.

Dread knotted his middle. He'd thought things had

improved with the children, and Cooky had seemed less distant toward Olivia since she'd returned after tending to Katy. Had he only seen what he wanted to see?

Had she given up and left? If so, how had she gone home, in the dark and in the cold?

She couldn't have. It made no sense, and Olivia struck him as an eminently sensible woman. Before he let himself worry, or think the worst, he had to search the house more thoroughly.

Parlor, dining room, kitchen, larder—nothing. He tried upstairs. Randy's room, Luke's, Cooky's—even his own, although he couldn't imagine she'd be there. Once again, he knocked on her door.

Silence.

Again.

He tried the cook's door. She opened, pale and worried. "Mr. Whitman, sir! Oh, dearie me. Is it my Katy-girl again?"

"Not at all." He placed a hand on the woman's shoulder. "I can't find Miss Moore. I've looked everywhere in the house, but there's no sign of her. I don't feel right going into her room, and I'd appreciate your help. Could you check there?"

"Sure, and I'm glad to help." She shook her head. "Where could that child have gotten off to? This isn't one bitty-bit like her, no sir, and it isn't."

"I know, Cooky. I wouldn't have troubled you if I weren't concerned."

She grasped the doorknob, paused, and gave him a comforting smile. "Ah, Mr. Eli, sir. Let's not be a-fretting yet. Maybe she's sleeping real hard-like. Some folks are like rocks, you know."

He nodded, not at all convinced.

When the older woman entered the room, she gasped. "It's empty! Miss Olivia's not here. Oh, dearie me—"

"I was afraid of that."

"Are you a-thinking she'd up and go for good? Surely not. I'm sure, and she wouldn't do such a thing. I've gotten to know her mama a little—from church and such, you know? I can't be imagining Elizabeth raising a girl who'd leave the children just like that, and all."

"Did she take her things?" he asked.

"Well...I didn't get a good look, or nothing such. I'll be after looking again." She slipped into the room a second time.

When she came out, she wore a puzzled look. "You can be resting easy, Mr. Whitman, sir. Her nightgown's all folded-like on the bed, and all. Plus her hairbrush is on the bureau. No self-respecting woman'd leave that behind, I'm a-telling you, I am."

"Since you're a woman, then where might she be?"

She laughed. "I'm after telling you, these young girls these days leave me a-scratching my head, sir, they do. Can't be figuring a thing out about a one of them."

Frustrated, he thanked her. "I suppose all we can do is go to bed and pray she appears by morning."

"If you find her, don't you be a-keeping it to yourself, you hear? You come and tell me or send her to do so, and right quickly, at that. A body can't be sleeping too good, all worried-like."

"I'll make sure you know the moment I see her, if you don't see her first—"

"I'll be a-telling you if I come acrosst her first."

"We're agreed. You'd best catch some of that sleep you need to be up as early as you rise every morning."

"Good night, Mr. Eli, sir."

" 'Night, Cooky."

Although he was reluctant to let things stand as they did, he didn't know what else to do. Eli locked the front door then went out back to use the privy.

As he approached, unusual noises—rough, choking sounds— came from the small structure. He groaned.

It never ended well when an animal found itself stuck inside the privy. Still, he had to take care of it. Holding the oil lamp high over his head, he reached for the door and found it stuck in place.

A gasp came from inside.

Eli froze.

He pulled on the door, harder this time, and called out, "Olivia—Miss Moore?"

"Mr. Whitman! I'm so glad you've come out. Please help me. I can't open the door. And I—I don't know why."

When he lowered the lamp he noticed two large rocks wedged against the bottom of the door. He kicked them away.

She tumbled out, hair disheveled, eyes huge in the lamp-light. He caught her in his free arm to keep her from falling.

"I'm afraid I do know, Miss Moore, and the two culprits will face quite a punishment. It's cold out here tonight, and you could have come down with some kind of grippe."

She frowned. "Oh, no, sir. Please don't punish them. I'm trying to win them over, and punishment will only set me back."

"I understand, Miss Moore. Believe me, I do. But this time, they've gone too far. Silly pranks like grasshoppers in drawers and honey on a seat don't normally hurt anyone. This, on the other hand, could have had a much worse outcome. They're fortunate I found you when I did."

She bit her bottom lip, a gesture he was coming to know as a sign of her discomfort. Moments later, when they stepped into the kitchen, his hand holding her arm to lend her support, she shrugged.

"I'll defer to you, sir, since you're their papa." As soon as he closed the door, she stepped away. "Thank you for your help, but now, I'd better get in bed and warm up. Good night, Mr. Whitman."

"Good night, Miss Moore."

Once she'd left and he headed to alert Cooky as to the outcome of his search, Eli had only one thought in mind. Grippe and influenza were deadly. She could have come down with either one. They could have lost her because of a prank. Just wait until those two came down for breakfast in the morning.

Just wait.

After a night of tears, restlessness, and prayer, Olivia rose late, for the first time since she'd come to the Whitman home. She rushed through her morning toilette, then went down to the dining room.

No one was there.

In the kitchen, she found Cooky. "Where are the children?" she asked.

"Oh, my dearie-girl!" Cooky bustled over and wrapped Olivia in a spice-scented hug. "Mr. Eli told me what those two hooligans were after doing to you last night. It's happy, I am, to see you're fine today."

"Thank you, but...where is everybody?"

"Oh, Miss Olivia, you shoulda heard that man, I'm after telling you. He gave the hoodlums a tongue-lashing fit to blister the whitewash right off the privy walls—" She covered her mouth. "I'm so sorry. Can't believe I said that today of all days."

Olivia smiled. "That's fine. But, where are they?"

"When he was done telling them how bad this one was, and how he would not be standing for any more of these shenanigans, or such again, he was after telling them they had to shape up or he'd be shipping them off to boarding schools, and—and—and then he marched them to school." She gave a firm nod, which set the knot of snowy hair at the crown of her head to bobbing. "Gave me orders to let you sleep to your heart's content, he did."

Olivia's middle sank near to the floor. Surely now, after last night and her failure to come down in time to take the children to school this morning, Mr. Whitman would be sending her back.

The only question that remained was how soon he would do so.

That evening, Olivia hurried back to the parlor after she'd listened to Randy's prayers and tucked Luke into bed. Mr. Whitman had asked her at supper to meet him once she finished with the children.

She'd already made sure her belongings were ready to return to Mama's satchel before walking the children home from school. Both had the grace to look chastened. They returned home in silence, and once in the house, both children ran directly to their rooms.

Olivia had slipped inside her own, collapsing on the bed and letting loose the tears she'd fought all day.

Now, everything in Olivia feared what might happen next.

Her stomach a knot, she breathed a prayer as she walked down the hallway, knowing full well he'd probably decided to let her go.

Then where would she be?

Not only would she become a burden to her parents once again, but if she had to leave the Whitmans, Olivia knew a hole would open in her heart. The family had built a nest there, and she doubted she'd fill it again anytime soon.

Gathering what courage she could muster, Olivia entered the cozy room. "I'm done with the children, sir. How can I help you?"

Mr. Whitman leaped to his feet. "Please take a seat, Miss Moore. I'm sure you've had a long day and wouldn't mind the chance to rest a bit." He gestured to the side table next to his armchair, where a coffeepot, sugar bowl, cream pitcher, and two cups and saucers had been set out. "I had Cooky make us coffee. How do you like yours? Unless you want tea, that is. In which case, I'll have her bring you some instead."

To her admittedly inexperienced ears, the banker seemed somewhat nervous. Olivia had never heard him ramble before. Her anxiety grew.

"Coffee will be fine." If she had to pack after their conversation, she'd need help to stay awake.

He gestured her toward the comfortable sofa as he poured the fragrant brew. "Sugar?" he asked. "Cream?"

"A bit of both, please."

Once he'd given her the cup, he sat in his well-upholstered armchair, stirred his beverage again, took a sip, placed the saucer back on the table and the cup on the small plate. Only then did he look Olivia's way.

"How do you like living here with us, Miss Moore?"

Such a peculiar question. "I—ah . . . like it fine, sir."

"I understand you and Cooky get along."

Olivia smiled. "We're becoming friends. I'm finding I even enjoy working with her. More important, as you must know, she loves the children, and they're just as fond of her."

He nodded as he took another sip. "After last night, how do *you* feel about the children? They are a handful, I'm afraid."

Again, she smiled—nervously. "Nothing I can't handle, sir. Last night was an exception. Things have been going quite well. They're wonderful, bright, lively youngsters. I've grown to care for them. I hope they haven't had complaints about me."

"In spite of last night, they tell me they're quite taken with you."

"Really?" *And how about you?*

The thought sprang to life before she could catch herself. At least she hadn't blurted it out. That would have been awful, improper, embarrassing. For both of them.

Still, Olivia had often wondered how Mr. Whitman felt about the stranger in his home. But it wasn't the night for questions like those.

"Well then, sir," she went on, "I have to wonder if you have any complaints with my work."

"None whatsoever." He set down his cup and saucer with great deliberation. "In fact, Miss Moore, your influence on my family is why I've asked you to join me tonight. I must say," he added, "you remind me of your father. Stephen Moore has always shown himself to be a fine, decent man who knows his mind, is fair, and prefers to bring negotiations to a close in a way that benefits all parties involved. If you are as much like him as you appear, I believe we will work very well together."

Pleasure ran through Olivia. "That is the loveliest compliment anyone has paid me. I'm proud of my parents, and can think of nothing better than to be considered like either one of them."

"From what I've seen, you're a credit to them. I suspect, since you're so like Stephen, that you just might be the right woman for this season in our family's life. I'm mighty glad you were clever enough to think of this arrangement, and then come seek me out."

This time, the blush on her cheeks came from pure pleasure.

"Which leads me straight to the reason we're here. I've . . . a proposition for you."

"How intriguing, Mr. Whitman. I must say, this is most unexpected. I thought perhaps you'd decided you didn't need my services any longer."

He stood, clasped his hands behind his back, and began to pace the room. "Not at all. I'd be a fool if I were to let you go. It's a rare thing for a man to come home to a peaceful supper at the end of the day without a thing to worry about. For the most part, you've made a difference in my children's unacceptable behavior—again, in spite of last night—and it's a pleasure when a man can spend quiet evenings at home without having a fight on his hands to get his youngsters to mind their manners."

His words painted a sad picture. She knew the difficulties had existed for a while, but for how long? Had there perhaps been trouble between him and the late Mrs. Whitman?

It was possible. And possibly painful. For all of them.

It was also none of Olivia's business.

She chose her words with care. "I'm glad my services have been satisfactory, sir. I've appreciated every minute I've been here."

He grinned and arched a brow. "Every minute? Even the grasshopper greeting? How about the honey?"

Olivia laughed. "I expected pranks, since I knew they'd given their previous nannies trouble."

"I'm surprised by how few objections my scoundrels actually have put up."

A touch of hope for her future began to glow. "I suppose children do need a woman's touch, sir."

His blue, blue eyes latched on to her face like the beam of light from an oncoming locomotive. Olivia's breath caught in her throat.

"A woman's touch..." His voice echoed pensive, his attention still fixed on Olivia.

She felt the urge to squirm under that scrutiny. Somehow, she resisted.

"A woman's touch," he repeated, "is indeed what we've lacked around here. You've brought it to us, with excellent results. As a businessman, I've learned to spot a good bargain, and you, Miss Moore, are one far better than even a windfall. I suspect you're more along the lines of a godsend, and I'd be a fool if I didn't recognize it. Which I do."

From his formidable expression, she recognized there was

more to his comments than met the eye. She couldn't guess what that more might be, but the statement puzzled her.

Still, Olivia recognized a compliment when she heard one. "Thank you for your kind words, Mr. Whitman."

He resumed his pacing. "As I said, I'd be a fool if I let you go. That's why I've come up with what I think will be an excellent business arrangement for the both of us."

Now she was downright bewildered and at a complete loss. "A business arrangement?"

"Indeed." He stopped in front of her, his relentless stare on her face. "When you came to my office you said you needed employment. I assume you, or rather your family, is still suffering the effects of our drought and grasshopper disasters."

She winced. "I can't begin to put it into words."

"You've done well by hiring yourself out as a nanny—companion, right? Since I don't imagine the financial situation will change much in the immediate future, I expect you're interested in a permanent situation."

Relief filled Olivia with a sense of calm. But not for long. Those intense blue eyes did strange things to her. They made her feel as though her every nerve ending had just awoken, as though her every sense had just become more exquisite in its sensitivity. While unexpected and uninvited, Mr. Elijah Whitman's gaze made Olivia feel more feminine, more a woman than she did in his absence.

She feared her unusual awareness spoke of danger. Not some kind of bodily danger, since no sensible woman would ever fear the gentlemanly banker, but rather danger of the riskiest sort. Olivia feared her response to her employer might speak of danger to her feelings.

She offered up a silent prayer then took a deep breath. "Yes, Mr. Whitman. I would appreciate a permanent position in your home. But please understand, it's not for my sake alone. I care what happens to your children, and would love to be here for them as they encounter the normal challenges of growing up."

His shoulders appeared to relax a fraction, and a hint of a smile lightened the intensity of his expression. "That is excellent. It looks as though this will work out to everyone's best advantage. Miss Moore, in view of all those benefits we've discussed, I would like you to marry me."

Olivia gasped.

Gulped for air.

Looked at the fireplace. At the rug. At anything but the man who'd just asked her to be his wife.

"You—you *what*?"

"I hope I haven't offended you, but, yes. I did ask you to marry me."

"But, why?"

"A number of reasons. The first, of course, is for my children. They need a mother, and you're the only person they've begun to accept. Then, there's my need for a social hostess. On occasion, I must entertain business guests. Those needs bring me to my last reason. And that's you."

"Me!" She leaped up. "Pray tell, what do you mean, Mr. Whitman? I might be unmarried, but I'm no desperate spinster, pining after you. I'll have you know, the very notion has never once crossed my mind."

To her horror, he laughed. "Indeed, Miss Moore. As you

say, you might be unmarried—yet—but you're no one's notion of a spinster. That might be your finest quality. You're intelligent, courageous, no one's fool, and you're willing to take a risk. But that's not what I meant."

When he grew serious, Olivia guessed what he meant. She grew mortified. "Oh, dear. You've heard."

"If you mean about the gossip, then, yes. I have heard. Reverend Alton came to urge me to consider my options. This is the only one that makes sense. For both of us."

Olivia crossed her arms. "I'm glad you've come to that decision, sir, but you've done it by yourself. Not only have you thrust this idea upon me out of the blue, but you've also not considered what I might think of it. You must realize I cannot give you a serious response right away."

"I do. Because of the situation, however, I suggest you don't take long to mull it over." He sat in one of the armchairs. "There is...um...another detail to discuss. A very delicate detail."

Olivia just stared. She collapsed onto the sofa. How could he think to discuss something like *that*?

"Oh," he said, his cheeks as red as hers felt. "That. No, Miss Moore. That's not a subject to discuss. Ours will be a business proposition. You need not fret about it."

Relief nearly drowned her. "Thank you. Then what?"

He grew serious, grim even. "It's business of another sort. My work, my business. My bank, if I must be blunt. I insist on keeping matters of the home and those of the bank completely separate. Under no circumstance will you involve yourself with the bank. Ever. It's not a matter for negotiation." His sudden smile appeared forced. "As my wife, however, you'll have full authority over household matters and you'll manage everything related to the children. Of course, I'll retain normal authority as their father, but otherwise, you'll be their mother and see to their daily needs."

"I see." She didn't, not really. "Again, sir. I must have time to pray about this before I can give you a response."

To her relief, he agreed.

Then she fled to her room, where she could do nothing but think about his proposal.

She also thought about Mama and Papa. She even thought about the scandal Addie had said swirled around her these days. Hours later, Olivia couldn't believe she'd heard right. Mr. Whitman wanted her to marry him.

His children needed a mother. She needed to salvage what was left of her reputation before it became damaged beyond repair.

So...did she have a choice?

More important, what was the wise thing to do?

Finally, what was the Father's will for her life? Did God intend for her to become the new Mrs. Elijah Whitman?

Was she ready to marry?

Was she ready to marry him...Eli?

Chapter 11

Dear God...Father in heaven. What have I done? What did I get myself into?

Olivia stood before the altar at the Church of Bountiful dressed in a store-bought light blue dress with white stripes hurriedly fitted to her. She glanced at her groom, admiring his fresh-shaven good looks, the perfect fit of his black coat, the blue eyes that never failed to catch her attention.

The whole congregation, including her family and the Whitman children, sat in electrified silence, drinking in her every word, her every gesture. It had only been a week since Eli's proposal.

She'd known the suddenness of their engagement, not to mention its planned brief duration, would raise many eyebrows. But, as she'd heard from Addie, it would seem she and Mr. Whitman had already raised more than their fair share. In spite of the chatter, she knew the reality. It spoke loudly of the reason behind their arrangement, and she hoped their wedding soon silenced all those who cared to look.

Because that was precisely what their union would be. A business arrangement. She prayed their decision brought only beneficial consequences for everyone.

She knew a number of successful marriages were born from emotionless decisions after tragic losses. Theirs was as good a reason to marry as any, the most common of all. A convenience-based endeavor, it would not involve matters of the heart; their union would never be the emotional entanglement many forged when they sought a partner for life. Neither was infatuated with the other. It was best if they kept things that way. Their handful of shared conversations gave her no illusions about a grand romance, certainly nothing like the deep love her parents shared. And yet, she couldn't extinguish the flicker of anxiety in the back of her mind.

Was this the right way to enter into the marriage covenant? Was this right in God's eyes? The building of barriers to exclude any action on the Father's part that might somehow, someday transform their marriage as He saw fit?

Just as discomfiting, her family had only seen what they'd wanted to see when she'd told them she'd be wedding her employer. They'd wanted the illusion, a sweeping, starry-eyed fiction, much like what one found in the dime novels folks enjoyed reading. Olivia could afford to indulge in no such fancies.

"...until death do you part?" Reverend Alton said.

Olivia blinked. Oh, dear. She'd lost track of the ceremony, and now Reverend Alton was asking her to take her wedding vows. A glance at the man at her side increased her anxiety.

She couldn't deny he appealed to her...just as she couldn't

deny how odd their imminent marriage seemed to her, even in spite of the apparent logic to the entire thing.

Could she do it? Could she enter into this covenant?

"Olivia?" her pastor said in his gentle voice. "Are you well, my dear?"

The memory of her parents' ill-concealed relief when she'd announced her impending marriage and her dislike of the frills, bows, and fuss some girls favored for their wedding burst into her thoughts. Luke's and Randy's sweet faces joined those of the elder Moores. Finally, as unbidden as ever, the handsome features of her husband-to-be overlaid everything else.

"Yes, Reverend Alton. I'm fine. And yes, sir. I do take my wedding vows. I will make Mr. Whitman as good a wife as I'm capable of being. I will also make Luke and Randy as good a mother as anyone could ever wish."

From behind the shelter of her eyelashes, she saw her groom's eyes widen at her words. He turned his gaze full on her, and the blue of his eyes snagged her full attention. Nothing could have made her turn from him.

They stood there for long moments, silent, staring at each other, a rare awareness flying between them. As though from a far, far place, she heard Reverend Alton voice Mr. Whitman's vows. Then, in that deep, resonant baritone, the banker pledged his troth to her.

Eyes still boring into hers, he said, "I do."

"By the authority vested in me by our heavenly Father and the laws of our nation," the reverend continued, "I declare you husband and wife. You may embrace your bride, sir."

Olivia gasped.

Mr. Whitman blinked. Slowly, with determined deliberation,

he reached out and took Olivia into his arms. With that same purposeful gentleness, her new husband pulled her close to him then pressed a soft kiss on her cheek, unbearably close to the corner of her mouth.

The heat of his lips...the power of his strength...the delicious sense of protection and shelter and comfort she found in his arms stunned her. It came at her like a revelation, one that sent her thoughts into a whirl, made her head spin, and snagged her breath in her throat. Olivia knew she'd never felt anything so exquisite in her life.

For a moment, she let herself relish his warmth, his strength, his caress. How wonderful it would be if it were all real.

If only...

No! She couldn't let herself play that disastrous game. She had to be thankful for the blessings the Lord had already poured down on her. She especially had to be grateful for Mr. Whitman's willingness to bind his life to hers.

She wouldn't—couldn't—go through that life longing for something that would never be, something that would only lead to misery. Their vows affected too many of their loved ones. None of them deserved misery.

She had to trust the Lord. Only he could have brought them to where they were today. Only he knew what their future held. It was up to her to trust.

And obey.

Days after the wedding, Olivia placed a hand on the shoulder of each of her children, again filled with the glow of her sudden and, to her mind, miraculous motherhood. To her amazement, the pranks had disappeared. She didn't know if they were gone forever, but she was enjoying the unexpected calm and the confidence she could handle any new pranks. "Time for bed."

She still struggled to believe the many changes three short months had wrought in her life. Not only had she wed Eli Whitman, but she'd also gained Randy and Luke in the bargain—an excellent bargain, as her husband—

Oh, my! *Husband.*

She gathered her thoughts again, refusing any tendency to drift down that fanciful path. Yes, she had made an excellent bargain by marrying Elijah Whitman. He had been right when he proposed, at the very least as far as that went.

As she headed to the hall, Eli cleared his throat. "Would you care to join me for coffee once the children are in bed?"

Her cheeks heated. "I'd be happy to."

His nod dropped a lock of thick black hair onto his high forehead. "Coffee and good company are always welcome at the end of a busy day."

Butterflies fluttered in her middle. "I'll be back once Randy—" The girl's dismay had Olivia squelching a laugh. A glance at Eli showed a matching twitch at the corners of his mouth.

"Excuse me," she said. *"Miranda."*

Her new daughter smiled.

"As I was saying, I'll return as soon as Miranda and Luke have washed and said their prayers." She gave the children gentle nudges. "Come along, now. It's getting late and you'll regret dawdling in the morning."

Luke turned those Whitman blue eyes on Olivia as he went up the polished oak stairs. "It's not the going to bed that's the problem, Miss—*Mama*. It's the rising and going to school."

Olivia chuckled, thinking she'd have to get used to her new role. To think, she'd gone from Miss Olivia to Mama in only a week. "Why am I not surprised to hear you say that?"

At her side, Randy gave a sniff. "Because we're fairly sick of hearing him complain about school every day, *Mama*. At least, I'm sick to death of it."

Olivia fought against another laugh that wouldn't benefit their budding relationship.

"Perhaps," she told Randy. "But Luke knows his duty, wouldn't you say? He goes each morning, even though he doesn't relish it."

Reaching the upstairs landing, Randy rolled her eyes and bobbed her head from side to side. "I suppose. Still, he's such a *child*."

Olivia lost her battle against the laughter. "We praise the Good Lord for that, don't we? What else should a ten-year-old boy be but a child?"

With a shrug, Randy sailed into her room. Out of the corner of her eye, Olivia caught sight of Luke's protruding tongue and crossed eyes. "Now, Luke. Is that your most polite expression?"

Luke shuffled on the fashionable hallway runner. "No, ma'am. But Randy's not the most polite person, neither."

"Either."

" 'S what I said."

Olivia placed her arm across his thin shoulders to guide him toward his room. "I meant that the correct word in your sentence was either, not neither."

"Oh. That again."

"Yes, oh. That again. And again until you remember more often." She turned the boy to face her then dropped to her knees. "What do you think Jesus would say about that face you made at your sister?"

Luke's lids shuttered his eyes. "Oh."

"Once again, yes, oh. What would the Lord say?"

He shuffled some more, his thin fingers knotting. "I don't rightly know *egg-zackly* what he'd say, but I reckon he wouldn't be too pleased." Then Luke frowned. "Still, Randy's the worst stuck-up goody-goody that ever was."

Olivia took the boy's face between her hands. "Look at me, Luke. Would Jesus call Randy what you just did?"

Again, those beautiful eyes closed. "No, ma'am, He wouldn't."

"Then why don't you worry about becoming more like the Lord than about your sister's attitude? I can help her with that—it's one thing mothers do well."

Luke clasped Olivia's forearms. "Yeah, I guess I can." He squeezed. "I'm glad you married us, Miss Olivia...Mama."

Sitting in a pool of her plum wool skirt, Olivia pulled the rascal onto her lap. "Oh, Luke, I am, too. I haven't stopped thanking the Lord for you and Randy, especially since the wedding."

Thin arms wrapped around her neck. "Don't forget Papa. You married him, too."

Olivia caught her breath. "No...I don't forget your papa. I most certainly married him."

She shook her head a tiny bit. She really didn't want to dwell on doubt. She'd understood his terms and had accepted them. She'd had no alternative. Well, she could have said no, but then she'd have been where she'd started. And . . . had she really wanted to say no? Yet, on a regular basis, the misgivings she experienced at the altar came back to haunt her.

The morning she'd accepted his proposal, Eli had thanked her, and more. *"You'll lack for nothing as my wife . . ."*

Just then, she noted her new son's heavy-lidded eyes and deep, slow breathing. "My dearest Mr. Lucas Whitman." She tapped the tip of his nose. "Time has come to wash up and say your prayers. There's no getting around that scrubbing—and make sure you work behind those ears."

He stood. "Aw . . . all right. I'm goin'. Will you still be coming in?"

"I'll come pray with you and tuck you in—*after* you've washed. As I always do."

With a lopsided grin, he scooted into his room.

"G'night, Mama . . ." Luke and Randy's voices echoed in her thoughts.

Flushed with the joy the children brought her, Olivia hurried back to the parlor. The rich cocoa fragrance of Eli's pipe tobacco teased her senses as she crossed the hall.

She drew a breath and closed her eyes before stepping inside. *I don't know what Eli wants, Father God, but I know you can help me through the evening. Give me the best words and seal my lips against any others.*

Despite her trepidation, she couldn't help but marvel at her blessings. She had a sturdy roof over her head, wholesome food at her table, fire in the grates, even lovely clothes.

As Mrs. Whitman, the fine walnut and velvet furnishings were hers, as Eli had said a number of times. He'd suggested, more than once, that she move into the large guest room, but she preferred her own cozy, familiar bedroom.

There was also the measure of peace she'd achieved when it came to her family. She was no longer a drain on them. Mama and Papa at first had objected when she'd given them her earnings, but she'd persevered, and her wages had bought the family a reasonable supply of food. She never could have dreamed of this future for herself.

The Lord evidently had, and she thanked Him day after day for His provision.

Eli waved her forward. "Come in, come in. You were gone a while. I hope those two didn't give you much trouble."

Olivia sat on the wine velvet sofa and clasped her hands in her lap. "Oh, no. Not a bit, Mr. Whitman—"

"Surely you can call me Eli now."

Her eyes widened. Call the president of the Bank of Bountiful by his first name *to his face*? The most respected man in town? The wealthiest?

Her...husband?

As she fumbled for a response, that spouse of only a handful of days smiled. "I'd be honored if you would."

The twinkle in his blue eyes invited agreement, even though she had to work to keep her voice from shaking. "I'll try, but it might take some doing."

"I hope not from fear."

"Of course not. It's just that you're...well, you, and I'm... me..." Oh, dear, what a hash she'd made of that.

Eli chuckled. "Well, I certainly hope we're who we're supposed to be. After all, we are home, and have family matters to discuss."

Family matters. *Her* new family's matters. What a thrill!

She smiled. "What might those be?"

Eli gestured toward the steaming pot on the table by his easy chair. "Would you care for coffee first? Or Cooky could bring you tea."

"I drink both," she answered, "but coffee's fine. Thank you."

He handled the heavy silver vessel with confidence, underscoring the contrast between his sturdy fingers and the fine, graceful metal. Seconds later, she again thanked him for the cup of rich, dark brew.

He sat back, right ankle atop his left knee. "The holidays are only weeks away. I'd like your opinion on the gifts for the children."

She nearly choked on the hot coffee. "My opinion?" How astounding.

"Of course. You're their mother now. I think the gifts should come from the two of us."

"That's a lovely idea. What did you have in mind?"

"Have you noticed my son's interest in trains?"

"I'd have to be deaf, blind, and a fool not to."

Eli sent her a satisfied look. "You're none of those. That's why you will make such an excellent wife."

"Why...thank you." A most unusual evening, this.

"You're welcome to the truth. And because you're so aware of the children's needs, I can appreciate your opinion. What would you think of a wooden train set for Luke?"

"He would love it. But where would you find one? It's too late to order one from back East."

"I'd have Tom Bowen make it. The man's a marvel when it comes to working wood."

"Papa thinks a great deal of Mr. Bowen's talents. I'm sure the train would be a dream come true for any little boy, especially Luke."

"Then that's settled." Eli frowned. "I just wish Randy... er...Miranda were as easy to shop for as Luke."

"Miranda shouldn't be any trouble. She's become quite tall these last few months. Her dresses are much too short for a young lady. She's even straining the seams of last winter's coat."

Eli shook his head, a wistful smile on his lips. "I can't believe my little girl has grown so fast. I suppose longer skirts are appropriate now."

"I'm afraid so. She grows more interested in fashionable clothing by the day. Prepare yourself for your young lady, one with a young woman's tastes."

"Then gentlemen callers can't be too far off in my future."

Olivia took another sip of coffee. "With Randy's looks and her spunk, I suspect they'll come in droves."

"You're probably right."

His continued attention unnerved her. She felt more comfortable back in her room. "Do you agree with my suggestion, then? New dresses and a coat?"

"I'd rather keep her in pinafores and pigtails forever, but of course she must be properly dressed. I knew your opinion would help tonight."

She set down her cup and saucer. "I'm glad. They really are wonderful children. I've grown to love them."

"Then you don't regret our marriage?"

Olivia drew a sharp breath. "No. No, I don't."

It had only been a few days, but she didn't regret marrying him. At times, she did wonder if she would someday regret the business arrangement to which they'd agreed. Especially since the man she was coming to know had so many appealing traits. But she could hardly say that.

Eli cut into her thoughts. "I'm glad. That brings me to my last question. What would *you* like for Christmas this year?"

Olivia stood. "Me?"

Eli gave her a knowing look. "Indeed, Mrs. Whitman, you. A hint would help me choose something you'll welcome."

"Nothing. Nothing at all. I can't imagine more than you've already given me." She gestured toward the room. "I have more than I ever thought I would. The children, the home, easing Papa's burden...I thank God daily for these gifts. I can't think of a solitary thing more a woman could want."

Eli's expression darkened. "Try. I'm sure you can come up with at least one more. Women always do."

She'd never heard Elijah Whitman speak in any but the most respectful, kind, and gentle tone. Until now.

Well...and when, during his proposal, he'd warned her to stay out of his business matters. True, he'd wanted to delineate what her duties would be. However, he'd seemed unduly harsh and unbending about that issue. Had she in any way given him the idea that she possessed even a hint of interest in the Bank of Bountiful?

She didn't think so. Still, a serving of bitterness had accompanied his words. She couldn't help but wonder what lay behind it, but she didn't dare ask.

Her earlier happiness gone, Olivia set her cup gently down. "I'm most appreciative of all you've given me, Mr. Whitman. I don't have other needs, so please, don't waste another thought on a gift. I'm quite content."

She left the parlor, then in the hallway, paused again. "Good night."

In her room, she fell to her knees by the bed. "Lord Jesus, did I do something to displease him? Have I seemed ungrateful? Have I somehow crossed that invisible line he drew between us?"

She sifted back over her actions of the past weeks and found nothing to condemn her. Except...

Except that niggling sense of something missing, of emptiness. Feelings and emotions. Although she'd agreed theirs was a marriage of convenience, she'd always expected to find something else in marriage. Something more.

Olivia sighed. That something was nothing Eli could produce for the holidays. He more than likely never would be willing or able to produce it.

Until death do you part.

It would be a long time, indeed.

To her surprise, she suddenly wished for the warm tenderness her parents still shared, even after decades of marriage and five busy youngsters.

Nothing but affection. Although a twinge of sadness had pierced Olivia's heart, she'd come to see the various benefits in becoming Mrs. Elijah Whitman. They remained as strong as ever. Especially when it meant she'd never have to leave the children who were becoming so dear to her.

How selfish could she be?

God had blessed her with an upstanding husband, a respectful, sober, moral, hardworking man. Eli in turn had provided her with all the comforts a woman might need. Still she found herself longing for more.

Why? Why wasn't she satisfied with all she had?

"Forgive me, Father," she murmured. "Take away this discontent I never before knew might someday be a part of me. Help me find contentment in what I do have . . . in you."

A short while later, Olivia went to bed, her uncertainty eased, as always, by her faith. Her dreams, however, were filled with Eli's intriguing if distant face.

Chapter 12

"Afternoon, Missus Whitman," called Barry Woollery, Bountiful's blacksmith, as she crossed Main Street at his corner. It took a moment for Olivia to realize he was speaking to her.

"It truly is lovely," she replied with a smile.

As he stepped from his doorway onto the boardwalk, the large man wiped his shiny forehead with the back of a hand. "Just how I like 'em, ma'am. Cool and crisp and smellin' of winter, but sunnylike and bright."

Olivia took note of Mr. Woollery's flushed features and the roar of the fire behind him. "I can see where you would like the cold. It's hot work even now that the temperature has dropped."

"That it is, ma'am. That it is." He grinned and pointed with his chin. "Are you and the little missy out for an afternoon's walk?"

At Olivia's side, Randy bristled with impatience. "No, sir," she hurried to say. "We're on our way to Metcalf's Mercantile.

I need certain dry goods, and I promised Miranda a special treat once I'm done."

"Licorice drops were my boys' favorites. Would they be yours, too, Miss Randy?"

Randy took a step toward the mercantile. "I prefer peppermints."

Mr. Woollery tapped his brow and turned back toward the gleaming-red forge. "I won't keep you ladies, then."

Olivia smiled at her daughter. "Thank you for your patience. I promise not to take too long choosing my dress goods."

Luke, who'd watched the town's hustle and bustle from the boardwalk, frowned. "I sure hope not...hey! Can I go see Papa? Please? Just for a little while. I promise I won't be a bother. 'Sides, I don't like girls' dresses and stuff."

After a moment's consideration, Olivia nodded. "But only if you ask Mr. Holtwood if your father's busy before barging in on him."

Earnest blue eyes met hers. "Oh, I will, Mama. I promise. An' I won't bother one bit." He took off at a run, his footsteps pounding out his progress down the wooden walk outside the town's businesses.

"Such a child," Randy said.

Olivia ignored the comment and opened the door to Metcalf's Mercantile. "Let's see what we can find here. I have a fair idea what I'd like, but I do appreciate another lady's opinion."

Randy's blue eyes widened. "D'you mean...me?"

Olivia took a moment to study the girl. With her black hair, rose-tinted skin, and bright eyes, Miranda was already more than halfway to becoming a beauty. Blues and roses and whites would suit her better than the browns, rusts, greens, and occasional plums Olivia favored.

"I don't see why not. I'm sure you know what you like when you see it. I certainly don't want Mrs. Gallagher to make up any dresses in fabrics that will look foolish or dreadfully dull."

Randy stood taller. "That would be a waste, wouldn't it?"

To hide her smile, Olivia turned toward the table stacked high with rainbow bolts of cloth. "What about that periwinkle one?"

Under the pretense of gaining her daughter's opinion on new dresses for Olivia, the two of them went through the store's choices in systematic fashion. No cotton dimity went unnoticed, not a serge, calico, or wool. Randy forgot all about putting on her usual airs, and Olivia found the sweet side of the girl she tried so hard to hide. If only she could help her new daughter see she was most like the young lady she so desperately wanted to be when she relaxed enough to be herself.

As they narrowed their choices to six or so, familiar footsteps pounded into the store.

"Mama!" Luke cried. "I just heard the bestest news in Papa's office. I can't hardly believe our great good luck."

Holding her son by the wriggling shoulders, Olivia forced him to pause long enough to ask him a question. "Do you think you can slow down and let us in on your news?"

"Yes! But it's the best thing that's ever happened."

Here Olivia had thought, after last night, that Luke felt *she* was the best thing to ever happen. Trust the Lord to use a child to put a woman's pride in its proper place. "Tell me about it, then."

"Why, Mama, the railroad's coming to town. And Papa—
Papa's—the one bringing it here."

Gasps flew from various corners of the store. Olivia and
Randy had been so busy choosing fabric they hadn't noticed
the other customers in the emporium.

"The railroad?" she asked. "Are you sure, Lucas?"

Wide-eyed nodding answered her.

"But...Bountiful's such a small place."

"Won't be anymore," the boy crowed.

"The railroad..." Olivia stepped to the Mercantile's door.
She glanced out toward Main Street and watched the normal
midday bustle of their small town for a moment. Horses drew
neighbors' wagons to their business, while pedestrians paused
to chat with friends as they attended to errands. Everyone
knew everyone else and found comfort in that knowing.

But now...the railroad was coming. According to Luke,
her train-mad child. Could he have mistaken what he'd heard?
"Just what did you hear in your papa's office?"

"He said a spur line was coming through Bountiful, and...
and what a—a boon that would be for everyone. He said the
railroad would bring wonderful changes with it. Nothing will
ever be the same again."

Olivia took another look out the glass door. Reverend Alton
crossed the street at his usual brisk pace, his well-thumbed
black Bible under a brown-suited arm. Addie's mother, Mrs.
Hadley, and her dear friend, the recently widowed Mrs.
O'Dell, stepped up to the latter's home, probably discussing
the bakery the widow planned to open in the two front rooms
of her house. Hector Swope, the town ne'er-do-well, sat in his
usual spot outside the Folsoms' River Run Hotel. Every so

often, he persuaded a resident to treat him to a meal or give him a handful of coins. The rumbling wagons, the chatting neighbors, the busy street. Those were the sights of Bountiful, Olivia's home.

But now, if Luke were right, railroad tracks, locomotives, even a station, would come to change the landscape. The strangers who'd follow would change the flavor of their small community. When they did, Luke's statement would more than likely prove correct. Nothing would ever be the same in Bountiful again.

Unease nipped at Olivia.

On top of all she'd experienced in the recent months, especially the past two weeks, it looked as though still more change lay in her future. What would the traffic of a railroad mean to small, peaceful Bountiful?

Would it bring a blessing or a curse?

Eli watched his son tear out of the office in search of willing recipients of his good news.

It was good news. "What do you think, Holtwood?" he asked the serious man on the other side of his walnut desk. "It would appear our hard work of the past six months is about to pay off."

Mr. Holtwood nodded as he neatened a stack of papers. "Your vision, sir, was most clear. I appreciate working for a man like you."

He waved the compliment aside. "A good idea at the right time can make a man look wiser than he might really be. But I do believe God wants Bountiful to prosper, and for that to happen, we need a more direct link to larger cities."

Holtwood set the papers down on the desk corner nearest him. He nodded. "Perhaps we'll benefit from the cattle trade as well."

Eli's gut twisted. "Haven't seen benefit there but for the least ethical and most corrupt."

Holtwood winced, clamped his lips tight. "So sorry, sir. I'd all but forgotten about—"

"Please do me a favor and really forget it. Don't bring it up again."

Eli had tried to do just that for the last two years, keeping in mind the Apostle Paul's words about forgetting things past and pressing toward God's high calling in Christ. It hadn't been easy, and he evidently hadn't achieved true forgetfulness, as his response to Holtwood's reference revealed. He had, however, thought about his mistakes and others' betrayals less frequently of late, and he intended to continue that pattern.

He changed the subject. "How about looking into available land around Bountiful? We could find out who is interested in selling property at a fair price. Since the railroad is sending representatives here to investigate their options, we would do well to provide them with a list of potential purchases."

Interest brightened Holtwood's expression. "I'll certainly look into it, sir."

A knock at the door interrupted the men. "Come in, please," Eli said.

Larry Colby, the bank's other teller, entered the office, his skittish gaze flitting from man to man, one corner of the room to the other, floor to ceiling. "I have yesterday's tally, sir." He nodded and his spectacles slid to the tip of his nose. "And the letters to the railroad Mr. Parham wrote."

Holtwood nodded. "So glad Parham answered the advertisement for a secretary so soon. We really were in need of the help."

Lewis Parham had appeared in town, a copy of a Seattle newspaper in hand, Eli's advertisement for an experienced secretary circled, a sheaf of recommendations ready for his new employer.

"Oh, yes, Mr. Whitman," Colby said, setting the papers on Eli's desk. His nervous movement caused the stack, along with several of Eli's files, to slide, and all the pages poured to the floor. "Oh, no! I'm so sorry. Let me gather this for you, sir."

He went down on one knee, but his eyeglasses fell, as did the pencil he'd slipped over an ear. As he scrabbled across the rug, Colby offered a stream of additional anxious apologies and ran a twitchy hand through his already unruly red hair.

"Aha!" Colby cried, glasses back in place, papers gathered, pencil clutched in a fist. "No loss, sir. So, so very sorry. Don't know what's come over me this morning. Won't happen again, sir. Won't let it."

That would be a feat.

Exasperation chafed Eli. Colby had worked for his father and him at least a decade now. During that time, father and son had demonstrated their appreciation for Colby in multiple ways, and still his nervous-ninny demeanor continued. Eli didn't think he treated his employees in any way that might lead to such behavior, since none of the others displayed similar skittishness.

He tamped down his irritation. "Holtwood and I were just discussing potential land purchases to prepare the bank for the arrival of the spur line. It would be beneficial if we owned property we could offer them, or if it can't be bought by the bank, we can recommend the railroad buy it outright. Please help him look into who owns the most logical stretches for tracks both north and south of town. Let me know what you find as soon as possible."

With yet more rabbity movements, Colby headed out, leaving Holtwood to close the office door as they left. Relief replaced Eli's tension once the jittery man had gone. Despite Colby's anxiety and nervous tendencies, his ability to spot accounting errors had earned Eli's admiration and confidence, making the man a valuable employee.

Through painful past experience, Eli had learned to hoard his trust. From those who'd proven loyal, as Holtwood and Colby had, he could tolerate petty annoyances—even if at times he feared Colby's might drive him half-mad. Nobody was perfect, after all.

He shook his head, then tugged on his watch's gold fob. Hmm...a quarter past four. He'd intended to leave the bank early this afternoon to stop by Tom Bowen's, but he'd lost track of time, what with all the developments regarding the spur line. That left him little time for the carpenter, but Eli wanted to see if Luke's wooden train was possible by Christmas Day.

He dropped a pencil into the desk drawer, rose, and then, taking his black wool suit coat from the rack by the door, put it on and reached for his hat. Filled with the satisfaction of a job well done, he left the office with a bounce in his stride.

He paused at Holtwood's desk, where the two cashiers had spread a map. "I would appreciate if you would close for me tonight, Holtwood."

"Of course, Mr. Whitman."

Colby started and dropped his pen. "Oh, dear." He dabbed the offending ink smear on his gray trousers leg with a white handkerchief.

Eli averted his gaze from the man's latest mishap. "I'm on my way to see to a personal matter, but I will come in early tomorrow morning, as usual. Have a good evening."

"Yes, of course, Mr. Whitman," Holtwood said.

"You have yourself a good evening," Colby hurried to say. "You and Mrs. Whitman and the children."

Outside, the sun was already setting, bringing the day to its premature end now that the calendar drew close to Christmas. The air wore the nip of approaching winter even if white flakes had yet to fall. A solitary wagon trundled down the street, and Eli shared the boardwalk with only a scrawny stray dog. Bountiful's residents were busy elsewhere, most likely in the homes where golden light poured from the plate-glass windows.

Home. Where he would head once he spoke with Tom.

At the neat white clapboard house two blocks down Main Street from the bank, Eli struck the brass knocker on the black front door. Irma Bowen, Tom's good-natured wife, opened up.

"Well, now, how do you do, Mr. Whitman?" She gestured him forward. "Come in, please. What brings you here tonight?"

"Is your husband home?"

Irma nodded and gestured for Eli to follow her down the hall. "He's in his workshop outside, wouldn't you know? Can't get that fellow in unless it's for a meal or sleep." She shook her blond head, the curls that escaped the braided knot at the crown dancing at her temples. "Sure loves his woods and sawdust, my Tom does."

Eli chuckled. "I'd say that's good for a carpenter."

Irma gave him a shrewd look. "I'm not so sure it's as good for a husband. I've plenty of errands for him to run, but..." She shrugged. "Oh, well. He sure is happy working out there. Go ahead, then, Mr. Whitman. Tom'll be glad to see you. Me? I have to be getting back to my stove."

"Something smells mighty fine, there, Irma. But I do wish you'd quit calling me Mr. Whitman after all these years."

"Oh, get on with you." She flapped her floured apron at Eli. "I'm too set in my ways to call you anything else. Go along and tell Tom to come on in once you two are done with your business. I'll have his supper on the table in a half-hour, no more."

With a smile, Eli pushed open the door to Tom's workshop.

The carpenter looked up. "Hello, there, Eli. What brings you by today?"

"I have a special favor to ask you. But I don't want you to say yes if it'll be a problem."

Tom scratched his gingery beard. "I can't tell you if it'll be a problem unless you tell me what you want. Ask away. I'll be honest."

"You always are, and I appreciate it. What I'd like is a Christmas gift for Luke."

"Good boy, that Luke of yours."

Eli smiled. "Too spirited sometimes, but he means well." Remembering the boy's excitement when he'd learned the news about the spur line, he went on. "Luke's railroad crazy, and I was wondering if you could whittle him a wooden train—a locomotive, some cars, a caboose."

A smile lifted Tom's whiskers. "Why, sure I can. I like that idea a whole lot."

Glancing around the carpentry shop, Eli took note of all the work in progress. "What I need to know is if you have time to do this by Christmas."

Again the wood smith scratched his beard. "It won't be a big job, Eli. I've plenty of oddments left from other projects, so I don't need to buy lumber. As far as the whittling, why, I can do that at night while Irma rattles off all the things she wants me to do for her."

"I wouldn't want to get on Irma's wrong side." Eli chuckled. "You sure it's wise to work on this for me while she needs your help?"

"It's not really my help she wants. When I try to do for her, she pushes me aside seeing as I don't do things quite her way. I just figure she wants to talk matters through with me, see if I cotton to her notions before plowing ahead."

"Interesting..." Eli remembered how different life had been during his first marriage. "Think all womenfolk are like that?"

Tom arched a brow a shade deeper than his beard. "You wanting pointers on handling your new missus?"

Eli turned away from his friend. "Although you're too polite to mention it, I'm sure you remember what my life with Victoria was like. I don't know Olivia very well yet, and I'd like to keep things...cordial between us. A fellow could always pick up pointers from a good friend who's been married as long as you and Irma have. I'm hoping matters will go better this time."

Tom looked puzzled. "Cordial? You might be making a mistake keeping Olivia Moore as a cordial...what? Employee? Women need more than that—at least Irma does. Scripture says we're to love our wives like Jesus loved the church. Don't sound to me as if you're listening to that advice too well."

"Don't know that I can. That I can trust another woman again, I mean."

"But can you trust the Lord?"

Eli felt the impact of the question right in his gut. "I . . . don't know. I don't even know if I want to know."

Tom walked to Eli's side, slung a heavy arm around his shoulders, and gave him a good-natured shake. "Not every woman's like Victoria—praise the Lord for His mercy. So you can't go along thinking of Olivia as another Victoria. That would be the biggest mistake you could ever make."

"The biggest mistake I ever made was marrying Victoria Tyler."

"Maybe. If you let your emotions guide you instead of waiting for the Lord on your choice back then, why, I suppose that hasty, passionate marriage might could be a mistake. But Miranda and Luke weren't no mistakes, and don't you be forgetting that."

"You're right." Eli squared his shoulders. "It's time for me to get back to them. I wonder what Olivia had Cooky make for supper. Our menus are already much improved since she began managing the house. She keeps them varied and interesting."

"I think maybe the Lord had a hand in bringing Olivia Moore into your castle. Keep your eyes and heart open, Eli. God's plans are always perfect, even when they don't quite look to a man like they make much sense."

This time, Eli clapped a hand on his friend's back. "You might be right, brother. I'd best be going now, but I will see you at church Sunday morning."

"Bright and early, and marching in my troops."

"Give my regards to Irma again."

"Give mine to your new missus."

"Certainly will."

Tom's words lingered in Eli's thoughts every step of the way home. Was he making a mistake with Olivia? Goodness knew he'd made plenty with Victoria, the first of which had been to trust her. Still, he'd learned not a few lessons from those mistakes, in particular, to keep a woman as far from his business and personal affairs as possible.

Then he thought of Irma Bowen. Nothing about the plump whirlwind even suggested the kind of trouble Eli had experienced with his first wife. What did Tom know, and Eli didn't, that had prevented such problems?

Lord, am I making another mistake? I know what your Word says, but I also know what I know. What I learned from what I lived. Please show me what to do.

Chapter 13

Unsettled in spite of his prayer, Eli opened his front door a short while later. The scent of lemon oil greeted him. Against the right-hand wall, the small cherry table gleamed with elbow grease and polish, while the Persian rug Victoria had insisted on having shipped in from the East looked freshly beaten.

Eli hung his hat on the stand by the table, then stepped farther into his home. This time, Randy's laughter rang out from upstairs, while the clack of china chimed in from the kitchen. Although homey sounds and fragrances had become his welcome home in the time since he'd married Olivia, he had yet to be able to take them for granted.

The savory scent of chicken caught his attention. His stomach growled. Eli hadn't noticed his hunger before, and the enticing promise of the meal to come lured him further. He walked into the kitchen. "Hello."

"Oh, Mr. Whitman, sir." Cooky blushed, flustered as

usual by his invasion of her territory. "What would you be needin'?"

"Nothing. I just wanted to tell you how good supper smells. I hope it won't be long now before you're ready to serve."

The silver-haired woman's round apple cheeks reddened. "Only a whiley more, sir. Your new missus likes meals prompt-like. For the children, she says."

"So do I, I must admit."

"A man's got a hearty appetite after workin' all day's what I say." Her topknot bobbled at her nod. "And you work mighty hard for Bountiful. That Luke of yours came a-tearin' in here, more excited about that railroad'n a robin's about its first spring worm."

"I'm glad you're pleased." He turned back toward the doorway he'd just crossed. "Where's Mrs. Whitman?"

"She's likely upstairs with the children. She spends hours seein' to their school assignments. I'm sure she'll be happy to see you, sir."

Eli went up the stairs, headed to his bedroom, and hung his coat in the large armoire. He splashed clean water from the washstand pitcher into its matching bowl, then drenched his hands and face. After he combed his hair back off his forehead, he deemed himself presentable for supper. In the hallway, he called his children's names.

"Papa! You're home early."

A whizzing cannonball hurtled into his frame. Thin, wiry arms manacled his legs. "Thank you, thank you, thank you!"

"Goodness, Luke. For what?"

"For bringing the railroad to town."

"Whoa, there, son. I only said the Oregon Railway and Navigation Company will be building a spur line somewhere in our area, and that they're considering running it through Bountiful. I'm discussing the matter with the people involved in making the decisions, and it looks good for the town. But it's not a finished deal yet."

Olivia appeared in the doorway to Randy's room. "It isn't?"

"Not yet." The odd expression on her lovely face caught Eli's attention. "Why? Are you worried?"

She looked away. "No...not really."

Her response didn't quite satisfy. "I'd like to tell you more about the plans. Maybe over a cup of coffee after supper."

"That would be nice."

"Good evening, Papa."

Eli looked past Olivia's slender form, startled by his daughter's formal greeting. To his further amazement, Randy had coiled her long braids into a neat knot at the back of her head. His little girl looked more mature by the minute.

"Good evening, Miranda. How are you?"

Her regal nod would have done a monarch proud. "Very well, thank you. I understand you had a most successful day."

Choking back his laughter, Eli couldn't stifle a smile. "Indeed, my dear. I would have to agree."

To his increasing bemusement, the child-woman sauntered past him to the head of the stairs. "I'm certain Cook is about to ring us to supper. I shall head on down."

Randy descended, taking stately steps, and Eli arched an eyebrow at his wife.

"Go along, Luke." Olivia gave the boy a nudge in the right

direction. "Follow your sister and please wait for your father and me to pray before you even think to attack the food."

In a windmill flurry of arms and legs, Luke flew down. Olivia laughed. "Different, aren't they?"

"And how. But Randy...Randy's truly frightening. Are you certain that was my daughter?"

Cooky's silver bell chimed out its invitation to supper. Olivia headed down the stairs. "Oh, she most certainly is. I'm afraid this phase will last longer than you'll care for."

"Why do you say that?"

"Watching my sisters grow has given me some insight—not to mention my own experiences. Randy is busy becoming the woman she will one day be. It's a natural thing, even though not an easy one to go through."

In the foyer, Eli scratched his head. "Hm...I continue to wonder if I'm up to the challenge."

"With God's grace, every parent is."

"And with your help." He offered his wife his arm to lead her into the dining room.

Olivia lowered her head. "I'm glad I can help."

"So am I." When they reached the walnut chair at her end of the table, he seated her, then rounded the corner to his place, noting Luke's hungry expression.

"Slow down, son. First we give thanks"—he unfurled his napkin—"then we eat."

At the boy's nod, Eli went on. "Seeing how famished you are, Luke, please offer tonight's blessing."

This time, Luke's nod lacked some of its earlier eagerness, but he did as asked. "Dear Lord, thank you for this feast you helped Cooky make for us. Bless it and us and the rest of our evening." He reached for the biscuits. "Oh! And thank you for bringing the railroad to town. Amen."

The meal was as tasty as its aroma had promised. Eli paid Olivia and Cooky generous compliments, earning pleased smiles and rosy cheeks in response.

Luke and Randy helped Cooky clear the table, a chore the new Mrs. Whitman had charged the children to carry out.

Randy carried a platter and serving utensils, a look of distaste on her face. Still, she did as Olivia had asked, especially since the job came with a small wage. Randy favored hair ribbons from the mercantile, and the coins allowed her to indulge her fancy.

Olivia then sent them to their rooms to finish their schoolwork. Randy had reading to do, while Luke had subtraction problems to finish. On his way to the door, and with a pleading look, Luke turned to his new mother. "Could you please help me? You know how hard I've worked and worked on these ciphers and I still don't understand how to do them right all the time."

Randy sniffed. "I can do my work."

"But you struggled with it last week, remember?" Olivia replied.

Before she could answer Luke, however, Eli jumped in. "How about if I give you a hand, son? I'd say a banker has some experience with pesky numbers."

Luke's eyes opened wide. "Really? You would do that?"

A twinge pierced Eli's heart. Had he neglected his children so much?

Perhaps. What with the disasters he'd had to repair after Victoria's death, followed by all the negotiating he'd done to win the railroad's consideration for Bountiful, he had set his responsibilities—and joys—at home aside for a while. Time had come to fix that.

"I'd be happy to. I'm certain your new mama has plenty to keep her occupied." He turned to Olivia. "Until she's ready for that cup of coffee, that is."

Olivia smiled, watching the children head upstairs. "I'll see to Randy's composition, no matter what she says. She still has a great deal to go before she's finished, and it's a fairly advanced theme, at that." They parted ways, and soon all he could hear in the large home—aside from Cooky's clanging of kettles and china—was the sound of lessons being learned.

When the children had said their prayers, been kissed and tucked in, the adults returned to the parlor, where Olivia took up the wool wrap she was knitting for her mama and Eli his pipe. Cooky brought in the coffee, and the crackling fire put the finishing touch on the perfect time for a chat.

But even after he'd described his hopes for the railroad in detail, Eli failed to dispel Olivia's faintly troubled air. He tried to assure her he only had their hometown's best interests at heart.

"I do know that," she answered.

"But...?"

"But...I don't know. Bountiful seems fine as it is. We can't know what the railroad will bring with it. Questionable characters, dishonest folks, a complete change in the way we've always done things here."

Eli bit down against an easy reply. Olivia had conjured up the only reservation he'd had about the proposed venture. But he couldn't let fear stand between Bountiful and progress.

"I'll make certain nothing untoward happens in our

town," he said. "I'll help everyone benefit from the blessings of increased business."

She stood, clearly ready to retire, and said, "Is it really in your hands to determine that?"

As he listened to her footsteps on the stairs, Eli couldn't stop a shiver. He knew too well how little he could control in life.

His first marriage had taught him that.

"I'm surprised you're back in town so soon," Eli told Nathan the next morning. "You don't make the trip down from your mountain all that often and you were by a few weeks ago."

Nathan shifted in his chair. "You're right. I don't come down any more than I need to, but after assessing our situation at the camp, I've come to the decision I need to expand the flume."

Eli gave a wry smile. "You're going to have to explain that to me. You know I'm no lumberman."

"The flume is the channel I use to get the logs we cut down to where I can transport them to my markets. Some mills use rivers to let the water carry the logs down, others roll them over the terrain. I have to build a flume, a road for the logs, so to speak. And, if you do bring the spur line to Bountiful, I'm also going to have to expand in this direction."

Eli fought the knot in his gut. "I see. How soon would you need to do that? And how much would it cost you? If you don't mind my asking."

Nathan shrugged. "I don't mind. You're my banker, after all. I'd have liked to have done it this summer, but I was short-handed. I've hired a pair of men now, and they're working well. Ideally, I should start right away so that I can finish the higher portion before snow or ice hits."

"Are you telling me you need to withdraw funds for this project?"

"Precisely."

Nathan's need couldn't have come at a worse time. "How much are you looking at?"

Eli grimaced at the sum his friend named. "I don't have to tell you how tight we are right now. I—I don't know if we can do that. It would practically dry our liquidity. Can't do that to the bank."

"It's those mortgages, isn't it?"

"I won't deny I've loaned money to those affected by the drought and the insects. You know that—"

"Mr. Whitman?" Holtwood said after knocking on the office door.

A timely interruption. "Come in, come in. Nathan Bartlett's here with me."

Holtwood gave a brief nod to Eli's minority partner, then turned. "Colby and I finished our study of the local terrain. We have a path to suggest for the rail line, and I've tracked down the status of the properties involved. A number of them are heavily mortgaged with us."

Perhaps not so timely.

"How bad is this mortgage situation?" All ease vanished from Nathan's posture. "It sounds serious, especially in view of what you just told me."

It was serious, but Eli had hoped he could carry the bank to where the land at least showed signs of recovery. Perhaps now, with Nathan's need, he wouldn't make it that far. "We hold a number of large mortgages. They come due at different times next year."

"Excuse me, sir." Holtwood held out a ledger. "Take a look. Some could actually be called sooner rather than later, according to the terms of the loans."

Eli stood. "I suppose, but I've given my word to those men. They're counting on my patience, on my willingness to wait until they can effect some kind of profit."

Nathan also stood. "With the railroad's interest," he said, "it seems to me that it's time to call in those mortgages. I understand your unwillingness to go against your word, but if you don't take the opportunity to foreclose, take possession of the land, and sell it to the railroad for a profit, there might not be a bank by the time those men bring in a crop."

Eli felt ill. "I can't do it. A banker's only as good as his word."

"A bank's only as good as the funds it holds," Nathan countered. "And I need my money."

"Could you wait until the spring?"

"Will that make a difference?"

Eli shrugged.

"I could," suggested Holtwood, "begin by contacting the most delinquent property owners to see if there's any possibility of payment."

"That sounds sensible," Nathan said, his gaze on Eli.

"That puts more pressure on folks who are at the end of their rope," Eli argued. "We need to operate in a practical manner, true, but we must also show compassion when it's needed. It's needed now."

Nathan shook his head. "I understand compassion, but

this is business. Would you rather I contact them? I am a partner in the bank."

"What difference would that make? I'm the president of the bank."

"I don't mind if the landowners see me as the harsh and demanding one."

Holtwood cleared his throat. "If Mr. Bartlett is willing to wait, I could have Parham prepare the letters right away. That way, you wouldn't be the signatory."

Eli hated the very thought. "That doesn't feel right, not quite honest."

"Nothing dishonest about exercising contract rights," Nathan said. "I'm willing to wait. Especially if by doing so I can make sure we keep the bank on solid footing. I will admit, I have a personal need, but I also know the town needs the bank to survive this drought."

"Give me some time to think it over," Eli pleaded. "I won't take long, but let's not be hasty. If you need that flume so desperately, Nathan, then I'll advance you my own cash."

"Can't do that, Eli. I don't feel right taking your personal funds."

"Then let's wait. You won't be cutting down many trees in the snow, will you?"

"True enough. But there's still time before that happens—" He grimaced. "Never mind. I'll wait. But like you said, not for long."

Eli only allowed himself a sigh of relief when Nathan had left. He didn't have much time. Neither did the men who counted on him. He prayed the Lord had better weather in the coming months for their needy community.

Chapter 14

On a Friday in late November, after she'd left the children at school and she'd met with Cooky to plan the day's meals, Olivia gathered the gifts she'd made for her family and headed out toward the Moore farm. During the ride, she took yet another moment to thank God for Eli's generosity. He'd made his buggy available to her at all times.

Afraid the reasonably mild weather wouldn't last much longer, she'd decided to deliver her Christmas gifts early. Eagerness to see her loved ones' responses made her click her tongue to urge the sturdy chestnut Mabel to a faster pace.

Soon the familiar land came into view. A mixture of pride and sadness filled Olivia's heart. The whole Moore clan loved their homestead, knowing how much it meant to Mama and Papa and how hard they'd worked to wrest a living from it.

Memories of waves of golden grain flooded in: rippling in the wind, falling at the harvest, representing food, clothing, life.

Until last year.

Olivia also remembered the day Papa mortgaged the farm. Since then, not a morning or night had gone by without Olivia lifting the staunch man's efforts in prayer to the Heavenly Father, as she knew he and Mama did. Surely God would hear those pleas.

In the meantime, she was thankful she'd been able to help. She'd given her parents one less mouth to fill, one less child to clothe, and her wages to help tide them over. Now she welcomed the chance to use the last of her modest savings from her brief employment to bring a few much-needed items to her family.

Growing impatient, she jiggled the reins. "Come on, Mabel. It's only a bit farther now. See? There's the house."

Olivia would never forget the day the family moved into their new, permanent home. Neither would her brothers and sisters, she was sure. Mama had created a feast on the iron stove in her kitchen, taking advantage of the fruits of the garden she'd planted out back while Papa and some of their neighbors had built the home. She'd topped off the meal with a dessert of apple fritters, a favorite of the brood. If Olivia closed her eyes, she could still taste the crisp-fried dough morsels, heavy with chunks of tart fruit, drizzled with Mama's homemade sweet syrup.

Home . . .

Where she knew her work had always been valued, and where she'd always been loved and cherished as a welcome blessing.

Home . . .

What she longed to build for her own family, for Randy and Luke, with Eli—

Well aware of the dissatisfaction to which that thought could lead, Olivia let herself consider only the good things that might come in the immediate future. For the longer term she would wait on God.

Elizabeth Moore's walnut-brown eyes broadcast concern as she ran out the front door to greet Olivia. "Oh, my dear! Is something wrong?"

"Does something have to be wrong for me to visit?"

"I would hope not. Still, a mother can't help—"

Olivia reached behind her for a carefully wrapped parcel. "Of course, she can. Especially when the daughter comes bearing gifts, Christmas gifts. See?"

"Christmas?" Mama took the reins from Olivia and looped them around the lowest branch of the lone oak in the yard. "That's still weeks away, dear. Surely you didn't use Mr. Whitman's money on us...did you?"

Giving her mother a chiding look, Olivia pulled the box of wrapped presents from under the buggy's seat and lugged it toward the whitewashed house. "I would never do that. I used some of my savings from when I worked for Eli—Mr. Whitman."

Elizabeth wiped her hands on her crisp white apron. "Oh, dear. You shouldn't have. You worked very hard for that money. You should spend it on yourself."

With a chuckle, Olivia heaved her burden onto the porch. "You never change, do you? You'll fret about everything. But look, I have no need to spend money on myself. Mr. Whitman is most generous with me. I have everything I need, even the pleasure of giving my family gifts and sharing the season with them."

As she again wiped her hands, Elizabeth led the way in. The familiar scent of baking bread embraced Olivia.

Tears welled, emotion surged, and she threw her arms around the woman who had raised her. "I love you, Mama."

"Oh, child. I love you, too. We all do." Holding her daughter at arm's length, Elizabeth's damp eyes raked Olivia from head to toe. "Are you sure you're doing well? You do know there's nothing you can't tell me, don't you?"

Suddenly uncomfortable, Olivia extricated herself from the embrace. "I do."

But there was something she couldn't discuss. She couldn't tell her mother how odd things were between her and her new husband, about that…business arrangement of theirs. So instead she said, "Where are the others?"

After a final shrewd look, Elizabeth crossed the parlor and headed for the kitchen. "Come and have a cup of tea to warm yourself. Your father went to town today. I'm surprised you didn't cross him on your way here."

"If I know him at all, he left much earlier than I did."

Clucking softly, Elizabeth removed the teakettle from its preferential spot at the rear of the stove to pour hot water into a teapot at the ready. "The man does love his sunrises. He says it keeps him close to God, seeing the day born like that."

Olivia smiled, remembering the times she'd heard the same words from her father's lips. "And Leah? Marty? The boys?"

Mama poured the tea and placed one of the steaming, thick white cups in front of Olivia, who wrapped her chilled hands around the crockery.

"The boys are in the barn." Her mother took the chair across from her. "One of the cows gave birth awfully off-season, and the calf is runty. She won't suckle right, so your brothers are taking turns feeding her round the clock."

A sip of the fragrant brew warmed its way down Olivia's middle. "I imagine they're fighting to see who gets to do the honors. Which is probably driving Papa mad, since there's nothing he'd rather do than see to his own—human or animal."

"Just so." Bobbing to her feet again, Elizabeth grabbed a thick fold of towel and opened the oven door. "Hm . . . the bread needs a while longer, but the molasses cookies look done."

Olivia breathed in the sweet scent. "They smell done."

"Livvy's never refused cookies to go with tea," Leah Rose said from the back door. "Neither will I, Mama. I'm frozen!"

As Olivia embraced her youngest sister, Mama gave a dainty sniff. "That's what you get, Leah Rose, for following the boys to the barn."

"But the calf is so sweet, Mama. It's not fair that the boys get all the fun."

"If you think it's so sweet," Elizabeth countered, placing the dish of cookies on the table, "next time, you can fork out the old hay for Butterball and her babe. Don't forget how hard the boys work in the barn."

"I work awful hard washing their stinky clothes."

Olivia winked at her mother. "Seems a fair distribution of labor."

"Maybe. But it isn't when it comes to Marty," Leah Rose grumped around a mouthful of cookie.

"I heard that." The accused stomped down the front hall and into the kitchen. "I work, too. I help Mama in the garden—"

"So do I," Leah Rose cut in.

"I cook and bake and clean house—"

"I don't?"

"Sure, sure. But you run off to play with your colored threads and needles as soon as Mama turns her back."

"That's not fair, Marty. I sew. A lot. Try and tell me *you* do that. Especially, since I'm saddled with your needlework more than once in a rare while. True, I enjoy sewing, but it's not fair when you don't do your—"

Elizabeth tsk-tsked. "Truce, girls. No one can accuse Marty of skill with a needle and thread, but you both do work. And you've earned whatever gifts Olivia has brought."

Time flew as the Moore women chatted and opened presents. Leah and Marty oohed and aahed over the tucked, lace-trimmed blouses Olivia had made. Mama ran her hand time and time again over the warm wool shawl she'd knitted.

Eventually, they prayed for one another, for the family's menfolk, and especially for the future.

Olivia relished every second of her visit, even the good-natured sparring between Leah Rose and Marty, who was well meaning but somewhat flighty and occasionally careless.

Soon, though, Olivia realized it was getting late.

"I must be going," she said into the lull.

"Why so soon?" Marty asked.

Olivia donned her forest-green wool cloak. "Randy and Luke will be home."

Leah Rose followed her to the front door, a mutinous look on her still-rounded face. "But you have a cook. She'll be there..."

Mama's warning look hushed the youngest Moore child's protest. "Your sister has responsibilities now. Her children need her, and she does well to see to them."

Then she cradled Olivia's face between her work-roughened hands. "Don't forget what I said earlier. There's nothing you can't tell me, daughter. I'm always here, ready to listen and pray—and help, Lord willing."

"I know, Mama." Olivia averted her eyes. "I know. And I love you."

"I love you, too." As she always did before they parted, Elizabeth prayed a blessing over her daughter, then sent her on her way back to Bountiful and her new life.

Shortly after she'd returned from the farm, Olivia had a surprise. Cooky's daughter Kate, who had recovered from her burned arm and recently returned to her regular duties, entered Luke's room, where Olivia and the children had been discussing their day.

"Missus Whitman," she said, "your papa's here to see you. I showed 'im into the parlor."

How odd, Olivia thought. Papa in town this late? *Here?*

"Thank you, Kate. I'll be right down." She turned to the children. "Please excuse me for a while, but do keep on with your lessons. Especially that arithmetic, Luke."

On her way to the parlor, Olivia couldn't ignore the sharp pang of apprehension. Why hadn't Stephen Moore gone straight home after he'd finished his business?

Had he finished his business?

Or had his business concerned her?

"Hello, Olivia." The much-loved bass voice welcomed her into the parlor.

Launching herself into his arms, Olivia swallowed hard

against the knot in her throat. "Oh, Papa...it's wonderful to see you. I went to the farm and I missed you, even though I spent the day with Mama, the girls, and even saw the boys for a bit."

Papa's arms grew slack at Olivia's words. He stepped away and walked to the front window, his back toward her. "I'm sure your mother told you I had business in town."

"Of course, but I could figure that out when you weren't in the barn taking turns to spoil that calf with the boys."

A brief grin danced over Papa's lean face as he glanced over his shoulder. But then he turned his attention back to the darkening street outside. "You're right. I much prefer spending my days in the barn. A serious matter brought me to town today."

Her heart leaped into her throat. "And...?"

He released a deep, troubled sigh. "And things did not go well."

"Please tell me about it."

"I'm afraid that's why I've come to interrupt your evening," he said. "I'm terribly sorry about that, Olivia, but I believe you might be able to help."

"Me?"

Instead of responding, Papa handed her a single sheet of paper. As Olivia unfolded the page, she breathed a prayer. But with every word she read, more blood seemed to drain from her head. She dropped onto the settee, hands chilled and shaking.

"This can't be," she whispered. "There must be some mistake."

Papa shook his head. "No mistake, my dear. I came into Bountiful to see what I could do about it. As you can see, the letter demands repayment of the mortgage we had to take out on our land by the thirty-first of December. If we fail to meet that deadline, the bank will take the farm. You know I don't have the money. Won't have it until I can bring in a new harvest."

"Did you ask for more time? Until that next harvest?"

"Of course. But the answer was the same. New Year's Eve by closing."

"If you don't pay . . . ?"

"We'll be turned out."

"Where will you go?"

Papa shrugged and faced the window again.

Silence grew. A vise clamped over Olivia's heart. "Did you . . . ?" She paused, afraid of the response to her burning question. "Did you speak to Eli?"

Papa shook his head. "Your husband was in a meeting, but I spoke with that Holtwood fellow and the red-haired one, Colby. When it comes to matters at the bank, speaking with Holtwood is usually the same as speaking with your husband. Holtwood does nothing but carry out his wishes."

Her father's answer chilled Olivia. *Dear Lord . . .*

Winter had arrived, after all.

On the ride home from the farm she'd felt the change in the weather. The fierce wind had kicked up and the cold had pierced her woolen cloak. The air had grown redolent with the musk of snow, an invader who would attack at the time her family could withstand it least.

"Surely there's something you can do to stop this." She injected what encouragement she could dredge up into her words.

"There's nothing more I can do, but there might be one last ray of hope."

"What do you mean? Where do you see hope?"

"In you."

"Me?"

"You."

"What do you think *I* can do?"

Papa turned, a plea in his dark brown eyes. "You can speak with your husband. Ask him for mercy. We just need more time. Tell him about your brothers and sisters, your mother. He can't turn them out with nowhere to go in the dead of winter."

The reality made misery plunge deep into her middle. "You're wrong, Papa. I can't talk about this with Eli."

"Why on earth not?"

Her moment of truth lay before her. Much though Olivia had tried to carry on without thinking of her arrangement with Eli, all along she'd known much was wrong with her marriage. Now, when her loved ones needed her help, she found herself in an impossible position.

She'd promised to stay clear of her husband's business dealings. There was nothing she could do. She couldn't help her father.

Shame heated her cheeks. She squared her shoulders and stood. "There's something I have to tell you about my circumstances, Papa. Something I'd hoped I wouldn't have to share."

A shadow crossed Stephen Moore's face. He nodded encouragement, but said nothing.

She went on. "Ours hasn't been a...regular coming together, as most marriages are. When Eli first proposed, he made very clear that I couldn't meddle in his business affairs. At no time and for no reason whatsoever am I to bring up the subject matter. And this"—she waved the odious letter—"deals with bank business."

Papa's frown turned thunderous. He took a step toward Olivia. "Did that man threaten you?"

"Never. Eli wouldn't do that. He made himself very clear. His business is his alone. The children and the house are mine. I gave him my word, and I have to honor his wishes."

"As a child of God, Olivia, you're also called to help those in need." Papa's jaw hardened as he clenched the fists at his sides. "You've no idea how difficult this has been for me. I've always provided for my family, and this is…shameful. I need your help."

Oh, yes. She did know how hard it had been for him. Time after time for the last two years she'd heard his anguish when he'd talked with Mama late into the night. But she'd given her word. She couldn't go back on it, no matter the reason. Although Eli had never said so, Olivia feared he'd send her packing back to Papa if she went against his wishes. What good would that do?

None, but to make her husband feel betrayed—by her. And of course, she'd lose Luke and Randy. A pang struck her heart. From the moment she voiced her wedding vows, she'd seen the four of them, Eli, the children, and her, as a family.

But she had another family. How could she resolve this dilemma? How could she choose one family over the other? How could she fail one family or the other?

She couldn't.

Besides, Eli would never listen to any plea she presented,

not when it referred to the bank. If that happened, more than likely, all she would accomplish would be to make the situation even worse. That was not an option she could consider.

After a deep, ragged breath, she forced the words past her lips. "I . . . can't."

"You must." Papa gestured around the attractive room. "Even though you live here now, this letter will affect you. You're still a part of us, Olivia. You're our daughter and the younger ones' sister. I know how tenderhearted you've always been. If we end up homeless—if we suffer—it will affect you, too."

"But—"

"And I trust God. If you don't act, He will. He'll work out His plan in the end—with or without you."

"Well, then, why not wait for Him—"

"Oh, child, listen to me. Don't you think this might be the reason the Lord brought you into Eli's home? For Him to work through you? For such a time as this?"

After Papa left, Olivia went through the motions of supper, where she picked at the ham, creamed potatoes, and honey-glazed carrots she'd planned with Cooky that morning—a lifetime ago, or so it felt. She oversaw the rest of the children's schoolwork, but her attention drifted so much that Randy had to correct her mistakes when she tried to help with Luke's mathematics assignment. Sooner rather than later she hurried the children through their bedtime routines, unable to think of much but her family's troubles. Finally, she fumbled through her last chat of the day with Cooky as though she were lost in the depths of a cloud.

A cloud. Indeed. Thick and vast and bearing storms.

Feeling like the worst of cowards, Olivia slipped from the kitchen to the stairs, eager to reach her bedroom before Eli caught sight of her.

But she wasn't quick—or furtive—enough.

"Olivia," he said as she went to take her first step up. "I'd hoped we could end the day with our usual cup of coffee. Will you be back down soon?"

She turned slowly, searched for acceptable excuses, but failed to come up with even one. "I'm sorry, Mr. Whitman—" At the raised eyebrow, she revised her words. "I'm sorry, Eli. It's been a long day, and I'm exhausted. I would like to make an early night of it. Please excuse me."

"Are you unwell?"

"No." *Not really.* "I'm fine. It's just…as I said. I'm drained. From going to the farm and…" She made a vague gesture with her free hand. The other clung to the polished oak banister. "And, well, everything."

It didn't take much to discern his thoughts, as they were right there, legible in his bewildered expression. "I…well," he said. "I suppose then…the best thing for you would be an early night, as you said. I hope you sleep well. And that you feel better in the morning, of course."

She couldn't face him. Not with everything she'd learned from Papa looming large and ominous in her thoughts. She took that first step up. "Thank you. I hope so as well."

Olivia doubted she'd feel better after a few hours' sleep. With all her concerns and fears growing greater by the minute, did she have any hope of sleeping?

Not likely.

Before Eli could say another word, she flew upstairs and into her simple, private, peaceful room. Once she closed the door, she sagged against it, as drained as she'd told Eli, her strength sapped.

Her emotions clotted into a knot in her throat, and the tears that had threatened from the moment she'd read the loathsome letter rained down over her face. Where had her courage and boldness gone? Had she used them all up when she'd approached Eli for the nanny job?

How could she find herself in this position now?

"Oh, Lord, how could you!" The words ripped from her lips in a raw, low, guttural rasp. "How could you put me in such an impossible position? You know I can't do this. I can't go against my husband." And yet...it was her beloved family's fate that sat in Eli's hands. Could she just cower from questions that needed asking? Could she just let Eli turn Mama and Papa, her brothers and sisters out of their home for the sake of his bank's profits?

Could the man she married have such a cold, unfeeling side? Nothing she'd come to know about him suggested such a possibility. Was that behind his demand that she stay out of his business? Was he, in a way, two different men? The husband and father at home, and the single-minded, cold banker at work?

It didn't make sense. Eli's request didn't make sense.

Eli...

Eli, Eli, Eli.

He stood, tall as one of the evergreens in the nearby mountains, solid as the massive mountain itself, successful in their small town as...as any railroad magnate from back East. How could she, the daughter of a farmer beholden to Eli Whitman, challenge one of his business decisions?

Especially since Eli, as a condition of their marriage, had extracted her promise to never do such a thing.

Impossible.

There was nothing she could do.

As she crawled into bed, however, a Scripture much repeated by her mother over the years took shape in Olivia's worry-battered mind.

With men this is impossible; but with God all things are possible...

Disappointed at the way his evening had turned out, Eli returned to the parlor and his favorite armchair. He poured himself a fresh cup of coffee. His mind echoed with so many questions that he scarcely felt the heat, much less tasted the beverage.

Amazing how much a part of his evenings Olivia had become in such a short time. In the three months since he'd hired her he'd come to look forward to spending time with her, and after their wedding, discussing the children and all the details of life in the Whitman household. It never would have occurred to him to discuss such things with anyone before she came along. Not even with his first wife. Theirs had not been that kind of partnership.

Although he didn't know how to reach out to Olivia, how to breach the divide that now lay between them, he did know something was troubling his wife—

Dear heavens! She *was* his wife.

Almost.

The intimate, emotional aspects of marriage? Well, he didn't want to consider those, knowing now where they could lead a man if he let his heart take the reins. He'd traveled that path before, and it had led to disaster and near destruction.

Still, he'd thought they were building an excellent union, one rooted in an easy companionship where they could discuss all kinds of things.

He drank more coffee, cooler than before.

Perhaps he was looking for too much too soon. While Olivia had been under his roof since the beginning of September, and even though she had fit in with an ease that still surprised him, the children's initial objections and tomfoolery notwithstanding, only three months had gone by. They'd only been married for a matter of weeks. Not much time at all.

Had he become so greedy that he already wanted more and more of the closeness he knew had begun to grow between them? Before they'd had the time to build the level of trust necessary?

"Very well, Lord," he murmured as he set down his coffee and took up his pipe. "You've been patient with me. While I can never come close to You, I need to be patient. I need to give Olivia more time. I need to give us more time."

He lit the well-tamped tobacco and took a long pull of the aromatic smoke, his thoughts still on his wife.

In the middle of the night, Olivia again heard Luke cry out, followed by hushed whimpers. It had happened a time or two since she'd come to care for the Whitman children, but she hadn't felt he would welcome her presence. He'd likely have thought it meddling on her part.

This time, however, was different. She was his mother now. She slipped from the bed, threw on a housecoat, and hurried to his room.

"It's me, Luke," she whispered from the doorway. "May I come in?"

The silence left her wondering if he might try to pretend he hadn't heard her, but then the bedclothes rustled, and the boy sniffled. "Sure."

Olivia sat on the edge of his bed, reached a hand to smooth his tousled hair. "Want to tell me what's wrong?"

"Nothing much. Just a bad dream. I woke myself up when I screamed. Silly. Just like a girl."

"Oh, I don't know about that. All kinds of folks have bad dreams, grown-ups even. I've had them, too."

He sat up. "Really? Wha—what do you do about 'em?"

She smiled. "I pray about them. I tell God to take the bad dream and replace it with a good dream. Most of the time, that's all it takes for me to fall asleep again."

"That's it? That easy?"

"That easy." Olivia took his cold hand in hers. "Would you like to try?"

"Well, sure. Of course, God's big enough to do anything, right?"

"That's right, Luke. He can hear your prayers, and then replace the bad dream with a good one." She scooted over a bit. "Here. Why don't you sit next to me, and we'll pray."

Luke scrambled to her side, and Olivia wrapped an arm around his thin shoulders. He leaned into her, the gesture warming her heart. He was a rascal, but he was also a charming, lovable boy. Her boy.

"Heavenly Father," she said, "you know all about these nasty dreams bothering Luke. We know you're the God of all comfort, and he needs comfort right now. He also needs your peace through the night so he can dream good dreams and rest as he needs to do. We love you, and we thank you, Amen."

"I know you've not lost your hearing overnight, dearie," Cooky said the next morning, exasperation on her rosy-cheeked face. "Something's a-troubling you. I've called your name three times, and you've answered not a one of them. I hope you know you can trust me to talk to."

Olivia blushed. "Of course. I do know that, and I'm so sorry. I didn't mean to ignore you. It's just..."

"I'm thinking it's to do with your papa's visit yesterday."

A deep breath. "Yes, it is related. I'm not sure how much I should say, since it's not my problem to begin with, but I can tell you it affects my new family here as much as it does my old one."

"Now that's odd. Have the families been friendly-like all these years?"

"Oh, no. Not particularly. Papa has known Mr. Whitman for years, since he's done business at the bank, but friendly? No."

Cooky gave her a penetrating look. "Ah...business. That's a right sticky matter for Mr. Whitman, I'll have you know—if you don't already."

Olivia averted her gaze. "I do know. He's made his feelings far more than clear."

"Come, sit a spell, dearie." Cooky pulled out a chair from

the small square table in the middle of the large kitchen and plopped down as she often did these days. "Take a chair. Have yourself a cup of that tea you're so partial to, and let's be having us a little chat."

The last thing Olivia wanted was to have Cooky—anyone, really—pry and prod. But she realized there was no decent way to turn down the invitation. She'd never do anything to hurt her new friend's feelings, so she took a teacup from the shelf near the range, and then poured boiling water from the teakettle Cooky had begun to keep full and ready after she and Olivia reached a truce.

Cup in hand, she sat across from Cooky. To keep from meeting the wise woman's stare, Olivia focused on stirring honey into the tea. Finally, when she couldn't keep that up any longer, she set down her spoon and glanced up.

The kindness and affection on her friend's face warmed a shadowed aching corner of her heart. "Oh, Cooky...it's so complicated."

"Oh, pshaw! I'm sure and it's not. But folks always choose to look at things their way rather than God's way. From where He's sitting up there on His throne, things are mighty simple, don't you think?"

"Of course, but I'm not there—"

"Yet. And still and all, our sweet Jesus is there at the Father's side, stepping in and a-praying for you all this time. I'm sure He can handle this problem of yours, just as He's been after doing all these long years."

Olivia chuckled. "I suppose when you put it that way, it seems silly to be so troubled. If God can make this world work, no matter how irksome it must seem to Him at times, then I'm sure He can guide me to the right solution."

"Even if the trouble has to do with the mister's business."

Olivia's stomach gave a little flip. She sipped some tea in an effort to settle her nerves. "It's a difficult subject for him, and I can't see why it should be. He's such a successful man."

A horrid thought occurred to her. "Oh, dear. Is the bank not doing well? Is Eli having trouble there? Is that why he's so touchy about business matters?"

"No, dearie." Cooky waved, as though to shoo away that concern. "I don't think there's been much wrong at the bank for a good long while now. All's what's wrong is with Mr. Whitman, himself, it is."

"I feared as much."

"Now don't go an' be taking that wrong, Miss Olivia. In some ways, that poor man has his good reasons to feel like that, he does. He's had more than his share of troubles in the past."

"In the past? But if his business is no longer suffering difficulties, then why would he be so—" She caught herself. She didn't want to appear critical of her husband, even to Cooky, who clearly knew Eli better than Olivia did. "I suppose what I'd like to know is if those troubles you mentioned are resolved, then why would he still be . . . oh, I don't know. Why would he be closed up so tight about his business matters if it's all working well?"

Cooky shook her head. "Can't be saying as it's that easy, dearie. The first Missus Whitman . . . why, I reckon she nearly cost Mr. Whitman his business and his good name, she did."

Olivia gasped. "How could that be possible? How could a wife do that?"

"Well, child, it happened. Missus Victoria had a greedy streak to her, she did. Her family did even more so. She had herself a passel of brothers, and they were all the time making deals, promising special favors, and buying and buying and buying. Oh, yes."

Cooky fell silent, her thoughts in the past. When the moment drew out, grew uncomfortable, Olivia figured it was time to leave. As she was about to stand, Cooky shook her head.

"And all them deals and favors? Whoo-ee! They cost Mr. Whitman a-plenty, they did. He didn't know a thing about 'em until everything just came a-calling on him a coupla days after Missus Victoria died. Why, they—*she*—was always going behind his back."

"But Eli's so cautious, so clever and capable. How could they go behind his back? How did he not know?"

"Tsk-tsk-tsk!" Cooky shook her head. "Our Mr. Whitman, dearie, he's just a man like all other men. Why, he trusted his wife, he did. Missus Victoria, she was pretty like an angel, I tell you. She smiled at him, and he sure danced along, talked him into going in with her brothers in their investments, and all."

To Olivia's surprise, the older woman's normally happy expression changed, her lips clamped down, they thinned, drew a white rim around their edges. She smacked her hand on the table.

Olivia started.

"And then she up and died on him," Cooky said, her voice heated. "But what's worse, Miss Olivia, is how those brothers talked big, promised big, and all. They took money to put in businesses in California and deals in Washington—Mr. Whitman's money, and other folks', too. He was left with nothing but all kinds of papers, his and Missus Victoria's names on those papers—she did all the signing, even his name, you know. That money her brothers promised?"

Olivia nodded.

"Oh, no sirree, no. No dollars came like that riff-raff said would come, especially after they took off with everyone's last penny. Left Mr. Whitman holding the bag, they did."

The story of theft and betrayal horrified Olivia. It enlightened her, too. "Poor Eli. She signed his name? Forged his signature?"

Cooky nodded. "It was his name, but it was her signing like him, wouldn't you know? Those other folks taken in wouldn't believe Mr. Whitman, no matter how he explained, how hard he argued, she did it so good. I tell you, all kinds of strange folks came by and demanded to be paid back what they put in, since their schemes and such never had a payday. To protect the bank and his good name, Mr. Whitman stepped up and cleaned all that mess. Took him the better part of a year, but he paid every cent, he did."

In spite of how little she knew of the situation, how brief a time she'd known her husband, Olivia's heart ached with sadness for what Eli had gone through. Another part of her glowed with pride at his determination and persistence and decency. That was the man she was coming to know. Not one who could turn her family—and others, too—out of their homes in the dead of winter.

There had to be something she could do, some way to

appeal to Eli's better side. He couldn't have died to compassion, regardless of what his first wife's family had done to him.

Olivia would have to pray and pray and pray. Surely, the Father would guide her to the right solution. She believed the Lord would show her the best plan to put into motion.

But for her to have any chance to put a plan into motion, she would have to let Eli come to know her folks better. The more time he spent with them the sooner he would see what deserving, upright people they were.

Sunday dinner would fill the bill. Maybe many Sunday dinners would be needed. That was something she could handle.

"I do say," Cooky went on, "I can't begin to tell you how happy I am he's taken you for his bride. I never ever expected him to even think of wedding again. Not after what all them Tylers did to him. Never. I never would have given it the slightest chance, knowing what I know about what happened here starting three, maybe four years ago."

A cold lump landed in Olivia's middle. "How long has the first Mrs. Whitman been dead?"

"Am I hearing you right, Miss Olivia?" Cooky sagged back in shock, nearly upending her chair. "Why, she's been gone about a little less than three years now. Git on with you, dearie. Here, and you're telling me you don't know even that much?"

She shook her head, dreading the answers she might get.

As the bubbling sound on the range turned to a hiss and a sizzle, Cooky rushed to check on her supper makings. She snagged a wooden spoon and a thick piece of towel. Once she'd uncovered the iron kettle, the savory scent of lamb and barley soup teased Olivia's senses.

"Oh, my! That does smell good."

Cooky shook the long-handled spoon at Olivia. "There is good, and then there is not. It's plain wrong to have brought you into this family here all blind-like. I never would have thought Mr. Whitman would do such a thing. Just goes to show, and he's still a-hurting something fierce. It's glad I am you're here. Seems to me the good Lord knew what He was after doing when He had that pig run right out there in front of you."

Olivia's unease grew.

Cooky went on. "And here folks think pigs are such horrid, stupid critters. Nuh-uh. This one knew just what he was doing when he crossed your path."

"I wouldn't be putting any guilt on the pig, Cooky." Olivia stood. "Luke was the one who chased the poor beast out into Main Street."

Cooky planted her fists on her plump hips. "And you're after telling me the Almighty couldn't just have picked up that animal and turned him round to where He wanted it to go? God always knows what he's after doing, it seems to me. And see, dearie? God knew what He was doing when He brought you here. You're the right one for us, you are."

Olivia's unease grew with every step she took. Now it wasn't just Papa telling her God had brought her to the Whitman home. Even Cooky, a woman of great if earthy and uncomplicated faith, believed she'd been guided here by the heavenly Father.

With a quick excuse for her friend, Olivia left the kitchen, everything Cooky had told her filling her thoughts.

"Why me, Lord? Why now?"

As she went up to her room, the silence in the house seemed to deepen and turn as rich as velvet cloth. If the Father had indeed brought her here for a purpose it was as plain as could be that He was not ready to answer her questions or reveal that purpose to her.

Not yet.

Chapter 15

The next day, after she left the children at school, Olivia put into motion an idea that came to her in the middle of the night. Perhaps if Eli became accustomed to seeing her at the bank from time to time, he would grow less wary.

She walked in, and again was struck by the elegance and the heavy quiet in the air. Near the front of the building, on opposing walls, were the two cashiers' windows. At the far end of the large room sat a pair of desks, one on either side of the door to Eli's office. Two men looked quite busy at the desks, as did the two at the brass-barred windows. Moments after she stepped in, a gentleman with slicked-back brown hair, wearing a sober gray suit, approached.

"Mrs. Whitman," he said. "I don't know if we've been formally introduced before. I'm Samuel Holtwood, the bank's head cashier. How may I help you?"

She smiled. "It's a pleasure to meet you. I've heard a good deal about you."

A line appeared across his brow. "None of it bad, I hope."

"All of it good. I hear you're my husband's greatest help."

He gave her a modest nod. "I appreciate my position and my work with Mr. Whitman." He gestured around the bank. "Again, how may I help you?"

She blinked, thought fast. "Oh...ah...yes. I had hoped to stop in and have a word with Mr. Whitman."

Without a change of expression, Mr. Holtwood replied, "I'm afraid that won't be possible. He's busy at the moment, and cannot be disturbed."

Olivia was relieved. She hadn't come up with an excuse for her appearance at the bank, but at least she wouldn't need one. Not this time.

"I understand," she said. "I suppose I'll wait until he returns home this evening."

"I trust it's not an emergency, then."

"No," she said. "Just a few questions I need answered. But at least I've had the pleasure of meeting you. Thank you for your time, Mr. Holtwood. I'll be on my way home now."

Olivia hurried out, shaking her head. She certainly hoped her husband's right-hand man was as efficient as she'd heard, because he came across as cold as a winter blast and stiff as frozen laundry on the line.

Next time she came, she intended to meet the two at the desks—if she somehow got past Mr. Holtwood.

That evening, Olivia was still not ready to face Eli with the matter of her family's situation, but she was just as unwilling to refuse to meet him for their after-dinner coffee, so Olivia stopped in her room to pick up the dress she was making for

Randy. With her sewing basket over her arm, she made her way into the parlor as soon as the children were in bed.

Eli smiled when she walked in. "I trust you're feeling better than the last few nights."

She lifted a shoulder. "I'm not as tired today."

He gestured toward the fabric draped over her arm. "What do you have there?"

She set the sewing basket on the sofa, then shook out the fabric. "This is one of Randy's new dresses. I want to finish everything but the hem. I'll measure her and put that in after we've surprised her with her Christmas gifts."

Olivia took her seat next to the sewing basket and puddled the deep rose wool across her lap. She'd trimmed the luscious cloth with cream-colored lace at the throat and wrists, as well as six parallel rows down from the shoulders to the waist. It was becoming a smart and beautiful garment.

"You have quite a talent," Eli said. "I can imagine Randy will be overjoyed when she sees it."

Olivia kept her gaze on the dress, still perturbed by what she'd learned from her father. "Mama taught us girls to sew from the time we were little." Then, remembering her determination to help Eli become comfortable with the idea of her family, she went on. "I should say, Mama has tried to teach us, but I'm afraid the lessons have not taken well with Marty— Martha Jean, the older of my two younger sisters."

"How's that?"

"Well, Marty would rather do anything but pick up a needle and thread. She's happiest in the garden. That girl can coax masses of green out of even the worst plot of ground."

"Then I would imagine a couple years' drought and the two grasshopper plagues have been difficult for her."

Olivia sucked in a sharp breath. How could she have taken them down that pitfall-laden conversational path?

"Oh, Eli." Her voice rang with the miseries of the last two years. "The drought and the plagues have been devastating for everyone, not just Marty. Can't say as I know anyone around this area who's gone unscathed."

"We can hope the worst is over."

"If only it were..." She shrugged. "Anyway, Leah Rose, my youngest sister, is the one truly gifted with a needle. I'm just competent."

"I can see from here that you sell yourself quite short, Mrs. Whitman. I hope Randy's happy cries prove that to you Christmas morning."

His compliment pleased her more than it should have, especially in view of the conditions on which she and Eli had based their marriage. She couldn't be foolish enough to let kind words go to her head. They would only lead to heartache someday down the road.

To draw his attention away from her, Olivia asked Eli about the progress on Luke's train set, her gaze fixed on the buttonholes she was putting into Randy's dress. He launched into enthusiastic descriptions of every piece and minute part. Clearly, the father was as enchanted by the project as the son would be with the finished product.

Olivia was thrilled to have shifted Eli's focus away from her. She would have to develop the skills needed to do so on a regular basis. She couldn't spend evening after evening dreading her conversations with Eli, nor could she reveal more than she should until the proper time. She had to build his trust.

The only way she could see any hope of success was if she bided her time until she could recognize, by Eli's broader scope of conversation and the easing of his demeanor, the deepening of the friendship between them. Only then would she know he was ready to trust her. Only then would she be able to approach him about the mortgage.

She prayed it didn't take too long.

Soon, Lord Jesus, please. Sooner rather than later.

A short while after her silent prayer, she failed to suppress a yawn. "Oh, Eli, I'm sorry. I didn't mean to be so rude. It is getting late, and I'm ready to retire. If you'll excuse me?"

He smiled. "Don't let me keep you. I confess I'm something of a night owl, myself. I don't expect you to try and match my hours, especially if you're going to keep up with the children the next morning. We'll have another opportunity to spend time together tomorrow evening."

As the blush crept up her cheeks, Olivia sensed a return of her earlier boldness. "That would be *all* our tomorrows, Mr. Whitman."

He laughed. "You do have a point there. It is a matter of all our tomorrows, *Mrs.* Whitman. Good night."

Feeling better than she had since Papa showed her Eli's letter, Olivia made her way up the stairs. She opened the bedroom door, slipped inside, and put away her sewing.

This latest conversation between her and her husband gave her hope. Oh, yes. She was indeed prepared to wait upon the Lord. The prize, relief for her family and an excellent marriage for her, was well worth the required patience.

Again, she hoped it wouldn't be for long. If for no other reason than her folks didn't have much time.

As Olivia walked out of the parlor, Eli stood. He couldn't quite put a finger on what might have caused it, but he did know something had brought about a change in Olivia. As a result, it also had changed things between the two of them. He was certain the change had occurred either during or right after the time Olivia's father had spent with her when he'd come to visit days before.

That visit had been the trigger.

The moment he'd seen that horse tethered out front, an unwelcome mass of dread had dropped into his gut. It hadn't budged since. As much as he'd tried to dislodge it, it had, instead, strengthened.

The last couple of nights, Olivia had begged off their pleasant evening chat. He had always felt she enjoyed those times as much as he did. For her to scuttle off to her room right after she'd put the children to bed like that...something had to have been troubling her. Then tonight, instead of sitting in the armchair not three feet from his, as she usually did, Olivia had ensconced herself on the sofa all the way across the room. While he'd known she was working on the dresses for Randy, he hadn't expected her to use her needlework as an excuse to avoid meeting his gaze. Her evasion alarmed him.

What was she hiding?

What kind of trouble had he married this time?

Eli paced across the parlor, his thoughts rushing. Could his fears be coming true? Could Olivia's family have begun to pressure her to act on their behalf? And what manner of request might theirs be? If his suspicion was correct, it could only mean one thing.

History was repeating itself.

This time, however, he wasn't as gullible as he'd been during his first marriage. He'd learned the lessons, and he was well known for his excellent memory.

Whatever Stephen Moore had in the works, Eli wasn't about to let the man bring it to fruition at his expense. This time there would be no shady buying and selling of cattle herds, no investment in far-away property he didn't need or want, mines with yields that vanished the moment Eli's investment—as well as those of others—was effected. No, indeed. There would be no more questionable investments. None at all.

And absolutely no special favors at the bank, just because the Moores were now Eli's "family."

He wouldn't set himself up for another too-close brush with financial disaster while someone else skimmed off profits that should have been part of the bank's assets. No one would ever enrich himself while Eli wound up face-to-face with ruination.

Never again.

Not for anyone. Not even for Olivia.

No matter how much she appealed to Eli.

At least he knew better than to fall in love again.

He was no one's fool.

On Sunday morning, Olivia couldn't shake the knot of anxiety in her middle. She knew she'd see Mama and Papa at church, and she dreaded the worry she would read in their faces. Even more, she feared the question she would read in their eyes. They'd want to know if she'd spoken to Eli about that miserable letter.

Then, to her mortification, Reverend Alton's message that morning seemed tailored for her. With verse after verse, he stressed the point that God intended His children to trust Him, really trust Him. In its purest form, true trust blessed the believer with a life beyond the bondage built on the foundation of worry, anxiety, and fretting. Olivia had become much too familiar with those three building blocks in the last two years.

She'd fretted and worried about the family's situation since the start of the drought, since the first night she overheard her parents' worried conversation. Then, when the grasshoppers descended, her fears had escalated. Finally, when Papa had shown her that fateful letter, she'd lost all measure of trust.

Reverend Alton brought his point to its logical conclusion. A believer who indulged in worry and fretting revealed a lack of trust in God, he said. Lack of trust in the heavenly Father proved a person's weak faith.

Could Olivia set aside those common tendencies and truly exercise the faith she professed? Could she fully trust the Father?

What if Papa were right? What if the Lord had brought her to the Whitmans to help her family, and others, at the time of their greatest challenge and need?

If that were the case, however, she knew she'd have to trust the Father to guide her, to show her how to trust His leading. It would require total surrender. After all...she hadn't succeeded in her own strength. She still wasn't at that point. Worry continued to flog her on a regular basis.

As she stepped out into the crisp, clear late fall day, Olivia asked the Father's forgiveness on her way down the steps to the brick walkway up from the street. Partway there, she heard her name called. "Livvy! Please wait."

She stepped aside to let other worshippers leave. She smiled and voiced vague comments as they bid her farewell, her gaze on her mother. The look on Mama's face told Olivia loud and clear what topic she wanted to discuss. To her relief, neither Eli nor their children were near enough to overhear.

Her mother gave her the warm, loving embrace Olivia knew to expect. "How are you, dear?"

"I'm fine, Mama. How are you all? How is Papa's new calf?"

The two women discussed every subject but the one that loomed between them. When there was no reasonable way for Olivia to distract her mother any longer, Elizabeth asked her question.

"Have you done as your father asked? Have you spoken to your husband about the letter?"

The hope in those loving brown eyes made Olivia's heart ache. She couldn't bear the thought of watching the effect her answer would have, so she averted her gaze.

"No, Mama. It's not that simple."

"You gave your father your word."

"I know."

Olivia glanced around. Eli stood in the doorway of the church with Reverend Alton, the two men engaged in an animated conversation. She had no idea where Randy might have gone, but she could see Luke and another little boy chase each other between the buggies and wagons in the bare plot to the right of the church.

"I will speak to him," she said. "But it's not something I can just bring up at any time. I...Eli is quite particular about certain things. He has made it clear he doesn't want me involved in any way whatsoever in his business matters."

Parallel lines appeared between Mama's brows. "Asking a question is far from becoming involved, child. You could always point that out to him."

Olivia tightened her grip on her Bible. What more could she say, since she couldn't describe the true situation, all Eli had suffered at the hands of his late wife? The betrayal he feared might happen again. She knew it would distress Mama to learn the state of Olivia's marriage.

"I understand, Mama, but I would ask that you also understand that Eli isn't Papa. I understand you've always felt free to discuss anything and in any fashion you desire with Papa. But...well, Eli's a different man. I promise to speak to him, but it will have to be when he's receptive to my questions. Otherwise, I'm afraid I might make matters worse."

Her mother shook her head, a sad expression on her still youthful features. "What, dear one, could be worse than being turned out of our home when the weather starts to change? Snow is a possibility, and not a good one."

"I understand, Mama. I will speak with him. Soon."

Even to her, the answer came across as weak, made her sound mealy-mouthed. But it couldn't be helped.

Olivia knew she had to put her plan into action—or rather, to further the action she'd earlier put in place. She'd already asked Cooky to make enough to serve company at their midday table.

"Have you and Papa accepted a luncheon invitation?"

"For today?"

"Of course."

Mama gave her a weak smile. "No, dear. We're free."

"Wonderful! I'd like to have all of you to our home for dinner. Cooky's been making some lovely meals, and I've missed all of you an awful lot. Please tell me you'll come."

"I would love to." She glanced at Papa, who stood with a pair of other local farmers. "But I can't make the commitment without speaking to your father. If you'll excuse me, I'll go see what he has to say."

Before Mama had taken more than a couple of steps, Papa turned and headed toward them. Olivia caught her breath. She knew that determined expression only too well. She would not escape his questions.

"Good morning, Olivia," he said as he hugged and held her close. "You look quite some peaked. Are you ill?"

Ill? Didn't he realize the strain his request put on her? Still, she couldn't talk back to her father like that. He hadn't asked her to do anything another woman, in a different marriage, would find impossible to do.

"I'm well. Just a mite tired. Cooky and I have begun to prepare for the holidays, and I most likely overdid. Nothing a good night's sleep won't fix."

He gave a single nod. "Then I'll be brief so you can head home right away. Have you spoken to your husband about that matter—"

"No, Papa." She couldn't stand to hear more. It was enough to have to say no. "I—I did tell you it wouldn't do to simply ask without giving any thought to the timing or what might be the best approach. I do give you my word—again.

I'll speak to Eli about the letter. But I won't do it when it's likely to bring about a bad outcome. That won't help anyone."

Her father's jaw tightened. "Very well. I suppose there's nothing else for me to say. You know what we face, and you know what I've asked you to do for us. But, yes, yes. I do accept your promise to do whatever you can."

Hoping he would see her efforts as moving in the right direction, she went on. "I've come up with a plan, and even set it in motion this morning. But I will insist I cannot believe the man I married, the Eli Whitman I'm coming to know better each day, is capable of such cruelty. The man I know is generous, kind, and caring. He would never do this. Something about this letter isn't right. It doesn't fit Eli's nature."

"Olivia." Exasperation sharpened his voice. "You saw the letter yourself. How can you doubt what you've seen?"

She shivered. "I don't know, but I can't see him doing something so inhumane to a group of people who've done nothing but suffer.

"Besides," she said, "from the date I saw on that letter, Eli and I had already married. It's very recent. He has to have known you're my family. He must have realized that hurting you would hurt me, too. Something isn't right."

"I'm thankful you're so confident of your husband's affection for you." Mama's lips curved in a gentle smile. "I've worried, you know, what with that marriage as sudden as it was, and you hardly knowing Mr. Whitman to begin with. There was talk in town, Olivia. I know you, but I also had a number of difficult moments, there."

She blushed. "I'm sorry, Mama. I...well, Addie told me

about the gossips, and even Eli told me Reverend Alton spoke to him about the talk. He proposed right away."

"I'm thankful he's a decent, caring man," her mother said. "His feelings for you are right, then, since he stepped up to protect you with his name. And his love."

Olivia had to look away. She couldn't meet those perceptive brown eyes. With only one glance, Mama would have known Eli did not love her.

"Eli's a good man," she said. "I understand he has good reasons to not discuss his business with others, even me. Many folks have tried to take advantage of him and his generous spirit. Some have succeeded. He's cautious, is all."

Stephen Moore ran his fingers through his thinning hair. "I suppose I'll have to be satisfied with your opinion of the state of affairs. You're closest to Mr. Whitman, after all. I'll wait for you to act."

"Thank you, Papa." She glanced at Eli, who was still involved in his conversation with the pastor. "Now, about that plan I mentioned. I have an invitation for you. I told Mama already, and she was on her way to ask you."

Her father looked perplexed. "An invitation? Your plan?"

"I asked Cooky to make Sunday dinner for everyone— both families. I'd love to have all of you join us for the meal. I've missed you, and it would be a blessing to spend the time together."

Papa's lips tightened and thinned. "But—"

"It's also the perfect opportunity for Eli to get to know you better. He needs to see you're the upright and honest folks I know, how you'd never try to take advantage of him."

Mama placed her hand over Papa's clenched fist. "I think her idea's a good one, Stephen. It can't hurt anything for her young man to see we're not anyone to fear."

Papa thought for a moment. "I suppose that's sensible enough. But I will admit it sticks in my craw to think of breaking bread and making regular conversation with a man set to take from me what I've worked for all these long years. He sure isn't one bit like his father before him. Eli, Sr., would never send a letter like the one I got." He shrugged. "I've heard tell of a railroad spur coming somewhere through here. There's money to be made by selling them land. I suppose that explains why the son's no longer the man his father raised. That's why I want to talk to him, why I tried to go to the bank. But that Holtwood guards your husband's office door as if it were a fort."

"I'm sure there's been a mistake," Olivia repeated, ready to say the same thing over and over until her father came to share her opinion. "I will get the answers you need, but I will also respect Eli and his request—somehow. I don't know yet how, but I do trust the Father to show me how to go through these challenging times."

Her father sighed. "I have to admit, it's only right. He is your husband. I only hope Mr. Whitman recognizes his responsibility toward you half as well as you have toward him."

Olivia met Papa's gaze full on this time. "Eli treats me very well. I have no complaints."

Wishes? Dreams? Perhaps. But no complaints.

She glanced toward the church door and saw her husband approach. She caught her breath.

Once again it dawned on her what a fine figure of a man

Eli was. Good-looking, built tall and lean, but with a muscular solidity that brought to mind the picture of strength. He also possessed an unmistakable confidence, as he walked with a stride that made known to those around him how at ease he was with himself, how well he knew who he truly was.

More important, that outward assurance and strength were mere reflections of the inner man. Olivia considered it a privilege to find herself in a position where she was coming to know the true Eli Whitman. He was a man of character, decent, hardworking, devoted to his children, and a regular churchgoer. Everything about him attracted her.

A shiver of appreciation...of pleasure...of pure awareness ran through her. He was, after all, her husband. The handsome, powerful Eli Whitman had married her. Under irregular conditions, true, but he'd still chosen her.

Did she have any chance of changing his mind about those mortgages? Did she have any chance of making a difference, since his mind seemed made up?

Chapter 16

Eli's stomach turned an unsettling flip when he saw Olivia stop to talk to her parents that Sunday morning. Standing next to the serious Stephen Moore, she faced her mother, all three lingering outside the church. He knew his wariness bordered on the unreasonable, since the Moores were his new wife's parents, after all, and it was perfectly normal for her to want to speak with them. However, he had learned from his experience.

This time, he wasn't about to let his wife spend a great deal of time alone with her family. Whatever contact the Moores had with their daughter, he would make sure it happened while he hovered in the vicinity. He had to protect everything he'd worked for all those long, lean years.

More to the point, he had to protect himself. And his children.

A thought sped through his mind—for what seemed the hundredth time in the past few months, more often in the last weeks. Olivia had nothing at all in common with Victoria. She didn't resemble his late wife in the slightest way.

Still, his father-in-law's serious expression made Eli uneasy. It didn't look as though father and daughter were in the middle of a pleasant, Sunday morning chat about the sermon, about their family, about any of the normal things most folks he knew would talk about. Olivia's father looked intense, as though he had a purpose to his speech. Had he made a request, a demand of his daughter?

Eli sped his footsteps enough to cut the distance between them down to nothing in seconds. He nodded toward Olivia's mother, held out a hand to Mr. Moore. "Good morning."

Out of the corner of his eye he noted the pretty blush on Olivia's cheeks. Her forest-green jacket and skirt made her eyes appear to sparkle more than usual, and she seemed to glow in the cool, late autumn day.

It struck him again. His wife was an appealing woman, and not just because of her even features and simple elegance. Eli couldn't believe his great good fortune. For one thing, she'd learned to love his children. Then, too, she'd shown herself quite gifted as she turned the Whitman home into a haven. Without any fuss, but with grace and skill and ease, she'd become the lady of the house in what felt like no time at all. Her results spoke for themselves.

That she was so easy on a man's eyes didn't hurt one bit.

As though from a distance, he heard her voice and realized she was speaking to him.

"...asked them to come to the house for dinner," she said.

That wrenched his attention to the moment at hand.

Olivia continued. "I asked Cooky to prepare enough for

company, hoping Mama and Papa hadn't already made plans for this afternoon. And they haven't. It'll be splendid to have my two families become better acquainted."

The vague sense of unease Eli had experienced earlier burst into full-bodied alarm. "I see..."

Olivia hooked her mother's arm with hers. "Then let's go home, shall we?"

Eli clamped his jaws to control his automatic reaction. It wouldn't do to say something untoward when he had no justification. Under normal circumstances, a woman who'd just married would indeed want to have her family spend time getting to know her new husband and his children.

But his life hadn't been normal for a long time.

"Yes." He turned to leave. "Let's go home. I see Luke over by the Griffiths' buggy. I'll go fetch him then catch up with you, probably at the house. I don't suppose you know where Randy might be."

"I'm not sure, but she did walk out of church with Audrina Metcalf. I wouldn't be surprised one bit if they're at the Mercantile, looking at the new shipment of belts and silk purses Mr. Metcalf has on display in the front window."

He nodded. "That does sound like our Randy." Olivia sent him a radiant smile that, to Eli's irritation, shot straight to a cold and lonely, aching corner of his being. He steeled himself against the warmth it lodged there. "Why don't I stop by the Mercantile to see if she's there? I'll see you at home, then."

"I'll have Cooky ready to serve when you get back."

They parted ways, and he went to collar Luke. He hurried the boy home, which effort became especially easy after Eli reminded Luke a tasty dinner would be ready when they arrived. On their way down Main Street, he saw no sign of Randy outside the Mercantile, and when he spoke with Zebediah, the man said she'd only stopped for a moment. Once he walked through the front door of his home, however, he heard her chuckle in the parlor. A heartbeat later, Olivia's husky laugh joined in.

Again, he fought the effect it had on him.

He took off his hat and hooked it on the hall tree. Then his coat. He stepped into the large, welcoming room where his wife and children had gathered with the Moore clan. They'd all spread out, some on the sofa, others on the armchairs, one girl on the piano bench, and the two Moore boys sprawled on the thick carpet in the center of the parlor.

"I see we're the last ones—*I'm* the last one, since Luke ran ahead of me." He looked around, taking in the two younger Moore girls' animated chatter with Randy, as well as Luke's guarded stare for the somewhat older Moore boys. "Let's move into the dining room, if everyone's ready. I'm eager to do justice to one of Cooky's feasts."

Once everyone was seated around the large dining room table, Eli asked the Lord's blessing for the food. As though on cue, Cooky wheeled in the fancy cart Victoria had insisted he purchase for just such an occasion. He'd thought it silly at first, with its wrought-iron whorls and curlicues. Today, for the first time, it struck him as practical. Especially when the heady scents from the numerous platters and serving bowls it bore tickled his nostrils.

"Smells wonderful," he told the plump lady at the cart's handle.

"Ah...pshaw!" Cooky blushed with pleasure. "Do get on

with you, Mr. Whitman, sir. Plain old hoping here you enjoy your food on this Lord's day, is all."

Moments later, everyone did just that. For a while, nothing much happened but the dishing up of delightful treats and polite requests for more.

Then Cooky removed the empty china and passed around pots of coffee and tea. Cups were filled, beverages stirred, drinks sipped. Into the silence, Eli began the process—awkward, in his opinion—of getting to know Olivia's family.

He started with the man he knew from a number of business transactions at the bank. "So, Mr. Moore, how long have you been in the area?"

His father-in-law put down his cup. "Oh, we came out when Olivia was but a little thing, five years old, maybe? It was shortly after I came home once the war ended. The war left Maryland devastated, especially the Battle of Sharpsburg. I—I'd seen enough during the fighting."

No one spoke. Respect for the man who'd fought for his country carried the moment. Eli nodded his recognition.

Stephen composed himself and continued. "We didn't come straight to Oregon Territory. We stopped in Nebraska for a spell—two years—but the cruel weather didn't suit. We were spoiled by the milder Baltimore winters. And you?"

Eli nodded. "My family came from Boston when my father decided to try his hand at mining. Mama, my sister, and I stayed in Iowa—Kanesville, they call it Council Bluffs now—while Papa chased gold in barren places. His search didn't last long, but long enough that he turned his findings here in Oregon, at the Jacksonville fields, into the beginnings of a successful bank. Mama died shortly after we settled here; she suffered a bad cut that never healed. Papa sent my sister to live with an aunt in Boston, since there was nothing where Bountiful has now grown. She's still there, married with three little ones."

"Ah…separated family. I understand. It's never an easy thing to cross the country like that, and start all over from nothing." A soft smile curved the older man's lips. "Olivia didn't do so well on the trip. Don't know how any young-ster would, seeing as they want to play and not sit in a small wagon, bouncing over rutted trails and all the rocks in the hard dirt, day after day after day."

"I was eleven or twelve, so I remember our journey well. It was a trial for my mother, keeping my sister and me out of mischief. I can see how days in the confines of a wagon would have irritated Olivia." Eli glanced at his wife, whose embar-rassment showed in the pink circles on her cheekbones and the mild frown on her brow.

He smiled. "Perhaps that's why she has such a way with children. She must have learned quite a bit on that trip."

"I suspect," Mrs. Moore said, "she learned what she knows from helping me with Jonah and Peter. They were a handful, I'll say. What when I was with—well, ah…Martha Jean was on her way, why, I couldn't do a thing, I felt so sick for so long—months, even. Olivia was a great help, even as young as she was."

"Aw…we're not so bad, Ma," one of the Moore boys said. "'Sides, Marty's worse."

Olivia laughed. "Well, she has had a way of finding mis-chief, hasn't she?"

"Hey!" the accused objected. "They're crazy. I'm no worse'n the boys."

"Now, now. No need for that bickering," Mr. Moore said, his voice calm, gentle but firm and full of authority. "You're all older now, and I hope you've outgrown such goings on. Certainly while we're visiting."

Murmurs of apology and a wash of sheepish expressions came forth. Eli was impressed. Who wouldn't be? It might seem he could learn a thing or two about being a father from Mr. Moore. Just a firm word brought about the desired results. Clearly, this was where Olivia had learned her ways with children, by watching her mother and father raise them all.

Maybe she did have a point. Maybe the two families should grow closer.

Randy stood. "Papa, may I please be excused? I'd like to take Marty and Leah Rose up to my room to show them the dollhouse you had Mr. Bowen make for me last Christmas."

Fighting a smile, Eli nodded. "Go ahead. I'm sure they'll enjoy all the tiny pieces Tom whittled to fill the rooms in that house."

As the girls headed out of the dining room, they held themselves tall and composed. But when the youngest of the Moore girls stepped past Luke, Eli saw her glare at him and stick out her tongue.

"What . . . ?" he asked.

"One of the victims of the pig episode is Leah Rose's dearest friend," Olivia answered.

The girls sauntered out, but, as soon as they reached the hall, their footsteps pounded up the stairs, all three in a rush to reach the dollhouse.

He arched a brow in Olivia's direction. "I see Randy has left 'Miranda' somewhere else today."

Olivia smiled. "I'm sure we'll have her back once my sisters are home again."

He laughed. "More's the pity. I much prefer the girl Randy, you know."

"Oh..." Olivia said in a thoughtful if amused tone, "I find both quite charming. I'm thinking I must have done the same to Mama and Papa."

The elder Moores laughed.

"At least she's honest," Stephen said. "When Livvy was that age, she seemed older than the hills one minute, and then she became a moody handful of a youngster the next."

The pleasant afternoon wore on, the chatter centered on the two families' experiences in a new region, the challenges posed by raising children in the raw West, and the steady, welcome growth Bountiful was experiencing. A short while later, when it seemed they'd exhausted all conversational avenues, the older Moores stood and called for their children. After they'd left, Eli noticed the sudden silence, without any warning missing the cheerful hum the visit had created.

"Thank you," Olivia said.

"For what? You and Cooky did all the work."

"You were very gracious and didn't object to my inviting them before I'd spoken to you."

A twinge of guilt zipped through him. "I must admit, I was surprised, but this is your home now, Olivia. They are your family. You should feel comfortable enough to have them here. I'm glad you do."

He prayed he would stay glad.

Only time and a deepening closeness between them would tell him if he'd made a huge mistake.

*   *   *

The happiness she'd felt at her luncheon's success stayed with Olivia for the rest of the day. She spent time with Luke and Randy, she sewed for a while, and finally, in the early evening, they all enjoyed a light supper of leftover roast, Cooky's delicious bread, creamy butter, and crisp apples.

"Will you be joining me in the parlor tonight?" Eli asked as she stood to follow the children from the dining room.

"If you'd like." Pleasure fluttered in her middle. "I hope you don't mind that I'll have my sewing with me. I've a lot to finish before Christmas, and quiet evenings are a perfect time for me to make progress."

"It should be interesting to watch you finish the dresses for Randy. It's been years since I've seen anyone do any amount of sewing. My mother died when I was sixteen."

Olivia noticed his failure to mention his late wife. "I hope the memories I bring back are good ones."

"They are, indeed—"

"Mama!" Luke called.

"I'll be right with you." She turned to Eli. "If you'll excuse me, I'll be back as soon as they're settled for the night."

"I'll be waiting with our coffee—*my* coffee and your tea."

She blushed at his obvious effort to please her. "Thank you. I'm looking forward to our evening."

"So am I. I do have something I'd like to discuss with you. But it'll wait until you come back downstairs. It's not urgent."

She hurried to help Luke with his schoolwork, a nugget of joy glowing in her heart. Maybe their marriage had a chance to work out after all.

That thought carried Olivia through the bedtime routines,

to her room to gather Randy's gift-in-the-making, down again, and into the parlor.

"Good," Eli said as she walked in. "You're back. Here. Let me get your tea."

Olivia sat in the same corner of the sofa as she had the past two nights, sewing basket at her side, Randy's dress spread over her lap. The pleasurable glimmer within continued as she threaded her needle while Eli brought her the hot beverage. He set the graceful cup and saucer on the small walnut table to the right of the sofa.

She smiled at her husband, then took a sip to show her appreciation. He had cared enough to make sure Cooky steeped a pot of tea for her. His attention to her preferences touched her. While she did drink coffee often enough, her choice was always for a good, bracing cup of Earl Grey.

After she'd replaced the cup, she took up her sewing again, her attention on Eli, since he'd said he had something to discuss with her. He didn't make her wait long.

"I'm sure you remember Luke's enthusiasm about the possibility of the railroad bringing a spur through town."

A chill ran through her, stealing a good measure of her happiness. This was not a subject dear to her heart. "Of course," she said. "It would be difficult to miss how much he wants that to happen."

Eli lit his pipe, drew a long pull at the aromatic tobacco, and watched a curl of smoke rise above his head. "I have to admit, I agree with him."

The cocoa-laced scent reached Olivia, and for the first time since they'd begun their evening conversations, it failed to please her. She waited for Eli to continue.

"The railroad will be sending various officials to investigate the land, the town's needs, and the financial practicality of the project. I'm their host while they're in town—"

"What? You're having them stay with us? Here?"

Eli laughed. "No, no. They'll stay at the River Run Hotel in town. But I did extend the original invitation, so I'm responsible for the success of their stay in Bountiful."

Olivia sat back, a rush of weakness sending a shiver through her limbs. That had been too alarming for her comfort. "I understand. What will it mean to the family?"

"Nothing much to the family—the children—but plenty to you and me. You see, I'd like to host a Christmas party while these gentlemen are in town. The brunt of the planning and preparations will fall on you. Are you willing to help me with this?"

Olivia opened her eyes wide. "I see. That is something, isn't it? Um...I suppose it will take a good amount of work, as you said, and..." She set her misgivings aside and squared her shoulders. "Very well, Eli. I don't see too much of a problem with your plan. Cooky and I can handle it."

Relief broke out across his face. "I had hoped you would agree. Thank you. Please let me know if there's anything I can do to help you and Cooky prepare for the event."

She slanted him an amused look. "I don't think you'll be much help once I begin to stitch up a grand new tablecloth, nor do I think you'll accomplish much in the kitchen...unless you decide to help Cooky peel potatoes."

He laughed. "I can see you want to keep this a job for the ladies of the house."

"Of course. And if you don't mind," she added, "I'll ask

Mama to help. She learned a great deal about proper entertaining while she grew up in Baltimore. I can still remember the lovely dinners she held when we lived back East, even though I was very young, and it was wartime. She made a little seem like a lot of nice."

Moments crawled by, and then, after what she experienced as a short eternity, he gave a brief nod. "I can see where you would want her help. It makes a good deal of sense to bring her expertise into the planning. Are you sure you can manage such an event?"

So that must have been what prompted the strange look. Her suggestion to seek her mother's help with the party must have made it appear as though she couldn't pull together the affair. Olivia became more determined than before to succeed, to provide her husband with the most appropriate, elegant, and delightful Christmas party possible.

"By the Father's grace, Eli Whitman, I can do all things through Christ, who does, indeed, strengthen me."

"Ho-ho! I see you've taken my words as a challenge of sorts."

She set the rose-colored dress aside, stood, and marched to her husband's side. "And pray tell, sir, how else should a woman take your comment? Those came close to sounding like fighting words."

He stood as well, his superior height seeming to dwarf her. Before she could step back or say anything further, he chuckled again.

"I have no interest in fighting with you, my dear. Instead, I'm particularly interested in working with you. Whether we deal with the children or tackle a business soirée, we can do it together."

My dear . . . my dear . . . my dear . . .

His words sent a shiver through her as happy warmth expanded close to her heart. "What is it you plan to contribute to the party preparations, dear sir? Especially, since I don't see you cooking or sewing or even polishing silver before the coming day—"

A thought brought her up short. "Oh, Eli! There is that, you know. When do you plan to hold this party?"

His blue eyes twinkled. "The actual date of the soirée would help your preparations, wouldn't you say?"

As she sputtered, he reached out and took hold of her hand, the smile still curving his lips. "I'm sorry, Olivia. I can be a bit of a tease, and I was having fun at your expense there. I'd like us to hold the event on the twenty-fourth of December. The gentlemen plan to be in town over the holiday, and I feel sorry they'll miss the time with their families."

A touch of disappointment struck Olivia. She'd been looking forward to a cozy Christmas Eve supper, an early night for the children, another quiet evening for Eli and her, and then the joyous morning, when they would celebrate the Lord's birth as a family for the first time.

On the other hand, Eli was paying her a great compliment by trusting her with such an important matter. "Of course," she said, her fingers curling into his, her every fiber aware of his nearness and his gentle touch. "We must do whatever we can to help them over the sadness of the separation. Cooky, Mama, and I will treat them to the most charming dinner party they've ever attended."

His thumb caressed the back of her hand, and another shiver ran up her spine.

Oh, my!

What a sensation he sparked off inside her. She'd never experienced such a reaction to any other person. Then again, she'd never been married, had never been this near to a man before. And this was Eli.

"I have a feeling," he said, his thumb's gentle motions doing lovely things to the sensitive skin of her hand, "that your words don't stem from mere bravado. I suspect you regularly come up with splendid results once you set your mind to something."

She squeezed the hand holding hers. "I won't let you down, Eli. I promise. I only want to help you, to do what will be best for you."

As though she'd thrown a cup of cold water at his face, the look of admiration and his caring touch vanished. Her suddenly empty hand hung limp at her side, and she experienced a deep sense of abandonment.

Dear Lord! Please show me. What have I done?

Before she could marshal the courage to ask, Eli turned from her and sat back in his chair. "Please see that everything is ready for my guests. It is important, and whatever affects me will, of course, affect you in the end."

Olivia didn't dare comment, now that the friendly, companionable air between them had disappeared. She went to the sofa, gathered Randy's new dress and her sewing basket, then crossed the room to the door. Before stepping into the hall, she paused, met his gaze with all the dignity she could muster.

"I gave you my word, Eli. I was raised to always keep my word. It's who I am before the Lord. You can trust me."

Before he could say anything to delay her departure, she

hurried down the hall, fighting the sting of tears. As she took the first step up to the second floor, she thought she heard him speak.

Unless she was much mistaken, he muttered, "I hope that word is good. I certainly do."

Worry and a touch of fear took up residence in Olivia's heart.

Chapter 17

Much to Olivia's surprise, Eli invited her to keep him company after supper the next night as though nothing unusual had happened. At first, they each kept to themselves, he smoking his pipe, she working on Randy's new dress. After a while, he brought up the subject of the Christmas Eve party, and the awkwardness began to dissipate. Eventually, however, he made a comment that alarmed her.

"You want to do what?" Olivia's voice rose, growing panicked and more piercing with every word she uttered.

"I'm inviting the local tradesfolk, and even some of the farmers from around the area. I don't understand why you're so surprised. It would seem the most natural thing. The railroad will help them all."

She hoped.

Olivia caught several stitches on her needle, her gaze aimed down to keep Eli from reading her feelings. "Well then, how many people will we be hosting at your gala?"

"There will be five gentlemen from the railroad. Besides them, I would like to invite Tom Bowen, Barry Woollery, Reverend Alton, the schoolmarm, Mrs. Selkirk now that her millinery is doing so well, Richard Folsom from the hotel, and even your father and some of his fellow farmers. Their wives, too."

Olivia felt the blood drain from her face. "That...many?"

He narrowed his eyes. "Do you think we'll have a problem? I thought you said you could handle this."

"Yes, but...I didn't know you meant to have most of the town here for Christmas Eve!"

"I'm sorry," he murmured. "Did I overstep before talking to you? I'm sure there must be something I can do to lighten your load. Yours and Cooky's, too."

Olivia's head spun as she considered the tactics such a massive maneuver would require. "There's so much to coordinate. There are the decorations outside the house, boughs of holly and ribbons, the Christmas tree, and all the different candles—"

"Is all that necessary—"

"Of course. You said you wanted a festive Christmas party, didn't you?" At his nod, she went on. "Then there are the serving pieces and tableware. Do we have enough for that many guests?"

"I wouldn't know. You'll have to ask Cooky—"

"All those supplies, Eli!" She stabbed the needle into the dress and stood to pace. "How about the food? You do remember we've had two failed harvests in Hope County, right?"

A slight frown creased his forehead. "Well, yes. But I must confess I hadn't thought about that with regard to our Christmas party. Will it affect—"

"Will it affect...?" Her voice neared a shriek. "Where do you expect us to find enough food to serve an army? On relatively short notice, at that."

It finally seemed to dawn on Eli. "I suppose I must place an order for various foodstuffs from...oh, I don't know. Would Seattle be better, or maybe Portland?"

"I wouldn't know." She spun and marched across the room toward him. "I don't even think Mama could help with this part of the preparations. Shops in Baltimore were everywhere, and they were full of everything one could need for even the most elegant gala."

"Why don't you talk to Cooky? I remember Victoria held a number of events, and she always relied on Cooky's knowledge."

Olivia nodded. "I suppose she is the one who'll handle the meal itself, so she should know what we'll need." An idea occurred to her. "You know, Eli, Hope County is blessed with various flocks of sheep. Don't you think a nice roast lamb would be good to serve?"

He nodded. "Perhaps a turkey, as well. That shouldn't be too hard to come by."

"Not at all." She ticked off her fingers one by one. "Flour for breads and cakes, eggs, milk, cheeses, dried fruit, carrots, cabbage—things that store well...they shouldn't pose too much of a challenge either."

"Most of that you can find around here, right?"

"After the drought, I hope so. What if I worked with Cooky to serve our guests a meal that displays the local bounty? Surely the gentlemen from the railroad will want to know what's available in the area, don't you think?"

A broad smile brightened his face. "I think you're a very wise woman, Mrs. Whitman—as I've mentioned a time or two."

Pleasure sped through her. "Do hold off a bit on those compliments, Eli. I don't know yet if I can pull off this particular idea. Cooky and I have to look into what we can get this time of year, and then...well, you can see what you think then."

"Fair enough. You mentioned a tree and evergreen branches, didn't you? Could I help you with those?"

"That would be excellent. Perhaps you could help me string some wreaths and garlands. Wire—I'll need it to weave the branches together. You can help me with that, too, since I'm not sure what kind might be best."

A crooked smile tipped up the corner of his mouth. "I can't say I have much experience with decorations and such, but your ideas do make me look forward to getting started."

"It's never too late to learn something new." She picked up her sewing. "Now, if you'll excuse me, I'm going to find Cooky right away. She and I have a great deal to do if we're going to have a chance to do this right."

"I'd best go hunt out some tools to work on those wreaths and branches and garlands and...well, and any other thing of that sort."

Olivia smiled as she headed out of the room. "Well, Eli, it's only right, you know. The whole thing was your idea, so you should do your part."

"Wait, wait!"

When she paused, he approached, a question in his gaze. "You still haven't told me what you'd like for Christmas. Time is running short, and I do want to give you something you'll truly enjoy. You've done so much for us, for our family, and I want to show you how much I appreciate it."

Olivia shrugged. "You've given me more than I ever could have expected. I don't need anything more. I'm happy with my new life."

"Please humor me. Take your time, think about it, and let me know. I want to do something special for you, and Christmas is the perfect time."

"Oh, all right. I'll give it some thought. But I honestly am quite content." She patted his forearm. "Have a good night, Eli. I'll let you know what Cooky and I decide."

Sewing basket slung over one arm, and Randy's dress draped over the other, Olivia headed down the hall. But as she hurried to find Cooky, the beginnings of an idea began to take shape. There was something she wanted, something only Eli could give her.

It wouldn't be a gift of any traditional sort. But it was the one thing Olivia's life currently lacked. Maybe...maybe there was a solution to her worries. Maybe Eli had given her the way to approach him with the question she as yet hadn't dared ask.

The next morning, Eli called Holtwood into his office. "Have you looked into the county's available land as I asked?"

Holtwood tucked the papers under his arm. "I'm working on it, sir. I expect to have a proper list for you to look over by tomorrow or the day after—no more than that."

"Any details you can offer ahead of the list?"

"There's land, and plenty of it, as I'm sure you know,

Mr. Whitman. We just need to decide what will be most profitable for us, sir."

"You mean for Bountiful, right?"

"Of course, Mr. Whitman."

A soft knock at the partly open door caused both men to look that way. Lewis Parham, the new secretary, held a thick stack of papers in his hand. "I have today's correspondence ready for your signature, Mr. Whitman. You said you wanted it right away."

"Come in, come in," Eli said. "What do we have?"

Holtwood cleared his throat. "On top of the letters you dictated to Parham, I suggested he write a number of tentative missives to local landowners. They invite the farmers and ranchers to consider the bank if they have to think of selling out."

"I thought we'd agreed on this. I don't want any pressure applied to them. Not a one of those men is responsible for his situation. They had nothing to do with the weather, much less the grasshoppers."

Parham glanced at the papers in his hand. "The missives only suggest a possible solution." He met Eli's gaze, his eyes intent, his expression attentive. "No pressure at all, sir."

"Let me see one, please."

Parham handed Eli the top page. As he scanned the message, Larry Colby stepped into the office.

"I have the map Holtwood and I have been using to plot out the most probable route for the spur line. I thought you'd want to see it."

"Show me what you have there."

Colby spread out the map across Eli's desk, then as he

studied the depiction of the region, his spectacles fell right off the end of his long, thin nose. He bent over almost double, reached for the glasses, and in the process, knocked the stack of papers Parham had set on the corner of Eli's desk to the floor. Eli made a mental note to avoid putting papers in that spot, as it seemed to be particularly tempting to Colby's clumsiness. The man scrambled around, gathering papers and his belongings, his movements typically nervous and jittery. Finally, he stood again and, with jerky movements, polished his glasses on his jacket sleeve.

To deflect everyone's attention, Eli turned to Holtwood again. "You are keeping in mind that this project is to benefit the town of Bountiful, right? It's not just a matter of the bank making money off the backs of hardworking folks."

For a second, Holtwood looked offended. Eli wondered if he'd gone too far with his comment. Then his right-hand man composed himself again.

"Of course, Mr. Whitman, sir. We need to make sure the railroad deal profits Bountiful."

"Are you certain this is the map we discussed? Nothing looks familiar, and the list of properties won't help me if I can't show the railroad folks where they're located within the county."

"I'm seeing to that, too, sir. This was the best we could find. I'm waiting for the post to bring a better one I ordered. I hope to have it and the list for you within the day." He gestured toward the confusing paper Colby had brought in. "We've tried to flag on this one the properties we think will offer the best profit for the investment, but of course we'll see them better on a clearer map."

"You mean profit on investment for the railroad, right?"

"Of course!" Colby said. "I'm sorry we haven't made it clear. I've been dreadfully distracted, what with all the paperwork I've been doing for this deal."

Eli struggled to keep from rolling his eyes. "Go ahead, then, Colby, Holtwood. Finish up what you were doing, and bring the whole thing to me when it's done."

"Very well," Holtwood said.

Colby nodded. "Will do, sir." He caught his spectacles on their slide toward the tip of his nose. "Will do."

Eli turned to Parham. "I suppose these letters are acceptable to send. Leave them here with me, and I'll have them signed for you in a short while."

As the men left the office, Eli breathed a sigh of relief. Holtwood he could handle, and Parham was proving to be an asset to the bank. But if Colby were any less efficient, he'd have replaced the fellow long ago. Yes, at times Eli found him humorous, but after a small dose of the man's fidgeting, his nerves staged a revolt. Sometimes Eli was tempted to ask the other employees if he made them nervous. But when he walked among the men and spoke with them, he noted no similar jumpiness.

He sighed. Colby's problems couldn't be helped, and Eli had a great deal of work to finish. Time to put his second cashier out of his mind.

It was also time to think again about the Christmas party he and his new wife were preparing to host. At the thought of Olivia, anticipation filled him. He couldn't wait to see what new details she'd put together. Working with Olivia was turning out to be more pleasurable than he had expected.

Olivia herself was turning out to be a splendid wife. He settled back to work, a satisfied smile on his lips.

"Oh, Mama, I need your help!" Olivia cried as soon as her mother let her go. "I don't know a thing about entertaining, soirées, galas, or fancy parties. What am I going to do?"

Elizabeth clucked. "First thing you'll do, my dear, is take off your cloak and have a cup of tea. Then you should be able to see things more clearly, since I doubt you'll be so agitated about a simple thing."

"A simple thing? Perhaps for you. I've never been to a soirée, never mind organizing one. Eli trusts me to do a good job of it. How am I going to do this?"

Mama placed the cup of tea in front of Olivia, together with a pot of honey and a silver spoon. "Go ahead. Drink up. You'll feel better, child."

Although Olivia savored her sip of tea, she didn't feel any less anxious about the upcoming gala. "How does one go about putting on such an event? I don't even know what I should serve all these folks."

"Have you spoken with your cook? That dinner on Sunday was simple but tasty and well-prepared. She strikes me as a capable woman."

"Cooky is a treasure, Mama. She and I have put our heads together and, with your recipes and ideas in mind, I've made suggestions that have improved our meals considerably. Now we've come up with some possibilities, but I'm not sure those dishes will be elegant enough for such important guests."

"I've found that well-seasoned, well-made simple food,

served beautifully, is often better than the fussiest of fancy fare. Tell me about these guests, dear. Who will your husband invite?"

Olivia related the details of her conversations with Eli, explaining the railroad spur line under consideration. As Olivia spoke, Elizabeth listened, a thoughtful expression on her face. When she finished, Mama gave her a quick nod.

"I think your idea to showcase the blessings of Hope County is excellent. It will make your supper choices much simpler. Will Cooky handle ordering the foodstuffs you can't find locally?"

"She says she'll go through Metcalf's Mercantile."

"Zebediah's always reliable. I'm sure he'll take care of finding whatever you need."

"Even the food, dishes, and dinnerware we're missing?"

"Oh, sure." Elizabeth pointed toward the generous-sized tureen on a nearby shelf. "He ordered that from San Francisco for me three years ago, and I must say, it arrived in perfect shape, well packaged, and it's lovely, don't you think?"

Olivia nodded. She'd always admired that piece. "If he can do as well for us, then we should be fine. But do you think we still have enough time for him to have what we need shipped here?"

"That question speaks volumes for your husband's foresight. I think the spur line could be a blessing for us all. That is, if…"

If the family held on to its land. If they hung on for another year. If Olivia persuaded Eli to postpone the foreclosure proceedings.

But this wasn't the time to fret about those things. She

had been charged with a monumental task, and she was determined to carry it out successfully. Then...well, asking her husband for anything might prove easier then.

"What should I do first?" she asked her mother.

"After you order whatever you need from Zebediah, you mean, right?"

"Of course. All that will take time. Then what?"

"Then I would send out your invitations. You might want to make the invitation a part of the message in your Christmas cards. It would help to know just how many you'll be expecting for supper. After that..."

Olivia took note of the many projects she would have to complete before the twenty-fourth of December. All that, and she still had to finish one more dress for her daughter. Perhaps she could persuade Randy to help with preparations, especially since she'd be given "grown-up" tasks to tackle.

After the two women divided the looming project into building blocks, Olivia felt she could at least start her preparations. She donned her cloak and gloves, slipped her purse-strings onto the crook of her elbow, and then headed for the door.

"I don't suppose you've had a chance to ask your husband yet," Elizabeth asked.

Olivia didn't need any more information to know what her mother meant. "No, Mama. But I have been working on it, preparing for the moment, trying to set it up as soon as possible."

"I don't understand all the drama, dear. You just ask your husband a question. Especially since it's such an important matter."

"Yes, it's important, but, Mama, I did tell you he's asked

me to stay out of his business dealings. I can't go against his wishes."

"His wishes, Olivia? A wish matters more than what might happen to us if he has his way?"

She gasped. She'd never known her mother to make such a harsh statement before. While she understood Mama's concerns, the way Elizabeth had framed the situation struck her in a way she'd never faced.

"That's not how it is, Mama."

She really should give her mother more details, a better understanding of the situation, but she dreaded revealing the truth of her marriage. Especially to a woman who'd lived her entire adult life with the man she loved, respected, and admired, the man who returned her love and respect and admiration. Mama often said Olivia's father was her closest friend.

"Yes, dear. That is the way it is. At least, that is something you must consider."

"Eli..." She stopped, then took a deep breath before going ahead. "I gave him my word not to interfere in his business, Mama. I can't go back on it."

"While I understand your commitment to your husband, something I will always encourage, I hope you don't forget your duty as a daughter and sister. You must find a way to balance both."

"That's what I'm trying to do."

"See that you find a way to achieve it soon, dear. I...I don't know what will become of us otherwise."

Something occurred to Olivia. "Now that he's coming to know Eli better, has Papa tried to speak with him again? At the bank?"

"His plan is to try and meet with him at the bank tomorrow. I'll have him let you know how that goes."

At the front door, Olivia gave her mother a quick hug. "I'll pray that Eli responds well to Papa's request. And I'll be back soon, I'm sure. I'm going to need all the help you can give me to carry off this gala."

"I'll do my best, Livvy. Be careful on your way to town. The wind's got a sharp nip today, and the horse might struggle in the cold weather."

"Don't worry, Mama. I will take care on the way home."

Feeling as if she was fleeing from her responsibility to her family, Olivia nevertheless prayed all the way home. She prayed for her parents, for Eli, for herself.

The Lord knew what needed to happen. But she still had to trust and wait. As difficult as it might be, she recognized the Lord's timing as far superior to her own.

That evening, Olivia took a notebook with her into the parlor instead of Randy's almost ready rose wool dress. She wanted to update Eli on the notes she'd taken during her discussions with Cooky and Mama, and get his approval for her plans.

But when she reached the door, she found Eli unpacking a large box. "Oh! Are you busy tonight?"

As she walked in, he turned from where he knelt on the plush carpet and gestured her close. "I have something for you here."

"For me?"

"Well, for us."

Us? Her heart skipped a beat. "I'm intrigued."

From the depths of the box he withdrew a newsprint-wrapped parcel, about the size of one of Cooky's fresh-baked loaves of bread. "Here. Take a look."

Olivia took the object, carefully cupping it in her hands so as to protect it. Eli had handled it with care, and she wanted to do the same.

As she unwrapped the item, excitement made her heart rate speed up. What could it be?

As she removed the last bit of wrapping paper, she saw. The piece was a rustic wooden manger, carved by hand and painted with great detail. It awaited its usual inhabitants, and Olivia knew that within the still-packed box, a holy infant nestled in protective paper.

She ran a finger over the old wood. "How lovely!"

"There's more," he said, not meeting her gaze.

In a short time, they'd removed all the animals, Mary, Joseph, and the cradle as well. Finally, with great care, Eli withdrew the baby Jesus from where He'd lain, swaddled in paper, in a corner of the crate.

Olivia took the bisque statuette from her husband's hands. "This is wonderful, Eli. Just beautiful. It looks old, too."

A faint wash of color covered his high cheekbones. "It belonged to my mother. I remember her setting up the pieces every year right before Christmas. She always took great care to place them all just so."

Olivia felt the emotion in his voice. "What a treasure you have here. Something this special is even more extraordinary because it once was hers. I'm so glad we have it for our family."

"You don't think it's too old? Too shabby?"

"Shabby?" She shook her head. "It's a family heirloom. A

treasure for you, the children, even for me. Besides, like I said, it's absolutely beautiful. Why would you think it's shabby?"

He shrugged but wouldn't meet her gaze—again. "Victoria never wanted to set it out. She didn't feel it was smart enough for us. She always wanted things just so, quite perfect."

"Forgive me, Eli. I do not care to speak ill of the dead, but that is silly. Perfection belongs to the heavenly Father. Of course, we'll display your mother's Nativity. I'm proud we have such a special part of your family history."

He reached out and covered the hand that held the miniature holy infant. "I'm not one to wear my feelings on my sleeve, but I must tell you how glad I am you agreed to marry me."

A prickle of tears burned the inside of Olivia's eyelids, and the warmth of his hand spread all through her. At that moment, she felt able handle anything life brought her way. Their way.

Together.

The two of them.

Through the veil of her tears, she found Eli's beautiful blue gaze ready to meet hers. "I'm thankful you asked me to become your wife."

As they sat like that for long moments, Olivia wondered if he could hear her galloping pulse. She felt his touch to the very depths of her heart, and hope soared within her.

Then, slowly and carefully, as though to give her the opportunity to escape, Eli leaned forward, bridged the space between them, and placed his lips on hers.

Chapter 18

The heat of Eli's lips against hers made Olivia's pulse race faster, her skin tingle, ripples of awareness soar from her middle right up to her head...and made her want the moment never to end.

The earth tilted beneath her. Her head spun. Still, Eli's lips worked magic on hers.

Finally, after what seemed like the most marvelous eternity, he eased away.

She sighed, slowly opened her eyes.

He smiled.

She blushed.

He reached up and ran a finger down her cheek, curved it over her jaw, brought it to a stop on her lips. Once again, his touch was gentler than the graze of a feather and sweeter than her mama's pure sugar syrup.

Olivia forced air into her lungs. "Eli—"

"Mama!" Luke cried from the top of the stairs.

She drew back from her husband as though his touch scalded her skin. With the moment ended, a furious blush sizzled up her cheeks, and she cast glances in any direction but at Eli, who still sat on the floor by the box and the mounds of packing newsprint.

"What is wrong, dear?" she called to Luke, mortified at the quiver in her voice.

"Those dreams again..."

"Oh, I'm so sorry, honey. Go ahead. I'll meet you in your room..."

She ran from the parlor as though a pack of angry dogs were after her. But there were, of course, no dogs chasing her, just her embarrassment. And niggling thoughts about tomorrow.

How would she face Eli in the light of day? She'd never been kissed by a man before.

Especially since he'd said, when he proposed, that their marriage was to be one of convenience for the both of them. That kiss they'd just shared had *not* been in any way convenient.

It had, in Olivia's opinion, complicated matters a whole lot more, and they'd been complicated from the start. Especially when it came to Eli and his determination to keep hearth and home separate from business and the bank.

She reached Luke's bedroom door, paused to compose herself, then knocked and went in. "I'm here, Luke. Why don't you tell me what scared you this time?"

The next morning, Eli walked to work, a jaunty bounce in his step, a cheerful look on his face, and a happy whistle on his lips. Last night, the sweet memory of Olivia in his arms, her lips warm, soft, and yielding beneath his, had lulled him to sleep.

The kiss had been unplanned, an unexpected turn of events. From the start he'd envisioned a business venture to benefit the two of them, but this attraction? This he hadn't envisioned. Perhaps he should have. Olivia was quite a woman. He knew himself blessed to have her as his wife.

From her response to him the night before, he knew she didn't object to him. But not objecting wasn't enough. He didn't know how she felt about him. Not really.

Was she coming to care for him as he was for her?

Although the random twinge of fear struck him every once in a while, Olivia's favorable attributes reappeared regularly and wiped it away. Would she also wipe away the pain-filled memories Victoria and her family had left in their wake?

"Good morning, Mr. Whitman!" Mrs. Selkirk, the milliner, called out as he stepped past her store.

"Oh, Fridays are always good," he answered, doffing his hat to the tall lady. "They mean I'll have half of Saturday and all of Sunday free to spend at home with my children. The weekend is a fine thing, indeed."

With a mischievous twinkle in her green eyes, Mrs. Selkirk stopped sweeping the sidewalk at her front door, then cupped both hands on her broom handle and leaned on it. "I reckon now that you have yourself that nice new wife you have more reason to enjoy your time away from the bank than before."

Eli's cheeks warmed. "I do, indeed." He donned his hat again. "I do still have to get to my office today, though, so have yourself a good day now."

"Will do, sir. Will do."

A handful of other acquaintances greeted him before he reached the bank, which served to increase his sense of well-being. He again whistled a lilting tune as he loped up the front steps of the bank and drew open the door.

" 'Morning everyone—"

"Don't come in!" Holtwood cried, panic in his voice.

"Holtwood! What do you mean, man?"

Heart pounding, Eli stepped farther into the room. Out of the corner of his eye he caught sight of Colby frozen in place behind his window. The man generally had a ruddy tint to his rotund features, but today he matched the whitewashed wall behind him.

Eli started toward Colby, but stopped when the man gave a minimal shake to his red-haired head, his eyes wide open with alarm. "Colby?"

Eli spun as a flurry of activity came from behind Holtwood's cash window across the room. Suddenly, a man ran at him, a bag in one hand, a pistol in the other.

Eli lunged at the fellow to stop him. At the moment he made contact, a deafening explosion assaulted his ears. Searing pain bit into his upper torso.

He gasped, fell, aware he'd been hit. He also realized he'd fallen on the bandit. With all the strength he could muster, he wrestled the thief for the pistol. Unable to grasp the weapon, he managed to land a good blow or two on the man. As he fought, he shot a glance toward Colby.

"Go!" he said on a gasp as he prepared to land another blow. "Get help."

The man grunted and fought against Eli's weight. Despite

Eli's greater size, the crook managed to buck and kick and thrash, making his injured chest burn ever worse. Blood spurted at every move he made.

With a wriggle up, he pinned the bandit's gun arm, knocking the weapon out of his hand. The gun skittered across the polished floor, well out of reach of either of them. As he strained, Eli realized his strength was beginning to suffer from the pain. Maybe the loss of blood, too.

Oh, Lord, get us help soon.

From behind Holtwood's cashier window, Eli heard a pitiful moan. At the same time, beneath him, the robber gave a rabid growl. He bucked, twisted, and turned, sensing Eli grew weaker by the moment. He'd soon be able to fight free. With tenacity Eli had never known he possessed, he culled every bit of his determination, and hung on.

"Enough!" a man's voice roared from the vicinity of the front door. "You can get up carefully now, Eli. I got you covered. Just Eli. Wouldn't want to hafta plug this thief before I get him his trial, and all."

Relief sapping from him whatever strength he had left, Eli rolled off the man, taking the cash bag as he went. The thief let out another of his brutish growls. He was covered in Eli's blood, but didn't move with Marshal Blair standing over him. Eli reached up and patted his upper chest where the pain burned the worst. He pressed with his flat palm against the blood flow, and prayed Larry would think to get the doctor.

"Now get up!" the marshal hollered. "And be quick about it. Don't have all day to waste on the likes of you. Why'n't you try working for your cash every once in a while?"

A slight smile curved Eli's lips as the marshal subdued

the thief, but not for long. The pain and the blood seeping through his fingers had him praying for the Father's mercy. He couldn't make Olivia a widow and the children orphans.

Scant seconds after the marshal marched his captive out, the steel-gray-haired, mustachioed doctor marched in, black leather medical bag in hand. He checked briefly on Holtwood, then hurried to his other patient.

"Now then, Eli Whitman, let's see what kind of trouble you've gotten yourself into this fine day."

Eli's every muscle gave way to an incapacitating weariness utterly foreign to him. "Thank you for coming so quickly, sir."

And thank you, Father, for answering my prayer.

As Doc Chambers dug around in his injured chest, the only thing that pierced through Eli's fog of pain was the thought of the moment he would return home. Even though he'd stopped the thief from getting away with any funds, he knew he was in no shape to work the rest of the day. Colby wasn't either, and goodness only knew what Holtwood's condition would turn out to be. His unusually salty verbiage from where the robber had felled him suggested he hadn't been injured too badly. Clearly Doc thought he could wait.

Eli was glad. All he could think of was returning to the haven Olivia had created.

Olivia found herself chewing on the wooden end of a pen and staring off at nothing more times than she cared to count. She was supposed to be finishing the Christmas cards she meant to send to family and friends, including the handful of invitations they still needed to distribute among the business folk of Bountiful. But thoughts of Eli held her attention captive, and she wasn't quite sure she wanted to do anything about it. She smiled at the memory of Eli's gentle caresses, of his warmth and care toward her.

Although he'd only left home a short while ago, she couldn't wait until he came back at the end of the day.

She chuckled at her foolishness. Surely Eli would not be too pleased if she spent all her time daydreaming about him instead of working on the preparations for the Christmas Eve party. She dragged her attention back to the notebook, and began to skim what she'd jotted down when she and Mama had worked out the latest lists of must-dos.

A violent beating at the front door shattered the morning's peace.

"Missus Whitman! Open up, please."

Olivia rushed to her feet, hurried forward, breath caught in her throat, pulse pounding at her temples, fear chilling her hands. The woman outside sounded frantic.

More pounding struck the door. "It's me, ma'am, Irma Bowen. I need to speak to you—"

"What?" Olivia said, panic rising. "What's happened to Papa? Mama? My children?"

Mrs. Bowen twisted her calico apron between plump fingers. "No, ma'am. Nothing's wrong with your family—or your children. It's your husband. A bandit at the bank. I don't have much of the story yet. Marshal Blair sent me after you. You must get to the bank—"

"And so you've fetched me, Irma." Olivia grabbed the wool shawl she'd left on a small console by the door when she'd returned from walking Luke and Randy to school. "Let's go. I don't want to waste another second."

The two women rushed down the street, and to Olivia it seemed as though the block and a half distance had just lengthened by miles. She couldn't run fast enough to her husband's side. Over the years she'd heard horror stories about bandits of all kinds. They just as often killed their victims as let them live.

When she reached the bank, a crowd had gathered outside on the sidewalk. An eerie silence hung over the folks. Bile chased up into Olivia's throat.

"Excuse me." She edged people out of her way. "My husband…"

They all backed away from her as though she bore some dreaded disease. Fear warred against her determination and almost derailed her ability to walk. In the end, however, her determination won out.

She pushed forward. At the top of the steps to the front door, Larry Colby, Eli's second cashier, met her and ushered her inside.

"It's good you're here, Mrs. Whitman," he said, blinking madly, his hands shaking, his spectacles slipping down his nose. "He's going to need you some for a while."

Olivia gasped, but didn't bother to ask what Mr. Colby meant. Before her knelt Doc Chambers, and beside him, a pair of long legs in a familiar pair of brown trousers sprawled out toward her across the floor. She flew to Eli's side.

Her heart leaped into her throat at the sight of the large quantity of pooled blood. "What happened?"

Doc glanced over his shoulder. "By the grace of our Lord, not much, missy. Your man's blessed, indeed. An inch or two lower, and he'd'a been gone already."

Olivia's knees gave way as she crumpled to the floor, her gray skirt puddling around her. She pushed it aside and reached for Eli. He held his hand out to her. They both tightened their grip once they touched.

"Oh, Eli..." Her breath caught again in a sob, while tears fell down her cheeks.

"Hush," he murmured. "Don't cry. Please. I'm going to be fine. Just ask Doc, here." He gave her a crooked grin. "He'll tell you whether you want to hear it, whether you're ready to believe it, or not."

Her eyes ran over his prone body, searching for the source of the bleeding, which she found a short distance above his heart. Her middle twisted, and the nausea rose again.

"How can you say you're going to be fine? Look at all that blood! No one's going to be fine when all his blood's spilled out over the floor." She patted her skirt pocket then pulled out her hanky to dab her flooded eyes. "Just look. Look at the mess, and then tell me again how you're going to be fine."

His middle jerked and his lips widened into a broad smile. "See, Doc? No one's going to believe me. So are you done sewing me up so I can stand and show her I'm fine?"

He was injured and he dared laugh at her? "How—"

"Now, you listen to me, young man," the older gentleman scolded. "I'm the one who'll say when you can get up." He turned to Olivia. "And you, missy, listen to me, too. I'll admit it looks much worse than it is, what with all that blood, but he's going to be fine. That is, he's going to be fine if you both do what I say."

"Anything," she said, her fingers tight around Eli's. "We'll do anything you feel will speed his recovery."

Eli rolled his eyes. "It better not have much to do with lying about like a lazy old cow."

Olivia glared. "You're the one who's hurt. Doc's the one who knows what's best. And I'm the one who's going to make sure you do it."

Her husband's jaw jutted like a block of chiseled rock. "What makes you think you're going to—"

"Well, well, son." Doc Chambers gave a roar of laughter. "Seems to me you've met your match in our little Livvy, here. I can go home and rest now, sure as I am that you'll be doing what's right. I trust that stubborn streak of hers any day, just as I trust your stubborn streak to prod you to try and do whatever you wish. Can't wait to watch the battle."

From where Olivia sat, it looked as though Eli tried to stifle another grin. "I'm doomed," he said. "You've formed a mighty gang of two. You're both gunning for me."

"Now, you listen here, Eli Whitman," Olivia said, taking her hand from his and planting it, as well as her other one, on her hips. "You pay attention to getting well, and I'll pay attention to getting you well. I'll listen to Doc, and you'll do the same. I'm quite experienced with bull-headed, disobedient, mischievous youngsters, as you well know."

Doc Chambers laughed again then rose to stand at Eli's side, a wide hand extended toward the patient. "Let's see if you can get up from there, son."

"Of course, I can, Doc." Eli leaned on his uninjured side to help himself stand. When he rose to his knees, however, he grew lightheaded, visible in his inability to sit upright, and he planted his hands to help support him.

"Oh!" He grimaced at the pain that must have shot straight up his bad arm from the effort.

"No!" Olivia said. "Here. Let me help you."

Doc positioned himself on Eli's injured side, while Olivia took the other. Together, the three of them got him to his feet.

"Not so cocky now, are you?" The doctor sent a chiding look to Eli. "Looks like maybe I might know a thing or two. You listen to me and to your fine lady wife here. It's time to behave and mind your betters."

When Olivia glanced at her husband to see how he took the old doctor's words, she was stunned to see the warmth in his gaze, all of it aimed at her.

"Thank you," he said, his voice quiet, all silliness gone.

Her cheeks heated. "You—you're welcome." Her voice shook. "But I'm not sure what for."

He slipped his arm across her shoulders, then eased her closer. "For coming here. For sassing me into doing what you think is best for me. For loving my children and keeping my house and . . . and just for being you."

Doc Chambers gave them a knowing look. "I'll be right back. See if you can keep yourself upright, Eli. Don't want to see your young lady wife worried about you needlessly."

As he strode away behind one of the cashier's windows, Olivia smiled at her husband. "It's not much, Eli. I haven't done any more than any other woman would have."

He grimaced then shook his head. "Don't be so sure of that. I doubt Victoria would have done half as much."

She blinked at the bitterness in his words. "Oh, surely you're remembering through all the pain of your losses—"

"No, Olivia. I'm speaking as a man who was betrayed by the woman he loved. Believe me. Victoria never thought of anyone besides herself."

Not knowing what to say to that, Olivia stood close to Eli, her arm around his waist to offer her support. She shivered at the intensity in his voice, prayed for the Father's help and blessing as they went forward as husband and wife.

Otherwise, she didn't know if she could live up to the image of her Eli seemed to be building.

Chapter 19

With great care, slow pace, and in spite of his constant objections to their babying, Olivia and Doc Chambers helped Eli go home. It irked to find himself like this, weak as a babe in arms. At least he'd prevented the loss of his customers' funds. It would have been nearly impossible to replace any amount the robber and his lookout accomplice outside might have stolen.

Once he found himself in their welcoming parlor, Eli took a stand. "Look, I'm home now, and as you said, Doc, not at death's door. So please, both of you, enough of this absurd babying." He waved the overzealous physician toward the door. "You can go on now. Especially since you've sicced my own wife on me."

"Now, Eli Whitman," Olivia said, a frown line between her brows, "Doc Chambers did no such thing. I 'sicced' myself on you all on my own. Now we're here, it's time for you to lie down." She gestured toward the sofa. "There. Let's get you comfortable here in the parlor. No need for you to trudge up those stairs while you're injured."

The doctor chuckled again. "I can see you're in excellent hands, son. I'll be heading on back to my place." He turned to Olivia. "And you, missy, you send someone to fetch me if anything—you hear? Anything at all—changes. Right?"

"Absolutely."

Eli scoffed. "Won't happen, Doc. I'm fine."

The older man shook his head on the way to the door. "Oh, for the love of good peach pie! For once, Eli, you should just take off that hard crust of yours and enjoy the sweet filling of life. I'll be back tomorrow morning if all goes well and you don't need me during the night."

Eli knew further objection would net him nothing. As Doc Chambers opened the front door, Olivia took a step forward, away from Eli's side. He had to strain to keep his hands from reaching for her, pulling her back, and drawing her close.

"Let me show you out," she said.

The doctor shook his head and stepped out onto the covered stoop. "Don't bother yourself with me, Livvy. I'm here already."

When the physician closed the door behind him, Olivia turned to face Eli. He saw the color leach from her face as though a hand had run over it, and then a shudder ran through her. Her eyes grew wide as horror distorted her even features.

"Oh, Eli…" She stepped toward him. "I can't stand the thought of what that man did to you. That we might have lost you—"

"Hush," he said, his voice soft and low. He held his arms open wide, in spite of the knife-stabs of pain in his chest at the motion. "Come here."

For a moment, when rosy dabs appeared on her still-white cheeks and she aimed her gaze at the floor, he feared she would turn and run away. But then, to his enormous relief and burst of joy, she stepped up and slipped her arms around him. A fresh new sense of peace poured through his whole body, and he sighed with satisfaction.

Olivia laid her head on his chest as her exhalation echoed his. He closed his eyes to savor their closeness, the sense of belonging, the depth of comfort he drew from her proximity, the pull of attraction he felt for his wife.

Once again, those needles of fear, that impression of *I've-been-through-this-and-barely-survived-it* stabbed through him. And yet, again, his more logical side reminded him how different his new wife was from Victoria, as he had told Olivia about an hour earlier.

She nestled closer, bringing her face right up to the side of his neck. That was when he realized she was crying. The tears, evidence of her feelings for him, moved Eli. He tightened his arm around his wife then leaned his head down to rest on hers.

"I'm fine, Olivia. We're going to be just fine."

Her tears continued for a while. They clung to each other even longer. Something new was forged between them as a result of a bank robber's evil plan. A fragile bond that he came to realize meant the world to him.

Later that night, curled in the armchair Eli used most evenings, Olivia watched her husband sleep on the sofa she'd made up as a bed for him. After the tender moments they'd shared in each other's arms once Doc Chambers had left, she'd spent the rest of the day feeling cherished, treasured, and more like a wife than she had up until then. The day had flown by, even though a cranky Eli had bickered with her over every last detail with which he could take issue. Her robust, normally active husband made an awful patient.

She'd had to call on every drop of her mercy and restraint. And humor.

Still, she'd felt every bit of the changed texture of their relationship. A new closeness and a fragile, deepening bond had begun to bloom where before only polite interaction existed.

"Thank you, Father," she murmured. "I see you answering my prayers for my marriage. Now, when will you see fit to answer the ones for my family's plight?"

Eli groaned. He twisted and turned on the sofa. The blanket slipped off him. His restlessness revealed his failure to find a more restful position, and he moaned again.

Olivia's compassion for her husband deepened, seeing as how there would be no less bothersome way for him to sleep on the moderate-sized piece of furniture. Eli was a tall, broad-shouldered man. The cushions, while the perfect size on which to sit, weren't constructed to provide adequate support to an injured gentleman.

She slipped off the chair and knelt at her husband's side. With light, tender gestures, she smoothed the blanket up over his shoulders and around his back, fluffed his pillow, and tucked it more fully under his head. As she made the adjustments, he smiled, nuzzled her hand, and let out a soft sound that in Olivia's opinion revealed an easing of his previous difficulty.

His eyes opened a sliver. His hand slipped up from under the blanket and took hold of hers. As his eyes closed again, he drew her hand higher to place a kiss on the back. He sighed, and then, slowly, as his breathing grew deep and even again, he whispered, "Olivia..."

Peace settled over her. A smile curved her lips. Gratitude again flooded her, and she gave the Lord thanks—yet one more time—that Eli had been spared in the confrontation at the bank.

Slowly, gently, she tried to remove her hand from his clasp, but at the lightest tug, his fingers twitched, clenched around hers, and she stopped her efforts. Eli seemed to want her at his side right then, and that struck her as mighty fine.

The feelings this man had awakened in her had come as a surprise. She hadn't expected them, even though she'd hoped—prayed—for affection between them. This didn't feel like something as bland as affection. Her heart swelled with foreign emotions, and chills ran through her every time Eli's gaze landed on her.

Other times, she felt flushed, as though she'd run blocks down Main Street, when he grazed her hand. Then the other night, when he'd kissed her, she hadn't been able to fall asleep, treasuring the tender bond they'd forged.

What an amazing gift the Lord had given her with this marriage. She could no longer imagine life without this man in it, near her, holding her close. She hoped and prayed he'd begun to feel at least a little like she did.

With a sigh, she laid her head on the sofa cushion, right next to Eli's. A fresh sense of belonging kindled an ember of hope in her heart, and she relaxed. Warmth and drowsiness struck at the same time. She yawned, surrendered bit by bit to slumber.

So this was what love felt like . . .

By the Tuesday after the attempted robbery, Eli reminded Olivia of a cat intent on fleeing to freedom. He argued, paced, and had the house in an uproar for the most part. For that reason, she didn't object too strenuously when he insisted on going back to the bank. Both Holtwood, who'd only been knocked hard on the head, and Larry Colby, who hadn't been hurt at all, had kept the place open for business in Eli's absence.

After he'd left, she went to the kitchen to work on the day's menu with Cooky. The older woman let out a merry laugh when Olivia walked into the gleaming room.

"Oh, Missus Livvy, I couldn't love that man of yours more than if I'd borne him myself." She rolled her eyes. "But oh, my dearie, anyone with half a teacup of common sense woulda thought we'd stuck him in my nice little wire egg basket and latched the door shut just by looking at him fuss. I gotta tell you"—she wagged her finger—"I'm right glad he's off to work today, I am."

Olivia chuckled. "It's hard to put into words how wonderful it is to have him home evenings and on the weekends. Then, as soon as we brought him home to recover, why...he set my nerves on end, he was so restless."

Cooky nodded. "I loved my Mr. Goodwin to pieces, and I still do all these years since the Lord welcomed him home, but my, my, my! How that man could drive me mad. He got so antsy when he had nothing to keep him busy that he was worse than Luke with his fidgety boy ways, I'll have you know."

"I'm beginning to understand why Mama shoos Papa from the kitchen every morning even though she loves him to bits."

"She's smart, all right, a woman who knows how to keep from going mad."

"Well, for me to keep from going mad, you and I need to get to work now."

The hours sped by for Olivia. She worked on a number of the decorative pieces for the holidays and the Christmas party; she received and paid for the delivery of two sacks of wheat flour she'd ordered at Metcalf's Mercantile; she cut out pieces for the silvery blue, lightweight wool dress she wanted to finish for Randy's Christmas gift now that she'd finished the rose-colored one; and then she hurried to meet the children when school let out.

She enjoyed her daily stroll through town, the opportunity to greet the neighbors she met on her way. Even more, she loved to see the smiles on her children's faces when they saw her waiting for them. Spirited descriptions of the day's events in the schoolroom always accompanied the return home.

Once she had the children settled with their schoolwork, Olivia's thoughts turned to Eli. She began to track the path of the tall case clock's arm across its face. She couldn't help but wonder how her husband had fared on his first day back at work. Anxiety nipped at her, each time sharper, more than ever when she remembered how he had moaned in his sleep the night of the attempted robbery.

Had he struggled with a great deal of pain today?

Would he admit it if he had?

Just when she thought she would explode from fretting over him, the front door opened and his footsteps echoed as he went to the peg rack down the hall to hang his coat. She ran from her room to the top of the stairs and got there before he'd made it up even one step.

"How are you?" she asked, her voice strained even to her own ears. "How is the wound?"

He looked up, and when she caught sight of the twinkle in his blue eyes, she sagged against the newel post. "Well enough that there's no chance I'm going to let you chain me here again when I need to be at the bank."

Olivia was coming to know him and his fondness for teasing better each day. She planted her hands on her hips, fought a smile, and gave him a mock glare. "If you mean that, then don't go giving me any more great ideas, Mr. Whitman. As it is, I might just deposit that one about chains into my bank of notions for future use."

He crossed his arms. "I'd love to see you try to chain me down. You'd have to catch me first."

"I've always been light on my feet—"

"Ah, Mr. Whitman, sir," Cooky said from the doorway to the kitchen. "Looks to me like she's already caught you but good, and *for* good, at that. Can't tell you how happy that makes me."

Eli blinked. He seemed frozen for a moment, and then he glanced back up at Olivia. "Hm…I'm not feeling hog-tied one bit, Cooky. Matter of fact, life has been remarkably peaceful and most enjoyable around here of late."

Olivia's heart gave another of those flips it had turned for the first time back when Eli started to share his evenings with her. These days, that heart of hers seemed to spend its days in a state of dizzying whirls.

A sensation she was coming to appreciate.

"S'what I said," Cooky answered between hearty chuckles. "Things are mighty fine around this house, I tell you. Mighty fine, and I'm praising my good Lord in heaven, I am."

Olivia hadn't taken her gaze from her husband. Neither had he looked away from her. The gleam in his eyes appeared to heighten with every moment that went by. That intensity sent currents of awareness from the top of her head to the ends of her toes, the tips of her fingers.

The night of the attempted bank robbery, Olivia had recognized she'd fallen in love with her husband, with Eli. Could his breath-stealing stare and his heart-warming words mean he was coming to care for her as much? Could he...could he be falling in love with her?

It was her fondest wish.

She prayed it might be true.

"I'll be back down as soon as I wash the day's dust from my face, and pen ink from my fingers," he said as he ascended.

Olivia held her breath as they met in the middle of the stairs. He reached out, placed a gentle finger on her cheek, then ran it down to trace the line of her jaw.

"Soft..." he whispered.

A shiver ran up Olivia's body to spark a fizzy feeling in her head. She felt powerful, all-capable, as towering as a mountain, stronger than steel, invincible. She felt she should respond, but she didn't know if she could get a sound out past her emotion-tightened throat.

She stood tall, and with what she feared might look like a silly grin, she met Eli's gaze. "Thanks..."

He tapped the tip of her chin. "I'll be back. I hope supper's ready. I'm famished!"

As he ran upstairs, she floated down and into the dining room. What an extraordinary moment. She couldn't wait until she and Eli met alone in the parlor once again.

At supper, Olivia couldn't stop stealing glances at her husband, anticipation leaving her a bit impatient with the leisurely pace they always took. Later, once the children had cleared the table and Cooky had taken over the dining room to clean up, she marshaled her family upstairs for their normal evening routine. As soon as Luke finally whispered his "Good night, Mama," she took a moment to smooth her hair, tidy her white blouse into the waist of her skirt and, happier than she'd been in a long while, she sailed into the parlor.

"Come here," Eli said, gesturing her to his side.

Once again, he had a crate on the floor, this one without a cover. Olivia could see wrapping paper crumpled to the top.

"What have you brought home with you tonight?"

"I didn't bring it. Tom Bowen stopped by just as you went upstairs with the children. That's why I took a few minutes before heading to help Luke with his mathematics."

Olivia dropped down onto the elegant deep rose, cream, and black wool rug, close to Eli, smoothing her skirt around her. "Then this must be Luke's Christmas gift."

Eli shot her a grin. "Can't wait to see it, but I wanted to wait for you. I have to say, I didn't expect Tom to finish it so soon."

"He must have rushed to get it done, then. It's only the middle of December. I didn't expect to see the train set until the week before Christmas."

"Exactly. He caught me by surprise."

Olivia gave him a mischievous smile. "So are we to sit here and flatter Mr. Bowen's speedy work or are we going to see the fruits of his labors?"

He chuckled. "I'm not stopping you. Why don't you unwrap the pieces?"

In minutes, they'd hooked the train cars together. For the next while they entertained themselves running the train over the rug's colorful swirls and anticipating Luke's excitement come Christmas morning. Then, reluctantly, they wrapped the pieces and packed them away.

"I can't wait for Christmas morning," Olivia said, leaning on her hands, propped behind her.

"So you like it?" Eli asked, a hint of vulnerability in his voice.

"I love it. I thought you had an excellent idea when you first suggested a train set for Luke. Now that I've seen it finished, I think you know our son quite well."

His smile widened. "Think about it. I was a boy once."

She laughed. "Once? I seem to remember a very restless child recently."

A smoldering light brightened the spectacular blue of his eyes. "A child, huh? I don't think so, Mrs. Whitman."

He leaned closer to Olivia, and before she knew it his arms closed around her and his lips covered hers.

This kiss was something beyond Olivia's wildest imagination. As tender and caring as his earlier caresses had been, this one said her husband was all man, one who saw her as all woman—his woman. The kiss heated, passion soared, and by the time Eli pulled away, Olivia knew their relationship had changed once again.

Heavens! She couldn't catch her breath.

Blinking, she caught sight of Eli's satisfied expression. Before her head quit spinning, he stood. "I'm not about to apologize. I meant to kiss you, and I'm glad I did."

Her jaw gaped. "Well!"

Unsure of what to do, Olivia went for what felt most familiar. She'd been working so steadily on the decorations for the upcoming holidays that she turned and reached for the basket she'd earlier lined with scarlet fabric and was filling with pine cones, a pair of gourds, and balls of tightly wrapped green wool. The gourds had looked wonderful for Thanksgiving dinner, and would be equally appropriate for the more festive Christmas holidays, once she added fresh touches of green and red.

"This will be perfect for the hearth, don't you think?" she asked Eli, proud that her voice didn't shake. Not too much.

"It's very nice." He faced the fireplace. "The mantel will look good if you do what you mentioned before. An evergreen garland will be very festive."

"I plan to weave red ribbons with the greenery."

"Excellent."

They chatted, and the easy friendship that had grown between them overtook the heightened attraction Olivia felt for her husband. They worked on a centerpiece for the table where a number of pristine white candles of varied sizes were the main attraction.

As they worked, thoughts buzzed in Olivia's head. She'd seen the evidence of how fiercely Eli had fought to defend the business he and his father had built, and she couldn't help but wonder about that part of her husband's nature. Was he as ruthless in his work as he was protective? Was the businessman she'd married also the tender, kind, and generous man she saw daily at home? Could Eli, a man who professed to love God, have no regard for Christ's teachings on love and charity? If so, what was to become of her family? Of her?

Her heart told her he didn't have it in him to return his customers' trust with cruelty. Certainly not Eli, the man who'd been betrayed by the woman he'd loved, the wife he'd trusted. He would never betray the farmers.

She saw him with his children, with Cooky, she knew how

he treated her. Even before they'd begun to grow close, he'd offered her everything that belonged to him—except the bank, of course. He'd withheld nothing, not his lovely home, not his safe and secure buggy, not his horse, or his money. He'd turned his account at Metcalf's Mercantile over to her.

The more she thought about the situation, the more certain she grew that something was wrong, that Eli would never have done anything so out of character. The man she'd come to love would never turn her family, or any other family, from their home in the winter.

Even so, she'd seen the letter Papa had received. The letter had been written. She'd seen Eli's signature. How had that happened?

Could it have been another instance of forgery, as Victoria had done before? If so, who had done it? Who had access to the bank customers' information?

The men who worked for him, of course. But which one would do such a thing? She'd learned from Eli that only one was a new employee. Had that newcomer taken it upon himself to—to what? Harm strangers? That made no more sense than to think Eli could have done it. What would be the point?

The only way for her to help would be if she could find a way to talk it over with Eli. Could the blooming relationship between them mean she could ask now about the foreclosures?

Nerves made her stomach tighten, and she turned to silent prayer.

She didn't see an opportunity where she could ask. So she spent the rest of the time telling herself that suspecting Eli of such a thing was foolish. That Eli was the man who played with his son's train set, who helped his wife with frivolous decorations for an upcoming party, the man who teased her and held her and kissed her senseless. The rest of the evening flew by in a pleasant blur.

When the stately, tall case clock in the entrance chimed eleven times, Olivia's nervousness returned. How was she going to say good night to him? How were they going to part after that spectacular kiss? After his outrageous statement afterward?

In the end, Eli took over. He reached for her hand, and they went up the stairs together. At the landing, he turned, wrapped his arms around her, and kissed her again.

This kiss told Olivia, in no uncertain terms, that her husband, the man who'd captured her heart, was staking his claim. His passion left no doubt about his desire for her. He wanted her. For more than a convenient solution to a household problem.

He wanted a wife—his wife.

He wanted her.

When his lips lifted a fraction from hers, she sighed, a smile widening her mouth. He kissed her again. And again.

Then, without any warning, he swept her off her feet. He grunted from the strain on his chest.

"Eli, have you lost your mind?"

"It's not my mind I've lost." He strode down the short upstairs hall. "It's my sanity. And my heart."

He kicked open his bedroom door, shoved it closed behind them, and then placed her on his bed. Her wedding night had finally arrived. Months after the ceremony.

That night, she and Eli became husband and wife.

In every way.

Chapter 20

On Monday, Olivia floated down the stairs and sailed through her regular routine on a cloud of happiness. Her heartbeat sped like a galloping pony each time she saw Eli. Her skin sizzled every time they grazed each other as they crossed paths, and her breath hitched each time he looked her in the eye, smiled, then gave her a private wink.

Each shiver of joy left her anticipating their next meeting, their next conversation, and their next kiss. She caught herself more than once about to start spinning happy circles like a little girl, celebrating the fresh, new love she couldn't quite contain.

Not that she wanted to contain it.

Tuesday's only change was ever greater joy.

Wednesday, still more.

Olivia wondered if married life would keep getting better, if it could possibly bring her more contentment and delight. She didn't think so, and she thanked the Father for blessing her with a husband like Eli. She thanked Him for the wonder she'd found in the clear affection Eli showed her in his caresses, in their conversations that lasted into the wee hours of the night, her head on his shoulder, his arms secure around her, in their sweet but brief honeymoon. She prayed for it to never end.

Eli whistled as he walked to work on Monday. Although it had dawned a chilly, windy December morning, the glowing love in his heart held the outside cold at bay. He never could have imagined this turn of events. Still, he wouldn't say falling in love with his wife was anything but wonderful. Olivia... well, she had been the most delightful, unexpected surprise from the first day they met.

Now? A man couldn't ask for more.

As he loped up the bank steps, he realized he was happy—happier than he'd been in years.

He prayed it lasted for the rest of his life.

He also prayed her large family would continue to conduct themselves in the manner in which they had so far. While the Moores had been nothing but charming the times they'd met, Eli couldn't shake his concern.

He prayed for the Father's protection. Not only had he suffered from Victoria's treachery, but his children had also been deeply hurt by their mother's selfish, criminal actions. This time, he prayed the Lord would bless them with the peace, love, and joy all the Father's children were meant to have in their lives.

For his children's sake.

And for the sake of his mending heart.

Olivia had come to mean the world to him. He much

preferred to look forward to the joys he hoped to live through in the years to come with her at his side.

He was a man in love.

Later that morning, Eli called Holtwood and Colby into his office. "So tell me. What have you found? Any update on properties we might purchase for the bank? The railroad's plans for the spur line are moving along quite speedily."

Colby reached for the nearest armchair and, when he tried to drag it closer to Eli's desk, it caught on the edge of the rug. As he moved to lift it over, the papers and ledgers he'd carried in slipped from his grasp. When he tried to catch them, the pencil he'd tucked behind his ear flew off and rolled across the polished wooden floor.

Eli glanced at Holtwood, who sat in the other chair in front of Eli's desk, his fingers laced together. Eli had rarely known two more different men, and yet, both were still excellent employees.

In his newfound serenity, Eli felt more inclined toward indulgence for his nervous-Nellie cashier than he otherwise would, just as he found more patience for his reserved and somewhat distant right-hand man. He donned a smile and waited for Colby to gather his belongings and settle down in his chair.

After an awkward hunt on hands and knees for his pencil, which Colby found had rolled under the corner of Eli's desk, he finally took his seat.

Holtwood watched the whole episode with no particular expression.

"Oh, dear me, sir," Colby said. "I'm so sorry." He jabbed

his spectacles up to the bridge of his nose as usual, and in the process made the ever-present ink smudge a shade darker. At Eli's shrug, he went on. "Yes, well," he cleared his throat, "we have taken the liberty to look into some areas that would seem the most suitable for a superb railroad track. I've now flagged them on the new map we received of Hope County."

"Splendid!" Eli held out a hand, but Colby only stared at it. Eli waited, then said, "Could I see the map, please?"

For a moment, Eli feared his anxious assistant would bolt up and out of the office. But Colby just blinked, one...two... three more times. He gave Eli a jerky bob of the head before he sat up straight, wound even tighter than before.

"I left it on Colby's desk," Holtwood said.

Colby cleared his throat. "Indeed, Mr. Whitman, sir. I'll be certain to bring it to you once we've closed up the banking lobby and counted the cash at our windows this afternoon."

Eli gestured at the sheets of paper the cashier had dropped all over the floor. "It's not one of those?"

"No, sir, regretfully. I thought I should update you on the prices I've been privileged to discuss so far with a number of the property owners before I showed you the map. I mean... begging pardon, of course—if you do not consider those sums agreeable, why, I would search elsewhere for the bank's sake. I do know, however, that as profitable as the sums under consideration might be, we can do better still, Mr. Whitman."

"Better?"

"We've had opportunity to meet with some of the farmers," Holtwood offered, his voice calm, his expression cool and unruffled. "I had Colby and Parham work on these lists for you."

"You got this far?" Eli asked. "Just from a handful of letters?"

Holtwood nodded. "The letters opened up the conversation, and landowners are anxious about their future."

Colby's red hair quivered as he nodded in earnest. "Indeed, Mr. Whitman. It was a matter of diligent investigation. You see, I learned during my inquiries that many of these lands are those of property owners on the brink of selling out. They need the cash we could pay them. It—" He gestured broadly and his spectacles slid down his nose again. He shoved them back up. "So sorry, Mr. Whitman. It's just a matter of...ah... uhm—working...er...them." He winced and shook his head—"working *with* them."

Eli rubbed the spot on his right temple where a headache had begun to take root. By now, Colby's flustered conversation and mannerisms had become tiring. If only he weren't so efficient in his work and always reliable. At least, usually.

"I can see how much you and Holtwood have done about all this already. Good. I suppose we'll be best served if we wait until later so you can show me what you have. Don't forget. The men from the railroad will arrive here in little less than a week and a half."

The warning only served to make Colby even more jittery. His eyes burst into a blinking storm. The stack of papers slithered off his lap. He caught it, but as he looked down, the pencil fell out from behind his ear again. Eli called upon all his patience not to suggest the man keep his pencil elsewhere. He did not want to make his cashier's jumpiness any worse.

Holtwood stood and headed for the office door. "Oh, for goodness' sake."

"Why don't you both go ahead and tend to the customers in the lobby? I'll see you back here later."

Holtwood dipped his head. "Thank you, sir."

More of the usual squirrelly crawling over the floor ensued until Colby had retrieved all his belongings. He then nodded toward Eli and left the office, closing the door as he went.

When his cashiers walked out, Eli breathed a prayer for the men. He hoped the Father had a lovely lady in store for each man's future. It would do them a world of good, would probably bring them the peace and comfort that would begin to ease one's fretfulness and the other's aloofness. The joy Eli had found with Olivia was something everyone should experience.

A smile curved his lips, and he leaned back in his chair, arms crossed across his chest. Closing time wouldn't come soon enough for him.

As the sun outside Eli's office window began to set, a knock came at the door. "Come in, come in!"

This time, Colby carried only a small map and a pen. As always, he wore the frameless—and hapless—spectacles. Eli hoped his cashier had settled down since their earlier meeting, certainly now that the work day had come to a close.

"Let's see," he said. "Spread out the map here on my desk, and you can show us what you have."

Colby tucked his pen behind his ear, streaking ink across his temple to match the smear on the side of his nose. He spread the map on the desk, knocking a ledger over the edge.

"So sorry, sir."

Eli waved away the apology. "Go on, Colby. Show me what you have."

"Of course, of course, Mr. Whitman." He tapped four of the red marks, marks that drew a rough line through the area. "These are the ones I believe we can pick up the fastest—and as excellent bargains."

Studying the indicated properties, Eli couldn't quite make sense of what his assistant saw in those particular tracts. "I don't understand. They're not even next to each other. How do you reckon the railroad can use them?"

Colby shook his head, a finger on his glasses. "No, no, sir. These are just the beginning. We start here, since these are the folks who most need the money. Then we move on to negotiate the adjacent properties, sir."

Eli turned to the map again. If he wasn't much mistaken, one of the properties belonged to the Roberts family. The last thing he'd heard, Hugh Roberts had been forced to sell off some, if not all, their sheep, after losing most of their crops the last two years.

But if Eli remembered correctly, they had mortgaged the property so the funds would see them through the coming winter. The family was looking forward to a fresh start in the spring, and paying back the balance on their loan in as short a time as possible.

He scratched his chin. "Are you sure they're looking to sell, Colby? I was under the impression that Hugh wanted to work the land with his five boys, to leave them a legacy. I don't understand."

Colby shrugged. "I wouldn't know for certain, sir. Folks do change their minds. I suppose that might be the case with the Roberts. I just know what I told you."

Eli studied the map some more, unease tightening his stomach. Something didn't quite sit right with him. Then another detail caught his attention. "I do know some of these farms and ranches have gone through tough times, but the others? Those unmarked spreads mixed in among the ones with the red marks? I can't imagine any of these men would be willing to sell their land. Not for any sum."

Holtwood walked in. "Not yet, I'm sure. If some of their neighbors, who've faced the same disasters, consider selling, it's likely they'll do the same once they see others freed from financial fear."

"Yes, yes," Colby said. "A—and…" He snapped his spectacles off as they started to slip and used the bits of wire and glass to gesture. "We haven't yet begun to tell them how they'll benefit from selling out."

"I'm not sure I see how they'll benefit at all. Not from leaving their homes with nothing but a pile of cash in their pockets."

"Cash goes a long way, Mr. Whitman," Holtwood offered.

"Always has, always does," Colby agreed.

"Not if a man has children to raise."

"Oh," Colby said. "Well. I suppose there is that."

"Tell you what," Eli said. "What if we look at an unmarked map first? Then perhaps we can identify a logical route for the railroad folks to lay the tracks. Only after we figure that out should we look into the property owners' financial circumstances. I can't see how I can do anything that might take advantage of our neighbors."

"Of course, sir." The head cashier folded up the map.

With pen and his spectacles clutched in his fists, Colby

headed for the office door. "Whatever you say, Mr. Whitman. You're the boss!"

Sometimes Holtwood got ahead of himself in his efforts to please Eli. As did Colby. It was something he would have to discuss with them at some point in the near future. But it wouldn't be that night. That night he had a terrific family waiting for him, and a beautiful new wife he couldn't wait to see again.

Time to pack up and head on home.

Eli locked up his desk and pocketed the key. He donned hat, coat, and wool muffler, then, whistling again, strode into the banking lobby. As he approached the door, however, he heard the unmistakable sound of an escalating argument. To his surprise, and unless he was much mistaken, Parham, the new secretary, was one of the men involved.

No, it was not a surprise. It was a shock! Eli never would have thought Parham capable of such behavior.

He hurried to the front door. "What is the problem here, gentlemen?"

Startled, Parham nearly stumbled off the stairs. He clutched the banister to right himself on the landing.

Down on the sidewalk, Wilbur Ruskin spun and glared. "Of all men, Whitman, *you* should know—"

"It's fine, Mr. Whitman," Parham said. "I've spoken with Mr. Ruskin, and I'm sure either Mr. Holtwood or Mr. Colby—or I—can take care of the matter. No need for you to give it another thought, not this soon after your injury..."

The farmer glared again, then, as he muttered under his breath, he stomped off. Before he got too far, he paused. "You better do that, young man," he snarled. "I'm holding you to your word."

Out of the corner of an eye, Eli saw Parham swallow hard. "Let's talk again in the morning, shall we, Mr. Ruskin? We'll resolve this then."

"Don't fret another minute, Wil," Eli told the angry man who'd resumed his stomping pace. "My men will take good care of you. They're good men, decent, hardworking, and trustworthy. If Parham says they'll handle the matter, well then, I'm satisfied they will."

Ruskin kept on going, but before he got too far, he gave a dismissive wave then spat out a scoffing "Bah!"

Eli felt the urge to go after his customer, but he knew this wasn't the right time. Wil Ruskin needed to calm his temper. Besides, if Parham assured him he would handle Ruskin's problems, he felt his new secretary would do just that. If not him, then either Holtwood or Colby would. Eli's father had taught him the importance of leadership and delegating responsibility. He had said he'd learned the hard way he could not effectively manage every detail himself as the bank grew. With the railroad representatives due to arrive so soon, time was even more of a luxury for all of them.

"Whatever happens tomorrow, Parham, please see that you consider every possible option to help Wilbur settle the situation to his best advantage. We always aim to satisfy our customers as best we can."

"Of course, sir. We'll offer him every alternative available to us. No need to waste another thought on the matter at this present moment." He sent Eli a quick flash of teeth, something he assumed the man meant as a smile. "I'm sure you don't want to be late getting home to your family."

Eli's earlier calm returned. "You're right about that. I must tell you, Parham. Family life is a joy. Especially when a man is blessed with a good woman at his side. I'm sure you'll see what I mean when you find a wife and settle down with her."

For a moment, a twinge of longing crossed the secretary's face, but it was gone just as quickly. "I suspect you're right, Mr. Whitman. Haven't found the right lady so far. I mean to keep on looking."

"You do that. Now, I'm going to take you up on your suggestion. I'm going home to Mrs. Whitman, our youngsters, and Cooky's supper. I'll see you in the morning."

"Bright and early."

As was his habit, Eli locked up. Although he and Parham had decided on the plan of action with regard to Ruskin, something still didn't sit right with him. But no matter how many ways he turned the facts over in his mind, he couldn't put a finger on it. Still, he was sensible enough to realize he wouldn't do anyone any good by fretting about things. He'd have to remember to ask Holtwood about Ruskin's specific circumstances in the morning. Surely they would come up with a solution that satisfied everyone.

Feeling somewhat better, he accelerated his pace. He couldn't wait to be back with his family.

He couldn't wait to get home to Olivia.

Chapter 21

On Saturday evening, Olivia nestled closer to Eli on the sofa in the parlor. She'd put away Randy's dress-in-the-making, and Eli had set the book he'd been reading on the small walnut side table to his left. For a while, they watched the fire burn down in the hearth, sipping the hot cocoa she'd made as a change to their coffee and tea routine. The peace in the room was a balm to her spirit and a boost to her courage.

She'd decided to ask Eli about the foreclosures that night. She couldn't in good conscience put it off any longer.

As soon as Eli set down his empty cup, Olivia breathed a prayer for courage, for wisdom, and for the right words to say. She also prayed the Lord would soften her husband's heart and turn it into fertile ground for her questions.

A tremor of fear shook her. She didn't want anything to mar the beauty of the love now growing between them, the happiness she treasured at his side. But it was now or never, and her family's fate would turn bleak if she chose the latter.

"Eli?"

"Mm-hm..."

"Could I ask you something?"

He turned partway at her side, curiosity in his expression, the fingers of his right hand drawing tender patterns on her shoulder. "This sounds serious."

Another pang of apprehension shot through her. "I'm afraid it is."

Concern drew his dark brows together and his finger stopped, frozen in place. "Are you unwell? Is it about the children? What's wrong?"

Oh, Lord Jesus, help me through this. "It's about my family. A business matter."

If she'd seared him with a hot branding iron, he wouldn't have reacted any worse. He bounded to his feet, darts seemed to shoot from his eyes, disgust twisted his mouth into a grimace. But he didn't speak. He merely stared at Olivia, waiting for her next words.

She swallowed against the sudden dryness in her mouth. This wasn't going the way she'd hoped and prayed it would, but rather the way she'd feared it might. After all, he had warned her. More than once.

But she had a responsibility to her family. She couldn't just quit and take the easy road. She had to talk to Eli.

Olivia stood and smoothed her skirt over her hips. Facing the man she loved, she took a deep breath. "Papa told me about the letter he received from you—from the bank—asking for—"

"Enough, Olivia." Eli's voice was deadly soft, his hand held out in an unmistakable gesture of refusal. If she'd feared a shouting outburst, she'd been much mistaken. He wasn't that kind of man. He continued in a voice a notch above a whisper. "Before you agreed to marry me I made clear to you that I would not tolerate any interference with my business affairs. While I realize our relationship has changed, the line I drew hasn't moved. Now you're trying to cross it, and I must stop you. My business remains my business. Nothing you should insert yourself into, nothing for you to question or challenge."

"But, my family—"

"No."

This time, while his voice remained soft, it had an icy, sharp edge to it, and it sliced through Olivia's emotions. A knot formed in her throat and tears burned her eyelids. But she refused to let Eli see how deeply his rejection hurt her.

"Very well. I understand you still only want me as your wife for the purpose of serving you. I'm still not someone you cherish, much less respect, not someone with whom you intend to become one...as our vows stated, as I thought we'd begun to do."

"It's not like that at all. We had an arrangement, an agreement. You accepted it, and I expect you to keep to your word. If you think about it, I've been scrupulous about keeping the worries of work far from the comforts of home. The bank does not concern you one bit. Please make sure you keep it that way."

She turned her back to him and stared at the still-glowing embers of the dying fire. "I understand what you're asking of me, Eli, and I do keep my word. I was raised to honor my commitments. I...I will do my best to continue to live by that agreement."

And to bury my dreams and wishes for a true marriage.

The tears began to flow then, and she clinched her hands at

her waist. As though hanging on for dear life, she twisted her fingers, made herself draw breath...exhale...repeat the pattern. She also refused to turn around and show him the depth of her distress.

"Olivia—"

"I gave you my word, Eli. There's nothing more I can say. Please...please go now."

The absolute silence that followed her request spoke volumes about his reluctance to do as she'd asked. But then, just as she felt a cry of pain rising up inside her, his footsteps, heavy, plodding, utterly unlike his usual firm and decisive tread, headed for the door.

Moments later, those steps made their way up the stairs. When his bedroom door closed, she brought her knuckles to her mouth to muffle the moan that broke through.

A series of shudders shook her. Her knees refused to hold her. She wilted down into her skirts, the thick wool rug cushioning her fall. She didn't know how long she sat there, as soft sobs wracked her, and a depth of loneliness she'd never before known settled in, bit by bit by bit.

How could the man who'd loved her so tenderly now thrust her away, as though she were worth no more than an emptied flour sack? Still...she loved Eli.

Obviously, he didn't love her in kind. He hadn't ever listened to what she had to say. He had no intention of sharing his whole life with her, only those parts he...what? Dared?

What was holding him back? Why couldn't he trust her?

Was he comparing her to Victoria? Or was there something about Olivia that had proved objectionable to him?

What was she going to do?

Right then? Not much. Hours crawled past. She wept herself tearless. Still, two truths remained.

First, she loved her husband.

Second, she didn't know how she would continue to live with the man he was proving to be.

Eventually, with a broken heart, she went upstairs to her old room, the one with the adequate but small and lonely bed, the one now empty of even a trace of her presence.

She'd been a fool to marry within Eli's boundaries.

He'd been a fool. He'd known all along what the chances were. Time had proved him right. It was just like before. Victoria had done the same. Starting innocently, asking a question now and then, a few months after they were married, and becoming increasingly involved, along with her family. Making suggestions, offering to help him, to ease his burden...

Now Olivia had tried to insert herself into bank matters, and for the sake of her family. He didn't know her reasons or what she'd been after. That she'd tried at all was enough. Enough to prove himself vulnerable to the possibility of ruin again.

Eli paced the length of his room, turning the matter over in his mind. He couldn't lose Olivia. As long as he kept her separate, as long as he didn't let her become even slightly involved, she couldn't do any harm. Everything would be fine between them, just as it was. How could he make her understand that? What was he going to do?

Now that he'd fallen in love again.

*　　*　　*

The next morning, Olivia went through the motions of getting ready for church. When she heard Eli go downstairs, she gathered fresh clothes from among the items she'd moved to their—*his* room, dressed, urged the children to hurry, and barely nibbled a bite or two of toast at breakfast. She knew she wasn't at her best.

On her way out, when she glanced at the mirror in the entry hall, she cringed. But there wasn't much she could do about the dark smudges under her eyes or the faint redness in the eyes themselves. At least her nose didn't look like a red beacon anymore.

Then there was the bone-deep weariness. It seemed almost more than she could bear to take step after step after step toward the church. Her leather-bound Bible felt as though it weighed more than those sacks of flour she'd ordered for the Christmas dinner party.

During the service, she stood to sing the morning's chosen hymns like a puppeteer's marionette. When she sat back down, she needed all her determination to keep from crumpling into a heap and maintain a semblance of self-respect. Not only did she not want Eli to see the effect his rejection had on her, but she also wanted to keep the town from noticing something amiss between them.

To her embarrassment, she couldn't focus on Reverend Alton's sermon. In spite of her efforts otherwise, her mind turned to the state of her marriage time and time again. Soon, she gave in to her unruly thoughts, and turned them into prayers. As the pastor droned on, she prayed for her marriage, for Eli, for the farmers, for her parents, and for the Father's will in the matter of the foreclosures.

Although she believed the Lord heard her prayers, and she took the Bible seriously when it urged believers to ask in order that they might receive, she couldn't overcome her restlessness, her anxiety, her fear for her family's plight.

When Reverend Alton asked the congregation to rise for the closing prayer and hymn, she felt the first glimmer of something other than the crushing pain of betrayal. She felt the urge to hurry back home as soon as possible. She didn't want to face her mother's perceptive stare. There was no way she could hide her misery from Elizabeth Moore, not even if she'd worn the empty flour sack over her head.

As the last note of the hymn faded, she turned and placed a hand on Randy's shoulder. "Let's go, dear. I'm sure the pot of whatever Cooky left simmering on the stove is full of goodness. I must admit, I'm feeling hollow right about now."

It was true. She did feel hollow, but it wasn't due to hunger. Instead, she felt as though Eli had torn a part of her right out from her deepest self. Olivia didn't need to elaborate for her daughter. Time enough for Randy to learn about heartbreak years from now, when she was older, much, much older. Maybe, if the Lord had mercy on the young girl, she wouldn't have to experience anything like what Olivia was going through.

While she managed to get the children outside in record time, she didn't get far. The woman she'd most wanted to avoid ambushed her.

"Livvy!" her mother called out. "How are you this morning?"

Olivia drew a deep breath. "Fine, Mama. We're all very well."

Her sisters rushed to her side, each one chattering about a dozen things. Then her brothers arrived, each with a story to tell. Finally, Papa strolled to Olivia's side, hugged her, and placed a kiss on her forehead. The familiar gesture touched the hurt corners of her heart, and tears threatened to flow.

Her brothers and sisters, together with Luke and Randy, left after a few minutes, all six of them talking and laughing and looking for additional friends. Olivia was left alone with her parents.

Before they could ask the question she wanted to avoid, Eli arrived. He greeted her parents, his voice chillier than she'd ever heard it. Clearly, he hadn't thawed since the night before. Swallowing again became difficult. Moments later, he stepped away, ending the awkward silence after the initial greetings.

Mr. Roberts, Papa's friend, approached as Eli walked off, a somber expression on his weather-beaten face.

"'Morning, folks. I don't reckon you've heard the news yet, so I figured I'd best tell you before it turns into some kind of tall tale. My missus, our boys, and I are packing it in. We've family back in Iowa, and they're looking forward to us returning. They can use help on the farm, and there's nothing much to hold us here anymore."

"But, Hugh," Papa said, his face pale despite his healthy tan. "Surely you're not about to just give up. Didn't you tell me you felt led here to work the land? Don't you trust the Lord to see you through?"

Mr. Roberts shrugged. "What if all I did was mistake my own wants for the Father's leading?"

Papa's hands fisted but he kept his expression calm and his voice quiet. "What if you're turning and running just as He's about to work it all out?"

"I don't know, Stephen. It could be, but I can't put my wife through this trouble, all these worries and difficulties, any longer. Plus my boys need to have a way to make a living.

They're of an age where they'll soon be looking for young ladies to marry, and we have nothing much left here. Not now that the bank's coming after the land. You and the good Lord both know I don't have the money to pay the mortgage. I would need a miracle, and soon."

He stared at the sky, at the church, and Olivia saw him swallow hard a time or two. Then he faced Papa again. "Whitman knew I wouldn't have cash until I sold off my harvest." He nodded toward her. "Begging pardon, Missus Whitman. No disrespect meant for your man."

Olivia froze. No matter how hard she tried, she couldn't come up with a response. She struggled to nod and look anywhere but at her parents. She knew only too well what was running through their minds.

She couldn't report the dreadful results of her efforts the night before.

"At any rate," Mr. Roberts added, "Whitman and I had agreed he'd take what I could scrape up each month until the harvest. We'd planned to settle accounts then. But that letter I got—we all got—changed everything. I can't pay back that mortgage by Christmas. So before the weather turns really sour I'd like to be on our way back to Iowa. Storms on the plains can be brutal, and they come at their worst right after the holidays."

Mrs. Roberts strode up. "Have you told them, Hugh?"

"Of course, Ella. They know now."

"Well, then," Mama's dear friend said, more subdued than Olivia had ever heard the bubbly woman sound. "There's no point drawing this all out. It's best if we say our farewells fast, like ripping a crusty bandage from a sore wound."

Olivia winced at the lady's words. As the two couples

embraced and urged each other to hold on to courage born of faith, Randy called out to her.

"Mama! Are you ready to go home? Luke's hungry."

"I'll be right there, dear. Just saying good-bye." Olivia hurried through her hugs to prevent any further sadness. She had all she could handle at the moment.

The matter of the foreclosures was wrong. No matter what Eli said, she couldn't just stand by and let him ruin all those lives, not after he'd reached agreements like the one with Mr. Roberts. That didn't sound like the Eli she knew. Her husband was an honorable man, not a cruel, parsimonious miser. He would never dangle a carrot before a customer, then yank it back. Never.

She believed that from the bottom of her heart.

Nothing about the foreclosure nightmare made any sense. There had to be something she could do. Even if he refused to hear her out. Even if it meant the death of her marriage after she was done.

She knew the difference between right and wrong, had to face herself in the mirror every morning.

She had to face God into eternity.

Her heavenly Father would have to show her the way.

After a miserable Monday and Tuesday, Olivia couldn't stand the overwhelming loneliness, the sadness, and the sense of loss any longer. On Wednesday morning, when she left the children at the schoolhouse, she decided to visit Addie Tucker and her sweet baby Josh. The two of them would provide the kind of distraction she needed.

After the first short while, when both women enjoyed the

little one's coos and smiles, they sat to cups of tea in the parlor while he slept.

"Now that you know how the new mama and son are doing," Addie said, "why don't you tell me how the newly-weds are?"

Olivia's tea sloshed over the side of the cup, and she had to set it down before she spilled it all over herself. "Um…well, like… ah…newlyweds, I suppose." Her blood felt chilled, but her cheeks blazed. "We're adjusting to each other as best as possible."

Addie arched a brow. "That's not the most resounding endorsement for married life I've ever heard."

"It has its ups and downs, as I'm sure you know."

"True enough, but right now, I would have to say it strikes me as though…well, you seem to be in a very deep one of those downs."

In spite of Olivia's most determined effort, a sob broke from her throat and tears flowed. Horrified by her inability to handle the situation any better, she covered her face with her hands, and just let the emotion take her.

In a flash, Addie came to her side, draped her arm around Olivia's shoulders. She didn't say a word, but rather just held her. At the easy acceptance, Olivia only wept harder, her wounded heart hungry for the comfort of friendship and the gift of mercy.

Addie pulled Olivia's head down on her shoulder. "Go on, Livvy. Let the hurt out. You know you're safe here with me."

She did. Although she'd thought she'd cried herself dry on Saturday evening, and then again yesterday after she'd said her good nights to the children, she was stunned to realize that her aching eyes could still produce floods of tears at the snap of a finger.

Eventually, though, she lifted her head, sick of her misery. She shoved a hand into the pocket of her skirt and withdrew a hanky. She dabbed away the tears, patted her nose, and finally dragged up the courage to meet Addie's gaze.

"I'm so sorry," she said, her voice gravelly.

"Oh, hush, Olivia. I do remember you telling me not so long ago that you wouldn't be much of a friend if you didn't take care of my little one and me when I could no longer do so. What kind of friend would I be if I wouldn't come to your side when you're so sad?"

"But that's different—"

"No, it's not. The actual event might be different, but Scripture calls us to bear each other's burdens. It doesn't describe which burdens we're to carry for another."

"But—"

"I've known you too long now, Livvy, and you're not going to change the subject by cooking up an argument. Something has upset you more than anything I've known to trouble you before. I can't make you tell me what's bothering you, but I can promise you'll feel better once you let it all out. Plus, I can assure you I'll never breathe a word about it to anyone."

"Of course, you wouldn't Addie. It's not you, it's me. And . . . it's private. And embarrassing."

"And it has everything to do with your husband."

She drew in a sharp breath. "I can't dishonor him, Addie. You must understand."

"As if I'd ever ask that of you."

"You're right. You haven't. You wouldn't. It's just that I don't want to put him in a poor light."

"Your tears have done that, all on their own. He's done

something that's hurt you. I don't have to go too far to figure that out."

Then, because Olivia couldn't hold it in any longer, and because in a corner of her mind she knew she needed perspective, she told Addie the story of her marriage. She didn't like shattering the notion Addie had of her romantic, whirlwind courtship and wedding, but it couldn't be helped. It took a very short time to tell it all.

For a moment, the two women remained silent. Then Addie shook her head. "Well. I never would have imagined such a thing. I can understand his experience with Victoria would leave scars, and it was quite a scandal. I'm surprised you didn't know about it. I thought everyone in Hope County had heard."

Olivia shrugged. "I've never been one to mind others' business. I had plenty to keep me busy out at home."

"I'm not a nosy woman, either, but I heard about it at a church social, I think it was."

"At church socials, I usually spend my time making sure everyone one has plenty to eat," Olivia chuckled. "Doesn't leave me much time to chat—or gossip."

Addie leaned back, both hands raised shoulder height, palms out toward Olivia. "Whoa, there! I'm no one's gossip. And you know it. I'm just saying the matter of Victoria's criminal family was well known around these parts."

"I understand."

"I hope so." Addie stood and crossed her arms. "I also hope you'll listen to me. There is something wrong about Eli's stubborn refusal to listen. Especially since he's the one who created the problem. I never would have thought him the kind of man to go back on a business agreement. Then, for him to hold you to that same kind of agreement? No one's ever called him a hypocrite, and hypocrisy is what it all smells of. Something is wrong, Livvy, and I'm not sure it's a matter of a man who's changed his mind on a deal. Something stinks as bad as horse droppings on Main Street in late August."

Olivia wrinkled her nose at the image. "So I'm not making too much of this?"

"Not unless there's something you've left out."

She shook her head. "No, I've told you everything."

"Well, then. There's nothing more to be said. You must find out what is going on. Then you have to find a way to make Eli listen to you. You're not being unreasonable. He is. This is a serious matter. It could mean the difference between someone's life or their death."

"That, Addie, is what I most fear."

"Then you know what you have to do. One way or another."

"One way or another."

"I'll be praying for you."

As would she. Only God could work this out.

Chapter 22

Later that week, as Olivia strung berry chains and cheery red ribbons onto the evergreen garlands she planned to hang at the dining room ceiling, the doorknocker clapped against its brass plate.

She stood. "I'll be happy to see who that is, Cooky. I know you're busy. Don't bother coming out."

When she opened the door, the sight of her father on the porch sent a pang of alarm through her. "Oh, no! What's happened? Who's hurt?"

"Why is it, Olivia, that every time I come to your home, you immediately think it's for a disaster?"

She took a long, slow breath. "Because both times you've come alone I've recognized that look of worry on your face. Over the years, I've grown to know it more than well."

With a crooked smile, he gestured toward the door. "Will you let me come inside?"

"Oh, dear me. Of course, Papa. Come in, come in."

As they stepped into the entry hall, she took her father's coat and hat, then led him into the parlor. She laid the coat over the back of Eli's chair and set the hat on the seat.

"Please join me on the sofa," she said. "We can be comfortable while we visit."

When both were seated on the plum velvet piece, Papa studied his work-roughened hands for a moment before he dragged his gaze back to meet Olivia's stare.

"I must confess," he said. "I'm here not only to see you, but because I also have something important to discuss with you."

Olivia's stomach plummeted. "Oh, Papa..."

"Let me explain, dear." He took her hand. "While I can't tell you where I learned this—you know I would never betray a friend's confidence, right?"

At her nod, he went on. "I have learned that there's something shady about the letters we received from the bank. It has everything to do with that railroad spur line your husband's been working to bring to Bountiful."

Olivia's thoughts raced. Unfortunately, the race came to an end at an unsavory spot. Before she voiced her newest fear, she wanted to make sure she understood what her father was trying to say.

"First came negotiations to bring a railroad to town," she said. "A rail line that will need a great deal of land to run track. Then came the letters calling in mortgages the owners can't pay."

She paused and her father nodded.

"The railroad will buy that land," she added, "and one would expect them to want to buy it for as good a price as possible. Good from their perspective, of course."

Stephen Moore nodded again. "Don't forget, Livvy. The bank is in business to make money."

"Oh, I haven't lost track of that, Papa. Not one bit." Dread burned in her gut again. "What better way to offer the railroad land at the best possible price, while at the same time making the best possible profit for the bank, than to force struggling landowners off their property?"

"That's my fear."

The ever-present tears welled up in her eyes again. "How could Eli do such a thing? How could a man face God when he was capable of something so evil?"

"That, dear, is what I thought, too. That is, until I learned that Eli might not be the one who's behind this. The man who told me this information is certain someone else has been acting on his own. That person would have to be someone who stands to gain by swindling not just the farmers, but the bank and your husband as well."

The tiniest hint of hope lit up in her heart. Caution restrained her enthusiasm. "How could Eli not know about this? I saw his signature at the bottom of that letter you showed me."

"I don't know how it's happening, but there is the chance that someone got him to sign the letters without his noticing what they really were about."

Thinking back on his determination to never be a victim of a criminal's actions, Olivia couldn't give that possibility too much weight. "Never. Eli's too meticulous for that. He wouldn't sign anything he hadn't read. With great care, too."

"Don't say never, my Livvy-girl. All it takes is a determined crook, and one who knows his victim well."

"It's also possible someone forged his signature. I suspected that earlier. That means it must be someone close to him."

A slow nod from her father tightened the knot in Olivia's middle. "But, Papa. I can't see anyone at the bank doing that to Eli. True, I don't know everyone who works for him, but Mr. Colby and Mr. Holtwood seem loyal to him. I couldn't imagine either of those two men setting up my husband for such an awful thing."

"There are more folks who work for Eli," her father said.

"I don't know them. Perhaps it's time for me to take another trip to the bank, no matter what Eli has said about keeping business and family apart. I'll have to make sure I meet all his employees this time."

"Are you sure you want to do that? Won't Eli object?"

Her laugh bore no humor. "Oh, he'll object, but knowing what you've told me, I can't let his objection stop me. I need to do whatever I can to protect you. You, and everyone else. I could never live with myself if I stood by and let this happen."

"That's why I came today. I can't let a snake in the grass bring down everything so many have worked so hard to achieve. Not even Eli."

The spark of hope in her heart buoyed her. "The more I think about it, the more I believe there is someone working against everything Eli stands for."

"It could very well be, Livvy, but you should also prepare yourself for the possibility that your husband is involved."

"I'll try. But I can't see the man I—" Olivia caught herself before she spoke such a meaningful word, one that could again bring her to tears. "I can't see the man I married guilty of something so dirty, so cruel."

"I don't want to see you hurt, dear. A father's heart breaks when one of his children is let down by someone who matters as much to them as Eli does to you."

Once again, Olivia called herself a fool. Then, as Papa donned his hat and coat on the way to the door, she began to wonder if she really was a fool. It seemed Eli had good reason for wanting to keep his business separate from all other parts of his life. He'd been harmed by his late wife and her family, and now it seemed someone else was working to do it again.

Maybe she needed to be more understanding. And forgiving.

Then, too, Eli needed to learn she would never betray him.

Olivia felt God leading her to the best way to do so.

"Thank you for telling me this, Papa. It's not an easy subject to talk about, but you did it anyway. Maybe we can not only save you and the other farmers, but also keep Eli from being ruined again."

He hugged her and gave her his trademark kiss on the forehead. Olivia clung to her father for a bit longer than usual, blinking away tears, but then let him go. It was time for her to take action. Time for her to be not just the newlywed, but the wife she'd become.

It was time to tear down the wall Eli had put up between them. She just hoped when it came down, it wouldn't crush her.

The next day, Olivia made good use of the remaining Christmas cards she hadn't sent already. She took the time to write them out to various acquaintances, packed them into her purse, put on her forest-green cloak and the cream wool scarf Mama had knit for her, and then headed down the street to the bank.

Eli couldn't very well avoid speaking with her while his employees watched. He had too much self-respect for that, and, she hoped, too much respect for her to humiliate her by chasing her out to the street.

Her plan was to identify each employee of the bank and, at the very least, introduce herself to the ones she didn't know. She was still trying to think of a reason to spend time with them, get to know them better, when she found herself on the sidewalk outside the bank.

Unfortunately, nothing came to her.

Since she couldn't stand out in the chilly wind much longer, not if she didn't want to call attention to herself, she breathed a prayer for courage and for God's will to be done in the situation that grew more dire as the deadline approached. She then went up the six steps and opened the door.

The respectful quiet reminded her how significant the bank was to the town. Everyone brought their money there. It protected everyone's livelihood.

It was also her husband's legacy from his late father. No wonder it meant so much to him. Now some greedy someone wanted to steal from the bank to line his pockets. That would ruin Eli.

The longer she thought about the situation, the more certain she grew that her husband was not in any way involved in the swindle.

She had to ferret out who was.

She stepped further into the polished lobby. On either side

of the room, she saw the two cashiers, Mr. Holtwood on the one side, Mr. Colby on the other, both behind the protective bars on the windows of their enclosed booths.

"Good morning, Missus Whitman," Mr. Colby said, scurrying out of the cagelike space. "Let me fetch Mr. Whitman for you."

"You needn't bother," she hurried to say. "I can find my way. I've been here before, you know."

"Unfortunately, ma'am, I do know." He shook his head, making his glasses bobble. "It's not a memory a man will soon forget, meeting up with a bank robber like that."

"I understand." She'd never forget the gut-wrenching fear that struck her when she saw the quantity of her husband's blood on the floor. "I can't say I'll forget it anytime soon either."

Mr. Holtwood approached from the other side. "I still have that wretched knot on my head." He rubbed the spot. "I've half a mind to carry a weapon with me. I intend never to be ineffective or powerless again."

"We all had a horrid experience." She looked around the room, trying to find the other employees Papa had mentioned.

She spotted a man she didn't know at a desk toward the back of the room, studying an open ledger book. There were at least four other tomes spread out before him, while stacks of paper, covered in neat rows of small writing, littered the space between them.

She leaned toward Mr. Colby. "Who's he?"

"He's Mr. Whitman's bookkeeper." The cashier blinked furiously. "He's the one who knows where the skeletons lie."

Olivia shuddered. "What a dreadful thought."

Mr. Colby flushed all the way to the roots of his red curls. "Oh, I'm so sorry, ma'am. I've grown accustomed to our bankers' humor. My mistake."

"I'm sorry I'm unfamiliar with your kind of humor." She looked back at the bookkeeper. "Would you introduce us?"

"I'd be honored." Mr. Colby nearly tripped over his feet in his eagerness to help.

At the heels of his response, the front door opened. Mr. Mitchell, the owner of the best apple orchard in the area, walked straight to Mr. Colby's window. "Oh, dear. I'm so sorry, Mrs. Whitman." He swiveled his head from Mr. Mitchell to her much like one of Randy's porcelain dolls. "I have a customer, but I was about to introduce you . . . oh, goodness—"

"Go ahead," Mr. Holtwood said, his voice clipped. "I'll take care of Mrs. Whitman."

The young cashier made his way to his customer, his greeting loud, revealing his nervousness.

"Is Mr. Colby always like that?" she asked Mr. Holtwood.

"Like what? Restless?"

She nodded. "Nervous. Frightened."

"That's just Colby. Reminds me of my departed grandmother when she'd have one of her spells."

Olivia squelched a chuckle. "Poor man. It must be quite difficult to live like that."

Mr. Holtwood shrugged. "Here we are." He turned to the slender, balding man at the ledger-littered desk. "Andrews. Look up. I've someone for you to meet."

The introduction went smoothly, as did the pleasant chatter that followed. The impression Olivia got from the brief contact was that of a man devoted to his sums. Mr. Andrews flicked his gaze toward the ledger full of neat columns of numbers every few seconds. The whole time they spoke he held his pen at the ready. He clearly itched to return to his work, so Olivia excused herself and approached Eli's office door, a determined thought in her mind. This man could easily manipulate the bank's books. He knew, more than likely to the penny, what everyone owed and what they had in their accounts.

If only she could discuss her suspicion with Eli. But that wasn't to be. She knocked. Prayed.

When he responded, she let herself in. Half of her mission had been accomplished. From what she understood, she only had one more employee to find. That is, if Papa was correct about those who worked for Eli.

As she approached his desk, the line of Eli's jaw reminded Olivia of the craggy, stony mountains she'd seen when her family had come to Oregon all those years ago. Those hard and sharp peaks had posed a daunting sight, one never to forget.

He wasn't going to make this an easy meeting. "Good morning again, Eli."

"What brings *you* here?"

She held her head high and continued with her mission. "I finished more Christmas cards, and wondered if perhaps you could take care of sending them."

For a moment, she thought he'd refuse. Then he nodded and held out a hand. She placed the envelopes in his broad palm. He set them on the corner of his desk and met her gaze again.

"Anything else?"

She shook her head. "That was it. Thank you."

"You're welcome."

She squared her shoulders. "Oh...um...on my way in, Mr. Holtwood introduced me to another of your employees. Your bookkeeper struck me as a devoted worker. Mr. Andrews couldn't wait to get back to his ledgers. He seemed a very nice man."

"Andrews is a good worker. He keeps the bank's books in excellent shape."

"I'm glad. For you. I mean, I could never spend that much time worrying over figures, tracking down every last cent, staring at endless lists and numbers and...and...certainly not without making all sorts of errors. I'd wind up with tangled accounts in no time. I don't suppose your Mr. Andrews suffers from a similar affliction."

"No, Olivia, he's outstanding with figures, and honest to the penny. He stayed late one time to follow the trail of a mere forty-four cents missing at the close."

As Olivia tried to think of a way to ask more questions, Eli jammed his hands in his trouser pockets, tapped a toe, and arched a brow. While he didn't say a word, his stance broadcast his impatience.

"I'll be on my way now," she hastened to say. "Thank you so much for your help with those invitations."

"Again, you're welcome, Olivia. Next time you have something for the post, you can simply send it out with Cooky when she goes to the Mercantile."

Olivia used all her strength to prevent a wince. He knew she'd cooked up the flimsy excuse, but she'd felt she had no choice. He'd made things impossible between them, and she wasn't about to let anyone harm those she loved.

As she stepped to the door, she tried to smooth things over with a less touchy topic. "Cooky is making lamb stew with the leftover roast we just had. I know how you love her stew."

"I'll be sure to enjoy my supper. As I always do."

This time, she nodded and ducked around the door, closing it behind her. On the other side, she let out a huge breath, fighting the urge to lean back against the door until her legs felt more like bone and muscle than an unstarched shirt on washday.

That had been awkward. She hadn't fooled Eli. Clearly, the famous Mr. Alan Pinkerton would not come seeking her services for his agency in the near future.

Out in the banking lobby, Olivia looked around again. Another surprise met her gaze. At the opposite corner of the room from Mr. Andrews's desk, she noticed Mrs. O'Dell sitting across another desk from a total stranger. This man wore a gray suit, his dark hair touched with a sprinkle of silver, slicked down from a center part. Clearly, he worked for Eli.

Hoping for an introduction, she realized both Mr. Colby and Mr. Holtwood had customers to tend, and Mr. Andrews had returned to his ciphers. She was on her own. Fortunately, Mrs. O'Dell was Mama's friend.

"Good morning," she told the widow. "I'm surprised to see you here today."

Mrs. O'Dell rose quickly despite her substantial frame, bringing to mind the solid mahogany armoire in Eli's bedroom. "It's a pleasure to see you, Livvy, dear. Haven't but caught a glimpse of you since you married. The children must keep you busy."

Mrs. O'Dell's hug was tight, familiar, and welcome. "I'm sure you know. You had your own brood to watch."

"The boys are men. Martin went to Seattle, while Terrence lives in Cleveland. Very, very far."

"It must be difficult, now that Mr. O'Dell—" Olivia caught herself. "I'm so sorry. I didn't mean to bring up your sad loss."

"I do miss him," she said, "but I'm comforted knowing I'll see him again once I'm before the Father's throne."

"That is a comfort."

"It's his loss," the older woman continued, "that brings me to the bank today. I've come to sign all kinds of papers Harry left behind. Now that I'm opening up a bakery, your Mr. Whitman insisted we do this right. All the property and the little money we had, he wants to put in my name. Imagine that."

"I suppose it is all yours now, so it's right to have it in your name."

"Eli said this way no one can challenge me, no one can leave me out in the street. I hope you recognize what a good man you have there, Livvy," the older woman said, her voice gruff, her forehead lined with a frown, her eyes fast on the desktop. "I certainly hope you appreciate him. He's an upstanding gentleman, decent, honest, sober and dry as desert sand, and more loyal than most fellas' dogs."

"I know, Mrs. O'Dell. I know how blessed I am." Because she did, she would do everything in her power to help Eli, even in spite of himself.

She turned to the man behind the desk, hand outstretched. "We haven't met. I'm Olivia Whitman, and you are . . . ?"

The man stood and took her hand in a firm clasp. "Lewis Parham, the bank's new secretary."

"Indeed," Mrs. O'Dell said. "He's taken over Harry's position, and I see he's doing an admirable job."

Mr. Parham smiled. His keen brown eyes gave a hint to his intelligence, while his gray-dusted hair suggested well-earned experience. "With time, I hope to do work as fine as Mr. O'Dell did. He left everything in impeccable condition."

"That was my Harry. He was always after organizing even my kitchen. Cups and plates and spoons and all. It didn't matter. Everything had to be just so for that man."

It would seem this man also had his finger on all the information needed to swindle everyone. His newcomer status made no difference, since Mr. O'Dell had left all the documents in "impeccable" condition. How had Eli made the decision to trust him? Was he trustworthy? Or had he arrived, quickly identified the opportunity, then, when asked to write letters, he'd written whatever benefited him? He'd have access to all Eli's business correspondence. Surely the man had a hand in writing the letters to the mortgaged landowners. Maybe, just like Eli's wife before him, he'd learned to forge Eli's signature.

Anything was possible, and this man was a stranger. No one knew what he might do.

Now it was a matter of reaching Eli, not an easy thing for her. But as Mama always said, with God, all things were possible.

Chapter 23

As Olivia started to leave, the bank door opened before her and a mountain of a man walked in. As soon as he saw her, he removed his hat. "'Morning, Mrs. Whitman. Pleasure to see you again."

Olivia smiled at the bank's minority partner, whom she'd met on her wedding day. "Yes, Mr. Bartlett, it's nice to see you again."

"Please call me Nathan." When she nodded, he continued. "I hope Eli's rascals aren't giving you too much trouble. He's told me tales of their antics."

"If you'd asked me before the wedding you would have heard of the horrors of stray grasshoppers and honey-covered furniture. But now, they're quite charming."

"I'm glad to hear that," Eli said from inches away from Olivia's shoulder.

Shocked by his silent arrival, she turned and almost lost her balance. He caught her elbow. The usual rush of sensation flooded through her. Their gazes met, clung. Images filled her thoughts. Awareness charged the air, and longing lodged in her throat. Olivia couldn't have spoken if her life depended on it.

She loved him.

The strain between them hurt.

She wanted nothing more than to collapse into his embrace.

Eli gathered himself first. He released her arm, then turned to Nathan. "I'm surprised to see you in town again so soon. This is—what? The fourth time, the fifth?—in the last couple of months. I don't remember when you last spent so much time here. Did you need to see me?"

Her eyes still fixed on her husband, Olivia caught a momentary flare of worry, perhaps alarm in his eyes. But it came and went so fast, she began to wonder if she'd imagined it.

Nathan cleared his throat. "Matter of fact, I do. It's about that flume we discussed the last time I was here."

"I was afraid of that." Eli's jaw took on a stonelike rigidity. "Nothing's changed since then. Winter's almost here, nothing's been planted, much less harvested, and the bank's liquidity is as before."

"Something's changed. For me." Nathan glanced around the busy lobby. "But I don't think my finances—or the bank's business—is something we should discuss in public."

Although she would have loved to hear the men's conversation, Olivia knew the time had come for her to leave. "I'll let you gentlemen get on with your business. I'm sure Cooky's waiting for me." She looked at Nathan. "We will see you on Christmas Eve, won't we?"

"If the weather holds, ma'am. If snows come, then I don't know that I'll come down the mountain. Too much risk of getting stuck here in town or on the mountain trail. In either case, I can't be away from the logging camp too long."

She nodded. "Then I hope the weather holds."

As she stepped out the door, Nathan spoke again, this time to Eli. "It's time we—the bank—take a stance on those out-standing loans. I need my money..."

A noose seemed to tighten around her throat. Was this evidence of Eli's wrongdoing? Or did it point to Nathan Bartlett? As a partner, even though a lesser one, as Eli had said, he could take action. The logging camp owner had just said he needed money.

For that matter, just because Mr. Holtwood and Mr. Colby had worked for Eli and his father for many years, it didn't necessarily follow that they would always be true and faithful employees. Same thing went for Mr. Andrews, and loyalty could hardly be expected from the new Mr. Parham.

As Olivia set off for home, she found herself more confused than ever. It appeared her visit had solved nothing at all. She had more potential culprits than before.

And her family's time was running out.

Between the day Olivia went to the bank to meet Mr. Andrews and Mr. Parham, and the day before the party, she tried every way she knew to approach Eli again. He, in turn, spent his time eluding her every way he could. They became virtual strangers, and Olivia didn't know how much longer she could stand to stay in the Whitman home.

Her only other choice would be to confess to Mama and Papa how dreadfully bad things had become between her and

Eli, and then leave with the family when they went back East. No part of that scenario appealed.

Each time she thought of leaving Eli, she had to fight the tears that filled her eyes. He'd torn her heart in two with his refusal to trust her, so she didn't see how they could make a marriage work under those circumstances. How much could two people, husband and wife, share if one didn't trust the other? Her best example was that set by her parents. Elizabeth and Stephen Moore shared every part of the life they had built upon the rock of their faith.

She'd wanted the same for her marriage.

Now, with the way things stood, she saw no hope for sharing, much less growing old together. Still, she would miss him with every fiber of her being. She continued to love him.

And the children…

Although she felt torn to shreds inside, she'd promised Eli her best effort with the Christmas party, and she meant to keep every bit of her promise. She continued to work closely with Cooky to put the finishing touches on the myriad details, and she thought she'd done an acceptable job hiding her misery from the older woman.

That would be another wrenching good-bye for her, the day she was forced to part from the dear, dear woman. Olivia didn't want to think too much about it. It only added to the heaviness in her heart.

How was a woman to leave one family for the sake of another? She forced the troubling thoughts away, and continued her preparations, fasting and praying for favor.

"Is everything ready for the meal?" she asked Cooky that afternoon after the two of them, assisted by Cooky's daughter Kate, had stretched out the parlor rug on the back-yard clothesline and beaten every speck of dust out of it. "This is almost our last chance to tie up any loose ends."

"Everything from the kitchen is ready, I'm a-telling you. And I'm waiting until all these folks come see how hard you've worked. They'd *all* better be recognizing you for the fine, godly woman you are, too, s'what I say. I won't be having none of that bootlicking foolishness so many of these high and mighty important sorts are insisting on all their born days, I tell you."

Olivia wasn't about to comment on that. "You've worked even harder than I have, Cooky. After the table's cleared tomorrow night, you can take well-deserved time off for yourself."

"Oh, go on with you, Missus Livvy!" Cooky planted her fists on her hips. "What would you be having me do, what with no meals to make and none of you Whitmans to keep running along smooth-like? Why, I'm sure and I wouldn't have a notion what to be doing with myself."

Olivia didn't dare let a smile break forth. "I'd say we're ready then. The rooms look as pretty as a Christmas dream come true, and all I need now is to get the children and me ready tomorrow afternoon. Luke and Randy know they'll only join the grown-ups for a short while. I'd like them to have an early supper before anyone gets here, so that after they've greeted the guests, I can send them straight to bed."

"Sounds like a dandy of a plan, it does. I'll make sure and save a tasty treat for each one of them. That way, I'm thinking, when they have to go to their rooms, they won't be a-fussing and envying all those folks you're having in for that mighty fine banquet I'm serving up."

Olivia looked around the kitchen, at the bowl of apples left after Cooky had baked a half dozen pies, the sack of potatoes ready for peeling and mashing and serving with puddles of butter in nooks and crannies, bright green peapods ready for shelling, plump gold squash about to be baked, and deep red beets, pickled and canned and only needing to be warmed and served.

"It does look as though we're ready. My mouth waters every time I come in here. You're a treasure, Cooky, and you've done wonders with each of our ideas. Mr. Whitman will be so happy and proud when he sees it all."

Cooky crossed her plump arms and studied Olivia with all-seeing eyes. "And are you thinking that will chase away the mighty big black cloud he's been a-carrying over that thick head of his these last pair of weeks or so?"

Olivia gasped. She hadn't expected Cooky to bring up such a sensitive subject. She wished she had a way to fight the hot blush that singed her cheeks, but nothing could have stopped it. "I . . . why, I'm not sure I know what you mean—"

"Now, Missus Livvy!" Cooky's eyes snapped, her lips pursed, and she wagged a chubby finger in Olivia's face. "I tell you, I never woulda thought you'd try and fib like that at me. No sir, I did not. You and Mr. Whitman are on the out and outs, and anyone with eyes in their heads can see it, clear as fresh-cracked egg whites, at that."

Mortified, all Olivia could do was nod. "Yes, well, I'm sure he'll be fine soon enough—"

"He's not making things easy-like for himself, is he now? That frowning and fretting makes him look like a pinched-up prune. What woman with sense in her head would be wanting to hug and kiss a prune, I ask you?"

Again, Olivia's cheeks sizzled. "I really don't know what to say."

Cooky shook her kitchen towel at Olivia. "No need to be saying anything to me now. It's the man with the black cloud you'd best be talking to. I reckon plain talk's the best way to knock that cloud right out of your way."

Before Cooky could say anything more outrageous than she already had, Olivia came up with a feeble excuse and ran from the kitchen as fast as she could go. She kept herself busy the rest of the day, fussed with details that needed no additional care, helped the children wrap their gifts for Eli, and then lingered over supper far longer than she ever had before.

Later, when she could no longer avoid it, she kissed Luke and Randy good night and went out to the upstairs landing, certain she should try to break through Eli's stubborn silence, but unwilling to face another ugly quarrel.

"Oh, Father," she whispered. "I can't continue to be a coward and hide in fear. I didn't believe Papa when he first told me he felt you'd led me to Eli and the children for a time like this, but as the days have gone by, I've come to accept he spoke the truth. I still don't feel up to the task, but I know your Word says you'll never leave me or forsake me. Don't forsake me now."

When she walked into the parlor, however, Eli gave her no chance to speak.

"You've never told me what you want for Christmas. I've asked you a number of times, but each time you have put me off. Now it's only one full day and one night until Christmas Day, and you haven't said a thing."

Olivia wouldn't have been more shocked if he'd broken into

patriotic songs and a military march the moment she stepped into the room. How could he bring up the subject of a gift? Why now, after he hadn't said more than a handful of terse words to her since their argument?

On the other hand, at one point she had planned to ask him for mercy for the cash-strapped farmers and ranchers as a gift to her. While he'd waited until almost the last moment to bring it up, and he had done so after they'd had their first serious argument and an icy standoff of his own making, he once again asked what she wanted.

There was only one thing she wanted.

Now the Lord had opened a way for her. God had answered her prayer. She couldn't let fear overcome her faith in Him.

"I confess your question surprises me," she said, approaching Eli. "But after the last time you asked, an idea did occur to me. I never found time to mention it since. You have brought it back to mind now."

He raised his pipe to his lips, drew on the fragrant smoke, expelled it, and only then did he speak again. "What would that idea be?"

"The only gift I want, especially after all your generosity toward me, is the gift of mercy. But I don't ask for myself."

With a curl of smoke still rising from the bowl, he set the pipe in the small tray he kept on the table by his chair, and stood. "That is unusual."

He strode to the fireplace, placed a foot on a shiny brass andiron and an elbow on the garland-swathed mantel before going on. "I must say, you have captured my curiosity. Go ahead. Tell me everything."

His blue, blue stare seemed more intense than she'd ever

seen it, and it didn't flag. Olivia clasped her hands at her mid-section and nodded.

"Please show mercy to the farmers and ranchers who received the notices of foreclosure," she said. "I don't under-stand how you could demand full payment of those mortgages by the end of the year and threaten to throw those families from their homes when you know they won't have money until the next harvest."

While his jaw had tightened again in that now familiar stony line, when she mentioned the foreclosures his brows drew close and a puzzled expression came over his face.

"Please stop, Olivia. In the first place, you're again throw-ing aside our agreement. In the second, I don't have a clue what you're talking about. What foreclosures? What farmers and ranchers?"

She must have caught enough of his curiosity for him to question her in spite of the blasted agreement he'd imposed on them. She wasn't about to question the inconsistency, but instead thanked the Lord for the opening and stepped for-ward with what she had to do.

"Of course you do. Papa showed me the letter you sent with the demand for full payment of the mortgage by the thirty-first of December. Should he not pay—and you know he can't—he's to abandon the house and the outbuildings in three days."

Eli shook his head. "Absolutely not. I never sent your father any such letter."

Olivia's heart sped up its beat. Perhaps things weren't quite as dreadful as they'd seemed. Then she remembered the paper she'd held in her hands. "I saw it, Eli. I read what it said, and saw your signature at the bottom."

"That's impossible."

She spread her hands, then shrugged. "I know what I saw."

He ran rough fingers through his hair. "How could you think I would do such a thing? How could you think I'd go back on my word—a solid agreement—with your father? You know me better than that."

Pain struck at the heart of her misery. "Perhaps the same way I fail to understand how you would think I tried to ask about this to harm you."

"That's different. You'd given me your word."

"That should have shown you how important my questions were. My word is as good as yours. You should have trusted me."

"How could I trust anyone? Victoria and her family started out the same way. A question here, a request there. In the end, they stole me blind and left me on the hook for a number of cattle thefts and failed investments. I was betrayed by the woman I'd trusted, the mother of my daughter and son. If I couldn't trust her, then how do you expect me to trust a virtual stranger? A newcomer into my life?"

Olivia stood tall. "I think you knew from the start that I'm no Victoria, and Papa is no cattle rustler. Comparisons like those are unjust, and plain wrong. You need to learn again the difference between right and wrong."

"I do know—"

"Please, Eli, hear me out. *I* know what's right and wrong before the Lord. I also know the heavenly Father calls me to act when I see a wrong being done. Asking you to spare my family and the others was—is—the right thing to do."

His shoulders slumped. "Olivia, please. I know what's

right. Throwing folks from their homes in the dead of winter is wrong. I know the difference between one and the other. Besides, I would never break a contract in such an unscrupulous way. If word got out that I engage in such shady dealings, I'd be ruined in no time at all. Everything my father and I worked for all these years would be lost. A banker's integrity is all he has."

"A Christian stands before the Lord," Olivia countered. "I take that seriously. Please know that your trust in me is well-placed. Do the right thing, Eli. Set my folks free from the bondage of fear. Spare them, show them mercy."

He began to pace. "How can I show someone mercy when I don't even know what's been said? I need to make sure an unscrupulous letter is all that was done to them. I won't stand for trickery or cruelty. You can count on my word."

"So you suspect the same thing I do. That someone else is guilty."

"I'm certainly not the one who did any of this."

"Then hear me out." She prayed for strength and the right words. "One of your employees must have written the letters. Who would you suspect?"

His eyes pinned her with an unwavering stare. "Not a one of them. Even you mentioned their loyalty."

"Perhaps a better actor than you think is among them."

"Even if one of my employees were to fall on difficult times, they know I would never tolerate what you've told me. It's nothing more than a swindle."

Olivia lifted her chin. "The landowners aren't the only victims, you know. You're at risk as well. I hope you understand now why I couldn't stay silent. I couldn't let anyone do this to you. I can't let *everyone* be destroyed."

He glanced away. "Could you have your father bring the letter tomorrow night?"

"I'll get word to him, even if I have to ride to the farm to ask him myself. I know he's been praying for the opportunity to speak with you since he first received it."

"Why didn't he just come to the bank? I've never refused to meet a customer. Especially not a decent, honest man like your father."

"Papa tried, Eli. But you know Mr. Holtwood's devotion to you. Surely he would fight anyone who tried to disturb you when you've asked him to keep customers away."

Eli lifted a shoulder in a one-sided shrug. "Sometimes a man needs to finish a meeting uninterrupted. Interruptions, no matter how legitimate, do keep me from finishing. Still, Holtwood reschedules in those rare cases. I always welcome my customers."

"I understand. It's not anything you've done, or anything unusual on Mr. Holtwood's part that postponed this moment. He did what he usually does, but it kept Papa from speaking with you. Papa had no alternative. The letter told him he had until the thirty-first to pay the mortgage or he must leave."

With a weariness Olivia hadn't seen since the injury to his chest, Eli ran a hand over his face. "Let's not go over the details you know and those I don't know anymore. We need to see your father's letter before we say anything further, or do anything else."

As impatient as Olivia was to have the matter resolved, especially now that she'd managed to bring it into the open, she had to agree he had a point. "You're right. We'll wait until Papa brings the letter, and then we can decide on a plan."

A faint smile lifted the corners of his lips. "We?"

She glared and stalked forward, hands in fists at her sides. "If you, Eli Whitman, think I'm going to fade away after I've been so patient about this mess you created with your outlandish agreement, then you, sir, have to find some new thoughts. Here I've been trying to protect you and your bank and all you can do is question me—"

"I was only trying to make a joke." He placed a finger on her lips. "Not the best time, I suppose. I didn't mean to upset you."

As always, his touch melted her and sent waves of electricity through her body. The small gesture struck her as the first step back from their argument, but much wasn't right between them still. Beginning with trust.

She reached up and wrapped her fingers around his hand. "You must understand my need to be there when you and Papa decide what to do about the letter—letters."

He nodded. "Of course, but there's nothing more we can say or do tonight. Tomorrow promises to be an exhausting day. It only makes sense for you to get the rest I know you're going to need."

She knew sleep the night before a significant event was a matter of common sense, but the strain between them still bothered her. On the other hand, they had made progress. They were speaking again.

"Good night, Eli. You should rest as well. Tomorrow will be an important day for both of us."

She turned and walked out to the hall, up the stairs, and into her room. Only then did the tears fall.

Chapter 24

As the sun began its glide down the sky toward the horizon on Christmas Eve, light snowflakes began to dust Bountiful with their sugary sparkle. Wearing a new eggplant-colored wool dress, Olivia could scarcely control her excitement...or her apprehension.

On the one hand, she'd anticipated this evening for a long while, devoting hours to prepare her home for the event. On the other hand, since Eli had sent a message to her father that morning, she knew that at some point in the evening they would meet with him. Eli would see the letter that had set off so much trouble.

After that...well, it was anyone's guess what they would do after that.

When the doorknocker clapped against the brass plate for the first of many times, Olivia hurried to greet her guests. On the way to the door from the dining room, where she'd finished lighting candles, she called out to Eli. "They've begun to arrive. I'd like you here with me, especially since I don't know your railroad officials."

She waited and, when she heard her husband's steps on the stairs, she opened the door. The Bowens were the first to show up.

After the woodworking master, others came in a steady stream, including the five somber gentlemen from the railroad. Olivia offered them a warm greeting, took their oh-so-proper black coats and hats, and took the items up to her room. The men struck her as intent on their business and dreadfully dull.

By seven o'clock, the house rang with laughter and conversation, little of it contributed by the dour guests of honor. The rooms brimmed with folks enjoying the delicious treats Cooky had worked so hard to prepare.

A smile on her face, Olivia chattered with the ladies who'd come, glad for the feminine company at a gathering that would otherwise have been for the men. She joined Eli time and again, trying her best to keep her attention on their four special guests.

Then Mama and Papa appeared. Eli must have seen them the moment Olivia opened the door. He excused himself from the railroad men and joined her, his expression serious, his gaze, as it often appeared, intent.

"Good evening." He shook hands with Papa, then folded Mama's wool cloak over his arm. "I hope you don't think I'm terribly rude, Mr. Moore, if I ask to speak with you right away. Our kitchen's likely the best place for us to go since our guests are in other rooms."

"Not at all. I have the letter right here." Papa patted the pocket of his tobacco-brown suit.

The four of them made their way to the kitchen. There, Cooky and her daughter Kate bustled from table to stove to shelf gathering the platters and trays they would need when they took the food out to serve.

When Olivia closed the kitchen door, Eli held out Mama's wrap to Kate. "Could you please take Mrs. Moore's belongings up to Mrs. Whitman's room?"

She nodded.

"I would also appreciate it if you'd take a few minutes and give us some privacy in here. You, too, Cooky."

As soon as the two women left, he turned to Papa. "May I see the letter?"

Papa handed it over.

Eli scanned the page.

Olivia held her breath.

Mama prayed.

When he finished, Eli exhaled. But before he could say anything, Papa gave him another fistful of papers. "Here, Mr. Whitman. I gathered some of the other letters. The men I spoke to wanted to thank you for taking the time tonight to give these a look. Everyone knows how important your meetings with the railroad officials are to everyone in Bountiful."

Eli only nodded.

Although it seemed like an extraordinarily long time to Olivia, the clock atop the kitchen pie safe said it only took her husband seven minutes to skim the papers her father had given him. She couldn't wait for Eli's verdict.

Mama took hold of Olivia's arm, her fingers cold even through the fabric of her sleeve. She began to count the seconds.

"I can assure you of one thing," he finally said. "I've never seen these before. I didn't sign a single one of them. It is my name and it does look like my handwriting and signature, but I did not write these falsified documents. They're a good imitation, but, again, it's not my writing."

Olivia let out her pent-up breath. "Who could have written them?"

"I have my suspicions, but suspicions aren't enough to take to Marshal Blair."

"It is criminal, then."

Eli nodded. "They're forgeries. Whoever wrote them has worked with great cunning to swindle these men out of land that's rightfully theirs. While he's at it, he has done his best to implicate the bank in his thievery."

"I only have one more question," she said. "If the bank forecloses on the mortgages, don't the deeds come back to the bank? How can the thief profit from that?"

Eli shrugged.

Papa shook his head. "I wouldn't know."

"But I will find out." Eli's voice left no doubt. "Just like I saw earlier today that a number of files are indeed missing from the bank—Hugh Roberts's, for one." He shook his head. "I looked around, asked a few direct questions, and now I can see how Mr. Parham, who is new, wouldn't know any better. I just don't know how I didn't notice the missing paperwork. Of course, I don't check that material on a daily basis, but what's gone from the file drawers is substantial, including a number of deeds. Thank you for your patience, Mr. Moore. From what Olivia has told me, you asked her to tell me about this quite a while ago, but I kept her from speaking when I should have encouraged her willingness to help. I'm sorry for my stubbornness."

Although Eli had spoken to her father, his gaze had pinned Olivia's. The hope he'd done so much to extinguish over the last two weeks flickered again. She tried to tamp down her enthusiasm, since she didn't know what Eli meant by his intense stare. She needed to hear his words. And to witness his actions.

She'd have to wait him out.

Papa cleared his throat. "Mr. Whitman, could you indulge me a moment longer, please?"

Eli nodded.

"One of the men who received one of these letters mentioned someone, but the man he accused is someone I can't see as the culprit. Zealously loyal toward you? Oh, yes. He's guilty of that. But treachery and criminal acts? No. I can't see him do that to you."

Olivia brought the knuckles of her fist up to her mouth to keep a cry from breaking out. *Zealously loyal…access to loan papers, account balances, deeds…familiarity with Eli's handwriting.* She knew who it was. She turned to her husband.

"Now that I know you did not write this letter…" Papa paused, as if making up his mind. "When I came to the bank, the same man told me the correspondence should be clear enough, that it must say it all so there was no need for me to speak with you."

Eli's jaw tightened. He, even better than she, knew who Papa's friend had implicated in the crime.

No one spoke the name. No one had to.

"If you'll excuse us, then." Mama linked her arm through Papa's. "Now that we've related everything we know, we'll join the rest of the guests and leave you two alone. I believe you have a great deal to consider. And talk about."

"One last thing," Eli said before the Moores left. "Perhaps it goes without saying, but I want no more confusion. As far as your property goes, don't give the fraudulent notice another thought. We'll discuss everything at another time—the twenty-sixth, sir, if that's convenient for you. Rest assured the original terms on the loan stand as they always have, as does what we discussed about the extension. I'll get word to the other farmers and ranchers as well. In the meantime, please celebrate the evening with us and our guests, and tomorrow enjoy the day of our Lord's birth."

"Thank you," Papa responded, "and I wish you and Olivia a blessed Christmas Day as well."

Mama dabbed a tear from the corner of her eye.

Papa patted her shoulder, and then turned and extended his hand. The two most important men in Olivia's life shook on the agreement they'd reaffirmed.

From the corner of the kitchen where the monstrous black iron stove sat, a familiar voice piped up. "It's good and well past time for these two to do more than mope around this house, it is. Time for the sun to come out and shine right bright for this family again. I'm plumb sick and tired of that kind of tomfoolery, I am."

Eli turned to the cook. "I gather you slipped back in here without anyone the wiser, and you heard everything we discussed. I would appreciate—"

"Don't you dare insult me, Mr. Eli Bank President Whitman!" Cooky warned, a ferocious look on her plump, rosy-cheeked face. "I'd far rather chop a finger right off my hand this very minute than go out and flap my tongue about business that's none of my own. What's more, if you weren't so blind and deaf, you'd already know it right well, now wouldn't you?"

In spite of the gravity of the situation, Olivia couldn't hold back a laugh. Mama and Papa hurried away, chuckling as well. Once they were gone, Olivia dared a look in Eli's direction.

A sheepish expression and a ruddy flush on his lean cheeks proved Cooky's words had struck their mark. Perhaps it was time for her to follow her parents before her humor at her husband's expense canceled the progress they'd made so far. As she went toward the door, Eli stepped forward to stop her.

"Don't go yet. I want you to know that I may still pull Holtwood aside tonight. He owes me—everyone—an explanation. Depending on those answers, we might need to call the marshal out of the dining room before he's finished his supper."

"Why don't you wait until Cooky and Kate clear the table?" Olivia suggested. "I'll speak with the marshal, let him know you may need his help."

At first, she thought Eli would balk, but then, a smile brightened his face. "It may take me a while to get used to it, but I accept your help. Let's join our guests now, and then scare the snake determined to ruin us out of the patch of grass where he has hidden so well."

"Don't forget the farmers," Olivia added, torn between joy and alarm. "Just like you, they're targeted to lose everything they own."

In spite of the revelation of the culprit's identity, and how great a betrayal it represented, maybe things were about to work out as she'd hoped. Maybe the Lord would answer her prayers for her marriage the way she'd prayed He would as well.

When Eli held out an arm, she slipped hers into the crook of his elbow. Together, they joined their guests for a splendid Christmas Eve soirée.

When the guests had finished the last morsel of apple pie and Cooky and Kate entered the dining room with the handy cart to clear away the china and silverware, Olivia's gut tightened again. She glanced at Eli, who gave her a quick nod, a tight smile, and that private wink that had disappeared the night of their argument.

A rush of memories and a flood of warmth sped through her and lodged in the vicinity of her heart. *Please, God, please! May it be your will.*

She stood to look for the marshal, and found him chatting with one of the men from the railroad and Mr. Metcalf, the owner of the Mercantile. Although she hated to interrupt a conversation that could have an impact on the decision about the spur line, she knew she couldn't stand by and not alert the lawman.

They had a forger...swindler...thief—a crook—to catch.

Standing tall, she approached the trio. "Gentlemen."

Marshal Blair dipped his head. "What a table you set, Mrs. Whitman. Haven't eaten that well in a mighty long time."

Mr. Metcalf raised his hands and took a small step back. "Oh, no. I'm not about to step into that hole. If my missus hears me say something like what you just said, Adam, I'll be eating hay with the horses for the next six months."

The man from the railroad chuckled. "Well, I don't have to worry right now. With my wife back East, I can compliment your excellent meal, Mrs. Whitman. Made me feel right at home. Thank you for all the trouble you've taken to make this evening a pleasant experience."

By the time he was done, the heat of Olivia's blush reached her hairline. "Thank you, but you're all too kind. I didn't come to fish for compliments. I need a word with the marshal, so I've come to borrow his attention for a moment."

Polite murmurs followed, and then Olivia led the lawman to a quiet corner.

"As nice as I'm sure a conversation with you would be, Mrs. Whitman," the marshal said, "I don't suppose that's what you have in mind, now, is it?"

"No, sir. Mr. Whitman asked me to alert you that at some point this evening he might find himself in need of your services. Would you kindly stay for the next hour or perhaps even a bit more? Even after most guests have left?"

"Now, ma'am, you've managed to intrigue me, all right." He crossed his arms and studied her, a wide smile on his face. "A lawman's curiosity is something he values. I'll be happy to lend you and Eli a hand. Just be sure to fetch me right away. Wouldn't want to miss a bit of whatever he's cooked up."

Relief lent her a responding smile. "I'm much obliged, sir. It likely will turn unpleasant at some point, but we want to keep it as quiet as possible. We just don't want to let lawbreakers go without bringing them to account."

He tapped his forehead with two fingers. "I salute you, ma'am. Too many look the other way. Evildoers who go scot-free will be back at their tricks in no time at all."

The marshal rejoined his conversation, and Olivia checked on the other guests. She had just said good night to the Bowens when, out of the corner of her eye, she saw Eli approach Mr. Holtwood. With a nod toward her, he led the man toward the kitchen.

Mr. Holtwood. It seemed impossible. A part of her still hoped it was all a misunderstanding, that all Eli obtained was information from his right-hand man. Then they would confront the actual culprit. But her gut said otherwise. Eli's reaction had been immediate and decisive, not to mention what Papa had said. She trusted Eli's instincts, especially in this case.

Olivia scurried after the men, unwilling to miss a moment more than necessary.

"Good," Eli said when Olivia entered the kitchen. "I'm glad you're here." He turned to his assistant. "Mrs. Whitman and I have a few questions for you, Holtwood."

The bank's head cashier paled. "What kind of questions, Mr. Whitman?"

Olivia stayed near the door, in case Eli indicated the time to fetch the marshal had arrived. Her husband took his time unfolding Papa's letter. Eli held out the paper and Mr. Holtwood took it.

Before the man had a chance to read a word, Eli spoke again. "What is the meaning of this?"

When Olivia followed him and Holtwood into the kitchen, Eli felt capable of handling anything life—or his traitorous right-hand man—might throw at him. She hadn't been seeking his downfall, as Victoria had done not quite three years earlier. Her determination to do the right thing, by her family as well as by him, was something to praise, not put off.

God had truly blessed him when He'd brought Olivia into his life. Now if the Father would bless Eli with the wisdom and discernment needed to bring to justice the guilty party in this many-layered swindle, he would do everything in his power to mend the tattered edges of his marriage.

Eli leaned against the frame of the back door, hands in his pockets, right ankle over the left, eyes fixed on Holtwood. He wasn't about to let even a flicker of reaction from his head cashier go unnoticed.

The clock ticked the seconds away. Eli watched Holtwood read. As pale as the cashier had grown when he'd been handed the letter, he'd continued to lose color as he stared at the paper that shook in his hands.

Since there wasn't much to read on the page, after five minutes Eli grew impatient. "So, Holtwood. What do you have to say?"

Holtwood looked up, lips pinched. "I don't know, sir. Perhaps you should confer with Mr. Parham. He's the one who prepares the bank's correspondence for your approval and signature, isn't he?"

"Indeed, Holtwood. But after all these years we've worked together you know as well as I do that is not my signature."

"Are you sure, Mr. Whitman? It looks like your penmanship. Perhaps Mr. Parham has learned to approximate a good facsimile of your handwriting and signature, and signed these missives for you."

Olivia inhaled audibly.

Eli closed his eyes momentarily as he shook his head in her direction.

He turned back to his head cashier. "I must ask you to stop right there, Holtwood. Although he's only worked a short time for me, Mr. Parham will not even draft a letter from a handful of ideas I give him. He insists I hand him my written notes or dictate the body of the missive. He'll then turn what I've given him into a letter that he'll wait until I read word for word. He watches like a hawk until I sign each and every bit of correspondence that leaves the bank. This is not his doing, nor is it his penmanship."

"You scarcely know him, not long enough to know what he might or might not do. They do say there's always a first time for everything."

"There's also the fact that he has no direct access to mortgage information, foreclosure possibilities, or deeds, never mind the most important matter we have yet to discuss."

"What would that be?"

"It has not escaped my notice how these false foreclosure letters are dated from immediately after we began to look into the possibility of bringing a spur line through town. Whoever ends up with his name on the deeds to these properties, even one or two, stands to gain a respectable sum from the railroad."

Eli met Olivia's gaze.

Mr. Holtwood's eyes narrowed. "It's the bank calling in defaulted mortgages. Only the bank stands to gain from the reversion of the deeds. It's always good when the bank realizes a tidy profit, is it not, sir?"

"An *honest* profit, Holtwood. I'm afraid that detail has escaped your notice. But it won't slip that of the authorities."

The man's demeanor began a subtle but distinct change.

"The first group of landowners will default come January first unless they pay. The bank is in its legal right to foreclose at that time. When the deeds are processed, the new owner can approach the railroad and negotiate a profitable sale."

Eli had to leash his temper. He narrowed his gaze and took a step toward his assistant. "But the bank's not the only 'owner-in-the-making' as a result of these foreclosures, is it?"

Holtwood's wiry body tensed and his nostrils flared. "I don't understand. It says right here"—he waved the letter at Eli—"the bank, in its position as lien holder, is entitled to take possession of the land and all improvements upon it. The bank is the lien holder. I don't know what you are trying to imply."

From his pocket, Eli withdrew another set of papers. "Here are more letters. I don't have to imply anything. A number of deeds are missing from the bank. I suspect when I do locate them, the bank will not be named as the owner, now will it? The same with the lien documents. They'll also reflect a new lien holder, won't they?"

Holtwood stepped forward and snapped the papers from Eli's hands. A shot of pain struck his gut. A wave of nausea rose to his throat. All these years, and now it seemed Holtwood had played him all too well.

Another betrayal...

He forced his injured feelings aside and focused on the moment of truth. That was when he caught a flash of cunning in Holtwood's gaze. Eli wondered how many times something like that had slipped his notice over the years.

A guttural sound from Holtwood's throat broke into Eli's thoughts. "Despicable!" Holtwood said. His eyes darted from Eli and Olivia, as though gauging their reaction to his outburst. "Someone has indeed taken liberties with your signature."

Eli's patience was gone. "We both know who. I imagine when the marshal searches your home, he'll find your name on those documents."

He glanced at Olivia and nodded. She turned toward the door.

Holtwood lunged.

Before Eli realized what had happened, his head cashier came for him. On the man's way across the room, he grabbed Cooky's sharp knife from the work table where she'd left it. He aimed the slick blade right at Eli's throat.

He dodged the attack, then called out. "Go, Olivia! Bring Blair now!"

But Olivia had already left, most likely the very second before Holtwood had reached for the knife. Now Eli would have to fend off the enraged man's attacks, if only for a handful of minutes, minutes during which that sharp steel blade could do a world of harm.

"Out of my way," Holtwood ground out from between clenched teeth. His goal was to reach the back kitchen door against which Eli had leaned, and in front of which he still stood.

"Can't do that, my man. Hand over the knife. You've made too many wrong choices, and now you'll go nowhere but Marshal Blair's jail cell."

"Never. Not even if I have to make my way out over your bleeding body."

For Eli, the moment felt like something out of a fantastical dream. Nothing seemed real, especially not the enraged creature coming at him. This was a stranger, not the man he'd trusted for so long.

He stayed ready on his feet, hands up to present a defense.

Holtwood paused, biding his time, but when footsteps approached from the dining room, he bolted, knife leading the way.

"I meant it," he said, teeth bared, eyes wild, blade at Eli's throat.

The sting of the steel sliced into his skin. The thrust of Holtwood's hand met his healing bullet wound. Pain stole his breath.

"Now. Or the next cut will go all the way through!"

Eli did the only thing he could. *Father, help! Not now. Not when Olivia and I have a chance to make things right between us.*

He realized then he'd never told her he loved her.

Chapter 25

When Olivia saw blood on Eli's neck so soon after he'd been shot, she lost all sense of fear. Ignoring Papa's and Marshal Blair's cries behind her, she flew at Holtwood and grabbed the back of his shirt collar. She pulled—hard. He gasped when it did what she wanted and cut off his breath.

She prayed the buttons holding the collar to the shirt's banded neck stayed tight.

Eli took the opening to grab Holtwood's hand and twist. The man made a choked sound, reached up to loosen his collar, but didn't surrender the knife.

"Drop it!" the marshal ordered.

Holtwood ignored the command.

Olivia pulled harder, but heard a button pop off.

The collar loosened.

The cashier paused in surprise.

Eli renewed his fight for the knife.

Holtwood kicked Eli's knee.

Eli went down clutching his leg.

The traitor turned on Olivia. He grabbed her arm, trying to bring the knife around to her throat.

"Move, and she's dead," he told an angry Blair and her horrified papa less than five feet away.

Olivia fought, wriggled, bucked, kicked, and tried to bite any flesh that came near. It wasn't enough. Although thin, Holtwood had a wiry build that now, in his moment of rage, offered him enough strength to immobilize her. He countered her every move.

Unwilling to distress her father any further, Olivia donned as calm an expression as possible. She held herself immobile, praying.

What came next happened in a blur. From behind her and Holtwood, she heard Eli's growl followed by a thick, metallic thud. Olivia's captor let go. Her husband had attacked. Holtwood dropped onto her from the back, a string of curses on his lips.

In front of Olivia, Marshal Blair aimed his gun at Holtwood while Papa ran to her side. Before either man could reach her, Holtwood's knife hand moved. Olivia tucked her head into her shoulder and ducked to escape the gleaming blade, but she wasn't fast enough. While she did keep her throat out of the murderous thief's reach, he struck her temple, the top of her arm, and then sliced across her shoulder blade.

She screamed. The pain made her knees buckle. She collapsed in a heap.

Activity flurried around her, but she never had a chance to watch the commotion. As she lost consciousness, she prayed. She didn't want to die. Not yet.

She wanted the chance to hold her children, to lie in Eli's arms again, to tell her husband how much she loved him.

As everything turned from gray to black, she whispered. "Eli..."

When Olivia regained consciousness, silence reigned around her. While she was overjoyed to be alive, still the pain from her injury nearly made her black out again. When she forced her eyes to focus she realized someone had carried her to the parlor and settled her on the sofa. Now she lay propped on her good side with her hurting arm immobilized tight against her ribs.

She saw no one around her. "Eli?"

"I'm here with you," he said. "You're going to be fine. I'll make certain of that. Your father's gone for Doc Chambers."

"Did...Marshal Blair...get Holtwood?" she whispered.

"They're on their way to the jail."

She pushed past the pain and smiled. "Good."

Mama walked in, a large basin in her hands, a tight, pinched look on her face, tears in her eyes.

She set the bowl on the table next to the sofa. "Doc will want this as soon as he gets here." Then, when she noticed Olivia's open eyes, she let out a cry and crumpled down at her daughter's side, sobbing.

"Thank you, Father." She held on to Olivia's hand. "Oh, Livvy, honey. I was so afraid we were going to lose you."

"I'm so sorry...Mama. I hate...to see you...cry."

"Don't apologize, my dear. It's that animal who has so much need of forgiveness. How dreadful to think there are those in this world who can do such things to others."

Eli reached out a finger to smooth a strand of Olivia's hair away from her forehead.

A knock at the door startled them. Eli started to stand, but Cooky, running down the hall, stopped him with tear-wobbly words. "Don't you go moving from our angel's side, Mr. Whitman. I tell you, I may be old, but I can still do something helpful tonight yet. Lord, have mercy on the black soul who's done this."

Muttering as she went, the cook answered the door. A moment later, Olivia heard male voices out on the porch.

"Railroad or no railroad, gentlemen," Cooky told the newcomers, "we've had us a tragedy here in this house tonight. That's all what matters, I tell you. Now go on, get along with you. I reckon you can take yourselves on over to Mr. Whitman's office straight away when it opens again, if it's business you're wanting to do with him. Let the poor man see to his dear wife for this little whiley, now. Won't hurt you none to think of things from above at Christmastime, I tell you. It'll do your souls a world of good to ponder on the miracle of the sweet Baby Jesus' birth, it surely will."

"Oh, Eli..." Olivia said, feeling sympathy toward the men at the door. "Let them in...they're important."

"You're much more," he answered, his blue gaze intent.

"Please?"

He sighed. "I can see life will never be boring again." He walked to the front of the house. "I'll take care of our visitors, Cooky. Go ahead. Keep Mrs. Moore and Olivia company in the parlor. I expect Doc to be here any minute now."

Although the railroad officials tried to keep the volume of their conversation pitched low, Olivia heard every word. In spite of her conflicted feelings about the planned spur line, she knew how important striking a deal with these men was to Eli. So when she heard what they'd come to say, dread struck, filling her with misery.

She hadn't been able to avert this disaster.

"Under no circumstances," the gentleman told Eli, "can our good name be attached to anything so sordid as a scandalous swindle. We've decided that, in view of the cloud of suspicion that now sits over the Bank of Bountiful, we must withdraw any offer for the proposed spur line. We will not be running our track through your town."

A tear rolled down Olivia's cheek. "Mama, don't let the men leave. Make sure...Papa helps Eli when he gets here. They have to...listen to them."

"Oh, Livvy, dearie," her mother said, "don't fret about any of that tonight. I'm sure your father, Eli, and the railroad men will come up with the best way to smooth out all these tangles Mr. Holtwood left behind."

Papa and Doc Chambers finally returned. To the background sound of ongoing male conversation, Olivia surrendered to the haze of pain while the doctor began to patch her back up. It all improved when the physician administered a welcome dose of laudanum, and she dozed off.

Christmas was a day for the children. From her vantage point on the parlor sofa, between doses of laudanum, Olivia watched Luke and Randy give their father the gifts they had for him.

Randy glowed at his praise for the gray wool socks she'd knitted for him. Luke clapped when Eli's eyes lit at the sight of the finely bound copies of James Fenimore Cooper's popular *The Deerslayer* and *The Last of the Mohicans*.

Happy, and enjoying the peace that reigned over her family on such a blessed holiday, Olivia dozed off. Next time she awoke, she found Luke engrossed with his new train set, running the detailed cars over the carpet, as she and Eli had done the lovely night Tom Bowen had brought the gift from his workshop.

"Mama, Mama! Thank you so very, very much," the boy cried. "It's the most perfect present—the most perfect Christmas gift a person could ever and ever want."

Her pain still controlled by the dregs of her last dose of medicine, Olivia smiled. "You must thank your papa. He's the one who had the splendid idea of a train for your gift. Don't forget to thank Mr. Bowen the next time you see him. He's the one who did the excellent carving."

"Oh, I won't forget." The boy scooted over to her side, brought his face up close to hers. "But thank you, Mama. Thank you so much for being my mama. God couldn't have answered my prayers any better than He did. I'm so sorry you got hurt. You're the best mama a boy could have."

The hair-trigger tears flowed again. "I'm the one the Father has blessed, dear son. I couldn't ask for better children, a grander home—"

"And a more perfect husband, right?" that husband asked from the open doorway.

At his side, Randy giggled. "We're all the most perfect folks." She turned a pirouette. "And, see? Mama made me the perfect dress. We're the perfect family."

"Oh, Randy, dear," Olivia said. "There are no perfect

people in this life. Only those who love God, try their best to serve Him, and ask His forgiveness when we fail."

Luke nodded. "We're all like that, aren't we?"

Eli laid a caring hand on his son's shoulder. "We all try our best to live for the Lord, son. That honest effort to follow our Savior is what makes our family what it is."

Luke's earnest gaze shot up to his father, then back down to his mother. "I still say we're pretty close to perfect, and that's all I know. I love you, Papa, and I love my new mama, too."

Randy flounced over to where the other two stood, pert nose in the air. "You're such a child, Luke. Of course, you love Mama and Papa. You'd be a silly fool not to love them."

Olivia took that to be as close as she and Eli would get to a statement of their daughter's love. It satisfied her, and, when she glanced at Eli, she noticed the twitching corners of his lips. It satisfied him as well.

Before too much else happened, the pain began its by-now-familiar escalation, and Eli brought her the next dose of remedy.

She slept until the following day.

During the overnight hours, Eli watched his wife sleep the fretful slumber of the injured. He well remembered his own struggles when the bank robber had shot him a few weeks earlier. While serious enough, his experience with a glancing bullet wound paled in comparison to the long, deep gashes Olivia had sustained.

What did hang equally in the balance was the pain they both had suffered at the hands of those they trusted and loved.

He wished he could take back the hurt he'd caused Olivia, a woman who hadn't deserved the comparisons he'd made. He now knew the Lord had granted him another chance at happiness, and he'd nearly thrown it away.

He wasn't about to make that mistake again. He would fight with all he had to keep Olivia at his side for the rest of his life.

No matter what it cost him, he would make matters right for his bank customers who'd been wronged by a man with a spectacular lack of conscience. Eli had asked his father-in-law to spread the word that the bank would protect the landowners' rights to their properties until the elements went their way again.

Even if it cost him his very last cent.

However, under no circumstances was Eli about to leave his injured wife for very long. Not to go to work. Not to meet with his remaining employees to explain the circumstances. Not even to make things right between him and the landowners, especially the man who'd saved his business life. He owed a great deal to his father-in-law.

That morning, he'd been at the bank at seven o'clock, as always, and had greeted Larry Colby, Lewis Parham, and Ezra Andrews. He invited them to conduct business with him in the dining room of the Whitman home until such time as Olivia's condition permitted his return to the bank.

Although surprised, his truly loyal employees had expressed their concern for his wife and their enthusiasm for his plan. By ten o'clock they'd moved ledgers and steel lock boxes, receipts and cash onto the large table that so recently had displayed a bountiful feast for guests.

Wearing a lace jacket over a plain white blouse, torn to

allow Doc Chambers access to her wounds, Olivia had greeted them all with her usual smile and graciousness.

"I had my doubts about that weasel," Larry Colby stated, nodding vigorously, his red curls bobbing up from where he'd slicked them down. "There was something off about all that polite talk, and sirs, ma'ams, thank yous, and welcomes he waved about like a flag."

"Nonsense, Colby," Andrews responded. "All those were signs of good breeding and politeness. It was the money he always had at hand that bothered me."

Larry shook his head, sending his spectacles to the tip of his nose. "He doesn't have a family. He never had to pay for much but his rent and his meals. Of course, he always had money to flash around. He just never looked a man in the eye, not even when working together. That irritated me no end." Their good-natured bickering continued until customers arrived, directed to the temporary banking lobby by the sign Eli and Larry Colby had placed in the window of the bank. At that time, they resumed their work as though nothing had happened.

Eli returned to the parlor with a mountain of documents in hand. He sat in his armchair and began the tedious job of uncovering how deeply Holtwood's deception went.

Olivia smiled, and he felt the task dwindle to a mere irritation. She had that effect on him, more and more each day. In view of how much he really could have lost, he considered himself a wealthier man now than he'd ever dreamed of being before. He was rich in all that truly mattered.

"This is nice," she murmured. "I must say, I quite favor you working out of our home."

"At your side," he corrected, bringing a soft flush to her

cheeks. "Perhaps once we've sorted out this mess I can arrange to spend more time with the paperwork here at home."

"I would like that," she said, her voice tentative.

"As long as you can tolerate my presence in the house while you and Cooky go about your business, then I'm a happy man staying near you."

At that, his wife smiled again, leaned back onto the sofa cushions, and rested with the help of the medicines Doc Chambers had left with them.

By the next morning, Olivia refused to take another drop of the drug.

"I can't tell you how much I despise being at the mercy of that poison," she said, determination in every inch of herself. "It takes over my mind and my body, and I don't appreciate a forced surrender to anything but my Lord's will. I'll be having no more of that, Eli."

"I'm not sure how your stubbornness—er...willpower will affect your health," he said. "But I confess I can't see any reason to force you to take something that causes you so much distress. It's bad enough that you've suffered at Holtwood's hands."

"They're two different matters, Eli. I can't justify dozing my life away. I'm well enough to make it through the days on my own strength."

"Very well," he said, "but the moment you feel the worst of the aches return, let me know. You can't recover if you wear yourself out fighting pain."

"You said Mama and Papa are on their way here." She

turned the direction of the conversation to a tack she much preferred. "You intend to show them those documents you've been studying."

"Marshal Blair recovered the missing deeds from Holtwood's home, among other papers. He brought them by yesterday while you were resting."

"Have you found anything to celebrate among the devastation he left behind?"

Eli shrugged. "I'll make more of the facts clear once your parents arrive. I don't wish to put you through more than one description. At best, it's tiresome, sad, and infuriating, all at the same time."

Olivia waited in silence until Mama and Papa arrived. While Doc Chambers had approved her return to needlework, knitting didn't hold much appeal that day.

Finally, by midmorning, the doorknocker clapped three times. Larry Colby, who'd volunteered his services as doorman, hurried to respond. He ushered her parents into the parlor.

Eli directed them to the settee that normally sat before the window on the other side of the room, which he and Ezra Andrews had moved closer to Eli's armchair and the sofa where Olivia still reclined.

Through the open curtains, brilliant winter sunlight shed light on the matter at hand.

They exchanged brief greetings, but before Papa had a chance to speak, Eli took the reins of the gathering, and no one looked back.

"If you would hear me out," her husband said, "I have an offer for you, Mr. Moore. It will likely surprise you, but I've thought long and hard about it, and I think it will answer a multitude of prayers."

Apprehension tensed Papa's shoulders, tightened the corners of his mouth, and drew a line across his forehead. "I'm willing to listen and take anything you suggest to heart."

"Very well, sir, here's what I would like to do..."

Olivia prayed silently as she waited for Eli to proceed. Before he said anything, however, he walked across the room and handed her father a single sheet of paper covered with writing. From what Olivia could see, it also bore an official-looking seal and a number of signatures as well.

"What is this?" Papa asked.

"The deed to your land," Eli answered.

Stephen Moore looked puzzled. "But—but I don't understand. Why would you bring this out at this time?"

"Because, if you look closely, I've signed over to you any claims the bank ever had on the land."

Papa stood. "I don't understand, Mr. Whitman—"

"I think," Eli said, "it's time for you to drop the Mr. Whitman. We're family now, and I'd feel much better if you called me by my given name."

"I see." But Papa didn't appear to Olivia as though he did. "Then Eli and Stephen it is."

Her husband smiled in return. "Excellent."

"Now as far as this deed goes," Papa continued. "I'm mighty glad you married my daughter, and I can see you're doing your level best to care for her, but that doesn't mean I've reached the point where I look kindly at charity of any sort."

Eli nodded. "I anticipated your response, and I'll point out

I never offered charity, sir. What I have for us is a business transaction."

"A...business transaction," Olivia said.

"Precisely," Eli said, not a hint of doubt in his voice. "I'm sure it hasn't escaped your notice that my bank is now lacking a head cashier. After all that has happened, I'm leery of hiring just anyone to fill the spot. Since I know how desperately your finances have been ravaged by the last two years, I'd venture a guess you could use a steady income about now, right?"

Papa's brows drew closer still. "Yes, but I'm a farmer. I have plenty of land to work. That's all I know, all I've ever known."

"You have two sons. I'm sure you've taught them the ropes quite well by now. With just a bit of guidance from you in the morning, I'm sure they can handle most regular chores. Besides, it's winter right now. There's not much more for them to do than water and feed your stock. As far as the bank, you knew enough to spot a thief. All the years I've known you, you've kept your books in excellent shape. I suspect you'd only need to learn the particular routines of the bank, and once you grasp those, together with your basic understanding of profits and losses, I've no doubt in my mind you'll do a first-rate job for the bank."

"But—"

"I realize you won't make enough to clear the mortgage working for me through the cold months," Eli went on as though Stephen hadn't spoken, "but it will provide enough for you and the family until spring."

"I cannot accept charity—"

"I'm not speaking of charity. It's a legitimate job offer. But it's up to you. You can carry out Holtwood's responsibilities for as long as you wish—or need. Then we'll hire a new cashier."

"Eli, I—"

"I need your help, Stephen. Your integrity and courage speak volumes about the man you are. I can think of no one I would rather have look after my customers and my bank. Please, accept my offer. I trust you where I doubt I could trust anyone new."

For a moment, a long, silent moment, Olivia feared Papa's self-respect would force him to reject Eli's offer. But then, after the older man rubbed his forehead and met his wife's gaze, he turned to Eli again.

"I can only consider this if you allow me to work off the mortgage from my earnings. I will do my best for you, but I can't just take the title to the property, and your money as well. It wouldn't be right, Eli."

While Olivia understood her husband's desire to help her family, she also understood her father's position. For a brief span of time, Eli seemed to argue with himself, but eventually he shrugged.

"We can settle those details when you arrive in the morning for work. Right now, all I care is for you to understand my position. I give you my word, Stephen. I have never gone back on it or a signed contract, and I will never do that to a customer in the future. Not to you, not to any of the other landowners who have mortgaged their property. Not to anyone who will bank with us in the future."

Her parents' relief brought tears to Olivia's eyes. This was the man she'd married, the one she'd come to know better and better over the last four months. This was the man blessed with a generous heart, one full of kindness and decency and care.

This was the man she loved.

As Cooky cleared away the noon meal, someone clapped the doorknocker again. Larry and the cook danced around each other in the doorway, both of them intent on responding to the knock. In the end, Cooky sniffed and returned to her domain in the back of the house, while Larry chuckled as he hurried to the front.

The young cashier escorted Marshal Blair into the dining room. Olivia's breath caught as the lawman approached.

Eli rose to his feet. "How can I help you, Adam?"

He snatched his hat from his head, nodded a greeting to Olivia. "I'll be needing to borrow those falsified letters and deeds for a while. They're mighty strong evidence, and we must bring them forward at your thief's trial."

"I still don't understand how he thought no one would realize they were fakes," Olivia said.

"He only needed them to hold up long enough to get the railroad's money. The representatives confirmed he had been exchanging correspondence with them for some time, convinced them the land was his. He planned to sign over the deeds while they were here. A few more days and Samuel Holtwood would have disappeared with the railroad's money. I can tell you, they're none too pleased. But now, thanks to those papers, he's in for a long time behind bars. There'll be no claiming self-defense on his part when it comes to the skirmish in your kitchen this past Christmas Eve, either."

Eli's mouth took on a grim line. "I'm glad to hear that. Take them as long as you need. There's no hurry to return them. I intend to file them away only as a reminder of what a greedy swindler can do."

"I take it you've reached an agreement with the folks he hoodwinked."

"I'm settling those individual situations already. I'm just thankful I could persuade Hugh Roberts to stay put. I regret the distress he suffered, and if he'd actually pulled up stakes, I would have carried a heavy load of guilt for the rest of my life."

The marshal shook his head. "Don't take up what's not yours in the first place. That guilt belongs to Holtwood, and to Holtwood alone. You understand?"

Eli shrugged. "Thank you for all you've done on our behalf." He glanced around the room. "Have you eaten yet? I'm sure Cooky has plenty left in the kitchen, and nothing pleases that woman more than serving folks a meal."

Blair's eyes twinkled. "I'm not that big a fool. I'm not one to turn down one of your cook's plates. Let me follow her to her kitchen. No reason to make a mess out here again where it's clear she's finished her work."

As soon as he walked down the hall, his boots striking a sharp report against the wooden floor, everyone in the dining room laughed.

Olivia took the opportunity to ease out of her chair. "Cooky's a treasure. I don't know how I would have put together that dinner party without her help."

Eli gave her a penetrating look. "I think you would have found a way. You're not a woman who gives up at the first sign of trouble. It's one of the things I like most about you."

Olivia blushed. "Why, thank you, Mr. Whitman. I do appreciate your kind words."

As she left the bankers in the dining room with their sums and their cash, Olivia cast a final glance over her shoulder. Her effort was rewarded with another of those heart-stopping winks Eli liked to send her way.

Joy in her heart, she headed straight for the stairs, intent on returning to her little room. Seconds later, she found herself battling Eli's and Cooky's strenuous objections.

"What do you think you're doing?" Eli asked.

"I'm tired of the parlor. It's time for me to return to normal life."

Cooky clucked. "Get on with you, Missus Livvy. That fiend cut you all up like some chicken for frying, and here you're talking about stairs. Not under my watch, you won't. Come along, and let's get back to that sofa. Time enough to head upstairs when you're well's what I say, it is."

Olivia avoided her husband's blue eyes. "None of that matters, Cooky. I'm well enough now, and I'm not about to live in the parlor for the rest of my days."

She dared a glance at Eli. His expression was a mix of exasperation and amusement. Exactly what she felt.

While things weren't fully resolved between them, she now had hope that someday they would be. Maybe at that time she could leave behind the lonely room for good, but until that moment arrived, it would serve her purposes quite well. Better than a sofa in a very public parlor, now that the bank operated just across the hall.

"I'll be back down shortly." She turned and took her first

step up. When neither followed, she continued. At the head of the stairs, she paused.

Cooky had retreated to her kitchen, but Eli still stood at the foot, a grin brightening his face. With a nod for her, he began to clap. "Bravo, Mrs. Whitman. I'm proud of all you've accomplished."

She took more from his statement than his mere words expressed. In spite of the twinges of pain at her arm and back, Olivia couldn't remember a better moment in her life.

Hours later, however, Eli managed to eclipse it by a mile.

After supper, he accompanied the children to their rooms. Soon, he returned to the parlor, and took a seat on the sofa at Olivia's side.

Her heartbeat kicked up.

He reached for her hand.

She slid her fingers between his.

"This is as good a time to ask your forgiveness as any," he said. "Everything you said was right. Not only did you suspect Holtwood's betrayal, but also, and more important, you saw through my stubborn determination to hold you at arm's length."

She blushed but couldn't eke out a word. Even her breath seemed to catch in her throat. Expectation put her in a heightened sense of awareness, a clear recognition of the magnitude of the moment.

Every crackle of the fire in the hearth seemed magnified to where she couldn't miss hearing it. From the corner of her eye, she caught each flicker of the candles. She smelled the crisp fragrance of the greens still strung across the ceilings and mantel, mixed in with the pine and the bay rum Eli used in his grooming routine.

Most important of all, she sensed the warmth of the leg pressed close to hers, the strength of the man at her side, the admiration in his blue eyes, and the tenderness in his smile.

"Nothing to say?" he asked, disappointment in his words. "That would be a new experience, I suspect."

Those words broke through and Olivia laughed. "I'm sure you know you're forgiven. By the Father, as well as me."

"I needed to ask, and even more, I needed your words."

"You have them." She covered his hand with hers. "As you always will."

"About a week ago," he continued, "I feared you were about to leave."

"I did give the possibility a good deal of thought." She shrugged. "I couldn't imagine life without trust."

"By God's grace, you chose to stay."

"You chose to trust."

He breathed deep. "I can't promise I'll never fall back on the stubbornness again, but I can give you my word, Olivia, that I'll never question your loyalty again."

"Thank you, Eli. I needed to hear those words, too."

"I'd be a fool to forget how you and your family saved me from ruin a second time in my life."

She smiled. "Goodness knows, you're no one's fool, now are you?" She took a deep breath. "As long as we're discussing forgiveness, I need to ask for yours."

Alarm widened his stare. "What have you done now?"

"Oh, don't fret. Nothing new, of course. I...well, I failed you just as much. I didn't find the patience within me to wait for you to come around and see the truth. I made light of your experience and wanted you to trust me right from the start. No one can do that. Not with a stranger. Not without sufficient time."

"I trust you now."

"Trust needed to grow, and it has."

"All the emotions in a man's heart need time to grow, to go deeper, and enrich his life." Then he stole her very ability to think. Eli slipped off the sofa and knelt at her knee.

She only felt...she felt overwhelming love for him. Tears filled Olivia's eyes.

He took her one hand, folded a kiss in the palm. "There's something else I've failed to do, but I refuse to let another moment go by without changing that."

He met her gaze. "I've never told you how much you mean to me, Olivia. I still can't quite understand how I've come to love you so deeply in such a short time. But that's the truth, and I'm proud to tell you. I'm sorry I kept silent when instead I should have told you right away."

A trembly sigh escaped her lips. "Like trust, love takes time."

"I hope it won't take you long to come to love me back."

Olivia did something she'd longed to do during their most awkward moments. She slipped the fingers of her free hand into his silky, shiny black hair, and pushed a disobedient lock back from his brow.

"I suspect I've been ahead of you on that," she said. "I can't remember the precise moment when I realized how much I cared—actually, I think I can. It was the night you were shot. I'm sure that was before the first kiss we shared."

He caught both hands, brought them to his lips. "I love you, Olivia."

Tears rolling down her cheeks, she leaned close. "I love you, too. I always will."

Eli pulled her into his arms, careful not to bump her wounds. Then, with the tenderness and passion that never failed to melt her heart, he kissed her. Over and over and over again.

Their breaths mingled, their tears blended as well, and in the quiet of the night, two hearts truly became one.

Epilogue

The next day, Olivia and Eli got precious little done in the way of work. As soon as the bank employees arrived, including Stephen Moore, the newlyweds returned upstairs, this time to Olivia's lonely room.

Amid laughter, kisses, and tender stares, they gathered her belongings, packed her clothes, shoes, books, toiletries, Bible, and hats, and one by one found a home for each in Eli's much larger room.

From behind, Eli wrapped his arms tight around his wife's waist. "I like the looks of my shoes right next to yours."

"You must admit my pretty hats look better than your dull brown and black felt ones ever could. Especially now that we can compare them side by side."

He turned her in his arms, never letting her go. "I hope you're not suggesting some outlandish sort of swap. I'm the first man to encourage Bountiful's businesses with my patronage, but no one's about to persuade me to shop at our new, fashionable millinery. Not even you, my dear."

She laughed. "There aren't enough silk roses or peacock feathers in the land to make one of Mrs. Selkirk's confections look right on you."

He grew serious. "Are you happy, Mrs. Whitman?"

"As never before, Mr. Whitman."

"Is the room to your liking?"

"Oh, perhaps white curtains will look cheerier at the windows. Other than that, I can't think of a place I'd rather be."

While they knew perfection didn't exist, they now knew they could face anything together. As long as they stood on their love for each other and their faith in Christ, they would overcome.

Their blessings were too many to count.

And yet, those blessings continued to mount. A year later, David Moore Whitman came to make their joy ever more full.

Two years after that, young Amelia Hope Whitman made their family complete.

Through the years, Olivia rested on the knowledge that the God she served had once led her to Eli's side for such times as the ones they came to share.

Acknowledgments

Writing is a lonely endeavor, but it becomes less so when you're blessed with good friends. Lynette Eason, Margaret Daley, Pamela James, Michelle Sanders, and Julie Ward, thanks for being the glue that holds me together. Pastor Ryan and Rebecca McDowell, thanks for the welcome, the friendship, and the anointed teaching. I'm also privileged to work with some amazing people. To my agent, Steve Laube, my editor, Christina Boys, the art department and the rest of the team at FaithWords, a heartfelt thank you.

Look for the next Women of Hope novel

Remember Me When

by

GINNY AIKEN

Coming from FaithWords in 2013